SAVAGE LITTLE GAMES

SIN CITY MAFIA, BOOK 1

LANE HART

COPYRIGHT

Cover Photo of Blaze by Wander Aguilar Photography
Cover Design by Wingfield Designs

SYNOPSIS

In the dark underbelly of Las Vegas, Dante Salvato reigns as a ruthless mafia king. Violence may come second-nature to him, but when he sees the bruised and battered face of his favorite cocktail waitress, his fury ignites to explosive levels.

Vanessa Brooks thought her makeup was thick enough to cover the beating she suffered until her inappropriately flirtatious casino boss noticed. She's always been on Mr. Salvato's radar, but now he's obsessed, demanding to know who hurt her and why, intent on making them pay.

When Dante discovers that Vanessa's boyfriend, Mitch, not only owes money to a vicious Vegas mobster but is also cheating on her, he offers him one hell of a deal—Dante will pay off his debt in exchange for the one thing he wants more than anything: Vanessa.

Vanessa is appalled by Dante's offer, which requires that she spend seventy-six days and nights with him, one for every thousand dollars of Mitch's debt. If she refuses, however, Dante promises to kill Mitch right then and there for being the one ultimately responsible for her bruises.

Desperate to avoid any bloodshed even after she's provided with evidence of Mitch's betrayal, Vanessa reluctantly accepts Dante's deal with one stipulation. She warns the arrogant mafia king that she will never, under any circumstance, sleep with him.

Now Vanessa just has to resist the mob boss for seventy-six days and nights while he uses every weapon in his arsenal to try and change her mind.

TRIGGER WARNING

THIS STORY CONTAINS GRAPHIC SEX SCENES, HEAVY
PROFANITY, AND DARK THEMES.

POSSIBLE TRIGGERS INCLUDE:

TORTURE
KIDNAPPING
MANIPULATION
PHYSICAL ASSAULT
SEXUAL VIOLENCE

DEDICATION

For all the good girls who love villains and have a trigger warning kink.

1

Vanessa Brooks

Dante Salvato sprawls in his booth like a king waiting to be served. I guess he is royalty in Vegas. He owns this casino where I serve cocktails, as well as dozens of other properties around the city. The man has more money and power than he knows what to do with. Not to mention he runs plenty of illegal underground businesses too. He has the type of law enforcement connections to make people disappear for good. Rumor has it that he's killed at least three of his lovers when he grew bored with them and that he'll put a bullet in the head of his own guards if he thinks they're disloyal.

All I know for sure is that he's technically my boss's boss, and today, his current throne is the booth in my section of the casino lounge.

The other girls I work with love to wait on him. There have been literal catfights in the parking lot when someone snatched up his table when it was not in their section. Normally, I would pass him off to Georgia or Jessica, but I'm in desperate need of money. Despite all the blood on his tattooed hands, Salvato is a very generous tipper. Not that giving servers hundred-dollar bills for a couple glasses of booze makes up for all the violence.

"His Highness is waiting for you, Van," Gavin, one of the casino's male strippers, says as he finishes his nightly round of shots. It's his ritual before he takes his clothes off for the screaming, greedy horde of women. "Hurry, before he decides to cut your heart out for wasting his precious time."

"I'm going." I sigh, then turn back to the pretty man, flashing him a small smile. "Hope you have a good night."

"You, too." He gives me his trademarked wink and grin that makes dollar bills rain down from the sky and slips a twenty onto the bar.

Pulling my long, straight blonde hair over the front of my shoulder to cover more of my face, I make my way over to the table. Salvato is sitting with two other men who are dressed in similar black suits to his own. One clearly looks like he's also an Italian mobster, while the other has more of a blond-surfer-stuffed-into-the-suit vibe.

"Good evening, Mr. Salvato," I say sweetly. I pull out my small notepad from my apron pocket, keeping my eyes down, using my hair to shield them from view. "What can I get you to drink?"

"A whiskey neat, scotch on the rocks, and an old-fashioned." When Salvato finishes ordering for himself and his friends, I can't help but peek up at the two men to make sure it's what they actually want.

Neither glances away from the screens on their phones, though, while Salvato stares at my boobs. Usually, I try to avoid looking directly at him in such close proximity. His jet-black hair, constant five o'clock shadow, and glacial blue eyes are too much. He's too much sitting down when only half of his big, muscular body is visible. When he stands up... well, it's not fair that God gave this one man good looks, power, and money. No one stands a chance against him.

"That'll be all for now, butterfly," he eventually says to dismiss me.

Butterfly.

Making my way back to the bar, I can't decide if I like or hate the nickname that he bestowed on me years ago. One night, when I first started working here, he came in while I was wearing an open-back dress, revealing the tattoos running diagonally down my back. Sure, butterflies are beautiful, but they're also fragile, which is probably what a man as physically and financially dominating as Dante Salvato sees when he leers at me. I'm five-foot nothing, one hundred and ten pounds, and a nobody waitress. I don't even technically own the clothes on my body because I'm still paying off the interest for them on my credit cards.

My life is the complete opposite of Mr. Mafia King's.

Today, I'm just glad Salvato didn't look any closer at my face.

As soon as I blurt out the drinks to our bartender, James, he turns his back to me to get started on them. "You lucked up and hit the jackpot tonight."

"So lucky," I sarcastically agree, with my forearms braced on the bar counter. A warm tingle of awareness down my spine causes me to glance over my shoulder. Sure enough, Salvato's eyes are still on my ass.

"Oh shit, Van," James says when he slides the whiskey in front of me and peeks around to see the ogling man behind me. "He wants you bad."

"He doesn't want me. He just wants a tight hole to fuck."

"Georgia said it was the best fuck of her life," he responds.

"Who was the best fuck of my life?" The woman in question appears beside me, sweeping her long, wavy brown hair over her shoulder.

I tip my head in the direction of the dirty businessman.

"Oh, yeah," she whispers. Biting her bottom lip, she lifts her fingers to wave at him. I bet my week's paycheck he doesn't even know her name, much less remember it from their "memorable" night. "He ruined sex for me. I would crawl on my hands and knees over hot coals just for another taste of his big dick." Her heavy sigh as she gawks at him is pathetic. Georgia is just one woman in a million who he's screwed and tossed aside. At least she survived him and is still breathing to tell the tale.

"I'll take their drinks to them," she offers when James finishes pouring the old-fashioned. "You can still have the tip, Van."

"That's okay. I can handle it."

The smart move would be to accept her offer and reap the benefits without the work.

I shouldn't want to be near him, to hear his sexist remarks as he gawks at me, but he's the only man who even bothers trying to flatter me lately.

The truth is, while I will never give in and won't ever encourage it, Salvato's flirting makes me feel good about myself. Special. Someone like him doesn't really want my thirty-six-year-old single mom body that's never seen the inside of a gym. I know it's all an act with him. He's a horny, tenacious spider, weaving a beautiful web to draw women in so he can devour them. He wants what's under my dress only because I will always deny him access.

Sliding the three glasses together between my hands, I pick them up and carry them to the table. My heart races, and my palms turn so sweaty I worry I may drop the glasses. Finally, I place the old-fashioned in front of Mr. Salvato's seat in the booth, the scotch to his right, and the whiskey to his left.

Again, I'm practically invisible to the other two men who are still engrossed in their phones. But Dante grins up at me before he swaps the two drinks, putting the scotch in front of the blond and whiskey neat before the other mobster.

"Sorry," I say. "Is there anything else I can get for you, Mr. Salvato?"

He doesn't answer right away. No, he makes me stand there waiting nervously until he lifts his glass and takes a slow sip. Only when the bottom of his glass returns to the table does he speak. "You could come sit that fine ass of yours on my cock."

And there it is.

"Jesus, Dante," one of his companions mutters. The guy with his long, dirty blond hair tied out of his face sounds like he can't believe he just said that. The other one just cackles loudly.

In any other workplace, Salvato's words would be considered sexual harassment. Here, at *The Royal Palace*, though, there is no human resources office. As my boss told me my first week, *"If you don't want to put up with the shit talking, then you better get the fuck out of here."*

I put up with it because I'm a high school dropout with no skills whatsoever. The tips are nice, even when some of the customers get handsy.

In some alternate universe, I may even be stupid enough to climb on Salvato's lap and ride him right here in the middle of his casino while his friends and everyone else watches. Just thinking about it has warmth pooling in my lower body. What can I say? I have an unfulfilled exhibitionist fetish. In real life, though, I wouldn't be able to look at myself in the mirror for being so weak and naïve.

Weak for letting a man have that kind of power and control over me. Naïve for believing I'm special and not like all the other women he's used.

"As usual, I'll have to respectfully decline, Mr. Salvato."

"Did she just shoot you down, Dante?" the laughing man in the three-piece suit asks. He wipes away tears from under his brown eyes and says, "God, I'm so glad I got to be here to witness this historic occasion."

Salvato glowers at his friend for a moment, then turns to me. His cobalt-blue eyes are gorgeous and dangerous all at the same time. Hot enough to burn you and cold enough to not care when he sets you on fire. I have absolutely no clue what's going on in his head right now during the silence. "Titus has a point. You're the only woman who has ever refused me. Why is that, butterfly?"

He's never asked me for a reason before today, just threw out an offer and accepted my rejection with amusement. Tonight, though, he actually looks puzzled and...aggravated by my blatant refusal.

Shit. Time for damage control. The last thing I want is to anger the beast.

"Maybe I would consider it if I wasn't currently seeing someone," I explain, since calling Mitch my boyfriend when I'm rounding up to forty sounds ridiculous. It's the best I can do to let the mob boss down easy.

"He doesn't deserve you," Salvato says arrogantly, as if he knows him personally. One of his arms stretches out along the back of the booth as if offering me the place to curl up next to his side. "I would worship you, treat you like a fucking queen..."

"Queen for a day? No, thank you, Mr. Salvato."

"Wow. Well said." The blond friend who wasn't cackling salutes me with his whiskey before swallowing every drop down. His handsome face is familiar, but he's never spoken to me before. All I know is that wherever Dante goes, he goes.

"One of these days, when you finally say yes to me, you're going to regret waiting for so long, butterfly," Salvato remarks. He watches me over the rim of his glass as he takes another sip of his old-fashioned. With his arm still raised, his suit jacket gapes open. The top three buttons of his sky-blue button-down are undone to draw attention to his broad chest and gun in a shoulder holster. It's easier than it should be to ignore it, to take in the rest of his upper body. There's no tie in the way and the dress shirt is fitted to his flat stomach. He probably bought extra abs and has like ten of them hiding underneath the snug material.

I don't bother disagreeing with him before I force my eyes to look away and retreat. Turning him down in front of his buddies could be enough to get me fired or killed on a bad day. There's no point pouring gasoline on the fire by asserting that I will *never* say yes to him. He could put a gun to my head and threaten to pull the trigger, but I would rather die than give in.

Even without the rumors of him murdering his lovers, men like Salvato don't respect women. Never has, never will. He'll spend his life moving from one willing victim to the next, using them and then throwing them away like garbage.

I have my hands full with Mitch as it is, thanks to the giant hole he recently dug himself into. The hole responsible for the extra two layers of concealer and foundation I had to use on my face today before I came into work. After a year together, I'm beginning to think it's time for my worthless live-in boyfriend to hit the road.

Dante Salvato

"I get the feeling that she doesn't like you very much," Titus remarks with a shit-eating grin. "Wonder if I would have a better chance..."

"Fuck off." If he wasn't my friend and second-in-command, I'd be tempted to shoot him in his face.

At first, getting rejected by the tiny blonde cocktail waitress was amusing because I'd had all the other waitresses except her. Now, years later, her consistent rejection is annoying as fuck, leaving me frustrated, distracted even. Her weak-ass explanation doesn't even make sense. I'm Dante fucking Salvato. Women have literally left their husbands to be with me for a night.

Of course, they all think that they'll be the lucky winner who turns one night into two, and two nights into a diamond ring. They don't realize that they would have a better chance of ice skating across the desert. Hell will freeze over before I marry anyone.

"Poor girl," Eli says without sarcasm. "The last thing she needs tonight is the two of you trying to get in her panties."

"What do you mean?" I ask him.

Ever since the MMA fighter forfeited his life to serve me last year, he goes where I go and does what I tell him to do. Lately, the thief seems to think that the forced proximity has made us friends.

We're not.

He tried to steal millions from me, from my customers. Now I own him. He's a reminder to anyone who may consider crossing me that there are some fates worse than death. Maybe he needs a reminder that I still hold his life literally in my hands.

"You didn't see the bruises?" Eli asks.

"Bruises?"

"On her face. Her makeup and lipstick were thick, but I could see the black eye, the busted lip, the bruises on her throat—"

"Wait," I interrupt him. "Who the fuck are you talking about?"

"The pretty little server who just rejected you," Eli says simply.

"Eh, it was hard to see around her hair, but I think he's right, boss," Titus agrees.

I search the room for her, finding her forearms resting on the counter again, showing off her ass under her short, tight black dress. How the hell did I miss seeing bruises on her face, on her full pink lips? I know that face like the back of my hand. I always imagine those lips stretched around my cock whenever someone else is sucking it.

Who the hell would hurt her? She said she's seeing someone. Was it her boyfriend? I'll slice his hands off and shove them down his goddamn throat.

7

"Get your ass up," I tell Eli. He immediately slides out of the over-sized booth, allowing me to stand and head for the bar. My steps feel heavier than usual, like the rage in each of them could make the fucking floor shudder.

The bartender sees me coming and freezes with a rag in his hand. His face goes a shade lighter. "Ca-can I help you, Mr. Salvato?"

She, however, doesn't see me coming. Hell, I don't even know her first name. When she peers over her shoulder, I'm inches away, towering over her. She has to tip her head back to see my face because I'm at least a foot and a half taller than her—even though she's in heels.

"Bathroom. Now."

"Uh, what?" Her wide, emerald-green eyes shift from me to the bartender, who shrugs. While her face is turned away, I finally see the shadow underneath her left eye, down around the side of her nose. And fuck, I can already smell the blood of the person who hit her.

At first, I don't understand why she hasn't moved her ass to do what I fucking told her to do. When I speak, people listen. The choices are either comply or die. Usually.

Finally, I hear her gasp. It's not the good kind, either. It's the sound men make before they beg for their lives. It only takes me a moment to realize her train of thought. She must be assuming that I'm tired of her refusing me and will take what I want from her. She's such a little thing I could easily scoop her up with one hand and carry her wherever I please. My dick likes that idea a whole hell of a lot. My head reminds me that there are probably more bruises I can't see, and picking her up would hurt her. The heads of whoever laid hands on her are going to literally roll.

"You're going to wash that makeup off, and then we're going to talk," I explain to her through my clenched teeth to try and ease her worry. Does she actually think I would force myself on her? Jesus. I get every-thing I want or need from willing women. Well, all except for her.

She winces when she finally realizes what this is about and looks relieved for about half a second. "I'm so sorry, Mr. Salvato. I tried to cover the bruises up so customers wouldn't see them."

What the fuck?

"Are you apologizing to me for someone busting up your face?"

"Yes," she answers softly, but with conviction.

This conversation is her real voice, not the fake sugary one she uses when taking drink orders, using sir or "Mr. Salvato." And now I really want to hear her chanting that same word over and over again when she's underneath me before I make her scream my name. My first name, not that proper boss bullshit. I want her coming under me screaming, "*Dante,*" at the top of her lungs.

Shit. My dick is always trying to distract me from handling business. I've purchased 737s, sports cars, and penthouses I don't want or need all for one end goal—pussy. I have a feeling that all those things together wouldn't even be enough to persuade the waitress.

And that certainty drives me fucking crazy.

"You're not in trouble, butterfly," I assure her, trying not to take my anger out on her. "We can talk in the bathroom down here or up in my office. Your choice."

She gives me a tight nod and then starts walking to the right toward the women's bathroom. I follow her inside. The fluorescent lights are brighter than the sun, which is why I wanted to see her face underneath them.

Without having to repeat myself, I wait with my arms crossed over my chest, leaning on the door frame as she grabs some towels, wets them under the faucet, and gently scrubs her face. I count every wince from the bruises for payback later. There are four of them. Her bottom lip is noticeably swollen, without any color on it.

"Put your hair up," I tell her when her face is bare, still beautiful, just a little damaged. Her eyes narrow slightly at my order, but she doesn't argue with me or look at me before piling her light blonde hair up in a messy knot on the top of her head.

When she turns to face me, I glide closer to her. Close enough to touch, but I don't. The marks are even worse than they were in the mirror's reflection. Dark bruises. Recent ones. It's like my past has come back to haunt me, but at least this woman is still alive.

Someone fucking choked her and punched her in her delicate face at least twice. I may break men's jaws, noses, and every other bone regularly, but seeing that kind of damage on an innocent woman's beautiful face makes my stomach turn. I want to do something to make it better, I just don't know what.

"Is this all of the bruises?" I ask. Her bowed head shakes side to side. I fucking knew it. I want to demand to see every single one, but I know she'll refuse if I ask. "Who did this to you? Your piece of shit boyfriend?"

"No. He wouldn't hurt me," she answers as her palm comes up to gently touch the right side of her ribs. Most likely, some are bruised underneath her dress. If her boyfriend didn't keep her safe, then he's still a piece of shit.

"Then who was it?"

"I-I don't know their names."

Names. Plural. Jesus.

"Was this a random act of violence or was it done on purpose?"

"On purpose," she says with a heavy sigh. "Look, Mr. Salvato, I'm sorry I didn't cover them up better, but I had to come into work. I need the money. I didn't think anyone would notice."

She's right. I didn't notice. I was too busy staring at her tits and ass. If Eli hadn't mentioned it, I would've never known.

"Do you owe someone money?" I ask, since that's the number one reason for a beating by strangers in this town.

"No. I don't owe anyone."

"Who does, then? Your boyfriend?"

"Yes." It's barely a whisper, but it tells me everything I need to know.

Son of a bitch. He's a dead man.

"Who does he owe, and how much?"

Shaking her head, she says, "I honestly don't know, but I'm guessing some mobster like you."

"It sure as fuck wasn't my men."

"Well, I was in the dark, too, until last night when two goons came into the apartment and ransacked it, demanding their payment. He didn't have it, or anything else of value for them to take, so they did this to motivate Mitch." She glances up, eyes wide, as if she didn't intend to give me his name.

"Mitch what?" When she holds my gaze, jaw clenched tight, refusing to open her mouth, I tell her, "I'll find out one way or another."

"Fine. Mitch McKinny. But it's not his fault!"

"Oh, I'm sure it *is* his fucking fault," I tell her. And he's going to pay for it. "Get your things. You're coming upstairs with me."

"What? Why?"

I'm not entirely sure what I'm going to do yet, but I have to do something. Any plans I had tonight no longer matter. Figuring this shit out, making sure nobody hurts her again, is now my priority.

"Call your boyfriend. Tell him to get his ass down here now. I'll be waiting for you by the elevator bank."

"I don't...I should get back to work! James and Georgia can't—" she starts, but I interrupt her.

"I don't give a fuck about James or Georgia." Shit. I don't even know her name. For years, I've lusted after her and only ever called her butterfly because of the dainty ink on her back. "I want to know your name."

"Vanessa."

She's lying.

"Vanessa what?"

"Vanessa Brooks."

I'm not sure why, but I'd bet my left nut that's not the name she was born with. People don't blurt their names out that damn fast unless they're made up and they have to practice using them.

"Go get your things. Don't keep me waiting, *Vanessa*," I tell her before I turn around, jerk the bathroom door open, and walk out.

I want to know everything there is to know about Vanessa Brooks and Mitch McKinny. Then, I'm going to figure out a way to keep her safe and make her mine.

2

Vanessa

S *hit, shit, shit!*
      The last thing Mitch and I need is to get Dante Salvato involved in this nightmare.

It would've been nice to have someone stand up to those thugs as they hit me and kept kicking me when I was down, though. The pain was bad but gasping for air while one squeezed my throat...I really thought he was going to kill me.

Today is too late for a white knight or dark knight or whoever Salvato thinks he is giving me orders.

Why did he have to be down here tonight? Sometimes I can go weeks without seeing him in the lounge. The one time my face is a mess, he shows up and causes a scene.

Taking my hair down because I hate that he gave me the order to put it up and wash the makeup from my face, I march back out to the floor and tell James, "I have to go. I'm sorry. Hopefully, he'll let me come back later..." I remove the few tips from my apron and lay it on the bar.

"I know. Mr. Salvato told me you're done for the night. He looked pissed. What's going on, Van?" the college-aged kid asks, then his jaw drops. "And what happened to your face? Did he do that?"

"No, he didn't do this, but he is pissed about it. I'll explain everything later. Please don't tell anyone what happened," I beg him, because I don't want to be dragged through the casino's rumor mill.

"My lips are sealed," he says. "Hope you're going to be okay."

"I'll be fine," I assure him with a smile. I have survived worse than Dante Salvato.

Back in the employee locker room, I open mine to grab my purse and dig out my phone to call Mitch.

"Hey, babe. Aren't you at work?" he asks, since he knows we can't have phones on us during a shift.

"Yes, and shit just hit the fan. Who do you owe money to, Mitch?"

"I told you not to worry about it. I'm handling it."

"Was that Salvato's men last night?"

"Fuck, no."

I guess that's a relief. "Well, Dante—Mr. Salvato—just saw my face and made me tell him what happened. He wants you to come down to *The Royal Palace*. Now."

"Me? What the fuck, Van? What did you tell him? Who the hell does he think he is?"

"I'm sorry. Just come down here. If you don't, then he'll probably send someone to pick you up."

"Fuck! You should've kept your mouth shut!"

"That wasn't an option!" I shout at him. "I have to go. He's waiting on me."

"Jesus, Van. I do not need this shit..."

"And you think I do?" I yell at him before I end the call.

This isn't my fault, it's his, and now I might lose my job, but Mitch doesn't seem to care about that. All he worries about is himself, probably because he's never had anyone that he's responsible for keeping alive. He doesn't have a twenty-year-old son in college with tuition that needs to be paid every semester.

I stuff my phone into my purse and throw it over my shoulder. Rushing out of the locker room, I make my way through the casino floor and to the hotel's elevator bank. Dante's leaning a shoulder against the nearby wall. His scowl says he's running out of patience while waiting for me.

He looks so pissed I expect him to yell at me for taking too long when he pushes off the wall and stalks forward. Instead of cussing me out, he simply says, "Ready?"

"Yes, sir, Mr. Salvato. Mitch is on the way."

"Good," he grumbles as he jabs his finger on the elevator's *up* button. I have a feeling it's not going to be a good thing for Mitch. Salvato wants to blame him for my messed-up face, and in a way, he's right.

I've never had any luck with men, not with the one who raised me, the one I was supposed to marry, the one who knocked me up, or any of the ones who liked me well enough to date me once or twice, but had no interest in dealing with a mouthy teenage boy. Mitch is my first and only serious relationship ever. He and Cole actually get along pretty well. It probably helped that Mitch didn't move in with me until Cole left for college.

The elevator finally arrives. Once it empties out, Dante waits for me to get in before he follows, swiping a card for the penthouse while a man and woman join us and press the number six. I keep my gaze forward, but it's impossible not to notice the tall, towering man's reflection in the mirrors staring back at me. He's eying me up and down while running his index finger over his lip slowly, thinking deep thoughts. Likely dirty thoughts.

When the man and woman exit on the sixth floor, he speaks. "You're too...delicate." He says the words as if they're an insult. "I'd have to be careful with you, wouldn't I, butterfly?"

My cheeks suddenly grow warm because I'm pretty sure he's thinking about us having sex.

"Good. Now you're thinking about it too," he says with a grin, shoving his hands into the front pockets of his suit pants.

"No, I'm not."

"Sure, you are."

Oh, come on! How many floors does this place have? Thirty-eight apparently. We're only on twelve.

15

"I would smother you in missionary," Dante remarks. "So, you would probably have to ride me."

I shake my head because there are no words. Insulting him won't do me any good right now when I'm at his mercy and he knows it.

"Putting you on all fours could work, too. I do love it from the back."

"This is the slowest elevator in the world," I mutter. And hottest. There's hardly any air flow. It has to be about two hundred degrees in here. Sweat is literally beading on my forehead and neck.

"You're blushing like a Catholic school girl, but I think you're older than you look."

At least talking about my age is better than the best sexual positions for us. "How old do you think I am, Mr. Salvato?"

Again, his eyes roam my body like elevators up and down, up, and down, from head to toe. "Twenty-eight? Twenty-nine?"

I can't help but smile, even though it hurts my damn busted lip. "Thank you."

"Well? Tell me." When I hesitate, he adds, "I could just take your purse and find your license."

"Fine. I'm thirty-six."

"Wow. Thirty-six? You're so petite it throws everyone off."

"How old are you?"

"Forty-five."

I nod and tell him, "You act younger."

"Hmm. That's not a compliment, is it?"

Thankfully, I don't have to answer because the elevator finally jerks to a stop. The door slides open. The first thing I notice in the hallway are the two huge men in all black. Guards, obviously, one standing on either side of the heavy, double metal doors. Dante walks up and punches in a code into the wall-mounted keypad. I hear the lock turn, and he opens the right side, holding it for me to go through first.

The penthouse is even bigger and fancier than I imagined. There are stairs that spiral up, up, and up some more. The marble floors spill into a huge kitchen where a small wall with a fireplace separates it from a dining room.

"Where's your living room?" I can't help but ask, as if that's my biggest concern at the moment.

"Second and third floors," Dante answers. "My office is this way."

We pass by the glass windows and door leading out to an infinity pool. The sun begins to set, and several beautiful women in bikinis relax in lounge chairs like they don't have a care in the world.

Must be nice.

Dante's office is just about what I expected. A cavernous room with two floors of books lining the walls. There's a leather sofa, some chairs, a giant cherry wood desk that's so large it looks like it was built in the room. Once inside, he gestures to the sofa and says, "Get comfortable," while staring down at his phone now in his hand, typing away. "Eli is on his way here to wait with you."

Being comfortable is apparently my latest command, and since there's nothing else to be done, I go and plop down on the caramel brown leather sofa to wait.

Dante

A few calls later and, thanks to my many sources, I probably know more about Mitchell McKinny than his girlfriend. If so, I can't wait to enlighten her. Unfortunately, there's not much background information available for her. Previous tax returns show her places of employment going back fifteen years. DMV records list addresses where she's lived. There's not a single blemish on her criminal record. It's all too squeaky clean for a thirty-six-year-old woman working in a bar as a cocktail waitress for a measly minimum wage and tips.

The only surprise my team uncovered was that Vanessa has a son. He's twenty years old, and there's no father's name listed on his birth certificate.

When I come in from the balcony, Eli is still standing as directed outside my office, where the little blonde bombshell is waiting.

"McKinny has arrived and been detained downstairs," he says.

"About time," I mutter.

Having overheard us, I see Vanessa stand up as if to join us. Buttoning my suit jacket, I tell her, "You're staying here for now. Yell for Eli if you need anything."

"Okay then," she agrees with a sigh before she sits back down and crosses her legs.

"Here's the document you wanted." Eli offers me a tri-folded slip of paper. Trusting it's exactly what I asked for, I stuff it inside my suit's breast pocket.

"Make sure she doesn't leave this room," I warn him.

"Yes, sir."

He remains in his sentry position next to the open doorway to wait while I head to the basement to have a talk with McKinny. Like the penthouse, it also requires a card, along with a fingerprint scan to keep tourists out.

When I step off the elevator, my dress shoes are loud in the quiet space, echoing around the concrete floor of the mostly empty open space. I make my way over to the single occupied chair in the room where a man sits with four of my guards surrounding him. In a word he's...messy. His brown hair and beard are long and shaggy, his clothes, a band tee and athletic shorts, are faded and wrinkled like he slept in them.

"Mitchell McKinny?" I ask when I'm standing in front of him, as if I haven't just downloaded his entire life history including photos and videos.

"Yes, sir."

"Did you just get out of bed?"

"Ah, yeah."

"Sleeping while your girlfriend works all night?" Sleeping instead of selling his soul or whatever he has to do to pay off his debt to keep her out of harm's way.

"I'm looking for a job," he says, which is probably a lie.

"You're a shitty boyfriend," I tell him.

"Excuse me?"

"You let her work ten, sometimes twelve-hour days on her feet while you fuck around behind her back and blow money on idiotic bets with very dangerous men."

18

"I'm sorry?"

"Are you?" I ask as I walk up to him so close, he has to tilt his head up to see my face. "Because I don't think you're sorry."

"How is that any of your business?"

"It's my business because I made it my fucking business. Vanessa is also my employee. You screwed up, and she took the fall for you."

"I begged them not to hit her!"

Tilting my head to the side, I examine him closer. "Unlike her face, yours is completely unmarred. Why is that?"

"They said they were hurting her to motivate me."

"Motivate you to pay off your debt to Kozlov?"

"How did you—"

"I had my people ask around," I reply. The Russians are not a group he wants to fuck with. I would know. They once put a hit out on me, one that I barely dodged by laying low in Europe until my father and the Russian boss Yuri Petrov reached a truce.

"How long have you and Vanessa been together?"

He shrugs. "I don't know. I guess we've been living together for a year or so now, dating for a little more than that." Yeah, he's definitely not a man who buys her flowers on anniversaries.

"And why are you stringing her along when you obviously want to be a free man again, screw who you want, do what you want?"

"I-I never said that."

"You didn't have to. The photos and videos I just received of you fucking at least four of Kozlov's strippers and whores says it for you."

"Oh, shit! Please don't show that to Vanessa. I'll-I'll do anything."

"Anything?"

"Yes, sir. Name it."

"My sources tell me that you owe Kozlov seventy-six thousand dollars."

"How? The girls were free!"

There's no fucking way that's true. In Vegas, men have to pay those women to even look at them.

"No, dumbass, they weren't free. No woman in Vegas is free."

"Shit."

"Well?"

"Yeah, I owe Kozlov a lot. I didn't know it was that much."

"I rounded up. You know how interest works with assholes like us."

"Jesus. I'll never get that much cash..."

"I'll pay off your gambling and whoring debt."

"You will? Why?

"Because I want Vanessa."

"Vanessa? *My* Vanessa?"

"Yes." Although, she won't be *his* Vanessa much longer.

"What do you mean you *want* her?"

"What do you think I mean?"

"Like how long do you want her? A night or what?"

He doesn't get angry or even look the least bit appalled that I just insinuated that I want to fuck his girlfriend. He's a selfish asshole who is ready to get down to the dirty details, not even concerned that Vanessa may be opposed to such an arrangement made without her permission. I have no doubt that for so much money he would be willing to stand back and let me take her even if she refused me. And when she finds out just how easily he would've sold her body to me like he owns it, she's going to be fucking furious.

"Well, if I were paying a whore a grand a night that would buy me seventy-six nights."

"Seventy-six nights? You want me to give my girlfriend to you for seventy-six nights?"

"Yes, but I want her days too."

"And you're going to..."

"Fuck her as many times as possible in those seventy-six days."

"What if she doesn't want to fuck you?" Now he finally asks the important question. "She seriously hates you, man."

She hates me? What the hell?

"If Vanessa refuses, then I'm out seventy-six thousand dollars and you get her back safe and sound in seventy-six days. If she still wants you by then." I should've let him think the worst, but finding out she hates me throws me off my game.

"She'll never agree to this."

Is he just realizing that now? God, he's an idiot.

"How long would it take you to pay Kozlov off at his interest rate?" I ask him.

"Fuck, I don't know. Years?"

"That's what I thought. Years. Decades, maybe, with the interest growing every single day. Unless he just decides to kill you and cut his losses."

"I, ah, I heard he's done that before."

"He has. So have I when collecting debts becomes too tedious."

"You'll really pay it all off? Tonight?" he asks, like he's trying to figure out the catch.

"I'll pay it off before you walk out of the building tonight. Do we have a deal?" I hold out my palm to him and he stares at it.

"Fuck. Van is going to kill me or-or leave me..."

"Hopefully both," I admit honestly. Then I bait him, knowing he'll take it. "At least Kozlov won't kill you. Hell, how much do you want to bet she willingly fucks me before the night is over?"

"Double or nothing?" he eagerly suggests with a grin before shaking my hand.

For his audacity and stupidity, I haul my left arm back and slam my fist into his fucking mouth.

"Ow! What the fuck?" He tries to stand up and my men grab his shoulders to sit his ass back in the chair. "You didn't say you were gonna hit me!"

"Didn't say I wouldn't either, you stupid son of a bitch. You still haven't learned your lesson about taking idiotic bets. You don't deserve her."

"Hell, I know that," he mutters as he dabs his fingertips over his lip. I'm happy to see them come away with crimson staining them since that was my non-dominant left hand.

"You better hope she gives a shit about you," I tell him. "Because if Vanessa refuses my offer, I'll just slit your throat right here and now."

His jaw drops, and I punch him in the eye so hard with my right fist that my knuckles split open.

"Fuck!" he exclaims as he clutches his face but remains seated.

"Just a few more blows to go. Stand him up," I tell my men who jerk him up by his elbows. I land a blow to his gut that would've doubled him over if not for the hold they have on him. I slam my fist up into his ribs a few times as he cries out.

"Drop him," I order them, wanting him sitting for the final part. When he's slumped in the chair, I wrap my fingers around his throat, squeezing hard, and tell him, "Don't you fucking dare drag Vanessa into any of your bullshit again. Do you understand me?"

His face turns red, then purple while he nods his head vigorously, as much as I'll allow. Finally, I relax my fingers and he sucks in a breath.

While I want to make damn sure Vanessa ends things with this asshole, I'm not just doing it out of the goodness of my heart.

I want her. I will have her. It'll be what she wants too. Eventually. I'm not going to make it easy for her to refuse me. I still find it hard to believe she *hates* me...

"Tell Eli to bring her down," I instruct my men while I pull out my handkerchief from my pocket to dab at the blood on my knuckles before it gets on my custom suit. "Now, Mitch, tell me you know the names of Kozlov's men who hurt Vanessa."

3

Vanessa

"Where are we going?" I ask Salvato's friend, or maybe assistant, Eli. He pushes the B button on the elevator and has to scan a card, then scan his finger. He doesn't answer but I can draw enough information from the B to figure it out. "The basement? Why are we going to the basement?"

"You'll find out soon enough," he says while staring straight ahead as the floors tick down. He doesn't look concerned. In fact, he looks...downright giddy as he rocks back and forth on his heels, humming a tune.

Again, the elevator takes forever. When the door finally opens, we step off into the grungy basement so at odds to the luxurious penthouse. I don't wait for Eli as I head for the group of men standing around. At first, I don't even recognize the one sitting hunched over in the chair. His face is too swollen and bloody.

"Mitch!" I exclaim, slapping a hand over my mouth. "Oh my god. Why?" I demand from Salvato who is staring at me expectantly from where he stands beside his chair.

"We were talking business," he says as he pulls something silver out of his pocket and opens it. A knife. A very big knife. "His face should at least look like yours, don't you think?"

"No!" I exclaim. To Mitch, I tell him, "I'm so sorry. I had no idea he would do this to you."

"It's fine," he replies, lifting the front collar of his white faded rock tee to dab at his bleeding lip.

"Fine?" He's no longer blaming me?

When Salvato goes around behind the chair, I already know what he's going to do before he does it. Still, I gasp when he grabs a handful of Mitch's hair in one hand, bending his head backward, and pressing the blade to his throat with his other hand.

"Please...please don't..." I beg without a clue as to what to say to stop Salvato from moving that knife.

"So sweet that she's worried about you after you just agreed to sell her to me," the arrogant mafia king says.

"What?"

"It's not as bad as it sounds," Mitch whispers.

"Mitchell here owes a bad man named Kozlov a lot of money, as you already know."

"The Russians? You owe money to the Russians? Oh my god, Mitch!" I exclaim. "I told you to stay away from them!"

"I'm sorry," he says, but it's too late now.

Last night, I wasn't sure who the guys worked for but knew it was bad. This isn't bad; it's a fucking disaster. Salvato is a saint compared to those monsters.

"How much does he owe?" I ask Salvato since Mitch never gave me an amount last night and probably won't now even with a knife to his throat.

"Seventy-six grand."

"Seventy-six..." I slap my palm over my gaping mouth. "How? How could you?" I ask Mitch, slightly less concerned about the knife threatening his life. We don't have that kind of money! Hell, I'm lucky if I have seventy dollars in my bank account when payday rolls around.

"I'm going to pay it off tonight," he says.

"Tonight? How? By selling both of your kidneys?"

"No, he's selling you," Salvato responds gleefully.

"Me? Selling me to who? The Russians?" God, my head is aching. This cannot be happening.

"He's not selling you to the Russians," Salvato says. "He's selling you to me."

"You?"

Suddenly, this whole clusterfuck begins to make sense. It's one big set up to screw me over thanks to a stupid piece of shit and a conniving megalomanic.

"At a grand for each day, that's only seventy-six little days," Salvato explains as if he's an info-commercial host offering me an incredible bargain.

"What is seventy-six days?" I ask in confusion.

"In exchange for me paying off Mitchell's debt to the Russians and letting him live after he let you get hurt, then sold you to me like a whore, you're mine for the next seventy-six days. And nights of course."

What. The. Hell.

Salvato thinks I'm going to be *his*? As in his property? Day and night?

"No. Hell, no. God, Mitch. You are unbelievable! And you," I say pointing a finger at Salvato. "You are one insane, persistent prick!"

The four men standing around, the mafia king's guards, go completely still as they turn to watch Salvato's face waiting for his response to my insult.

"So, I should just kill him and be done with it?" the asshole asks. "I can't say I really blame you."

He presses the sharp side of the blade to Mitch's neck so hard blood drips down his throat, causing the asshole to start sobbing and begging. The sight of blood makes me queasy. I don't want to be responsible for ending another man's life. I don't want more blood on my hands. And even if Mitch is dead, the Russians will demand I pay up his debt and probably kill me, too, when I can't.

"Wait!" I exclaim.

"See, *that* is loyalty," Salvato says to Mitch as he pulls the knife away, leaving the wound he made to continue dripping blood onto his shirt collar. "But I think we should be completely honest with

Vanessa, don't you, Mitchell? Make sure she still thinks you're worth saving after she finds out you've been fucking around behind her back."

The psycho mafia king wipes the knife blade on Mitch's shoulder, leaving a crimson stain behind, then stares at me smugly. The blood is so distracting I nearly miss the bomb he just casually dropped at my feet.

"Fucking around? How do you know he's cheated on me?" I ask.

"I have the photos and videos from various strip clubs and brothels on my phone. There are four or five different women. Hard to tell since they look so much alike. He really does have a thing for blondes. Would you like to see them?"

"No," I snap, swallowing around the growing knot in my throat. I believe him. Dante Salvato doesn't have to bluff. Mitch doesn't bother disputing the disgusting allegations either.

"I'm so sorry, babe," he whispers. "You work every night, and I get lonely. It won't happen again, I swear."

I can't help but scoff at his worthless promise. "Asshole! Now I'm glad he busted up your face."

"It was my pleasure," Salvato says triumphantly.

Once, about a month after Mitch and I first moved in together, I saw the texts between him and another woman. He blocked her number and swore then that he hadn't cheated on me, that they were just talking. Talking, right. Sure. I wanted to believe him, to give him the benefit of the doubt. With Cole in college, I was also lonely and needed his help to pay rent. Not that he's contributed lately since he got fired from his job working security at another casino.

"Well, butterfly, now that you have all the facts, what's it going to be?" Salvato asks, the knife glinting under the lights when he places it back in front of Mitch's throat.

Running my fingers through my hair, I tell him the truth. "I...I don't know. I don't really understand what you want from me."

Salvato arches an eyebrow, and his heated blue eyes sweep up and down my body to make what he desires very clear.

"I'm not going to sleep with you," I tell him.

Salvato makes a sound of disagreement. "We'll see."

"No, you crazy bastard, we won't see! I'm telling you it's *never* going to happen, so that's not going to be part of whatever deal this is you're trying to make."

Again, the guards all bristle as if I insulted them instead of their boss.

"Van, please!" Mitch huffs, brown eyes pleading with me. "Don't make this worse."

I glare at him, letting him know that he doesn't get to have a say in this. I'm not fucking some asshole whenever he wants for seventy-six days and nights just to pay off his debt. Nobody is ever going to *own* me, not even temporarily.

Although, if I absolutely had to, I would maybe sleep with Salvato one little time to keep Mitch's sorry ass alive. I would hate it, but I would do it. Once. Wouldn't mind doing it in front of the cheating bastard, actually...

I haven't had an orgasm in a very, very long time. And while Salvato is an arrogant asshole, he has the swagger of a man who knows he can pleasure a woman in record-breaking time with the slightest twitch of his pinkie.

"Here are my terms," Salvato says. "You live with me for the next seventy-six days and nights. If you leave this building without my permission, if you refuse any of my demands, I'll consider our agreement null and void, and I'll kill him."

"Sex is off the table."

"Sure. If it makes you feel better, then non-consensual sex is off the table. I won't touch you...*intimately* until you ask me to, whenever that may be..."

"I think you meant *if*. *If* I ask you to."

"I said what I said, butterfly," he replies with an arrogant smirk. "Breaking you is going to be so much fun."

"I hate you both," I tell the two bastards who have me backed into a corner with only two very shitty options to choose from.

"Mitchell here just informed me of your *hatred* for me," Salvato grits out through his clenched teeth. For a second, his eyes darken as if he's actually hurt and offended that I don't like him. A moment later, though, he seems perfectly fine again when he says, "The more hate the better since angry fucks are by far my favorite."

"You said earlier that you loved it from the back," I remind him.

"Why can't it be both?"

Angry sex from the back. Right. I'm sorry I brought it up.

Scrubbing my palm down my makeup-less face, I wince when I touch the bruises then take a deep breath. "Will you please let him go now?"

"In a hurry to get started?" Salvato asks.

"No. I just don't want to see his face anymore."

"Fine. He can go, just as soon as you sign my contract so I can send the payment to Kozlov."

At first, I think he's joking. "You don't actually have a typed-up agreement for this, do you?"

"I wanted to be prepared for when you agreed."

When, not if, like he knew I wouldn't let him kill the bastard.

"Just a moment," he says.

Lifting the knife from Mitch's throat, he doesn't put it away. No, he pulls up the hair on the top of Mitch's head and slices off a big chunk right down the middle, then tosses the fuzzy wad aside.

"Dammit!" Mitch hisses. He looks ridiculous but at least he's not bleeding from anywhere else.

Finally folding up his knife, Salvato slips it into his pants pocket. Reaching into his suit jacket, he withdraws a tri-folded piece of paper and a gold pen, then holds the paper out toward me.

I remember Eli printing something in his office earlier. Guess this was it.

Once I have the paper, I unfold it to start reading. It says exactly what we discussed— verbatim—but I still re-read the words three more times to make sure I'm not overlooking anything.

I, Vanessa Brooks, agree to reside with Dante Salvato for the next seventy-six days and nights with all meals, lodging, and reasonable expenses allotted, without any additional compensation unless otherwise specifically stated on an addendum. If I leave Mr. Salvato's vicinity or residence without his permission or refuse any of his demands before the agreed upon period of time, I understand that this agreement will be deemed null and void, forfeiting Mitchell McKinny's life.

He even added the consensual section, albeit it arrogantly:

Any and all sexual intercourse will not only be consensual, but enthusiastically enjoyed by both parties.

Then there's a place for me to sign and date it.

"You put a murder threat in writing?" I ask in disbelief.

"Yes. The document will only serve as a reminder for you of what's at stake in case you become...obstinate. Any other questions?" Salvato asks. I shake my head, at a complete loss for how to avoid this situation I've found myself in with him. "Great. Lean forward, Mitchell, so she can sign it on your back."

The bastard does as he's told so I take the paper over, accept the pen, and sign the next seventy-six days of my life away with one signature.

"You owe me, you son of a bitch," I say to Mitch as I hand the document and pen back to Salvato.

A moment later, Salvato types something on his phone. "Your debts with Kozlov have been paid. Now you can dump him in the parking lot," Salvato instructs the guards as they haul Mitch up out of the chair. "Alive," he adds, giving me a wink to make it clear he's holding up his end of the now signed agreement.

I'm so emotionally spent that it didn't even occur to me to ask.

Salvato's gaze lowers to my dress, then my heels. His voice deepens when he says, "Let's get you upstairs and into something more comfortable."

"I need to go to my place to get my things if I'm going to be here awhile."

"We'll take care of that tomorrow. I'm sure we can find you something appropriate to wear until then."

I have a feeling my version of appropriate and his are two completely different things. There's no telling what he'll make me wear or do before this is all over.

And there's not a damn thing I can do about it.

4

Dante

It took longer than I anticipated, but now I've got the pretty little blonde right where I want her, and I refuse to let her go.

She looks good wandering around my penthouse as Eli gives her a tour. I bet she'll look even better in my bed tonight. Not that she knows that's where she'll be sleeping yet.

Maybe it makes me a bastard to have used her boyfriend's life to twist her arm, but I don't ever throw away money without getting something in return. I'd be a shitty businessman if I did, and a dead gangster.

While Vanessa is insistent about turning me down, I've seen the way she looks at me. I've been inside women who have spent less time staring at my face and body than when Vanessa takes my drink order. She wants me, even if she hates me for some goddamn reason. I do plan to get to the bottom of that. Although, after a few orgasms I'm sure even she will forget why.

I know I'm an attractive man, that it's not just the money and power that draw women to me. Even if I'm not Vanessa's type, she would have to admit that I'm better looking than that hippie boyfriend of hers. Ex-boyfriend now hopefully. She would be an idiot to go back to that piece of shit who let men beat her because of his bad decisions.

"So, that should be pretty much everything you'll need," Eli says as he leads Vanessa back to where I'm still waiting in the foyer. "Don't go on the third floor unless you're invited."

"Invited?" Vanessa repeats as she looks to me. "Is there like a VIP club up there or something?"

"It's where—"

"Something like that," I interrupt before Eli can blurt out my personal business to her.

And really, I should've thought about how my girls would react to this situation before now. They probably aren't going to be happy about me having a live-in female guest. I'm sure Vanessa can handle them, but there's no reason to start a cat fight before I have a chance to spend at least one night with her. They can meet tomorrow at dinner if she hasn't bolted yet.

The next twenty-four hours is when I'll test our boundaries, see how much she'll put up with, how far I can push her under the "not refusing any of my demands" part of the agreement.

"You gonna take it from here, Dante?" Eli asks when we continue to stand around in the foyer.

"Yes. You're dismissed," I tell him. "Just don't wander off too far."

He nods and flashes me a grin on his way to his room. He also knows that Vanessa is a flight risk and that being unable to trust her will drive me fucking crazy. That and her constant rejection.

Why the hell does she hate me?

Her asshole boyfriend has been cheating on her and is the reason she was beaten, yet she didn't hate him enough to let me kill him. That may be the one life I'm grateful I didn't have to take because it would've meant losing this chance to be with her.

"Your room is down that hall." I point to the hallway on the left side of the open room where Eli just disappeared. Better late than never, I ask, "You don't have a fear of heights, do you?"

"No, I'm not afraid to be up this high." Vanessa takes a deep breath and then heads down the hall with me right behind her. "And I'll even admit that the view is amazing," she adds.

"Then you're going to love the floor to ceiling windows in the bedroom. Last room on the right. Eli's is on the left if you need anything."

I wait impatiently for her initial reaction to the spacious room that I've never shared with anyone.

"Holy shit," she says as she tips her head back up at the ceiling that's two stories tall, all glass and only sheer gray curtains hanging from the top but currently pushed back. The silver bed frame matches the wardrobe, and the navy bench at the foot of the bed accentuates the navy bedding. That's the only furniture I wanted in here because I didn't want to block the view. There's also a private balcony that's just mine with a chaise lounge. Now I'm wishing there were two for when Vanessa wants to sit out there with me. Because she *will* want to one day.

Seeing her standing in my dim, masculine room feels about as frustrating as trying to catch a lone firefly on a pitch-black night. She's tiny, delicate, alluring, and always fucking evasive. At least for now...

"Is this really where I'll be sleeping tonight?" she asks over her shoulder still taking in the glow from the lights of the Vegas strip now that the sun has set.

"Yes, you'll be sleeping in here tonight and every night...with me."

"Oh my god." Vanessa spins on her heel to glare at me. Her cheeks are rosy red again, just like they were on the elevator when I was considering sexual positions and logistics for us. I like to stay one step ahead, always prepared. "This is your bedroom? You expect me to sleep in here, with you?"

"Of course."

"There's no way I'm—"

I take a step toward her and clear my throat to interrupt her rant while keeping my hands in my pockets. They're not allowed to touch her yet, and it's really fucking frustrating. I'll have to work around the rules to manage some sort of contact before I go crazy. "Careful what words you say next, butterfly." She really should've gotten firefly tattoos instead, even if they're not as beautiful. "You *will* sleep in this room, *this* bed, with me every night. But don't worry. I won't touch you until you ask me to."

"If. *If* I ask you to. And I won't." She glances down at the floor. "No carpet, either, which means the marble floor would be miserable."

"You're not sleeping on the floor or on the bench," I add when her eyes dart to the long, soft velvet cushion. "End of discussion."

Vanessa squeezes her eyes shut and breathes deeply with her fists clenched by her sides as if reminding herself that I can still slice open Mitchell's throat. When those sparkling emeralds open again, she looks right at me to grit out, "Could I please have something to sleep in?"

"Help yourself. The closet is through the bathroom. Wardrobe is right there. I need a shower."

"That's it? You don't mind if I search through all your things?"

"What exactly do you expect to find besides clothing?" I ask.

"I don't know." She shrugs and licks her lips. "Money? Guns? Bloody knives? Other various torture devices?"

"Other than the gun I keep on me during the day," I reply while pulling the 9 mm out of the shoulder holster to show her, "the rest of my weapons, torture devices, and cash are locked up behind the safe built into my closet."

"Do you sleep with your gun?"

That's an odd ass question.

Does *she* sleep with a fucking gun? Is she that scared after those goons hurt her? I'll have to have Eli ask the guys who go pack her things tomorrow. And also see where we're at on bringing the Russian fuckers who touched her in so I can repay the favor.

"No, I don't sleep with a gun. The only people who could get through the casino's security and my own personal guards to attack me in my sleep are people I trust. And now you. Do I need to point out our size and weight difference if you were to try and kill me?"

"I'm well aware that you're a big, tough man."

"Exactly." She doesn't sound very impressed, so I shrug off my suit jacket and toss it on the bench, flaunting what's underneath. At six-five, it took years for me to fill out. Several more years of lifting weights before I bulked up and could handle myself in a fight. I'm up at seven a.m. every morning to run five miles on the treadmill and work out in my personal gym with a rotation of trainers from every type of martial arts.

Vanessa's eyes follow me as I make my way to the bathroom, my fingers unbuttoning my shirt. "Get comfortable while I take a shower."

"You're just gonna..." she trails off when I toss my shirt on the floor and pull the white undershirt up over my head.

"Am I just gonna what?" I try not to look smug when her eyes glaze over as she takes in my hard-earned six-pack, the ink covering both arms and spanning across my chest as angel wings. Hell, my biceps may be thicker than her entire waist. Petite as she is, I do love her hourglass figure. The black dresses she wears to serve cocktails are snug enough to hug every curve as tight as possible while barely allowing her to breathe. My father had a Dolly Parton obsession. I think I get it now. Vanessa, thankfully, doesn't look like she's about to topple over, though. I've got big ass hands, but I bet her breasts would fill them perfectly.

"Am I just going to what, butterfly?" I ask again to get her attention.

Vanessa shakes her head and glances away from me, drifting over to the windows. "You're just gonna throw your clothes all over the floor?"

I empty my pockets, leaving my wallet and phone on the bathroom counter to work on my belt buckle. "I pay people to pick up my clothes and clean them."

"Of course you do," she says as she keeps her head turned away. She even tries to cross her arms over her chest like she doesn't know what to do with her hands but winces and drops them to her sides because of the fucking bruises.

Until she's all healed up, I won't even try to convince her to give in to me. Because when I have her, it's not going to be a gentle fuck. When it finally does happen, I predict that we'll both be good and angry. Need it nice and rough. And it'll probably be over way too fast.

5

Vanessa

The asshole actually stripped down right in front of me. He knew I would look. It's hard to have a conversation when you refuse to face the person.

And while I may have imagined what Dante Salvato looks like out of the fancy suits once or twice, the fantasy was nothing compared to the real thing.

He's bigger than huge. Massive. Add a few of those colorful grips to his torso and he could be a climbing wall for kids and petite women.

I would've assumed the mafia king had a little ink somewhere on his body, but had no idea there was so much of it. Damn those obscuring suits. The tattoos on his arms are hard to make out but there's no mistaking the wings spread over his sculpted pecs with a cross between them. I get the feeling it's a memorial for someone he lost.

Somehow, I focus on my anger for him making me stay here, making me sleep in his bed every night, and manage to look away before his pants come off.

I want to look, but I resist.

Currently, he's standing under the shower that could easily wash four people at the same time, the bathroom door wide open, as if he wants me to look, to be tempted.

Sure, yes, he's got a gorgeous, perfect rock wall of a body. It's just fancy gift wrap for the cold-blooded killer underneath.

While he's occupied, I slip off my heels and go over to the wardrobe to try and find something to change into. I'm not sure why he wouldn't let me go to my place to get my things unless he thought I might run.

I'm pissed at Mitch for being a lying sack of shit, but I wouldn't try to flee town knowing Mitch would pay for my disappearance with his life.

In the wardrobe are four shelves of neatly folded clothes and four pull-out drawers at the bottom. One pile looks like jogging pants, so I grab a pair of light gray ones then take a plain white tee off the pile. On second thought, I reach for a dark blue tee so I can take my bra off without the shirt being see-through.

Before removing my dress, I slip the pants up my legs. The elastic waistband needs to be rolled three times to get them to stay on my hips. As quick as possible I then unzip and squirm out of my dress, nearing groaning at every move thanks to my bruised ribs. Finally, it's off. The giant cotton tee comes down to my knees and feels nice and roomy. The only problem is it smells like a rich bastard. A dangerous, rich bastard who uses delicious, expensive soap just because he can.

I'm so ready for this day to end but need to use the restroom before trying to get comfortable in a strange bed with a psycho mafia king. There's no way I'm going into that bathroom when he's naked, though, so I'll just have to wait.

The shower cuts off but a few minutes later I hear the sink running. Finally, his highness strolls out of the bathroom.

"All yours," he says when he notices me standing in the middle of the room being swallowed up by his clothes.

I thought he would've at least wrapped a towel around his hips. Why am I not surprised that there's not a stitch of clothing on him?

His dark, wet hair is slicked back, water dripping down his torso. The arrogant bastard strolls over to the wardrobe letting it *all* hang out.

And there is a lot of him to hang out and swing around. Thick as a soda can but I can't even begin to estimate the length. And he's not even hard!

He's not hard.

That's a good thing. Right?

Pushing all thoughts of his dick out of my head, I slip into the bathroom to take care of business.

While washing my hands in one of the two sinks, I notice the unopened toothbrush laid out, assuming it's for me. Once my oral hygiene is taken care of, it's time to find out if he has some damn clothes on yet.

Black boxer briefs are all he deigned to put on.

"Are you hungry? Thirsty?" he asks as he adjusts the elastic waistband.

Oh, I'm feeling a little thirsty alright. Unfortunately.

"No, I'm fine," I tell him since I had dinner before I got to work.

Wow. That seems like it was days ago with all that's happened since then.

I trudge over to the right side of the bed, the side closest to the bathroom, not caring if it's his side or not. He can deal with it. Removing a few decorative pillows, I pull back the thick bedding to get to the sheets. Before sliding into them, I glance over and find Salvato watching me. In his underwear. A giant, strapping, inked, killing machine with a significant package the thin fabric can't hide. He's watching me carefully with his hands on his hips, analyzing my every move like I'm a volatile science experiment about to blow up all over his bedroom.

"What?" I huff at him, mirroring his stance. Well, my hands are on my hips. I can't pull off the strapping, inked, giant part.

Biting back a smile he says, "You look like a homeless person who lost a hundred pounds after they put those clothes on."

"Wow. That sexy, huh?" I blurt out without thinking.

"Clothes are optional, especially if you're going for sexy."

"I'm going to bed," I mumble. Turning back to the bed, I gather up the throw pillows I put on the floor and begin making a wall down the center of the mattress.

"Do you actually think I'll attack you in your sleep or that a few decorative pillows would stop me if I do decide to attack you?"

For all his ruthlessness, I don't think he would actually go that far. "Just making sure all of your body parts stay on your side of the bed in case you flop around in your sleep."

"Right," he says with a sigh. Going over to the wall, he presses a button that makes thick curtains appear out of nowhere to cover the windows and dims the lights, throwing the room into complete darkness.

The bed shifting is the only way I know where Salvato is right now.

There's a *womp* of pillow fluffing and some squirming before he finally gets still. When he heaves a heavy sigh, it lets me know he's on his side, facing me.

I roll over to face the wall and hiss at the pain radiating from my side.

"Bruised ribs?" he asks softly.

"Yes."

"You want ice or a heating pad?"

"No. Thank you," I add since it was nice of him to offer.

"I am sorry."

That makes me scoff. "No, you're not."

"I'm sorry he hurt you, that his bad decisions caused you physical pain. But no, I'm not sorry you're here in my bed. I've been waiting a long time for you to give in, butterfly."

"Right. Sure," I mutter.

Then a thought suddenly hits me. The sheets look and smell clean but... "How recent was a woman in your bed before me?" I throw out another question without giving him a chance to answer the first one. "How many women have been in your bed? There are no bedposts so do you have to mark them all down on the headboard to keep count?"

"No women have been in this bed."

I would laugh if it wouldn't pull my rib muscles. "You're so full of shit."

"I don't appreciate being called a liar," he grounds out through what I'm guessing are clenched teeth because he's pissed. "And I own four hotels with plenty of beds, a dozen clubs with private rooms, as well as a car service with very roomy backseats. Why would I want to fuck anyone in the bed I have to sleep in every night?"

I consider that information for a moment. "You're telling me that you really don't have sex in this bed?"

"Not yet. There's still seventy-five nights to go after this one."

Sighing, I say, "Goodnight, Salvato."

"You can call me Dante. It's a little easier to scream than *Mr. Salvato* in the heat of passion."

"If you say so," I reply, refusing to use his first name.

"I'm not calling you Van."

"Fine with me." My nickname could be something worse than the one he prefers to use.

"Vans are not sexy vehicles, and you are very, very sexy," he explains. "Also, I don't think Vanessa is your real name, butterfly."

I stop breathing and my shoulders stiffen. "What?" I whisper hoping I misheard him.

"Your butterfly tattoos scream 'new beginning.'"

"They're just pretty..."

"Is Vanessa your real name?"

"Yes."

"Don't lie to me, and I won't lie to you."

"Vanessa Brooks is my legal name," I tell him. "Check my driver's license if you want."

Neither of us speak again after that. I wait. Wait for him to say something else. When he doesn't, I try to close my eyes, but it's impossible to sleep here in this strange room, strange bed, next to one of the scariest men in the city. It's not that I think he'll hurt me. No, I honestly don't believe the persistent bastard will touch me first. He wants me to make the first move and plans to wait me out.

If he were anyone other than Dante Salvato, I would probably have sex with him, tonight, and enjoy the hell out of it. Why not? Mitch and I are over. I should've left him last night, but I was in pain, and I think I was still in shock. Now that I know he's cheated on me and gambled away money we don't have and never will have, putting us in debt to a mobster, well, I'm fucking furious. There's no forgiving that. Just because I don't want him dead doesn't mean I want to see his lying face. He'll never touch me again.

"You deserve better than him," Salvato remarks softly, as if he knows what I'm thinking. I feel the mattress move as he rolls away from me and know I don't need to respond.

That's one thing we can actually agree on.

I deserve to be loved and cherished, and Mitch never did either of those things.

6

Dante

Thanks to the small crack I left in the curtains, there's enough sunlight shining through for me to see the face of the woman sleeping next to me. It took fucking forever before she relaxed enough to fall asleep. I know because I was awake and listening to her breathing, her huffing, her whimpering when one of her bruises caused her pain.

The fuckers who put them on her body are going to pay for them before I have dinner tonight. Dinner with Vanessa and my girls. I hope we all manage to survive that particular ordeal.

I should be more concerned about the fallout when Kozlov finds out two of his men are dead than a family dinner, but I'm not.

Fuck him. Fuck the consequences. There's no other acceptable punishment. It'll take time before anyone misses the assholes, much less traces it back to me.

Beside me, Vanessa mumbles something that sounds like *intuition* or *tuition*. It's hard to make out.

I like seeing her beside me, cuddled down in a big pile of bedding looking so...comfortable. If she were naked, it would be sexy, but I'll take comfort for now.

A rogue strand of pale blonde hair lying across her face must be tickling her nose, but I don't reach over to move it. Good thing, too, because her hand swats at it right before she cracks a green eye open. When it sees me, she groans and stuffs her head under her pillow. "Were you watching me sleep?"

"Yes."

"Why?"

"Because I can."

"Ugh. It's creepy," she grumbles.

"Didn't sleep much last night, did you?"

"No."

"Tonight will be easier," I tell her.

"If you say so." Heaving a sigh, she removes the pillow and rolls to her back. "So, what will you make me do today until I have to go to work?"

"Work?" I repeat in confusion. "You're not going back to work."

"Why not?"

"Because you don't need to."

"Ah, hold on there Mr. Mafia Moneybags. I think I know my finances a tad bit better than you do. I *need* to work."

"No."

Sitting up in a huff, her hair looks white in the sun, and it is a tangled mess. "I have bills to pay! Being at your beck and call certainly won't make them disappear."

"Reasonable expenses."

"What?" she snaps, eyes narrowed, so bright and beautiful in the morning light.

"Did you forget that part of our agreement? I'll cover whatever bills you have to pay while you're here. Rent, utilities, whatever. I'll give you a credit card you can use for them."

Vanessa opens her mouth, shuts it, then her tongue wets her busted lip making my morning wood turn to steel. "You're just going to give me a credit card?"

"Yes."

"I don't want your money."

"Tough shit. Where do you think your paychecks come from?"

"That's different."

"Why is it different?"

"Because I'm performing a job, putting in the hours to earn that money for your business."

"I've got a job you could perform for me right fucking now..."

Vanessa rolls her eyes at my suggestion and slams her head back down on the pillow. "Why do you have to be so difficult?"

"You think *I'm* being difficult? I offered you a limitless credit card to buy or pay for whatever the fuck you want, but you're pissed because you would rather work a ten-hour shift every night serving cocktails?"

"Yes."

"Why?"

"Because serving cocktails for money is that and nothing more. Taking money from you without earning it means I'll owe you... something."

"I'm guessing the something you're referring to is sex? While I feel no shame in paying for sex if it's worth the cost, that's not what this is between you and me," I assure her. "*When* you fuck me, it'll be because you want to, not because I paid for it."

Scrubbing her palms over her face she mumbles what sounds like "Presumptuous prick." At least she doesn't insist it's *if* not *when*. Although, I think I prefer the *if*. *If* means it's still a possibility.

"We have an arrangement. An agreement. I don't expect you to put your life on hold," I assure her.

"Yes, you do."

"Fine. I do. But I know you have responsibilities that can't wait for seventy-five more days. That's what the credit card is for, along with anything else you need while you're with me. I'm also taking you shopping this afternoon."

"I don't want to go shopping."

"Too fucking bad. It's not up for debate because *that* was also part of our agreement. You do what I say. I won't remind you again."

"Fine."

Why does she have to be so goddamn frustrating? Her obstinance makes me want to grab a handful of her hair and fuck some obedience into her stubborn mouth. My chest is still heaving by the time she concedes, reminding me where I should have been instead of watching her sleep like a fucking creep.

"Fuck!" I grit out as I fling the covers off my body to stand up. "You've made me late." Blaming her makes me feel better even though it's my fault for not setting my alarm. I don't even know what time it is because I left my phone in the bathroom last night. When have I ever gone to sleep without it in my hand?

"Do I need to get ready too?" she asks, sitting up again to watch me pull on a pair of jogging pants.

I should make her come to the gym with me. If I told her to run until she puked, she'd have to run.

But I'm not that much of a sadist. Her bruises are still dark, painful. One glance at her and I can see the exhaustion on her face. Without me beside her, she may actually sleep soundly unlike the fitful sleep last night. "No. Go back to sleep."

"Okay," she easily agrees with that, rolling over to turn her back to me.

I don't bother with a shirt. I do grab my phone after I take a piss before heading up to the gym. At least I didn't miss anything urgent. Eli's door is still closed since he doesn't usually get up until eight or nine unless I tell him to. I send him a text that I want Kozlov's men brought in today, whatever it takes.

Running and training won't be enough to work off the frustration that's got me so worked up I can't see straight. But carving into men who hit women will definitely calm me down.

Vanessa is still asleep even after I shower, get dressed, and leave to start my day. It's not easy to walk away rather than climb back under the sheets with her, but I have shit to take care of that can't wait. My men found and brought in Kozlov's guys this morning. Eli is waiting with them in the basement.

We still have seventy-five more days and nights together, I remind myself.

"Where are you off to?" Titus asks when he steps out of the kitchen with a steaming mug in his hand.

"Basement to take out a pair of assholes. You coming, or should I wait for you to finish your coffee first?"

"Fuck. I'm coming."

Outside the penthouse, I tell the guards, "The woman staying here with me may not leave the casino without my permission. If she even wanders around downstairs, there better be at least two men on her, and I need to know about it."

"Yes, sir," both reply.

I'm stepping onto the elevator by the time Titus puts away his mug. He has to run to slip inside before the door closes.

"Are you sure about this?" he asks as the elevator jerks and begins the descent into hell. "I know whose men were brought in. These guys are enforcers, handling Kozlov's business like ours do for us."

"Our guys don't hurt innocent women," I remind him.

"You're doing it for the little blonde cocktail waitress, right?" he asks. "The dancer I fucked last night was running her mouth about you whenever my dick wasn't inside of it."

"Oh, yeah? Bet you hated that." Being my second has plenty of perks the man enjoys. He doesn't enjoy everyone, in particular women, asking him to cough up details about me or my business.

"She said she heard you moved the waitress into the penthouse and have been beating the shit out of anyone who looks at her."

Flexing my right hand in front of me to stretch my still swollen knuckles, I tell him the truth since he's going to run into Vanessa at some point. "I only fucked up her ex-boyfriend. She is staying with me. Temporarily."

"She is staying with you? In the penthouse?" he asks. "That shit was for real?"

"Yes."

"Damn, Dante! Since when do you take chicks up there to fuck? In front of your girls, too?"

"My girls are not your concern. And I'm not fucking her. Yet."

"So, then what the hell are you doing with her?"

"She's staying with me. That's all you need to know."

"You keeping secrets from me now? When Kozlov goes ape shit about the two men you're about to lay into, will I need to know shit then?"

"There's nothing to know. His men shouldn't have touched her. They need to die for that mistake. She's staying with me. Now drop it, Titus. I don't owe you or anyone else an explanation." I straighten the sleeves of my suit to keep from clenching my fists. "Fucking obstinance must be contagious around here."

Shaking his head, it sounds like he mumbles to himself, "Not even fucking her," before he thankfully drops it.

I don't know why, but I don't want him or anyone else around Vanessa more than is absolutely necessary. One wrong move will scare her away.

And I will do whatever it takes to wake up beside her again tomorrow, and the day after that. All seventy-five mornings.

In the basement, the first thing I notice are the two men hanging upside down from the basement ceiling. They remind me of washed-up meatheads or underground fighters who aged out of the game.

Enforcers. That's what they are for Kozlov. Muscle paid to do his dirty work for him, so he doesn't get any blood on his hands.

I have a dozen men who do the same for me. They teach lessons to people who get out of line. With women, a threat to family members will usually get their attention. There are plenty of rumors out there to make them think I would go through with the promise. Enough to do the trick. Set them straight.

Men, though, usually require a beating before they see things my way.

When it comes to torture, it's either me, Eli, or Titus doing the dirty work. I don't trust anyone else. Everybody who works for me needs to know it could one day be them hanging in the basement getting carved up.

I trust Titus more than anyone else.

And Eli, well, he actually enjoys inflicting pain. Gets off on it. It's how he earned the nickname Eligor based on the legend of a demonic lord who sold warriors secrets to win their wars in exchange for their souls. Except in Eli's case, he extracts secrets from men before freeing their souls from their destroyed bodies. Since he knows his nine lives have all been used up, I don't worry about Eli ever crossing me. He also enjoys his work too much to give it up. He's fucking depraved, which works well in my line of business.

The most repeated rumor about Eli is that he once scooped out a man's eyeball and fucked the socket while the bastard was still alive.

I thankfully can't attest to the truth of that one since I wasn't there to witness it, but if I had to bet, it's all true.

Today, Eli has already gotten started on the two Russian enforcers. A puddle of blood is dripping under both of them. Along with the coppery smell is the lingering scent of urine in the air from where at least one has no doubt pissed themselves. Ah, the one on the left has a piss stain on his shorts probably thanks to the deep cut along the back of his knee. Some of the liquid is even dripping down his face since he's upside down.

"W-we'll tell you anything!" the other one stammers. His shirt has been torn, and it looks like there's only red, raw skin and blood where his nipples used to be.

"Jesus," Titus whispers. He doesn't enjoy inflicting pain but will do it when necessary.

"They think you want information from them," Eli explains unnecessarily.

"I apologize for the confusion," I remark as I glide closer to them. "You're not here to give me information."

"Then...wh-what do you want?"

"I just want you dead," I explain. "But I want you to die a slow, painful death." The pisser begins to cry at that, incapable of speaking discernable words. "Do you two remember a petite blonde woman from the night before last?"

"We didn't know s-she was one of your girls," the stammering one announces.

"You see, that's why you're both dead men. Going around hurting any woman, mine, or someone else's, is unacceptable."

"Our informant says they also grab girls for Kozlov's flesh trade," Titus informs us.

The sudden rise of my blood pressure makes my head throb. What if they had taken Vanessa and thrown her into one of those disgusting trafficking rings? I probably would've never seen her again or known what happened to her. Bastards like these guys are why I'm so protective of my girls.

While I want to put a bullet through both of their heads right here and now, slow and painful is what they deserve.

"How long do you want to keep playing with them?" I ask Eli.

"A few more days at least," Eli answers.

"Fine. Do your worst for the next forty-eight hours."

"And if they don't make it that long?" he asks.

"Try to keep them alive. I want to be the one who finishes them off."

"Yes, sir."

I don't bother touching them now. Seeing the fear on their face, the pain from what's already been done to them, it's enough for the time being.

7

Vanessa

When I wake up, Salvato is nowhere to be found, and it is nearly noon. I get my shower, with the bathroom door locked of course, then put on the dress I wore last night wishing I had clean panties and clothes.

Not that there is anything wrong with my panties. Seeing Dante Salvato naked and sleeping next to him didn't get me hot or anything. I barely noticed the constant throbbing ache between my thighs all night long. Hopefully he didn't feel the pelvic floor lifts that wouldn't stop on his side of the mattress. Once he left this morning, the pulsing stopped, and I was finally able to fall asleep.

Maybe it was the tone he used when he yelled at me this morning that made my hormones calm down.

Salvato is a pain in the ass, but I don't want him pissed off at me. Men have probably been shot for talking to him the way I have. Arguing with him. Calling him names. Since I want to remain bullet free, I make a promise to myself to try and be more agreeable and less bitchy today.

After all, it wasn't Salvato who cheated on me or punched me repeatedly. If anything, he's been weirdly protective of me since seeing the bruises.

I would prefer to work every night to get paid than take his money, though. The power imbalance between us is big enough as it is. The last thing I want to do is give Salvato something else he could hold over my head. In seventy-five days, I'll be free of him, and Mitch will keep messing up his life, but at least it won't be my fault if someone kills him.

When there's a knock on the bedroom door, I'm not sure why I expect Salvato to be standing on the other side. He doesn't have to knock before going in his room.

The door opens before I can walk over to it. The two women who start inside both freeze and stare at me, one with her arms full of towels and the other pushing a vacuum cleaner.

"Oh!" the first one with towels exclaims. "I am *so* sorry. We thought the room was vacant." They both gape at my face, the black eye that doesn't look any better today. There's no way to even try and hide it without my makeup.

"You're fine. I can leave if you need me to get out of your way," I tell them right before heavy footsteps sound in the hallway.

Apparently, the women are familiar with the stomp of those dress shoes because their eyes widen as they glance at each other in panic. They must have seen his bad side before too.

From this morning to now I had somehow forgotten how much room he takes up, not just his size but with the added arrogant swagger in his charcoal suit. Thankfully he doesn't look as angry as he did earlier when his gaze lands on me.

"Mr. Salvato! We didn't know you had a guest," one of the women blurts out. "Please forgive us."

"I should've notified you that Vanessa would be staying here. Do what you need to do, we're leaving," he tells them. "Ready?"

"Ah, yeah. It's just..."

"What?" he snaps as he pulls out his phone. His fingers fly over the screen typing a message, refusing to look at me.

"I, um, need some makeup."

Lifting his face to mine, he says, "No, you don't."

52

"No? So, you don't mind if everyone who sees us together assumes you did this?" I ask as I gesture with my hands to my face.

"Fuck," he mutters in understanding. "Give me a second."

He turns to leave, and I can't help but ask, "Any chance you could also find me a change of clothes and a pair of panties during that second?"

That has him putting his phone away as his gaze drifts to my lower body. I can see the question on his face. He's wondering if I'm wearing any panties or not. He rubs his index finger over his bottom lip in what I'm starting to think is his tell for when he's thinking dirty thoughts.

"You're going to be the death of me, butterfly," he grumbles before he strides out the door.

When the women continue to silently watch me, I realize there's a stupid, triumphant smile on my face. It's fun seeing Dante Salvato flustered. "He didn't hit me," I assure them.

"No. No, of course not," they reply like they never doubted it for an instant.

"We're not sleeping together either," I feel the need to inform them. "Well, we are sleeping in the same bed but nothing else."

"We'll just come back later," the woman with the vacuum responds before they both scuttle out the door.

Dante

"Do I want to know where this dress and the panties came from?" Vanessa asks in the elevator on the way downstairs.

"No. And I'll need the dress back."

"If you say so."

"I do."

I adjust the sleeves of my suit, wondering how much shit I'll pay later for stealing the emerald dress from her closet without asking. It matches Vanessa's eyes, which is why I picked it.

"Can I keep the makeup?" she asks.

"Yes." Eli's already finding the replacements for all of that shit. The designer dress isn't as easily substituted.

"I wouldn't need any new clothes if you would just let me go home."

"If I say you need new clothes then you do," I tell Vanessa as we make our way through the casino to one of the three boutiques. "I have to look at you all day and night for the next seventy-five days. I'm bored with seeing you in little black dresses. Butterflies are supposed to be bright and colorful."

"It's your dress code, remember?"

"So, I should've changed it just for you?"

"No. And you wouldn't even know I exist if I hadn't refused your offer for a quickie in the bathroom that first night."

"I don't know. I'm not sure once would be enough with you."

"Oh, but it's enough with everyone else you sleep with?" she asks as we weave through slot machines and game tables. She's so small next to me that my neck hurts when I try to see her face. I would love to know if she asked the question because she's jealous. Too bad she either has a damn good poker face or truly finds me revolting.

"Usually, yes. Not one time, though. More like one night. A lot can happen in a few hours."

Vanessa groans. "Women who are smart would be scared of you."

"But most aren't, are they?" I point out. "Are you scared of me? Is that why you refuse me? Do you think I would be too rough with you?"

I'm not sure if I would prefer that she hate me or fear me.

"No."

"So, you like it rough and hard?"

"That's...I'm not talking about this with you." I can see enough of her face to know she's blushing.

"Then what would you like to talk about while we walk across the entire resort?"

"Can't we just play the silent game?"

"You're the only woman I've shared my bedroom with, one of the few people I'm willing to converse with, who I'm completely honest with, and you just want me to shut up?"

"Yes. We're not going to be friends, or anything else, Salvato. I'm here because you manipulated me, remember?"

"I remember. If you weren't so stubborn, I wouldn't have had to manipulate you."

"Right, blame me for not being wise enough to see how amazing you are or whatever. Maybe, I just have common sense and know better than to willingly stroll into a hungry lion's den wearing nothing but Lady Gaga's meat dress."

Unable to help my grin, I say, "Oh, butterfly. You don't know me at all. Unlike a lion, I can't ever be tamed."

"How about lying down in a den of vipers?"

"There's no antivenom for my bite."

"Fine. You're a one-of a kind savage beast no one survives. Maybe that's why I've avoided you."

"Glad you finally have a better perspective," I say as we reach the boutique.

"Wow," Vanessa says as she stands outside the enclosed glass store. "I bet one dress costs more than everything in my entire closet at home. The closet that's just a few miles away from here..."

I don't bother telling her that I have men packing up her things to bring to her later tonight. She would only be furious that I directed them to break into her apartment.

Ignoring her, I begin to sort through the sizes on a rack of dresses, choosing petite smalls.

"You're not going to let me veto any selections, are you?" Vanessa asks with a scowl.

"No."

"I didn't think so."

Within minutes, my arms are full of clothing. I've never been a fan of shopping before but knowing that each item I choose will slide over Vanessa's bare curves is a nice motivator. I especially love picking out all of her new panties and matching bras.

"Pajamas, too?" she questions when I add a few hangers to the top of the pile. "Your choices for sleeping attire don't look like they'll keep me very warm."

"That's what I'm for."

"Ugh," she groans. "And the bathing suits?"

"Unless you prefer to skinny dip in my pool and hot tub. That's fine with me."

"No, I prefer a suit that covers me, not these tiny triangles and strings that wouldn't cover a mouse's tits or ass!"

Smiling, I tell her, "They'll cover the most intimate areas. I could require you to remain naked all day every day."

That threat finally has her shutting up.

When we've been through the entire store, I take her hand and pull her toward the dressing rooms. "Time to try these on." I choose the last room—the biggest one. It has an armchair squeezed inside as well as plenty of mirrors and a long leather bench.

After locking the door behind Vanessa, I dump the pile of clothes on the bench before heading for that chair since this is going to take a while.

"What are you doing?" Vanessa asks as I get comfortable.

"I'm paying for the clothes, so I'm going to watch you try each and every piece on before I buy them."

"Dante!" she exclaims, and we both seem to realize it's the first time she's called me by my first name. Progress already in less than twenty-four hours.

"Yes, Vanessa? That wasn't a complaint on the tip of your tongue, was it? Just to remind you, as part of our agreement, I didn't promise not to look at you, did I? Another rule you'll have to learn to deal with during our time together. It's the least you can do for your ex-boyfriend's life, isn't it?"

She stares at me, emerald eyes narrowed for one long moment. "You, sir, are no Richard Gere."

"Who the fuck is Richard Gere?"

"The actor from *Pretty Woman*? He wouldn't have insisted on watching Julia Roberts try on all the clothes he bought for her. While he may have been a rich prick, he was still a gentleman."

"I'm the furthest thing from a gentleman, though." Pulling out my knife from my pocket, I twirl it in my fingers. "So, take your clothes off. *Now.*"

"If you want to watch me try on clothes, then I guess I don't really have a choice in the matter, do I?"

"I don't just want to see you undress," I tell her honestly. "I also want to see where your other bruises are on your body. It's for your own good, butterfly."

"Right. Sure," she says as she turns to the pile. "I don't even know where to start."

"Anywhere you want, but we're not leaving this room until you try on every single item."

8

Vanessa

I thought shopping with Dante Salvato was bad enough. It never occurred to me that I would have to take off my clothes and try everything on, even panties and bras, in front of him.

At first, I tried to pull on one dress before fully taking off the one I'm wearing. It was more trouble than it was worth. Eventually, Salvato still got a peek at my bra, so I gave up. Changing as fast as possible became my new method.

I never knew how much I hated the word "wait" until I had to hear it from his mouth over and over again. Making me stand in front of where he's lounging in his chair like a king, he would stare at me for long, silent moments. This happened over and over, yet he always approved each piece for purchase, especially the dresses so tight across my boobs that I could've used the next size up.

The bathing suits go on over my bra and panties, yet they still feel too revealing as he inspects them on my body.

Not for the first time, his dark gaze lowers to my ribs.

"Those men will pay for what they did to you."

Oh, shit.

"That's okay. It's over and done with."

"No, it's not. You wince each time fabric brushes them."

"Then don't make me keep trying on clothes!"

"You're almost done now."

Shaking my head, I turn my back to him to remove the bikini and move on to the provocative sleepwear. Those are definitely going on top of my underwear.

"Seriously, Salvato. Please don't do anything crazy. You know, like start a war with the Russians over a few bruises?"

When he doesn't respond, I turn around in the short see-through white nightie to face him again. "Dante?" I ask, using his first name to get his attention off the lace around my bra-covered boobs.

"What?" he replies.

"Promise me you won't do anything to cause trouble with the Russians."

"I'm not promising you anything."

Great. Asshole. "I don't want you to go looking for revenge or whatever. Please? I'm not worth it."

"Are things over between you and Mitchell?" he asks, completely off topic.

"Hell, yes. Why?" I can't help but ask. "That doesn't mean that anything is going to happen between us."

"How did you end up with a loser like him?"

Turning around to remove the white nightie for a black one, I try to figure out how to answer that. "Ah. I don't know. I was lonely. He was sweet at first, affectionate."

"How sweet? How was he affectionate?"

"Well, he would..." I try to think of an example, but nothing comes to mind. "It's hard to remember now that I'm so angry with him. Mostly we just shared an apartment, okay? I depended on him paying half the rent."

"Until he lost his job?"

"Yes."

"Do you know why he lost his job?"

"Uh-huh. He was mouthing off to management. At least that's what he told me."

I turn around to wait on his approval for the black teddy and matching thong that I slipped on over the borrowed one.

"That may be partially true," Salvato replies as he examines the lingerie. "Mitchell most likely mouthed off to management, but it was after they fired him for not checking IDs."

"What?"

"He let some kids into Boltero's casino. One of them got into an argument with a regular during a poker game, and he got shot."

"Oh, wow."

Salvato's finger traces his bottom lip as he stares at the embroidered flowers across my boobs on the black nightie. "If the kid hadn't lived, your ex may not have either."

"I-I had no idea."

"I didn't think you did. But everyone else knows, all the other casinos. That's why no one will hire him. He's slack and makes bad decisions. He knew the kid was underage."

"How do you know all of this?"

"I have eyes and ears everywhere, even in other casinos. Also, it's in the police report. The kid told the cops Mitchell wanted a hundred bucks to let him sneak inside."

Mitch got a kid shot and lost his job for a measly hundred bucks? Shaking my head, I scoff. "I can't believe he would be so stupid."

"I can't believe you were ever with him to begin with, butterfly."

I can't tell him the truth, that Mitchell was the first man I dated seriously in two decades. I didn't want men coming and going from my bedroom while Cole was growing up, so I abstained. My son was worth the small sacrifice. But once he left for college, I hated the empty apartment so damn much. It was the first time I had been alone in my entire life. I thought Mitch was a good guy. Or maybe I just didn't want to see his faults.

It's unnerving that Salvato knows so much about Mitch, more than I did when I was living with the man. A thought suddenly occurs to me.

"Have you been looking into *me*, too?" I ask him.

"Of course, I have."

Oh, shit.

"Do you think I would just let you live with me without finding out everything I can about you?"

"And? What deep dark secrets of mine did you manage to find?" It's impossible not to hold my breath.

"I didn't know you had a son, especially one old enough to be in college."

I glare at him in warning. "You better leave my son out of this!"

"You have my word that Cole won't be harmed."

I wince when he says my son's name so familiarly, hating that he knows it at all. "Your word? And why should I trust your word, Salvato?"

"Because you don't really have a choice, do you, Vanessa?" Before I can respond, he says, "Is that everything?"

I glance around on the pile that was on the bench that's now in the done pile. "Looks like it."

"Great. Let's get all this paid for so I can get back to work." When he stands up, the dressing room becomes half the size it was when he was still sitting.

I press my back to the wall so he can leave, but he just finds the dress I wore down here in the pile and slips it over my head like I'm a child or his personal, life-sized doll to play with. Slapping his hands away, I slip my arms through the holes and even get it zipped in the back on my own.

"We're having dinner together tonight at seven. You should wear one of the new dresses."

"What's wrong with this one?" I ask, eying the front of the pretty green one. It's soft and covers more than any of the new options.

Salvato grunts something under his breath but doesn't comment. He just turns around to scoop up the pile of expensive clothing and walks out of the dressing room.

9

Vanessa

After our shopping is done, Salvato drops me and the purchases off at the penthouse before telling me he's got work to do before dinner.

I try to call Cole the second his footsteps fade away from the bedroom. Of course, my son doesn't answer. I send him a text hoping he'll be more inclined to type back a response.

How is everything going at school?

The rest of the afternoon is spent waiting for a response. One finally comes a few minutes before the required seven o'clock dinner.

Fine.

I gave birth to him, work my ass off to pay his tuition, and all I get back after hours of worrying is one word.

If anything was wrong, hopefully he would call and tell me. At some point I'll need to let Cole know where I'll be staying for the next few months, but not yet.

I wish I could trust Salvato not to harm my son, but I don't. Besides, there are other ways to inflict pain than by physically hurting someone.

I'm so busy worrying about the fucked-up things that the mafia king could do that I don't even notice he's in the room until he speaks.

"Ready for dinner?"

"Yeah. Yes," I say as I slip off the bed and slide my feet into my shoes.

"You're not going to change dresses, are you?" he asks when I walk up to him.

"No. What's wrong with this one?" I ask.

"Nothing. Let's go. Dinner is in the upstairs dining room." He has more than one dining room? Wow.

"Who cooks?" I ask as I follow behind him, trying to keep up with his long stride.

"Hired chef. Why?"

"Right. I didn't think you spent hours in the kitchen or anything."

He doesn't bother responding. In fact, his shoulders look tense as we walk up the stairs and into a formal dining room twice the size of the one on the first floor. There's a long table that seats twelve, but only five places are set.

Salvato takes the seat at the head of the table, of course. I pull out the chair to his right. He opens his mouth to say something as I sit down, just before three beautiful women file into the room, leaving me speechless. There's a brunette, a redhead, and one with jet-black hair. None of them look old enough to drink. And what the hell? Am I a blonde to complete his little collection?

They're all dressed up like it's a requirement, and they pull out chairs without thought, taking seats at the table as if they've done it hundreds of times.

"Who the fuck is she?" the redhead asks.

"Watch your mouth, Cass," the mafia king says in warning.

"She's in my seat." The brunette huffs as she jerks out the chair next to mine.

"Is she wearing my dress?" That question comes from the one with hair as black as Dante's. She's sitting on the opposite side of the table in a chair next to the redhead, glaring at me. "Why the fuck is she wearing my dress?"

"Sophie!" That warning comes out in a near growl from Salvato.

Oh god. That's where he got the clothes and makeup from? His... lovers? I thought he didn't have sex in his bed! And my god, they are so young...

Wait. Do they all live on the third floor? Is that why I'm not allowed to go up there? Ew, I'm wearing one of their panties?

"Vanessa, this is Madison, Cassandra, and Sophie, my lovely, occasionally respectful, daughters."

"Daughters?" I exclaim aloud, eyes nearly bulging out of my head. Trying to regain my composure, I lower my voice. "They're your daughters?"

Jeez. No wonder they're all so young. Where are their mothers? I'm guessing there is more than one since none of them look anything alike.

"Vanessa's going to be staying here with us for a few weeks," Dante tells them. *His daughters.* My mind feels like the exploding head emoji.

"Why?" the redhead asks.

"Because I asked her to stay," he grits out which isn't exactly true. He didn't give me a choice.

"Welcome to our prison," the brunette seated next to me mutters as she studies me. "Are you allowed to leave, or does he have you shackled here too?"

"Ah..." I look to Dante who rolls his eyes. "It's for your own safety," he says, as if what she mentioned is actually true.

"You don't let them leave? *Ever?*" I ask him quietly.

"Only if I'm with them, and we have guards with us."

"Wow. That's...sad."

The girls all turn down their glares by a degree or two.

"I have enemies every—" he starts.

"*They* don't have enemies, do they?"

"Damn. Did she just interrupt him?" his raven-haired lookalike asks.

"And no, we don't have enemies," the brunette answers. "Only the Don does, right, Daddy?"

Hearing him referred to as *daddy* is so freaking strange. In the

65

bedroom, sure, but as a father figure, no. But it's right there on his stern face, his love and protectiveness over them.

"This fucking discussion is over!" he roars in what I now know is not just the mafia king tone but his daddy voice.

All eyes lower to the empty plates obediently. Still, I can't help pointing out, "Hypocritical of you to get pissed when one of them says fuck." Maybe I'm still a little angry about him watching me try on clothes earlier. It was embarrassing, and it hurt my ribs.

"Exactly! Thank you!" his lookalike says.

"Why is she even here? I get the feeling that she doesn't like you very much," the redhead tells her father.

"Her name is Vanessa. And she doesn't like me," Dante replies as he glowers at me. His blue eyes are dark and threatening before he adds, "Yet."

"I am like, so confused," the brunette whispers with a sigh while rubbing the side of her head.

"I bet she doesn't last a week," the redhead says as she grins at her sisters.

"Three days," the brunette counters.

Smiling, the raven-haired one throws in her guess. "Five days at the most."

"Your father paid seventy-six thousand dollars to bail my ex-boyfriend out of a hole and made me agree to stay here with him for seventy-six days so he wouldn't kill him."

Three jaws simultaneously drop as they turn to stare at their father. Dante looks like flames or lightning is about to shoot out of his eyes to strike me down.

"Wow, Daddy. That's fucked up," the black-haired one remarks.

"They didn't need to know all of that, did they?" Dante grits out. "You and I are gonna have a chat later, butterfly."

"Butterfly?" the redhead repeats, her nose wrinkled in disgust. "Ew. She already has a pet name?"

"I've worked as a cocktail waitress downstairs in one of the lounges for four years. He saw the butterfly tattoos on my back and has called me that ever since."

"And she loves it," Dante declares.

"No, I don't."

"This is so weird," the brunette remarks. "It's like we're in the *Twilight Zone*."

"Anyway..." Dante says loudly. "Let's eat."

As if waiting for the cue, several servers appear out of thin air, bringing covered dishes into the room, placing them before each of us. Water glasses are filled for the girls, red wine for me and Dante. Then the staff all disappear.

When the servers are gone, Dante sounds slightly calmer when he asks, "What did the three of you do today?"

"Same old," they all say at the exact same time.

"I would love to know what you all did today," I tell them. "And to get your names again, one at a time instead of all run together."

"And I'd love to escape this hellhole, but I'm shit out of luck," the brunette declares.

"You know how you can leave," Dante tells her.

"I'd rather be here bored out of my mind than free and fucking some old guy!"

"What?" I ask in confusion.

A growl from Dante has the brunette slumping down in her seat. She sips her water, refusing to even pick up her fork. "Whatever. My name is Madison."

Brown hair is Madison. Got it. One down, two to go. Then I process what she just said.

"You want her to marry a random man?"

"He's not random, and this discussion is over," Dante grits out. He doesn't appear to be eating much either, just pushing food around on his plate.

In fact, the one who looks most like him is the only one shoveling food in as fast as possible. When she notices me watching her, she says, "I burned like thousands of calories on the tennis court today." Her blue eyes narrow and she adds, "And my name is Sophie."

The one who looks like Snow White is Sophie. The brunette is Madison. Which means...

"You must be Cassandra," I say to the redhead who rolls her eyes.

"No shit."

Ah, Cass is crass. Snow White is Sophie. The brunette is Madison. I definitely have it down now.

Not much else is said as I nibble on the chicken, pasta, and vegetables. Everyone declines dessert and then flees the table.

Even Dante is up and out of there, so I follow him back downstairs.

As soon as we're alone in his bedroom, I slip off my shoes. "So...that was awkward."

Looking out at the sun setting over the city he says, "Nobody bled, so it went better than I expected."

"Did you actually think they would attack me?"

He doesn't turn around when he answers. "You or each other. They've never got along very well."

"Do they all have different mothers?"

His head seems to droop at that question. "Yes."

"Where are they?"

"Dead."

"Dead?" I repeat. "All of their mothers are dead?"

"Yes."

Holy shit. I thought the rumor about Dante killing lovers was a dark exaggeration.

"What...what happened to them?" I'm compelled to ask.

"That's none of your fucking business," he snaps.

"You're mad at me because I asked a question or because of what I said at dinner?"

"I've got shit to do. Stay here," Dante tells me. Then he storms out, slamming the bedroom door shut behind him so hard it makes me startle. Which I absolutely hate. I don't want to be afraid of him. I reassure myself that I am not afraid of Dante Salvato. He's not really angry at me. I don't think, anyway.

Even when I don't mean to, I guess I just have a tendency to say things that piss the mafia king off. And why that bothers me, I have no idea.

But I have no plans to follow his command, to stay like I'm his freaking dog.

10

Dante

"You look stressed. Vanessa giving you problems?" Eli asks, looking too damn happy about my fury as I pace around my office, sipping an old-fashioned.

"What the fuck was I thinking? Her mouth...she pushes every one of my goddamn buttons!" Rubbing my temple, I tell him, "No pussy is worth the headache she gives me. I don't even know if *I* will last seventy-five more days with her!"

"You're horny," he says simply as his ass perches on the corner of my desk. "You just need to get off a few times and calm down."

"That's the problem, though. If I touch another woman, and she finds out, it's all for nothing."

"Fine, then how about this? She's sleeping in your room, so let her watch you handle business. No, *make* her watch."

"If she hated me before, making her do anything isn't going to help, especially waving my dick in her face."

"Then I don't know what to tell you, Dante."

"I spent an hour watching her change clothes when I took her shopping today. Sixty fucking minutes of her undressing in front of me. And I was hard for every single second, even when I saw the bruises on her ribs, on her hip..."

"You can't erase them, but they'll heal. You're doing what you can, getting vengeance. Making the fuckers pay."

Running my fingers through my hair, I give it a rough tug. "She wouldn't approve if she finds out they're about to be dead. Unless they already are..."

"Still breathing the last time I checked," Eli informs me with a grin. "And why wouldn't she approve? She certainly wasn't the first woman they hit and wouldn't have been the last."

I don't bother telling him that she asked me not to do anything to provoke the Russians. In fact, I don't get a chance to say anything before his phone dings.

A second later and his phone appears in his hand. "Fucking great. Big D said they brought up Vanessa's things to the penthouse."

"Yeah? Good."

"They put all the boxes in my fucking room because they didn't want to bother you and didn't know where else to put them."

"And that's where they'll stay for now. I don't want that clutter in my room."

"Of course not," he mutters, eyes still on the phone's screen. "Apparently, Mitchell was so nervous about the guys showing up at the apartment that he didn't bitch when they started packing up her shit."

"I want him out of there now, so Vanessa won't have to deal with him in seventy-five days when she goes home." I already hate the thought of her leaving, even if she drives me fucking insane.

"I'll pass on the message," Eli agrees.

"What about guns?"

"Guns?"

"Yeah, guns. Did Dozer say if they found any guns in Vanessa's apartment?" I refuse to call my number one enforcer Big D like everyone else, even if he is a giant.

"Let me ask." Eli's thumbs move on his phone, typing in the question. The *ding* of response is instantaneous. "Yes. There was a gun."

"In her bedroom? Under the pillow or mattress with the serial number scratched out?" I ask and he continues to type.

"Ah, the gun was...under the mattress. And yes, the serial numbers were removed too." Looking up at me, he says, "Damn, Dante. How the hell did you know all that? Big D said the boyfriend even looked surprised when they found the gun loaded and cocked with the safety off."

"Ex-boyfriend," I correct as I sip my old-fashioned. "And it was a lucky guess."

I shove my fingers through my hair in frustration, thinking about her lying in bed, so afraid to close her eyes she has to sleep while armed.

Locked and loaded and untraceable too? Jesus. Vanessa must've been expecting someone to come after her in the middle of the night if she sleeps with it within an arm's reach.

I fucking knew it. I just wish I knew who. There's no way she'll tell me if I ask.

My beautiful little butterfly may look small and fragile, but she's actually a badass. That realization makes me want her even more.

"If she had a gun at the ready, then why the hell didn't she shoot those Russian assholes who roughed her up?" I can't help but ask Eli.

"No clue. Couldn't reach it in time?"

"What make and model and where is the gun now?"

His thumbs go to work again, and the answer comes in a second later. "A Ruger .380. It's unloaded now. Big D will leave it on top of the boxes in my room." I'm already heading for the office door as Eli follows me. "Seriously, Dante, how did you know she had a gun and where it would be?"

"She asked me last night if I sleep with one. Only someone who has a gun under the pillow or mattress would ask that."

"Wow. I guess you're right."

Stopping at the office door with my hand on the doorknob, I glance over my shoulder to ask him, "Did you have our IT guys do some more digging on her?"

"Yes. They said they found everything that there was to find on her going back to her birth certificate, then when she was first issued her driver's license up until the taxes she filed for last year. The license photos are definitely her—blonde hair and green eyes, five-feet tall, and an organ donor."

Damn. Maybe my gut was wrong about her changing her name. Our guys are the best so if they didn't see anything suspicious then I trust them, and I want to trust Vanessa. Guess we'll see how it all plays out.

"But, um, Dante?"

"Yeah?" I ask as I open the door, heading for Eli's bedroom.

"Vanessa's not in your room, or in the penthouse right now. The guards said she left a few minutes ago..."

That stops me in my tracks. Turning around to face him, I growl, "Where the fuck is she?"

Eli cringes as if he knows I won't like the answer. "Two guards are with her, as required, and, ah, she's waitressing down in the lounge."

11

Vanessa

"So, you're actually staying with Dante Salvato, here, in his penthouse?" Gavin asks when I bring him another round of shots.

"Yes." I straighten my black dress I only wore for a few hours last night, wishing I had the rest of my clothes. And I really need to figure out where the washer and dryer is in the penthouse.

"But why?" the handsome young stripper asks, his brow furrowed.

"Because I made a stupid agreement with him to live here for a few weeks. It's no big deal."

That's not the entire truth, but it's the most I plan on sharing with anyone. Dante didn't give me a non-disclosure agreement to sign or anything. Still, I doubt he wants his business talked about all over the casino.

Frowning even harder, Gavin huffs, "You're not actually going to fuck him, are you?"

"God no."

"Good. But he doesn't seem like the type to take no for an answer."

73

Huh. Is he jealous? No, that's impossible. He's at least ten years younger than I am. The pretty boy stripper just hates Salvato as much as I do, and I guess we're sort of friends since we chat every single night before he goes on stage. That's when a thought occurs to me.

"Hey, is there some pill or whatever that male strippers take to keep things...calm down there? Something I could sneak into Dante's food, maybe?"

"Ah, not that I know of."

"Oh, well. I'll just have to rip his balls off if he tries anything."

Gavin throws back a shot, then says, "So what are you going to do all day up in his ivory tower?"

"Not much probably. It's boring as hell. He made me go shopping today." I withhold the fact that he watched me try every piece of clothing.

"He took you *shopping*? That's not very hardcore mobster."

"Ugh, you haven't seen the clothes he bought for me. He wants to control what I wear, what I sleep in. And the underwear..."

"You're going to let him tell you what to wear? That doesn't sound like you, Van."

"I, ah, I don't actually have a choice about the clothing. It's sort of all part of the agreement."

"He's manipulating you!"

"He's *trying* to manipulate me. It won't work. Two can play his game. I just need a few days to figure out which of his buttons to push to make him give up and back off."

Gavin's eyes widen at something or someone behind me. "Oh shit," he whispers, making me instantly guess the unwelcome visitor's identity.

Dammit. That took even less time than I expected. I haven't been down here for more than fifteen minutes. "Salvato is charging up behind me, isn't he?" I ask.

"Yep."

"What the hell are you doing down here?" Dante growls from behind me.

"Working," I reply when I frown at him over my shoulder. I can't help but notice that his dark hair is more rumpled than it was after dinner. Was he just with someone? Not that I care, other than not wanting to sleep next to a manwhore who could have every sexually transmitted disease under the sun.

"Why?" he grits out.

"Why am I working? Because I want to? Because I was bored sitting in your bedroom with nothing to do. There's not even a television in there!"

It sounds like Gavin makes a disapproving sound. Oh, right. I didn't mention to him that I was also staying in Dante's bedroom with him.

"It doesn't look like you were working. You were just standing here chit-chatting with the stripper boy."

"My name is Gavin."

Dante doesn't acknowledge the dancer at all, doesn't take his furious eyes off of me. "You're done, Vanessa. Get your ass back upstairs. Now." He actually looks furious with me for serving drinks in his casino lounge, which doesn't make any sense. Still, I know better than to refuse him.

"Yes, sir," I mutter sarcastically, even throwing in a mock hand salute. Turning back to Gavin I say, "Sorry. It looks like I have to go."

"Take care of yourself," he replies before I walk over to the bar and tell James, "Sorry for leaving you hanging again tonight."

"It's fine, Van. We've got things covered down here," the bartender says with a fake smile because Dante is still watching and listening. I can feel his large frame shadowing me, tight on my heels.

Turning back to the lurking mafia king I ask him, "Can I at least come down and visit my friends some nights?"

"If the guards come with you."

Right. Guards like the ones who followed me down and will tell Dante every single thing I say or do.

Untying the back of my apron, I toss it on the bar and wave goodbye to James, then Gavin. As I walk to the elevators, I can feel Dante's annoyed stare on my backside.

He doesn't say a word until we get on the elevator with my guards and his own that I didn't even notice.

"How were you going to get back up to the penthouse?" Dante asks me.

"I don't know. Ask one of the two security guys who followed me down?"

"Don't make me chase you all over the fucking casino."

"Don't make me sit around bored out of my mind. I'm used to working all night, Dante."

"Not for the next seventy-five days. I left a credit card on the nightstand in the bedroom for you. Find something else to occupy your time."

"I don't want your money."

"Too bad," he mumbles. There's heavy silence in the elevator, tension nearly coming off the guards in waves. Then, the asshole speaks again. "I paid-up your son's tuition for next year."

Spinning toward him, a puff of laughter escapes me. "Are you fucking kidding, me?"

"No."

"Why would you do that? I didn't ask you for a penny!"

Dante straightens each of his suit sleeves slowly, avoiding my gaze. "I did it because I can. I thought you would appreciate the gesture."

"Well, I don't!"

Now his blue eyes snap up to mine. "You make me fucking crazy; do you know that?"

"Then let me go! You'll never have to see me again. I'll find a job waitressing somewhere else!"

"Do you think I went to all this trouble to get you in my bed only to give up less than twenty-four hours later?"

"So, is that a no on letting me leave tonight?"

"It's a no."

When we make it back to the penthouse, Dante goes to the kitchen while I go straight to the bedroom. My luxury prison cell.

I get changed into one of my new, somehow already washed, pink pajama short set. It's one of the few pieces of nighttime attire that doesn't reveal everything through sheer lace or minimal fabric. I've just climbed into bed to apply some lotion to my legs when Dante walks into the bedroom.

The mafia king closes and locks the door softly, which is fine with me, then he walks over to stand at the foot of the bed. He looks somewhat calmer than he did on the elevator.

"Your things are here in boxes across the hall," he tells me.

"My things?"

"From your apartment."

"How did..." I trail off before it occurs to me. "You sent someone to go pack up *my* personal belongings?"

"Yes. You're welcome."

"You expect me to thank you for breaking into my place and robbing me?"

"I saved you time. Nothing is more precious," he responds. Then he lifts his hand from his side and there's a small, familiar black handgun gripped in it. "And what the fuck are you doing with this underneath your mattress?"

Oh, shit. Guess it wasn't hidden as well as I thought.

"*You* have the nerve to ask me why I have a gun?" I scoff at him.

"Who are you afraid of, Vanessa?"

Whoa, where the hell did that question come from? "No one."

"Not the ex. He didn't even know it was there." How does he know so damn much?

"It was just, ah, you know, an in case of emergency thing," I tell him, which is the honest to god truth.

"Why didn't you shoot Kozlov's guys with it?"

"Oh, I don't know, Dante. Maybe because they weren't actually trying to kill me. Or maybe I knew that if I shot them or killed them, then Kozlov wouldn't have stopped looking for me until I was dead."

He turns the gun over, examining it closely. "That's likely true. And pretty smart, actually."

"No, it's common sense. Is your first instinct always to kill?" I ask him.

"If it's warranted. I'm not afraid of anyone who might come after me in retaliation."

"That's scary and kind of sad," I admit.

Holding up my Ruger, he says, "This is unloaded now, and it's going into my safe."

"Are you going to give it back to me when I ask for it?"

"*When* not *if* for this instance, huh?" he asks as he watches me. His index finger rubs over his lip, and I know what he's thinking about.

"In this situation, yes, it's when. I will want *my* gun back."

"Did you know the serial number here has been scratched off?" he asks while pointing out where the numbers should be.

"Huh. Weird."

Dante's about to rip his bottom lip off as his horny tell goes from touching it to tugging it. What sort of depraved shit is he thinking about now? His blue eyes darken while he watches me like a predator trying to decide if I'm prey worth hunting or not.

"What?" I snap at him.

Finally, he says, "I didn't think you could get any sexier, but finding out you have a little gangster inside of you is hot as fuck."

That was not at all what I expected him to say.

And I wish his flirty remarks didn't make me so damn giddy in some small, buried deep, part of me.

"Have you ever killed anyone?" Dante asks, sobering me up fast.

I decide to tell him the truth about that one, if not for any other reason than in warning. "Yes."

"More than one person?"

"Yes."

Smirking like a psycho, he says, "You're just full of surprises, butterfly."

He actually believes me? "You're not going to call bullshit because I'm a petite woman?"

"With an untraceable, loaded gun in your hands, you're just as lethal as anyone else. More so if your opponent underestimates you."

I consider that statement the entire time Dante is in the bathroom taking his shower.

Tonight, when he strides back into the bedroom, his nakedness, along with the droplets of water covering his muscular body doesn't have as much of an effect on me as it did last night.

Well, at least that's what I tell myself when I force my eyes to glance away when he reaches into a dresser drawer to grab a pair of black boxer briefs.

"Why can't you take your underwear with you to the shower to put them on afterwards like a normal person?" I ask Dante when he's covered up, heading over to press the button on the wall to close the curtains. My head may have tipped a little to the left to check out his ass.

Chuckling, he says, "I can see you watching me in the window's reflection."

Dammit.

"And I'll put my underwear on wherever the hell I want."

"It was just an idea."

The lights in the room go out and then Dante climbs under the sheets from the other side of the bed.

"What are we doing tomorrow?" I ask him, not yet tired because I'm a night owl.

"We? I have some calls to make. Normal, everyday business to handle."

"Oh."

"You can tag along if you want."

"Really?"

"Do I need to tell you to keep your mouth shut about whatever you see or hear?"

"I think it's pretty obvious that if I talk about your business to anyone, you'll cut out my tongue or something equally horrifying to keep others from making the same mistake."

"Exactly," he says, blowing out a breath as he flops around getting comfortable. "I'd rather avoid tongue removal. They're a bloody mess."

I have no clue if he's speaking from experience or not, and I don't think I ever want to know.

12

Dante

Since touching Vanessa innocently isn't prohibited in our agreement, I plan to do more of it now that she's lasted two nights with me. I'll keep my hands off her big, beautiful tits and fine ass for now. I'm saving that for when the bruises disappear, and she asks me to put them in those places.

By the time I get done with my morning workout and return to the bedroom to shower, Vanessa is awake and even dressed in a pair of white pants and a black sleeveless top we bought when I took her shopping. Guess she was serious about tagging along with me today. Although, the sexy black heels on her feet will be hurting after a long day following me around the casino.

Her long blonde hair hangs over one shoulder, shiny and beautiful. She looks like a woman ready to do business, a feminine force to be reckoned with despite her small stature. And she doesn't even look remotely impressed by the sweat running down my chest and abs. I've had women

I've never met before ask to lick the sweat from me before they drop to their knees.

What the fuck does a man have to do get this woman horny? If I don't get my hands on her soon, I may actually go insane. But too much too soon will only chase this elusive butterfly away.

I have an idea, if I can remember where the black hair ties are stocked in the bathroom. I go in to retrieve one then come back to the bedroom to tell her, "Turn around."

Her painted pink lips open as if to ask why, but she wisely changes her mind. "Right here?"

While I'm glad the makeup hides her busted lip and black eye, she's like a different person with it on. More disagreeable, more distant. No longer the natural beauty who sleeps in my bed next to me.

"Yes, turn around right here."

"Fine," she says with a sigh, her hands braced on her hips. "But then can I go find some breakfast?"

"Yes. I'll shower fast and go with you," I promise as I gather up her hair in my hands and run my fingers through it. I can't resist inhaling the scent of her coconut shampoo either.

"Wow, you're being even creepier than normal today."

"Shut up and stand still."

Vanessa

I have no clue what Dante is doing to my hair, but I know better than to refuse or ask questions. It feels like he's separating it in sections and intertwining the sections. Is he braiding my hair?

His hands are gentle, and fast, as he winds the strands over and under each other until he reaches the ends. There, he uses a hair tie to hold it.

"Done," Dante says as he gives the end of the braid a tug. "Now I'll get a shower and we can find something to eat."

I follow him into the bathroom to look in the mirror while he pulls his phone from his shorts to type out a message or email on his phone.

It's a thick, loose, beautiful, Dutch braid that falls to the small of my back. He even left a few light strands on either side of my face. "How did you...You learned to braid hair for your three daughters?" I turn around to ask him just as he reaches into the shower to turn the shower on.

"Three daughters who never wanted to cut their hair but didn't want to brush it either."

He straightens with a smile that's breathtaking. I've never seen anything like it on his face. It's a sweet father's smile that's completely at odds with his usual power-hungry mafia king persona. Throw in the fact that there's literal sweat dripping down his massive, sculpted upper body into his athletic shorts and I have to ask myself why I haven't climbed on this man and ridden his big dick yet.

When he arrogantly, smugly, shoves his shorts and underwear to the floor with a smirk I quickly remember why I haven't.

Sure, his cock is as perfect as the rest of him. But getting too close to him is hazardous to one's health. It's not the possible threats from his enemies I mostly worry about. The real threat is Dante Salvato blowing holes through your heart and soul with a different kind of weapon—his power. Not just as a mob boss, but as a manipulative bastard who does whatever it takes to get the one and only thing he wants or needs from women before tossing them aside.

On the other hand, the only thing I can do to hurt him is to keep bruising his ego by denying him. Which I plan to do forever.

"I'll wait in the bedroom," I tell him before I turn around and walk away without another glance at his nakedness.

Every inch of him is unfortunately already imbedded into my brain, taking up more space than he should.

Whenever I think I've got one up on Dante, he goes and does something to throw me off my game.

Like, for instance, turning a simple breakfast later that morning into a power play.

The spread laid out on one of the long tables on the veranda looks delicious. There are eggs, bacon, pancakes, fruits, and pastries to choose from. But there's only one large, comfortable looking swiveling patio chair nearby.

Dante drags the chair to the table then sits down. With a tug on the end of my braid, I find myself being pulled down onto his lap. His thigh is rock hard under my ass, but at least that's the only hard thing I can feel.

Ugh. How he turned something as innocent as a pretty braid into a dog leash so fast is remarkable. I'm guessing he's already thought of other more salacious situations in which he would love to pull on it as well.

"You want me to sit here, on your lap, while we eat breakfast?" I ask in disbelief.

"Yes." He curls an arm around my waist to readjust my bottom and get more comfortable. I try to resist which results in unnecessary squirming friction.

Glancing back to the glass door, I tell him, "I doubt your daughters would appreciate the PDA if they come down this morning to eat."

Reaching for a strawberry, he presses it to my lips and says, "They won't come down. Open."

"I…" I begin to tell him I can feed myself when he shoves the straw-berry inside. "Ass," I mutter as I have no choice but to chew or spit it out. Thankfully, the leaves have already been sliced off the tops.

"Madison takes online classes year-round. Cass will be working out with her judo trainer. And Sophie will be on the roof playing tennis for as long as she can before the day turns too hot."

"You have a tennis court on the roof?" I ask, leaning forward to grab another strawberry.

"I wanted a helipad." Dante reaches for a blueberry muffin. He holds it to my mouth, offering me a bite first which I take because it has the sugar clumps on top that I love. "But Sophie's safer playing here than anywhere else."

"So, one of your daughters is a nerd and the other two are jocks?"

"That's fairly accurate." He's already halfway through the muffin when he says, "New rule. You sit on my lap everywhere we go."

"Everywhere?"

"Everywhere. And just remember that the more you squirm the more my dick likes it."

"Pervert," I say with a sigh of defeat as I finally lean my back against his chest.

Sitting on his lap is not that big of a deal. He could make me do worse as part of our agreement. Watching me try on clothes was more intrusive. While being on his lap makes me feel silly and childish, I'll tolerate it. That's really all I can do at the moment unless I want Mitch's blood on my hands.

~

A tinkling ring fills the otherwise quiet office later in the afternoon, and I'm so bored I feel the need to say, "Your phone is ringing."

I've been sitting on Dante's lap in here as well—for hours. At least the chair is cozier, and with the door shut, I don't worry about anyone barging in. Well, other than Eli, who is like a constant shadow. Sometimes I even forget he's still somewhere in the room. I glance around but don't spot him lurking around at the moment. Doesn't mean he's not hiding in some corner of the bookshelves.

"Drawer on the right," Dante instructs me, so I lean over to open it. I try to ignore his groan behind me as I lift my ass.

The drawer is one of those deep ones, and inside there are two rows of cellphones all plugged in a long charging base that must run under the desk.

"That's a lot of phones you've got there."

"Just grab the one that's ringing before it stops."

A middle one that has "AZ" as the contact's name is lit up, so I pull it free from the charger and hand it to Dante.

"Yeah?" he asks as he puts the device up to his ear.

I can't make out much of the muffled conversation on the other side. It sounds like a male voice and like he mentions something about "cargo" and "warehouse."

"Goddamn it. Anything on the security cameras?" Dante inquires.

"Fucking destroyed." Those words come across loud and clear.

"Who was on duty last night?"

The man provides names I can't make out.

"Their condition?"

"Only one survived with a minor wound," I hear the man answer, followed by something else.

"How fucking convenient," Dante grounds out through his clenched teeth, clearly not happy about the news. "Bring him to me before the end of the day tomorrow."

The man agrees. Dante ends the call, throwing the phone down on top of his desk.

"Bad news?" I guess, figuring he'll offer a vague confirmation before changing the subject.

Leaning his head back against the leather, Dante's hand that has remained on my side glides up and down slowly, over and over again. A moment later, his thumb slips up under my shirt to stroke the skin just above my waistband back and forth over the same few inches in the silence. He's so distracted I wonder if he's doing it on purpose or just absentmindedly.

Either way, it's not technically breaking the intimate touch rule, so I don't give him shit about it.

Finally, he says, "My warehouse in Arizona was just raided."

"In broad daylight?" I ask in surprise.

"Yes."

"Feds?"

"Doubtful since the fuckers took everything and killed two of my guards."

"Ah. Sorry," I tell him even though I know deaths are a common occurrence in his world. They probably don't even faze him anymore. "You think the one who survived might have betrayed you to the thieves?"

Dante's thumb stills. He rolls his head toward me with a half-smile on his face. "Exactly. The rat is also a murdering son of a bitch now as well, if he wasn't already one before..."

"How will you find out if he was involved or not?"

Staring straight ahead, his thumb begins again, circling now on my side. "Check his phone records, have IT look for any recent deposits that are unusual for his bank account, then talk to him."

"The kind of 'talking' that results in bleeding?" I guess.

Chuckling Dante asks, "Do you really want to know the gory details?"

It's hard to imagine the rich businessman ripping off fingernails or slicing into people. That would be the mafia king version of Dante. And seeing him do those terrible things would remind me exactly who he is, and will always be, no matter how gorgeous the package may look on the outside.

"Could I watch?" I ask.

"What the fuck?" His palm completely leaves my side, and I only miss it a little when his long fingers grip the chair arm instead and glowers at me. "No, Vanessa, you can't watch."

"Why not?"

Dante studies my face as he tries to figure out why I would want to observe him at his worst. It doesn't take him long to put it all together. "I'm not going to give you any new reasons to hate me."

"Hate you? I think you mean give me new reasons not to fuck you. You don't want to do anything to diminish whatever slim chance you think you may have with me."

"A slim chance is still a chance. Just wait, butterfly. I haven't even started trying to convince you to spread your legs for me yet. And I won't until all the bruises those assholes gave you are healed."

He hasn't started trying yet?

Jesus, he hasn't.

Not because he doesn't want me, but because he doesn't want to hurt me.

All he's done for the past two days is flaunt his body in front of me, which has been enough temptation for a lifetime. Will I be able to keep refusing him once he's actually *trying*?

Yes. I can, and I will. I will never give in to him. Never.

"We still have ten weeks to spend together, every single day and night," Dante reminds me. "Before this arrangement of ours ends, you *will* be mine, butterfly. And when that happens, you'll be begging me for it. You'll let me fuck you whenever and however I want, even if I need you in a puddle of my enemy's blood with the world burning around us."

"That's-that's awfully arrogant of you," I say, not bothering to point out it's another *if* not *when* situation. "I'm not going to fuck you. And trust me, I will never fuck *anyone* in a puddle of blood."

"Want to bet? You may still hate me even when I'm inside of you, but at least by then you'll hate me less than you want me."

He's not wrong. I do hate him. He's a murdering, domineering, arrogant, manipulative mafia king. I will *never* want him more than I hate him, though.

I just have to make sure my opinion doesn't ever change, which should be easy enough when it's impossible to forget the long list of his fatal flaws.

13

Vanessa

D ante told me I couldn't work in the lounge, but that I could go hang out downstairs in the casino as long as his guards are with me. So tonight, after I was left to have dinner alone, I decide to get a little dressed up to go explore.

After a quick shower to wash off, I cake on the foundation to hide the bruises on my neck and eye. Red lipstick takes care of my busted lip that already feels much better. Leaving my long, usually lifeless hair back in Dante's braid that's holding up well enough, all that's left is to put on the silver chainmail mini dress he bought me. It has a draped neckline, is low cut in the back to show off my butterfly tattoos, and there are slits on either side that go almost as high on my thigh as the thin, matching, silver thong waistband.

The two guards at the door follow me onto the elevator without a word, just phones out in their hands. I assume Dante told them to accompany me if I leave and let him know if or when that happens. Asshole.

They can follow me around all night for all I care—and report every second of what I do to the mafia king.

Not wanting to make it easy on them, I decide right then and there on the elevator where we're going.

I doubt the guards will enjoy watching men take off their clothes, but that's too bad.

I've never had a chance to see Gavin perform, so tonight is as good as any to watch him dirty dance on stage shirtless, hopefully pant-less, too.

God knows I've wanted to see his body from the day we met. But I was always working nights or too tired on days off to come for his eleven-thirty stage time. Oh, and I had a boyfriend who probably wouldn't have been happy about me ogling a stripper.

The male strip club is just a short walk from the lounge where I worked, which is why Gavin came by to have a drink or shots most nights when he was working.

Inside the male strip club, I ask for a table and, since it's early, end up as close to the front as possible during a bad cop's dance on stage. A moment later, there's a whiskey sour in my hand—put on Dante's tab of course. I glance around and find the two guards standing on either side of the doorway.

Unfortunately, I didn't come prepared with dollar bills. Still, I'm happy to sit back and enjoy the show, not inclined to be one of the rabid women surrounding the stage, waving bills, or stuffing them in G-strings.

A sexy fireman comes out after the cop, which isn't a big surprise. But then, I get to see the main attraction.

Gavin struts out on stage wearing a long, burgundy, silk robe. It's wide open in the front, revealing a teasing hint of his sculpted, waxed pectorals and washboard abs. The robe is paired with matching silk pants. Sure, he looks hot in the outfit, but it's not until his first hip thrust that I see the appeal of the extremely thin, smooth fabric.

The loose pants reveal the shape of his very long, very thick cock. Jesus, I can even see where his crown begins in the outline. He's not Dante's size, but damn. It's a lot to swing around, and swing it does. Up and down, right to left, left to right. His face is pretty, but his crotch is mesmerizing.

I'm not the only one entranced. Women are now flocking to the stage, three people deep all the way around it, waving more than dollar bills in his direction. Some hold up Benjamins, some wave their panties. A few hold up...condoms? Wow.

Now I get why he gets tipsy every night to deal with this sort of shit. How will they act when they get their hands on him?

Gavin is nothing more than a life-sized Ken sex doll for these women to play with for a night before they go back to their boyfriends, husbands, or single lives.

They just want to have sex with him, not get to know him. I doubt if they even want to know his name.

Men do the exact same thing to women every day in the real world, but that doesn't make it okay to do it to the men here.

I want to get up and leave, really, I do. But Gavin is always inviting me to watch him, so I plan to stay until the end of his dance so I can tell him I came.

After removing his robe, he drags a chair on stage, causing the women to shriek so loudly I temporarily go deaf. Throughout the next several minutes of his gyrating and floor humping, Gavin's eyes occasionally survey the room as if he's picking out the woman who will get a very public lap dance. When he's back on his feet, his gaze moves over to where I'm still seated calmly at the table behind the crowd of enthusiastic women. Gavin does a double take, then a wide grin spreads across his face.

He crooks a finger at me, making all the females in the room sigh or groan in disappointment.

I don't bother refusing. No, I enjoy the pretty man's attention way too much. Talking to him is one of the best parts of the nights working in the lounge.

Getting to my feet, I head straight for the stairs on the side of the stage.

Once I'm there, Gavin gestures for me to sit, then immediately straddles my waist, not sitting on me, but with only a hairsbreadth between our bodies. With his feet still planted on the floor, he does a full body roll, dragging his pajama covered crotch up my stomach and chest, all the way up until his hard cock smacks into the bottom of my chin through the silk pants. When I tense up, there's a twinge of pain in my sore ribs and then it's gone.

I would've been insulted if any other man slapped me in the face with his dick, but this man, not so much. The fact that he's rock hard also goes to my head. Gavin once told me that it's technically illegal for men to be in a "discernibly turgid state" in public, even if their hard-on is covered up, so the male entertainers try to keep calm as much as possible.

The stripper gives me a wink after showing me he's hornier than allowed tonight.

"It's your fault if I get arrested," he says, giving the end of my braid a tug. "You look delicious in this tiny dress. I could eat you up." His eyes lower to the dip in the front where I'm not wearing a bra. "What do I have to do for a taste, Van?"

Grinning up at him, I shake my head and laugh at his ridiculous flirting. No wonder he makes big bucks every night. When he stands so his erection taps my chin three times in a row, I grab his hips to pull him down to make him stop.

He plops back down, his weight and ass now on my thighs, his legs on either side of mine, hands gripping the back of the chair. While he's seated, I run my hands up and down his washboard abs and hard pecs that are smooth and slick with sweat and oil. He smells like a tropical paradise. One I could lick from top to bottom.

Jesus. Watching Dante swaggering around his bedroom naked has me more worked up than I realized, which is a major problem. It's only been two days! How will I survive seventy-four more?

Pushing those thoughts aside, I decide to enjoy myself now, in the moment.

"You've made every woman in here very thirsty," I inform Gavin, as if he's not well aware of that fact.

Grabbing the back of my head, he pulls my face to his chest forcing my nose and mouth to rub up on his slick flesh. I can't resist taking a deep sniff of him so close. "Drink up, Van."

I do want to, but I don't, at the same time. I'm so much older, and it's wrong to go around licking strange men. Although, I guess Gavin is sort of a friend. An acquaintance. It's inappropriate to lick acquaintances even when they have perfect bodies.

The most pressing thought in my head, unfortunately, is Dante. Sure, antagonizing him is fun, but I can't push him too far or he'll kill Gavin. Probably Mitch too, for spite.

That's the biggest reason why I keep my tongue in my mouth and shake my head.

"You know you want to," Gavin says while his hips dip and roll seductively.

I poke my index finger in his abs. "You're playing with fire, and you know it."

"But I've been waiting so long to play with you."

Before I can comprehend those words, he tips the chair backward, riding me, and it, down to the floor. My ribs protest loudly at the movement, but they can go to hell right now. I will not let those Russian assholes take this sexy moment from me, this feeling of being wanted.

As Gavin continues pantomiming fucking me, he, occasionally, spanks my mound with the bat he's swinging between his legs. Thankfully the bottom of the chair and his body blocks the audience from seeing up my dress since the hem is nearly at my hips thanks to those slits on the sides. But Gavin can see them. He stares down at the junction of my thighs says, "Nice panties. Are they wet yet?"

"What do you think?" I reply, a blush now spreading across my nose and cheeks as he keeps rolling his hips in that teasing way.

"I think I want to rip them off of you."

"Rip them off?" I repeat. Is this some part of his flirting or is he serious? I can never tell with Gavin.

It's becoming harder to think. Between his thin silk pants and my thong, there's not much separating where our lower bodies want to fit together. If he keeps slapping my clit, I'm going to come right here on the stage floor.

Gavin is panting above me, and I'm starting to think it's not just from the dancing. He's worked up too, which is unbelievable.

Suddenly, the screams and cheers are cut off like someone flipped a switch. The feisty crowd is suddenly so quiet it's eerie. All I can hear is the pounding of the bass in the song that's still playing.

"What the—" Gavin says as he glances over his shoulder. In the blink of an eye, the stripper's heavy body is lifted off of me, leaving behind a rush of cool air.

There's no elegant way to get up from an upside-down chair lying on the floor. I roll to my side, wincing. I stay on my hands and knees a moment before slowly getting to my feet because of rib pain. By the time I'm standing, Gavin is being forced backstage thanks to Dante's fingers that are wrapped around the back of his throat.

Just great. I knew Dante would be pissed when he found out I came down here. I just didn't think he would turn violent. Or catch me in the act.

I hurry to follow the two men, finding them in the hallway backstage where Dante has Gavin's face kissing the wall thanks to his fingers wrapped around his throat. Well, he would be kissing the wall if his cheek wasn't plastered to the surface.

"What the *fuck* do you think you're doing?" the mafia king shouts in the dancer's face.

"He was just doing his job!" I tell him while keeping a safe five-foot distance from them. The last thing I need are more bruises. "Let him, go, Dante!"

Without turning his head to face me, he growls, "Get back upstairs. I'll deal with you later."

"I'm not your child or dog. You can't command me," I remind him. "And you...you are acting fucking insane right now. It was just a dance!"

"The stupid son of a bitch was fucking you into the floor when you have bruised ribs!"

"I didn't...I didn't know her ribs were bruised," Gavin chokes out.

"I'm fine!" I assure them both.

"I'm not fucking fine with it," Dante grits out while still sharing breath with Gavin. In fact, he pulls him from the wall just to ram his face into it again and again.

"Dante, stop! Please!" I beg him before he busts the stripper's head open.

He gets in one more slam then releases Gavin who slumps down the wall onto his knees, gasping.

Dante barks out two names and guards appear from nowhere. "Take him to the basement and string him up."

"Dante, no! You can't!" I exclaim as the men in black each grab one of Gavin's arms to lift him up off the floor.

Now Dante's furious face turns toward me, his blue eyes colder than I've ever seen them. "I can't *what?*"

"You...you can't hurt him for having a little fun, doing a stupid little dance."

When the two guards stop, as if deferring to me, the mobster releases an actual growl. "Take him now!" he instructs them, and they instantly comply, dragging Gavin out the back exit.

"I'm so sorry, Gavin!" I call out. "I'll...I'll do what I can to get you out of there."

"Out?" it sounds like he asks, as if he has no idea the fate that awaits him in the basement dungeon. And it's all my fault.

Once the door slams shut behind the three men, Dante's voice deepens several octaves when he says, "I don't take orders from you or anyone else. Shall I send for Mitchell to go down and keep your friend company?"

"No." It's hard not to call him out for what he is, but I bite my tongue, knowing it's a promise not an idle threat.

"That's what I thought." A second later his phone is in his hand as he commands me. "Let's go."

When I hesitate, he glances up from the device to ask, "Unless you want to continue your night of fun so I can drag more men down into my basement?"

I grit my teeth to keep from calling him an asshole. His expression is smug when I start toward the exit.

95

14

Vanessa

When we're on the elevator, in the small, enclosed space together, Dante continues to be absorbed by his phone while I can't help but notice an unusual stench emitting from him. Despite the handful of guests on the ride with us, I tell him, "You stink like stale cigars."

He doesn't respond or look up.

"You're taking a shower before you get in bed with me."

"Still under the delusion that you can give me orders and I'll obey?" he asks while typing on his phone, most likely giving instructions to his men on how to hurt Gavin.

"Please don't hurt him," I whisper softly, hating that there are witnesses to my pleading.

"Fine. I won't."

That was way too easy. Of course, the mafia king doesn't have to get his hands dirty if he doesn't want to. He has people for everything. "Please don't order anyone else to hurt him either!" I quickly add.

"Eli doesn't require my orders to inflict pain."

"Dante!" I yell indignantly, drawing the attention of all the guests on the elevator. Trying another route, I tell him, "Punish me. Punish me instead of him. *Please.*"

"Why do you give two shits about the stripper boy?" Dante lifts his eyes to mine. "Are you so fucking naïve that you actually think he cares for you? He's a bisexual playboy who literally fucks anyone and everyone he meets."

"I know that," I say in a huff while crossing my arms over my chest. The words are a lie. I knew Gavin was a player; I just didn't know he played both sexes. Not that it really matters. I wasn't letting him play me. It was just a dance.

Neither of us say anything else as the elevator stops on several floors to let people off. Once we get to the penthouse, I try to go down the hall to the bedroom, but Dante steps in front of me, blocking my way.

"Move."

"No."

"What is your problem?"

"You're not going to bed yet."

"Why not?"

"Because my doctor is on the way up here to examine you."

"What?" I exclaim in confusion. He has a personal doctor to force on me? No freaking way. "I'm not letting anyone examine me!"

"Yes, you will. She's on her way up to check your rib injury."

"My...that's ridiculous."

"You do remember our deal, don't you?"

Our deal, meaning I have to do as I'm told. "Fine. I'll see the doctor, but you have to go take a shower. It's gross. I didn't know you even smoked."

"This isn't a negotiation."

"No? You just expect me to do what I'm told? Well, trust me, I hate that probably as much as you do!"

"I'm not the one who was stupid enough to date a prick who got so deep into debt you had your ass beaten."

Too tired to think of a comeback, all I can mutter is, "Touché."

That one word seems to diffuse most of the tension between us.

Since my feet ache, I go and sit down on one of the stools at the kitchen's bar to wait, watching as Dante runs his fingers through his hair, then heads for the refrigerator. He removes a plate of something and begins heating it up, rattling utensils loudly when he finds a fork.

"Did you eat dinner?" he asks while watching the plate spin in the microwave rather than look at me.

"Yes."

I start to ask how often he eats with his daughters, but I'm too tired and annoyed to try and have a conversation with the man who told his guards to "string up" Gavin in his basement dungeon. "What will it take to convince you to let Gavin go?" I ask him seriously.

Dante turns around to lean his back against the counter next to the microwave and bites down on the tines of the fork. It takes less time than I expected for him to throw out his proposition.

"Here's my one and only offer: I'll let Gavin go when the sun comes up, if..."

"If what?"

"If you'll agree to ride my hand and my tongue to completion, at least once. And at a time of my choosing." Whoa. He can't be serious. "Both at the same or on two separate occasions. My preference," he tacks on as if those details are important.

That's not at all what I expected him to say. I figured the selfish bastard would tell me to get on my knees and suck his cock or go big and demand that I let him fuck me. He didn't ask for either. No, he wants to not only finger me and lick me but do both until I come for him.

"That...that's what you want? S-seriously?" I can't help the stutter that escapes my mouth when I ask for confirmation.

"Seriously."

"Until completion is too broad. What about a time limit?"

"I'm not negotiating any further. I believe my offer is more than generous, so take it or leave it, butterfly."

As if on cue, the microwave beeps. "And this deal expires the moment I start eating." Now he grins at me, like a conniving devil who knows I'm about to sell my soul. Or at least what I know will be two soul-shattering orgasms surrendered to him, either now or at some other point at a time of his choosing.

He turns his back to me, opening the door of the microwave.

It could be worse, right? And I owe it to Gavin to do whatever it takes to set him free. Even this since I went down to the club and started shit I shouldn't have with him tonight.

"I accept," I blurt out.

"I thought you would," Dante says confidently before he takes the first bite of his dinner.

Thankfully, I'm saved from further conversation about my concessions for now when a guard escorts a tall, middle-aged woman into the penthouse. In her immaculate black pantsuit and heels with perfectly styled brown hair, my first impression is that she's well off.

At least it's a female doctor who I'm required to have examine me. She's carrying a little medical bag and all, making her look legit.

"Hello, Dr. Gates," Dante greets her without leaving the kitchen. He barely lifts his eyes from stirring his plate of food. "Feel free to use my office since I have business to attend to in the basement." I try not to think too hard about the "business" he'll be attending to. To me he says, "Go," shooing me away like an annoying gnat.

"Yes, sir," I mutter sarcastically before I walk over to meet the doctor.

"You must be Vanessa." Giving me a warm smile, she holds out her hand for me to shake.

"I'm sorry you had to come up here so late."

Her smile dims and her voice is tight when she replies. "It's always a pleasure to assist Mr. Salvato." Waving her arm toward the hallway, she says, "Shall we?"

"Yes, let's get this over with," I agree leading the way to his office.

Once we're both inside, she shuts the door, then locks it which immediately elevates my opinion of her.

Getting right down to it, she announces, "I don't know if he has cameras in here. It's a safe bet to assume so. Do you mind removing your dress so I can take a look at your ribs?"

"Sure, but my ribs are fine. Just bruised."

"I was told to examine them, so exam them I must," she replies.

"Right." As I undress for the woman I just met, doctor or not, I ask her, "So, how did someone like you get involved with Dante Salvato?"

She walks over to his desk to set down her bag and open it. "He took care of the men responsible for my husband's murder."

"Oh," I mutter in surprise. I'm assuming that "took care of" means he killed them. "I'm so sorry," I tell her sincerely as I ease my arms from the straps to shimmy the chainmail dress down my body.

"He was at the wrong place at the wrong time. Saw too much," she explains. "Now I come when called to help Mr. Salvato, no questions asked. Are you ready?"

Instinctively I wrap an arm around my breasts. "Yes."

The doctor heads for the light switches on the wall, flipping them on so I'm standing under a spotlight in Dante's office in nothing but my heels and panties. This is not how I expected the night to end. Although, I'm guessing Gavin didn't plan on being tortured tonight either...

"Those are some nasty bruises you've got," Dr. Gates remarks as she comes closer, her eyes zeroing in on the dark splotches along my side and hip. "Do you mind if I prod them?"

"Go for it."

Even though I'm expecting the press of her fingertips, I still hiss in pain.

"Sorry," she says softly. "I would need an x-ray to confirm, but I'm fairly confident there are no fractures."

"I figured it would hurt worse if a rib was broken."

She pokes around my bruised hip, then turns my head to the side to see my neck better. "Any trouble swallowing or speaking?"

"No."

"Good. The bruises should all heal within a few days. You can take over-the-counter pain relievers as needed."

"Right. Thanks."

When I reach down to pick up my dress, she gives me a hand, so I don't have to bend so far.

"Did Dante punish the ones responsible?" Dr. Gates asks as she returns to gather her bag from the desk.

"You're that certain that he didn't give me the bruises himself?" I ask her in surprise.

"Yes." Glancing over her shoulder at me, she asks, "Am I wrong?"

"No. It wasn't Dante. And I asked him not to retaliate."

"Why not? The next person they do this to may not survive."

"I...that's...I would rather take that chance than start a war with the Russians."

"Ah. Cooler heads do prevail. And Dante's temper could always use a little...refrigeration."

"Just a little?" I scoff with a grin.

"Fine. More than a little. But vengeance is a necessity in their world. A way to balance the scales, right the wrongs."

"And who decides what's right and wrong? It's just war after bloody war as they go back and forth, so nobody really wins."

"Only the strongest survive," she says. Walking over toward the door, she unlocks and opens it. "If it weren't for vigilantes like Dante, taking the law into their own hands, the men who murdered my Larry would probably still be walking around free to do as they please. Maybe it makes me a bad person, but I believe they got what they deserved. And I know for certain that they can't hurt anyone else ever again."

"What about the oath you took to do no harm?" I can't help but ask her. She seems like a nice, ethical doctor so it doesn't make sense why she would approve of the violence.

"I didn't harm anyone. Dante did. And I can never repay the debt owed to him for shouldering that burden for me. That's why I come when he calls. Be sure to duck on the way out."

"Huh?" I ask in confusion.

"It would be a shame if you hit your head from atop that high horse you're riding."

She's already out the door when I snort out a laugh. The bitchy doctor just defended Dante and called me out.

And I can't help but wonder if she's right.

What would I do if someone hurt Cole? Would I wait for the slow wheels of legal justice to churn or take matters into my own hands?

I hate how fast I'm able to answer that question.

15

Dante

Down in the basement I expected to find Gavin hanging from the ceiling screaming and bleeding. By now, Eli's been with him for about half an hour, and the former MMA fighter is always brutal as hell out of the gate. He gets off on inflicting pain, which is why he's my go-to man for the dirtiest work.

But the stripper isn't bleeding like the two captive Russians who are now restrained to chairs and gagged, scheduled to meet their maker tomorrow.

Gavin is, however, completely naked, hanging from the ceiling by chains attached to his wrists. He's definitely not in any pain. No, quite the opposite. His head is thrown back, and he's groaning in pleasure.

Strolling over, I bark at a kneeling Eli, "Why the fuck is his dick in your mouth?"

Eli doesn't act the least bit ashamed. He pulls his mouth off the other man's hard length, then gets to his feet, leaving Gavin panting as he brushes dirt off the knees of his pants and walks up to me.

"Well? Were my instructions unclear?" I demand.

"Look at him," he huffs with a wave of his hand toward the naked man. "He was too pretty to maim."

"Make. Him. Hurt," I grit out. "I don't care if you think he's pretty. He fucked with what's mine."

"Blue balls hurt like hell," Eli points out.

Going over to the work bench where I keep my box of cigars, I clip the end of one, then put it in my mouth to light it up while considering the best punishment.

God knows Vanessa has given me blue balls for days now. Being so close to her in my bed while being a world away from fucking her is a new kind of torture.

And fuck me, she's right. My cigars are stale. I need a new humidor down here. Placing the stick on a glass ashtray to burn itself out, I tell Eli, "Do what you want to him, but he doesn't get to come tonight."

"Of course not," he agrees with an evil grin. "If he does, I'll find new ways to punish him."

"Good."

"I'm sure I can figure out a way to hurt him without leaving permanent damage."

"Right, well, let him go when the sun comes up."

"Just like that? Let him walk out?" he says in shock.

"At sunrise. I made another deal with Vanessa." One I can't wait to fulfill, but not until her bruises are healed. "Let the stripper walk out if he can. If not, dump him outside in the employee parking lot."

"Yes, sir."

Walking up to Eli so the stripper can't hear me, I tell him, "Have our IT guys do a deep dig into his background. I want all the dirt they can find on him ASAP."

"Got it," he agrees.

As I walk away toward the elevator, Gavin cries out behind me from something Eli does to him. I really don't want to know what it was.

Kicking his ass would've felt good, but then Vanessa would've been pissed at me for fucking him up. Whatever Eli does to him will probably cause worse damage than my fists anyway.

Knowing I'm going to get to put my hands and mouth on her pussy has me in a much better mood. The dick who rubbed up on my woman is surely regretting his decision, so he won't ever do it again. All is right with the world.

On the elevator ride up to the penthouse, I read Dr. Gates report on Vanessa. Her bruises seem to be superficial, which is good to know. If the stripper had aggravated her injuries in any way, he'd be a dead man, just like the two Russians.

It suddenly occurs to me that before I end them, I should at least question the Russians about the warehouse raid, see if Kozlov or his boss, Yuri Petrov, had anything to do with it. I know they couldn't have found out we brought in their guys and retaliated that fast, so it probably wasn't them. Could've been the Irish bastard, Lochlan, messing with me because he's getting impatient waiting for Madison to agree to marry him. Their union, making Lochlan an ally, would be nice. If the wedding falls through, though, he'll quickly become another enemy. One of the things most mobsters loathe more than anything in this world is having someone back out of an agreement.

As soon as I get back upstairs, I head down the hall, aiming straight for the bedroom.

I'm happy to see that Vanessa is awake even at this late hour, sitting up in bed, doing something on her phone with the bedside lamp glowing. She doesn't look up at me or speak to me. Not that I expected her to. I do, however, hear her sniffing me from five feet away when I sit on the bench at the foot of the bed, removing my jacket and gun holster.

"You still smell like stale smoke."

"Yes, I do."

"Are you going to shower?"

"If you join me," I challenge her.

"In your dreams, Salvato," she tells my back.

Vanessa probably would've fucked the stripper, but not me. I don't think she's a prude, so why the constant rejection? Is she trying to hurt me by denying me?

Standing up, I turn so I can see her, studying her face in the soft light. It's impossible to miss the bruises on her neck as dark as the ones I know are on her ribs and hip. I would give anything for a peek inside of her head, to know what she was thinking tonight when she got on that stage in front of a crowd of women...

"You knew I would find out about the lap dance, didn't you?" I ask her. "You *wanted* me to find out."

"I didn't give a tiny rat's ass either way, Dante," she sasses right back without lifting her eyes from her phone.

"You didn't care about the consequences to Gavin?"

"I knew he would be safe because you know that you would have a less than zero chance of ever touching me if you try to torture him or kill him."

"You're not to see him or step foot in that club again," I tell her.

Her angry green eyes finally lift to meet mine. "You're just pissed that everyone in the casino will think you're a cuckold now."

"A cuckold?" I repeat with a scoff.

Fuck. She's right. All my employees know she's staying in the penthouse with me. Soon, they'll all hear about my violent outburst on stage tonight because I was jealous of Gavin, something I've never been in my entire fucking life.

I'm also pissed because I can't go fuck another woman to get even or I will lose every chance with Vanessa.

She's damaging my reputation that I ruthlessly earned, the one that warns enemies not to fuck with me. It's what keeps my family safe, and now it's in jeopardy.

This woman...I've been well and truly fucked by her in every way but the one my body aches for as badly as my lungs crave oxygen.

I think Vanessa knows exactly what she's doing to me. She's intentionally hurting me for forcing her into this agreement.

Before I can call her on it, she says, "Just to be clear, I will see who I want, dance with whom I want, and *fuck* whoever I want, and there's not a damn thing you or anyone else can do to stop me!"

Suddenly she's so enraged that her eyes are glistening like she's on the verge of tears.

I have never seen her get so worked up. Somehow, I hit a nerve of hers without realizing it. I need to know more, but I'm too pissed at her right now to ask her about it.

"You fucked around with him in my casino, on my stage, in front of my employees. You fucked with my reputation, made me look like a *cuckold*, as you called it. That's the problem here, Vanessa. You are *fucking* with every part of my life except for my goddamn cock!"

"Then maybe you shouldn't have manipulated me into being your prisoner! I'm not one of your daughters. You can't control me, my body, or what I do with it."

"Is asking you to stop humping men in public, in my place of business, too constraining on your bodily autonomy?"

"I...no, I guess not." Now she glances away to the darkness outside the windows and crosses her arms over her chest defiantly. She may not be one of my daughters, but she sure as hell is acting like a goddamn unruly teenager right now.

"Could you at least give me a heads up before any other men hump you during our time together?"

"Just because I had one dirty lap dance with a stripper doesn't mean I go around jumping on every man I see. And again, it's none of your business."

"It is my business while you're staying here with me, doing it in my casino."

She blows out a breath and says, "You're a hypocrite, acting like I'm some huge slut. I haven't even been with many people! I'm actually extremely picky."

"Why was Mitchell one of the chosen few?"

Vanessa shrugs. "Ah, I don't know. Because he was easy? Uncomplicated, I mean."

"How?"

"When we first started dating there were no games, just let's fuck, let's hang out, let's move in together and help each other out with the bills. There were never any fireworks like intimately. Just normal sex. It was mutually beneficial for a while."

"And you were happy with just normal sex?"

"Why not? I haven't had firework sex since I was a teenager."

She hasn't had good sex in decades? "Since you were a teenager, huh?"

Now she lowers her arms, and her fingers pick at some invisible lint on the comforter covering her lap. "I was a bit promiscuous for a few years, which is how Cole was conceived."

"Tell me more about this firework sex you had, butterfly," I say while toeing off my shoes, then removing my socks. Anything to take my mind off of that stripper air fucking her on the floor while she's still covered in bruises.

She scoffs. "God, no! I'm not telling you about that."

"You don't want to distract me from my anger at your boytoy? Should I go back down to the basement to spend more time with him?"

"I..." she starts then stops.

"What's the best firework sex you had?" I ask, now undoing the buttons on my shirt starting at the neck. "Or would you rather discuss torture techniques?"

Groaning, she rubs her forehead with both hands and says, "Fine. There was one time, and only one time, that I sort of had a foursome."

My jaw nearly hits the floor at her confession.

"*You* had a foursome? As a teenager?"

She nods and bites her lips, keeping her eyes lowered to her lap. "They were frat brothers who I guess liked to do everything together."

My fingers pause on the bottom button of my dress shirt. "Vanessa Brooks, I am fucking shocked."

"Swear you won't do any permanent damage to Gavin?" she asks.

I remove my shirt and start working on undoing my belt. "No permanent damage if you tell me all about this foursome you had." Here's hoping Eli keeps that promise for me tonight.

"I've never told anyone about this."

"Why not?"

"Because men would think it means I'm easy and women would think I'm a slut."

"Why did you do it? Just having fun?"

"I was rebelling mostly, proving to myself that it was my body, and I can be with whoever I want to be with." There it is again, her emphasis on it being her body to do what she wants with it.

"Strict parents?" I guess as I slowly lower the zipper of my pants, very aware of her unfocused gaze staring at my chest while she talks.

"Very strict. So, when I got my first taste of freedom, I couldn't get enough of it."

"So how did the foursome happen?" Down my pants go to the floor where I step out of them. There's a bulge in front of my black boxer briefs that Vanessa seems to be focused on.

Her tongue wets her lips. "I didn't plan for it or anything. There was a frat party I crashed while I was squatting in an empty dorm room. I was fooling around with a guy up in his room when his roommate and friend came in. They watched and encouraged us. There was a lot of flattery and alcohol involved."

"Obviously."

"After the first guy finished, they sort of took turns all night, doing things I had never even imagined. And I let them because it felt good. I liked being wanted by them. It was the first time in my life I felt sexy, like I was no longer a little girl, but a woman who men were finally attracted to."

"Exactly how old were you, Vanessa?"

Now she lifts her eyes to mine again for the first time since I started my strip show. "Ah, sixteen or seventeen?"

"Sixteen? And they were, what, college guys in their twenties?"

"No. Maybe. They didn't know how young I was. I lied and said I was older. They were probably nineteen or twenty."

"And you don't regret that night?"

"I wish I knew who Cole's father was for his sake. I'm certain it was one of them. And I'm so lucky I didn't catch any diseases. But no, I don't regret it. It was the first time I ever felt...free."

She felt free after having a foursome in her teens. Jesus.

I want to strangle the frat bros with my bare hands while simultaneously shaking their hands for a job well done, helping me unlock one of Vanessa's deepest secrets. There's a sexy little queen inside of her demanding to be worshipped.

"Would you do it again?" I can't help but ask.

"What? The foursome? Ha! No way."

"Why not?"

"That's not who I am anymore."

Even so, my sweet little butterfly deserves her fireworks. Just not with the stripper. At the reminder of that asshole, I tell her, "I received Dr. Gates report from her exam. Are you sore?"

"For the last time, Dante, my ribs are fine!"

"That's good. Because if he made them worse, I would've broken his as well."

"But you didn't break anything? You're definitely letting Gavin leave in the morning in one piece?"

"I said I would, didn't I?" I shove my boxer briefs down, letting my hard cock bob up to slap my stomach. Vanessa takes a long look at it before crossing her legs that are stretched out in front of her. I think our sex talk, and my nakedness is actually getting to her.

She lifts her eyes quickly though, now examining the ink on my chest. "And the, um, terms of our agreement? When, do you, ah, think you'll want to..."

She wants to plan for my side of the bargain, to prepare herself to try not to enjoy it.

"It's my decision. I don't owe you any notice for either or both," I tell her. "But I can promise you that I won't touch you until your bruises are all healed."

She nods but doesn't respond as she considers my words.

"Now, I'm going to take a shower because I want one, not because you demanded I take one. Feel free to think about how good my fingers and tongue will feel when you ease that ache between your thighs."

She scoffs, cheeks flushing red. "There is no ache!"

"Liar," I reply with a grin before I stride into the bathroom, certain she's staring at my ass.

Vanessa

I hate the way my traitorous body wants Dante Salvato, despite all the protests from my head.

My body doesn't care that he's a murderous mobster or vicious manipulator who trapped me into living with him. It's not bothered by the thought of an innocent man being restrained in the basement dungeon.

No, my body just sees Dante as an attractive, massively muscular man with a big dick who can make me feel good.

It's impossible not to think about his tongue or long fingers between my legs now that I agreed to those terms for Gavin's sake.

Although, two orgasms don't really seem like much of a concession to make.

One thought suddenly occurs to me.

If Dante lied, if he hurt Gavin more than he promised, then I'll have grounds to void the earlier agreement.

Since I can't go down to the basement without Dante or another authorized person's finger, I'll have to wait and call him tomorrow to check on him.

That has me thinking of another man who could be buried six feet under by now. If so, I could walk out the door right now since Mitch's life is why I'm stuck here.

Even though I don't want to hear his sorry ass voice, I still grab my phone from the bedside charger and call him.

The line rings and rings, until he eventually answers. "Hello? Vanessa?" He not only sounds fine, but he also sounds wide awake despite the late hour. I'm almost certain I can hear the sound of slot machines in the background.

"So, you are still alive. Pity," I mutter, even if I'm secretly glad he's not dead. Guess I won't be leaving the casino anytime soon.

"Look, if you're calling about the apartment, I'm trying to find another place."

"What do you mean?"

"Salvato's men told me I have to move out of our place by the end of the month."

"Oh. Well, good." I'm not sure why I'm surprised Dante would do that. I'm starting to think his goal in life is to keep all men away from me. "And I assume you've realized we're done, and I never want to see you again?"

"Oh, come on, Van. You're living it up in the rich bastard's penthouse. I bet he has people waiting on you, giving you anything and everything you want by now."

"There's only one thing he wants from me, and you fucking know it!" I yell at him.

"You haven't given in yet? Why not? What's the worst that can happen? He kills you afterward?"

I can't help but notice that Mitch doesn't sound the least bit jealous. Not exactly shocking since he cheated on me multiple times.

Rolling my eyes that he can't see, I tell him, "I'm touched by your concern for my wellbeing. Why are you even still in town? If you were smart, you would get as far away from Salvato's reach as possible."

"Where else would I go?" He huffs.

"Try not to get yourself killed," I say then end the call.

Asshole.

I know I deserve better than him. Cole certainly deserves a better role model than Mitch, too. He's never had a man in his life to look up to, which makes me feel guilty. And concerned.

What if I messed my son up by raising him on my own without a father? I was so afraid I would introduce him to jerks that I didn't date often. And I think I've always been too afraid of showing my real self to anyone. I don't deserve to live happily ever after.

Struggling to make ends meet, living alone without anyone I can count on, is the price I have to pay for the mistakes I've made.

If I can just get through the next ten weeks without being responsible for anyone else getting hurt like Gavin, then I'll consider that a win.

But going back to my life, the ten-hour workdays, and my lonely apartment, after being here, living the spoiled princess life in Dante's penthouse, is probably going to be harder than I could ever anticipate.

16

Dante

The next morning, by the time I finish my workout and shower, I get a text from Eli that Stevie Hudson, the guard from the Arizona warehouse that was raided, has been brought in for questioning.

The thirty-something man with thinning brown hair is already strung up from the ceiling right where Gavin was last night.

Eli assured me that the stripper wobbled out of here on his own two feet and that he would be thoroughly deterred from messing with Vanessa again.

Getting right down to business, I ask Stevie the usual warm-up question as I pace in circles around him with my hands shoved in my suit pockets. "How the fuck did you manage to avoid being killed or even seriously hurt in the unexpected raid that took out your two companions?"

"The bathroom. I was...I was in the bathroom when I heard the gunfire. I stayed there until the shooting stopped."

"How convenient for you," I mutter in response to his rapid

response. "You didn't think your comrades could've used the backup? That you should've done your job and protected my product?"

"I'm sorry!" he says. "P-please don't kill me!"

The man pleads some more, but I don't hear much of what he says. Instead of focusing on getting the truth out of him, I'm distracted, thinking about Vanessa.

Why doesn't she want me? And why the fuck does she hate me?

It's irritating the hell out of me. I know there are plenty of people in the world who abhor me, and I couldn't care less what they think. But with Vanessa...

Does she hate me because I hit on her all the time when she was a cocktail waitress? Because I fucked around with all of her fellow cocktail waitresses?

Whatever it is happened before I coerced her into the agreement for Mitch's life. He's the one who mentioned it, as if at some point in time, she came home from work and told him she hated me. Or she said as much to him multiple times.

Trying to figure her out is impossible.

"You need me to take over?" Eli asks, interrupting my thoughts from his literal front-row seat. Other than the two Russians still restrained in chairs with duct tape over their mouths, he's the only other witness to our question-and-answer session with Stevie.

"No. I'm sure you have your hands full already."

"Which is preciously why I wish you would keep going. You know I can't come until he screams a little louder."

The former MMA fighter is still jonesing for more torture even after spending all of last night with the stripper. It's like he can't ever get enough of that shit. I've found that letting him jerk off in front of the bastards I'm interrogating and torturing makes them even more uncomfortable.

"You should ask him how he can afford that new car our guys found in his garage," Eli says helpfully.

"Right," I agree. "No financing, Stevie? On your measly guard salary? Who paid for the Land Rover?"

"My wife," he lies. "My wife bought it. It's in her name!"

"Should we bring her down here and ask her ourselves? String her up right beside you?"

"No! No, please don't!" he begs between gasping sobs.

"Then tell me the truth or I'll have her picked up right fucking now."

The asshole is about to hyperventilate after my threat. He better figure out how to speak long enough to tell me the name of who paid him to fuck me over before the pain begins.

"Burn him with one of his cigarettes," Eli suggests, breathing heavily behind me.

Sighing, I mutter, "Fine."

Pulling out my knife from my pocket, I open it up and position the tip over the top button of his blue uniform shirt. The man wails when I slide it down the material to split it open, probably because I pressed too deep and sliced some skin. Whoops.

I then go over to the tool bench where all the man's belongings were placed when he was brought down and searched. There, I pick up the half-empty pack of cigarettes to shake one stick out, put it between my lips, and light it with his cheap red lighter.

"Stop! Make him stop looking at me like that!" Stevie begs.

I don't have to turn around to know that Eli is grinning at him like the psychotic bastard he is, his pants and underwear around his knees, not bothering to try and hide his hard cock he's jerking like he's watching the best porno ever.

"The more you scream, the closer he gets to finishing. Tell me who killed my men, your so-called friends, when they robbed my goddamn warehouse, and he'll stop getting off on your suffering."

It's a lie. Eli and I both know the man isn't leaving the room alive. Eli will either get to finish during the torture or when I take the rat's life.

I hate that I sometimes get aroused, too, from the power play. Knowing I hold a life in my hands, a sorry son of a bitch rat or enemy's life in my hands, and there's nothing they can do about it, makes me hard. It's nearly therapeutic having so much control in this chaotic world, even if it only lasts a few minutes. Vanessa would really hate me if she knew that detail.

Taking a draw from the cigarette on the way back to the waiting man, I remove it from my lips to blow out the smoke. Deciding where to start, I walk around behind him. Grabbing the hair on the top of his head, I pull it back and place the smoldering end of the cigarette on the side of his neck. It sizzles on his flesh, making him shriek.

In front of us, Eli closes his eyes, savoring the sound as his fist strokes his dick faster.

When I remove the cigarette from Stevie's skin to take another puff, Eli's heavy-lidded brown eyes stare at me with longing and loathing.

The once champion MMA fighter, living his dream, hates what I've made him—an evil bastard who lives and breathes at my whim, just like everyone else who steps into my basement dungeon. Part of him loves it, having the freedom to be as fucked up as he wants now. He just wishes his leash was a little longer. He's lucky I let him live.

I know that I can't force Vanessa to stay with me the way I did to Eli, giving him no other option. Butterflies were meant to fly free, not be kept selfishly trapped in a jar.

So, I'll just have to find a way to win her over and enjoy the time we have left together before I let her go.

Why do I get the feeling that finding out who is responsible for raiding my warehouse will be easier than catching one little butterfly?

I put the cigarette back between my lips as I stroll over to the two Russians. There's drying blood on the floor around them and bags under their bloodshot eyes. They haven't been able to sleep or eat in two days, so they're not long for this world.

Ripping the duct tape off the first one's mouth, then the other, I wait until the swearing stops and then ask them, "Do either of you recognize the man hanging from the ceiling?"

Both shake their heads no.

"Never had any business dealing with him?"

Again, they deny the allegation.

"If I go back over there and he tells me you're lying, I'll let Eli cut your eyeballs out and fuck the sockets."

"N-never seen him. I swear," one replies.

The other says, "Don't know him."

"We'll see," I warn them.

Going back over to Stevie, I pull out the pocketknife I keep on me.

Opening it, I place the point to the fresh burn wound, making him scream. "Do you know those two men in those chairs?"

I pull the knife blade away from his flesh so he can respond, but he keeps on sobbing.

"Oh fuck," Eli groans. "Fuck, I'm coming!"

"Talk or he's going to feed you every drop of his cum," I threaten him.

"No! No! I don't know who it was! Please! I swear!"

Homophobia can be one hell of a motivator.

"You don't know who raided my warehouse or you don't know who paid you to betray me?" I ask for clarification.

"Please don't hurt my wife!" he exclaims, telling me the answer. "She doesn't know anything!"

"Tell me everything, and I'll spare her," I promise. She was never going to be my victim anyway, but the promise has him confessing it all.

"Someone...I got a text with an address. The message told me to meet up last Thursday at seven-thirty, after I finished my shift at the warehouse."

"And you went?"

"They offered me an easy fifty K. I didn't know what they wanted until it was too late!"

"Too late for your greedy ass to return the money? Sure. Right. Who was it, Stevie?"

"I don't know! He was standing there waiting in a long, trench coat and hat, no car. I didn't get a name."

"Did he have an accent? Could you tell his ethnicity?"

"I don't know! He was just a pale white man wearing sunglasses, so I barely saw his face."

"And what did he ask you to do for the fifty K?"

"He wanted me to text when the next shipment came in. Said I'd get another fifty after it was done."

"Well, Stevie, was that quick hundred grand worth dying for?"

"No. I don't want it! I'll give it to you."

"I don't want your dirty money. I want the person responsible for killing two of my *loyal* men and fucking robbing me!"

"I'm sorry, I'm so...so sorry." He then starts bawling like a baby.

"We have his phone?" I ask Eli.

"Yeah," he says while licking his hand clean. Sick bastard. When he's done, he pulls up his pants to finally put his dick away. "IT is trying to track the texts."

Turning back to the rat, I toss my knife in the air a few times and catch it. "Tell you what, Stevie, I'm going to let your wife keep the cash. She'll need it when you don't come home tonight—or ever again."

I don't give him a chance to respond before I bury my knife into the side of his neck down to the hilt.

Blood splatters over my jacket and button-down, drips from my hand as I jerk the knife free and let the asshole bleed out.

It's not much justice for Mark and Eddie, the two men who lost their lives to his greed. I'll make sure their wives get twice as much as the rat's.

"You're gonna have your hands full again this afternoon," I tell Eli.

"Three bodies will take all fucking night for me to bury," he complains.

"Why don't you swing by and pick up your new stripper friend? Make him help. Two shovels are better than one."

"You really want me to show Gavin the dead men and where we bury them?"

"Yes. With a gun to his head if necessary. Then video him digging holes to use for blackmail. I think they'll be a bigger deterrent for him to stay away from Vanessa."

"Fine."

Ready to get this over with, I head for the two Russians. I'm halfway to them when Eli calls out, "Hey, Dante?"

"Yeah?" I ask over my shoulder.

"I, ah, need to tell you what was dug up on Gavin."

"Yeah?"

"The stripper's had a crush on Vanessa for a while."

That brings me up short. Turning to face him again, I say, "And? How do you know?"

"He's not a fan of Mitch's, and he's friends with Kozlov's girls."

"You're saying he had something to do with running up the debt?"

"He offered the girls fentanyl if they baited him into fucking. Wanted Mitch to think it was a freebie while adding it to his tab."

"Holy shit."

"Four of them took him up on the offer. Crazy, right?"

"Vanessa is going to lose her shit. That fucker is the reason they hurt her!" I exclaim while pointing at the Russians.

"Gavin's only responsible for about twenty-five percent of the debt Mitch owed. The rest was all on him gambling on shit."

"Good to know. You got proof?"

"Talked to two of the girls myself this morning."

"You've been busy," I remark. "Take tomorrow off after you finish cleaning up this mess."

"Hell, yes," he replies with a smile.

Turning back to the Russians, I use what's left of one of their shirts to clean the bloody knife in my hand before pocketing it again. This suit is fucked anyway.

Then, I pull out my gun from my holster, putting one bullet in each of the asshole's heads.

17

Vanessa

It takes longer than I had hoped to track down a coworker who was not only awake to answer their texts but also had Gavin's phone number.

I should've known that Georgia would come through for me. She's probably slept with the stripper.

Instead of texting Gavin, I call him. It takes three attempts going to his voicemail before he finally answers.

"I don't know who you are and don't care. Just stop calling me!" he shouts into the phone.

"Gavin, wait!" I beg before he hangs up.

"Vanessa?"

"Yeah, it's me. How...how are you? Can you walk? Is anything, you know, broken?" I ask.

He makes a grumbling sound. "I've been better, but nothing is broken."

"I'm so sorry, Gavin. I had no idea Dante would erupt like that in public or take it out on you. I shouldn't have gotten you involved..."

"It's fine. I don't blame you."

"You should. It was stupid of me to provoke him while I'm stuck in this...agreement with him."

"You're still staying with him?" Gavin asks with a scoff, like he's surprised by that.

"Well, yeah. I have to."

"You don't have to do anything, Van!"

"Trust me, Gavin, if I could leave here I would."

"Has he hurt you?"

"No."

"Well, he probably will. He's fucking demented. Him and the psycho who tormented me the entire night!"

"Eli? He tormented you? What did he do?"

Sighing, he says, "It's done and over with. Now I just want to forget it happened. I still want to see you."

"What? No, Gavin," I reply in a rush. Is he crazy? "You should stay away. Seriously. I'm not worth the trouble, and I feel guilty enough about last night."

"I'll be in the lounge tonight like usual," he tells me.

"Well, I won't. I can't. I'm sorry about everything, okay?"

"Vanessa, wait!" he shouts but I hang up on him.

Is he insane? Whatever was done to him last night wasn't enough to deter him, which is confusing as hell.

And one thing is clear from our conversation, Dante held up his side of our bargain. Which means one day, in the not-so-distant future, I'll have to let Dante put his mouth on me, endure having his fingers inside of me.

Both of those things are terrifying because I know I'll enjoy it, no matter how much my head tries not to like it.

I don't see Dante again until late that night, after I've had dinner alone again. Not that I missed him or was waiting up for him.

"What did you do today?" he questions me as he removes his jacket.

"Ah, I had a spa day. Got a deep tissue massage, a mud wrap, and had some waxing done." I didn't like using the facilities here on his dime, but after last night, I think I deserved a little indulgence.

"Waxing, huh? Where did you..."

"Nope. That's none of your business," I stop him. "Where have you been all day?"

"Working," he says as he begins undressing at the foot of the bed facing me, first removing his jacket then gun holster. Just like last night, he's doing it on purpose, making me watch him get naked while forcing me to simultaneously hold a conversation with him.

"Working?" I repeat.

Undoing his buttondown, he holds my gaze. "The guard who was unharmed in the warehouse raid was brought in this morning."

"Oh. So...you were, um, questioning him?"

Arching an eyebrow as he shrugs off the shirt, baring his broad, tattooed chest and stomach he says, "Torturing the information out of him. No point sugar coating it, butterfly."

"Right. How did it go?"

"He confessed, gave me a lead, so I guess you could say it went well." He adds that last part like he doesn't really consider it a win. I would guess not since two of his employees are still dead and all his product, likely millions in illegal drugs, are gone.

For the first time since I've been staying here with him, I realize how difficult it must be for Dante to not be able to trust anyone in his life. In the mafia world I'm guessing you could be friends with someone one day and enemies the next. Nothing is ever free. Everyone likely has ulterior motives. Even I'm sitting here in his bed out of obligation, not choice.

As Dante shoves his gray suit pants down his muscular thighs, I try to think about anything other than his package in his snug sky-blue boxer briefs. He put on white ones this morning. I saw him after his shower when I was pretending to sleep. Before I can help myself, I blurt out, "That's not the...suit you were wearing when you left earlier." I barely catch myself from saying underwear. But the suit this morning was also darker.

"No, it's not," Dante responds while reaching down to remove his socks.

He changed during the day. Which means he either got dirty... rolling around in bed with someone or..."You got blood on the other suit?" I guess.

"It got a little dirty. Why?"

I hate that I'm relieved to hear he gets dirty torturing and not whoring around. Although, he could be lying and did both.

"Why not do what it is that you do in something other than expensive suits?" I ask him.

Dante's hand lowers to scratch the fuzzier part of his lower belly, right above the waistband of his underwear as if intentionally drawing my attention to it.

"Who would you be more afraid of if you ran into them on the street? A homeless guy in dirty sweats you're certain doesn't have a dollar to his name or a man in a pristine suit who could have enough money, enough power to kill you without consequences?"

"Ah, fine. I get it, the intimidation factor. Do you at least take your jacket off?"

His shoulders slump slightly, as if he's mentally and physically exhausted from the long day. "Sometimes. Not always. It depends on how urgent the situation arises. Why are you playing the gangster version of twenty-questions with me? You going to write my biography when you leave here, butterfly?"

I shrug. "I'm just curious. And it's not like I have anything else to do since you won't let me work. Maybe I'll take up writing." It's not that I miss waiting tables, but having something productive to do every day is better than being alone and bored.

"What do you want to do besides serve drinks to assholes all night?" Dante asks, his hands now gripping his hips.

"I don't know. I've never really had any free time to think about it. I'm always either working or sleeping."

"That is just fucking sad."

"I know. I realized the same thing earlier," I reply quietly. "What about you? What do you usually do after your gangster and businessman obligations are done for the day?" I ask.

"Fuck."

"Ah." Should've known.

"I fuck away all the shit I had to do during the day, the shit I don't want to think about for a few hours."

One part of that confession is hard to believe and makes me roll my eyes. "Hours? Really?"

"I have incredible stamina," he says. "And I love eating pussy. That kind of foreplay takes time and is usually a prerequisite before a woman can enjoy my cock."

My eyes unintentionally lower to the growing bulge in his underwear. "Because you're...big. Got it."

When his tattooed hand slides under the band, fisting himself under the cotton, it causes an unfortunate throbbing to begin between my legs.

"Vanessa, do you remember that part of our agreement about no additional compensation unless otherwise specifically stated?" he asks while his hand moves up and down just out of sight.

I swallow hard. "Yes. What about it?"

"I'll give you ten grand right now if you'll use your hand to get me off."

My jaw drops in utter disbelief. Did he just ask me... When I recover, I answer him with a resounding, "No!"

"Fifty thousand?"

He would actually pay me fifty grand for a hand job, which is insane.

"Still a no." I hate that my rejection takes a little longer to come out of my mouth.

"A hundred grand?"

Now I scoff, but I stupidly, desperately, consider stroking his dick before finally shaking my head to decline and clear those thoughts from it. "No. I'm not now, or ever will be, your paid whore!"

18

Dante

I'm horny as fuck tonight, and Vanessa refuses to be bought. Since I paid off Mitch's loan for her to stay, she'll never fuck me. I can't put a price tag on her dignity, no matter what I offer. I'm not sure if I'm relieved or disappointed. Mostly disappointed at this moment in time.

"You won't put your hand on my dick for a hundred thousand dollars?" I challenge her while stroking my hard-on still contained, for the moment, inside my underwear.

"No! Never!" she exclaims. Despite her refusals, I think she wants to. She wants me but won't allow herself to give in yet.

"Your boyfriend gave you up for less cash than that. I bet he would've sucked my dick for seventy-six thousand."

"I'm sure the asshole would have done pretty much anything you wanted for the money, especially if you made it into a bet."

My hand stills on my dick at her response. How...how did someone so good and so beautiful end up with a piece of shit like him?

"You know he still hasn't learned his lesson, right? By the time you're free of me, he'll be up to his neck in gambling debt *again* and have slept with half the strippers in the city."

"Thank you for that reminder, Dante."

"Okay, fine. If you're not gonna help, then I'll just have to find some material to take care of my dick myself."

Removing my hand from my boxer briefs I pick up my pants to remove my phone from the pocket. Then, I pull up one video in particular, turning the volume up so we can both hear the moaning, groaning, and frantic bodies slapping together.

Holding my phone in my left hand, I shove my boxer briefs down my legs to fist myself again, now giving her a front-row seat.

"I hate you," Vanessa snaps, admitting aloud how she really feels about me. And that fucking pisses me off.

"That's fine, remember? Angry fucks are my favorite."

She scoffs and flops to her side in bed, putting her back to me. "Goodnight, you depraved prick."

When the moaning on the video gets faster, louder, Vanessa covers her head with a pillow.

"Don't tune out yet. I think you'll recognize some of the grunting," I say loud enough that I know she can hear me.

A second later, her boyfriend's voice fills the air. *"Oh, yeah. Take my fat cock, you dirty fucking bitch."*

"I'm guessing he was exaggerating. Does Mitchell actually have a fat cock?"

For a moment, Vanessa doesn't move, doesn't even breathe. Suddenly, she pops up again. Crawling over on her knees, she comes to the foot of the bed, and plucks my phone right out of my hand.

Sitting back on her heels, she blinks at the screen as if she doesn't believe what she's seeing. Her cheeks gradually redden more as each second passes. Then, her eyes glisten.

"That's..."

"Mitchell? Yes. The date and time stamp on the bottom is accurate."

Vanessa keeps watching with a scowl. I hate seeing her upset because of that son of a bitch, but showing her the type of man he'll always be is the only way for her to get over him for good.

She called the bastard just last night while I was in the shower. How do I know? I put a bug in his cell phone that my IT guys monitor. I heard the conversation earlier today, so I know she was just making sure I left him alive. Maybe even hoped he wouldn't answer; that she would be left with doubt in order to use it as a reason to bail on our agreement. I'm staying two steps ahead of her, keeping up my side of the deal despite wanting to put a bullet in his head.

"Her stage name is Raine," I inform her. "You can probably guess why they call her that. She charged him five hundred dollars, and it took him less than sixty seconds to finish even though he had an hour. The fucker didn't take any time for foreplay either. Is that his usual style?"

There's a long groan before Vanessa presses a finger to the screen to make the video stop. "He paid her five hundred dollars for *that*?"

"Well, he put it on his tab with Kozlov."

"I got beaten up not just for the gambling, but because he didn't pay the bill for the whores he humped on for a few seconds?"

"Yes. That's more than you make working the entire night, isn't it?"

Her response is to toss my phone down on the mattress in front of me, lips pursed. Thankfully, the cut on the bottom lip is starting to heal.

"You're angry and hurt. I don't blame you," I remark. "Do you want to know the best way to hurt him back? By fucking me."

"Go to hell, Dante!" I know her raised voice and blazing green eyes are directed at her moronic ex, not me, not really.

"That's not me in the video cheating on you," I remind her.

"He hasn't worked in months!"

"Why should he when he can sit around and let you bust your ass all night to pay his bills while he busts nuts in whores?" I can't help but point out the obvious, feeding her fury. "If you want, we could even send him a video of us fucking."

Tilting her head to the side, she looks at me through her narrowed eyes like I must have lost my mind. "You're an asshole. Men are all assholes. You...you get better looking as you age while women grow older, and saggy, and undesirable. We can never live up to the perfection of young, thin strippers and porn stars you all fuck!"

It takes me a moment to get to the bottom of what she's saying within that rant condemning my entire sex as a whole. "Do you think Mitchell cheated on you because he was no longer attracted to you?"

She throws her hands up in exasperation. "Obviously! And while I hate it, I still get it. I can't compete with any of them. They're in their early twenties. Every part of them is still all perky and shit, while I'm sneaking up on forty for fuck's sake!"

"No, Vanessa. You've got it all wrong. That fucker cheated on you because he's a selfish asshole who only thinks about himself. You are a stunningly beautiful woman who isn't afraid of anything, not even a murdering bastard like me. If you demanded what you were really worth for seventy-six days, even I wouldn't be able to afford you."

Vanessa huffs out a laugh and runs her fingers nervously through the front of her hair. I want to braid it again, but I doubt she'll let me.

"I'm not touching your dick no matter how much you try to flatter me, Salvato."

"And I'm not going to stop trying to change your mind," I tell her with a grin. Then, I figure now is as good a time as any to hit her with the information from Eli I've been saving up all day. "Would you like to know how Mitchell ended up with those women?"

She shakes her head and crawls back over to get under the covers on her side of the bed. Her side. From now on, it'll always be her side of the bed, even after she leaves. "No. I don't need the dirty details."

"I don't mean the play-by-play," I grit out, hating how much I dread her departure, even if it's still weeks away. "I recently learned that Mitchell was actually entrapped."

She frowns harder at me, keeping her eyes on my face rather than my nakedness. I guess talking about her ex extinguished whatever arousal I thought was there. "What do you mean entrapped?"

"Someone pushed those strippers on Mitchell. Think about it. He's not attractive. He's not rich. And he's obviously not spectacular in bed. So why were so many women so eager to spread their legs for him recently?"

"Because they were running up his tab with Kozlov."

"Yes, they were. Even though they told Mitchell he was getting freebies."

Vanessa resumes running her fingers through her hair as she considers that information. "I'm confused. If you have a point, please make it so I can go to sleep."

"The strippers, at least four that my sources could confirm, were offered fentanyl if they convinced him to fuck them."

"What? Who would do that?"

"Who indeed."

"Did you..." she starts, and I hold up my palm to shut that shit down real fast.

"It wasn't me. Ask the women yourself if you want. They'll all tell you who came to them."

"So? Are you going to tell me or just keep building the suspense?"

"It seems the stripper actually did have a thing for you."

"Who? Gavin?" She shakes her head vehemently. "No. There's no way he would do that."

"He did it, Vanessa. I was as shocked as you are, to be honest. So, it seems Mitchell may have only been responsible for about seventy-five percent of the debt with Kozlov. Gavin is responsible for a quarter of it, which means the stripper is also partially, if not halfway responsible, for your beating."

"That...that son of a bitch!" She huffs as her shoulders sag.

Her words are music to my ears. I try not to smile too broadly in satisfaction.

Going up on her knees again, she points her finger at me. "If you're lying..."

"I'm not." Holding my palms up, I tell her, "I swear it on the lives of my beautiful daughters. It's all true. The women were happy to talk for a little extra cash."

"Wow."

"Do you still think the bargain you made with me was worth letting him go?"

"Yes. Although, I do wish I had kicked his ass first."

"Trust me, Eli did enough physical and psychological damage to the stupid boy."

"What did he...no, forget it. I don't want to know."

131

"Honestly, I don't want the details either. All I know is that the stripper won't come near you again."

"Good."

"You're welcome."

"Oh, fuck you very much," she grumbles before lying down, turning her back to me again.

19

Vanessa

As a prisoner, I've been keeping myself busy enough with playing tennis in the morning with a quiet, withdrawn Sophie, taking self-defense classes with a reluctant Cass in the afternoons, then helping the cooking staff make dinner for us every night. Occasionally, I've ventured down to the spa for another massage, manicure, pedicure, facial, or wax since it's on Dante's dime.

The mafia king and I still sleep in bed together with pillows between us. I swear he sighs his frustration with me a little louder each night before he flops over on his side and goes to sleep.

I haven't been back down to the strip club since that night out of shame and because I'm still furious with Gavin. Too furious to even confront him yet.

I've been telling myself that it's better to concentrate on my anger with Gavin instead of Dante since I'm stuck with the latter.

Whether I like it or not, bills are coming due, so I used the credit card Dante left me in the bedroom for me to stay on top of them.

The one expense I don't have to pay is Cole's tuition for next semester since Dante already covered it for some unknown reason.

I've barely heard anything from Cole by text message lately, so I decide to check in on him with a phone call he probably won't answer. At least I can hear his voice when his voicemail picks up.

The line rings and rings, until I hear, "Hi, Mom."

I wait a beat for the rest of the joke on the recording, something like, *"Just kidding. You're the only one who calls me so leave a message and I'll call you back if you insist."*

"Mom? Are you there?" he asks.

"Sorry, I thought I got your voicemail."

He chuckles, sounding like a normal, happy twenty-year-old college kid. It's all I ever wanted for him. Everything I've done has been for him. "Did you call just to nag me for not calling?"

"No. I just wanted to talk to you, hear your voice rather than see a one-word, abbreviated text message like I'm an old girlfriend you're trying to ghost."

"I'm not avoiding you. I've just been busy. I sleep, I work, I go out with my friends."

"Hopefully you also find time to eat, especially before you start drinking with your friends."

"Yes, Mother. I eat too."

"Junk food no doubt."

"Food is food."

I heave a heavy sigh. "No, it's not."

"Agree to disagree. I'll worry about my cholesterol when I'm old," he says. "Anyway, I've been meaning to tell you that I'm coming home next month."

"Coming home?" In a month I'll still be here, playing house or whatever insane game this is with Dante.

"Yeah, some guys from high school I haven't seen since graduation are planning a trip to Vegas, so I told them I would join them. And don't worry, they're not crashing with us or anything. I know Mitchell would flip. They wanted me to ask about your employee discount before making reservations at the Royal Palace. If we stay there, then I can come see you in the lounge."

"Ah, I can send you my employee code for the discount, but I'm not working in the lounge right now."

"You quit?"

"No, not exactly. And I won't be at the apartment either when you get home. Mitch and I broke up. He's in the process of moving out."

"Good. I hated that prick," he immediately responds.

"What? I thought you liked him."

"Ah, no. I just tried to be civil because you liked him for whatever reason I couldn't fathom." Wow, my son sounds so much like Dante it's a little scary. "Where have you been staying while he gets his shit out? And why won't you be back in the apartment by next month?"

"Well, it's a long story that I know you don't want to hear. The short version is that I'm staying with a friend at the Royal Palace, actually."

Cole doesn't speak for a long moment. "A guy friend?"

"Yes."

He chuckles. "Wow, Mom. Already moving on from Mitchell? That didn't take long."

"It's not like that. We're just...friends, and he insisted I stay here for a while."

"Even after Mitch is out?"

"Yes."

"Why?"

"Like I said, it's a long story you don't want to hear."

"So, who is this guy? Do you work with him at the Palace? Why is he living out of a hotel room?"

Of course, the one time I don't want him to delve into a deep conversation before hanging up on me, he asks a million questions.

"He's not renting a room. Dante sort of owns the whole casino."

"Owns it? Holy shit. Did you say Dante? As in Dante Salvato? You're with Dante Salvato, the mobster mogul guy?"

"I'm not with him. We're just friends."

"Just friends with the rich mob boss you're living with in his casino. Yeah, right. That's badass, Mom."

My son hated the normal guy I dated and is impressed by the thought of me dating a gangster. This is why I worry about him while he's so far away, going to college in New York.

135

"Can I stay there next month when I come home?" Cole asks.

"You want to meet him?"

"Definitely. He owns a ton of properties, right?"

Cole is studying business administration and wants to get an MBA because he eventually wants to run his own business.

"I don't know if you staying here is a good idea. Besides, you'll have the whole apartment to yourself."

"Yeah, but you won't be there."

"True," I agree. "I'll talk to Dante..." I trail off.

"Yeah, Mom, talk to the multi-millionaire and see if I can have a sleepover. You're with a rich guy when we scrape pennies to get by. That's so crazy." I wince at the reminder of how poor Cole grew up thanks to me and my single, minimum wage income. "And you're not working right now?"

"No. At least not while I'm staying with him." I'm going to have to find a new job after my time with Dante is over. There's no doubt about that. And I hate starting over.

"Good. Enjoy your vacation," Cole says. "What do you do all day? Sit around the pool drinking cocktails?"

"Not exactly."

"Well, I can't wait to see his place. It's a penthouse, right? At the top of the casino?"

"Yes."

"I'm gonna look it up online," he says, followed by a long silence. Then, "Holy shit! The penthouse is worth like, thirty million dollars!"

"I'm not surprised. It's...impressive."

"We should FaceTime next time so you can give me a tour."

"Maybe," I say, not sure how I feel about wandering the halls of Dante's house showing it off to my son.

"I better go get ready for work. Tell me more later, okay?"

"Okay," I agree. "I love you. Stay safe."

"Love you too," he replies before ending the call.

~

Later that night, once Dante and I are both settled into bed, the room pitch black, I can hear and feel Dante breathing in my direction on the other side of the pillow wall.

"Could I make a request?" I ask in the silence.

"Let's hear it."

"My son, Cole, is coming home next month, while I'm still required to be here."

"And you want a pass to leave?"

Why didn't I think of that? God, this man really does mess with my head. "No. I was wondering, he actually asked, if he could maybe stay here too? At the hotel? Not necessarily the penthouse."

"You told him about us?" Dante asks, his voice lifting in surprise.

"I told him I was staying here with you."

"And what did he think about that?"

"Apparently, he looks up to you. As a businessman, not a mobster. He wants to run his own company, be in charge of his own business someday."

"Ambitious."

"Yes. There's no way but up from the lifestyle he grew up in."

"I'm sure you did your best, made up for what money couldn't buy with loving him."

"I tried."

"He can come see you anytime he wants while you're here. But he's not sleeping near my daughters."

"Of course not." I snort. "He's a twenty-year-old boy. All they're capable of thinking about is sex."

"That's not just a characteristic of a twenty-year-old. It's what men of all ages think about every second of the day. The longer we go without, the more volatile we become."

"No kidding," I reply with a smile.

"And yet you still deny me, even though I grow crankier by the day without a release?"

A smile lifts the corners of my lips. "I'm certain you'll survive."

Dante groans, then I feel the mattress shift as he flops over, facing away from me.

It shouldn't make me happy to have such an effect on the mafia king, but it does. Staying with him hasn't been as bad as I imagined. In fact, tormenting him by rejection is fun.

I hate to admit it, even to myself, that lying in his bed beside him, in the top of his crooked ivory tower, I've never felt safer.

20

Dante

"It's been fourteen fucking days," I complain to Titus before finishing the last sip of my third old-fashioned. "Two weeks of sleeping next to her, putting her on my lap all day, offering her a hundred grand for a hand job, and nothing."

We came down to the lounge where Vanessa worked to have a drink at the end of a long day. A long two weeks.

I still haven't figured out who was behind the raid on my warehouse, which is fucking infuriating. Not to mention that I've been so damn horny, which makes me even more irritable. Still, I refuse to fuck anyone who isn't Vanessa, and fucking my hand just isn't the same.

"Maybe it's time to try a new tactic, man."

"What's that?" I ask my second-in-command since I'm all out of ideas.

"Ignore her."

"What?" Does he think it's that easy to just ignore the beautiful woman lying in bed with me every night?

"Take Vanessa out with you tonight then put her in a corner. Flirt with other women right in front of her face while pretending she doesn't exist. It can be your payback for her fucking with that stripper."

"That's your advice to convince her to finally give in to me? Ignore her and flirt with other women in front of her as payback?"

"Yes."

"That's stupid fucking advice."

Titus shrugs his shoulders. "What do I know? Women jump on my dick wherever I go, and that's that. You have more experience with, what do people call it? Dating? Wooing?"

"Neither of those terms apply here. Not really. And I don't fucking date. I'm pretty sure I met Madison's mother at a brothel orgy where we were both drunk and horny. Cass's mother was Madison's live-in nanny, so I was basically paying her to babysit and fuck me on the regular. And Sophie's mother was my masseuse, so getting me off was all in a day's work for her."

"Wow, Dante. I thought you fucked classier women than that."

"Fuck you."

"I get it. The dirty girls fuck the best. Vanessa is...different."

"No shit."

"And you tried offering her money for more?"

"Yes. I could offer her every penny I have, and she would still reject me!"

"Then what do you have to lose by trying something different with her?" Titus asks.

"If I try this and it backfires..."

"Then you're no worse off than before with your blue balls, right?"

"With Vanessa, if it doesn't work, I'll be farther away from her than before," I grumble. "Why do you think she hates me?"

"Hates? That's a strong word. If I had to guess, it's probably because you tricked her into being your live-in...whatever she is, to save her ex-boyfriend's life."

"No, before that."

"Oh. Why do you think she hated you before the manipulation?"

"Because her motherfucking ex said she hated me before we made the deal. So, it's apparently based on shit I did before, while she was a waitress."

"You have screwed all the other waitresses who work here, right?"

"Most of them. That's enough cause for her to hate me?"

"Maybe. If she wants you, but doesn't want to want you, and then sees you constantly hooking up with a bunch of other women."

"You think she's jealous? That it's a jealous hate?"

"Sure."

"So, she hates me because I fuck around too much?"

"Some women, especially ones who have been cheated on, can't stand a wandering dick."

"I've never cheated on anyone because I don't do those types of relationships. And she hated me before she even knew her ex was screwing around behind her back."

"That's true. Then she's either just a fuckboy hater in general or there's another reason we're too stupid to figure out."

Gavin's a fuckboy who Vanessa gladly, enthusiastically let air-fuck her on stage in front of a crowd. I hate that I've watched the security footage of them at least five times, including the part where I rip him off of her looking like an enraged lunatic.

But back to my point, I have this feeling that there's another reason my elusive butterfly hates me, one that I can't even begin to comprehend.

Vanessa

I'm tucked in Dante's bed in my comfy pajamas, sitting against the headboard playing Sudoku on my phone, when Dante comes home. He missed supper earlier that I had with the girls. They ate faster than humanly possible in order to get away from me, not even offering to help clear the table or help with dishes.

"Dress up. We're going out tonight," Dante says while removing his suit jacket and gun holster.

"Out? Out where exactly?"

"*Nirvana.*"

"Your female strip club?" I ask for clarification.

"Yes."

"Ah, no thanks. I would rather stay in."

"I wasn't asking you. I'm telling you we're going. Dress up or don't. That is your only choice." He growls this all in his no nonsense Daddy voice as he continues to undress for a shower or to change clothes without looking directly at me.

"Why now, Dante? Why do we have to go tonight? I don't get it. And why the hell didn't you mention this earlier in the day?"

A second later, the warm comforter and sheets are ripped away from my body like a magician's trick. I barely get a look at the bedding piling up on the bottom of the bed when my ankle is suddenly in the asshole's grip. With a yelp of surprise, I fall flat on my back when he drags me all the way down the mattress. When both of my legs are dangling over the bench at the foot, Dante's enraged face appears above me. His arms are planted on either side of my head, caging me in, blue eyes glaring down at me. I'm surrounded in his scent of this morning's fading soap along with a day's worth of sweat.

I am not aroused by the scent of his sweat or the way he's hovering over me so close I can smell the whiskey on his warm breath. That would be ridiculous. Commanding my pussy to remain as dry as the desert in July doesn't work, unfortunately.

"Do I look like I'm in the mood to deal with your bullshit tonight?"

I shake my head. He's nearly as furious now as he was the day he caught Gavin giving me...a lap dance? A stage dance? Whatever you want to call it.

Perfect Gavin who wanted me despite being constantly surrounded by gorgeous women. Wanted me so much for whatever reason that he set up Mitchell to cheat on me multiple times.

What the hell is wrong with men? They're all broken, each and every single one, in their own unique, fucked-up ways. I was probably just a challenge to Gavin like I am to Dante. Otherwise, they would've both screwed me once, then never looked back at me again.

"I want to go out tonight, and you're coming with me. End of discussion. Be ready by eleven," Dante adds before straightening to his full height and striding off to the bathroom.

Eleven? That's like...twenty minutes from now.

But I don't speak a word of complaint. Clearly, Dante is in a bad mood tonight. There's nothing left for me to do but get ready by eleven.

I throw on one of the new dresses he bought. It's a short, flimsy red halter with an open back. The front strips of fabric barely cover my breasts so I should fit right in at the strip club. After brushing my hair, and adding red lipstick, I'm as ready as I'm going to get at the last minute.

Dante and I don't speak as he gets dressed in another suit without a tie, or in the elevator on the way down with his ever-present guards. He doesn't even glance at me or tell me I look nice. It's like I could be wearing a garbage bag and he wouldn't care.

I hate that I miss his ridiculous, over-the-top, horny compliments.

When we reach the main floor, he grabs my hand to lead me to the strip club, right past the bouncers, of course, who bow their heads at him like he's their god.

It takes a moment for my aging eyes to adjust to the dim, purple neon lighting as he drags me over to a long, plum velvet sofa. He takes a seat and pulls me down with him, right between his spread legs and onto the top of his lap. Holding me on his muscular thigh with a palm tightly grasping the outside of my leg, his other hand rests leisurely on my bare knee. It's not an intimate touch per the rules, but it's more proprietary than I would like. Unfortunately, what I like doesn't matter to the mafia king.

As I glance around the hazy interior, I can't help but notice that it's possibly the one place that it's not unusual to find a woman sitting on a man's lap. I'm just the only one who isn't topless. The spotlight and colorful strobe are focused on the woman twirling around the pole on stage in a skimpy nurse's outfit.

"An old-fashioned," Dante says in that commanding voice. I turn my head to ask him if he really expects me to go get his drink when I notice the pretty brunette twenty-something waitress. She's standing in front of us, waiting patiently with her tray against her hip wearing her required plain black dress. Tapping the outside of my thigh he's been gripping like he owns it because it's on his lap, he says my actual name to get me to give my order. "Vanessa?"

I don't usually drink because I'm not that fond of getting tipsy, and I don't usually have the cash to spare for it. But tonight, I think I'll need some alcohol, and Dante is paying for it. "Could I get a whiskey sour on the rocks please?"

When the girl leaves, I can't help but think that I'm way too old to still be a cocktail waitress. The tips are good though, and I'm not a morning person so...

"You're a whiskey girl?" Dante asks, his breath warm against my ear.

I shrug to hide my shiver. "When the situation calls for it."

He smooths my hair back over my shoulder as if he wants it out of the way to move his face even closer to my neck and ear when he speaks. "And this is one of those situations?"

"Yes."

I'm thankful when the waitress returns with our drinks, so I have something to do with my hands. The glass will also keep one of Dante's busy. Only, he takes a sip, then stretches over to set it down on a small round table before his palm is back on my knee. This time his fingertips are cool from the glass, especially his thumb. His thumb that he's apparently trying to warm up by rubbing circles on the inside of my knee.

Attempting to ignore his touch, I sip my drink while watching the nurse take off her white dress to Bon Jovi's "Bad Medicine." I swear there must be some rule about only stripping to big hair bands from the eighties. Oh, and how cute. The front of her white panties has a little red cross on the front of them. Ugh. Maybe the bartender will poison my drink. I finish it off and hold it up with a smile when the waitress walks by again.

She's just handed me my third one when Dante, who had been silent behind me, pats the side of my thigh and says, "Hop up."

"What?"

Instead of repeating himself, he scoops me up off his lap and plops me down beside him none too gently, like I'm an overcoat he tossed out of his way.

Before I can bitch at him, a tall, slender, topless blonde strolls up to him. She's smiling like she can smell the money on him. More than likely, she knows who and what he is too.

"Hey, there, big guy."

Big guy? Pul-ease. That's so pathetic. And, yes, I am definitely a little drunk.

"Bela. It's been too long," the gangster replies, even referring to her by her name. Jeez. Dante pulls a money clip with a wad of cash from his front pants pocket. He wrenches free several hundred-dollar bills to tuck them into the side of her purple G-string that matches the décor.

"Always so generous," she says with a smile before stepping between his spread thighs.

I may as well be invisible for all the attention the two of them give me as she dips and rolls her mostly naked body all over his crotch. I turn away to watch the new woman on stage sliding down the pole dressed as a cheerleader to try and ignore them. At one point, though, Bela bends over to touch her toes right in front of Dante's face and more hundreds are deposited into her G-string's bank account. From that point on, either her ass is grinding on his lap, or her tits are right in front of his face. He keeps giving her cash until she's danced for so long, she's out of breath, and there's sweat beading along her hairline about to ruin her makeup.

Running her finger down the buttons of his shirt, she asks, "Should we go...finish this in a private room?"

There's only one way to interpret how she plans to "finish this" for him. His dick must be ready to erupt after the tease she gave him. I can't tell by looking at the fly of his pants if he's even hard or not. He has to be, right?

For the first time in at least fifteen minutes, Dante chooses the moment I'm thinking about his dick to acknowledge my existence. I don't know if he's about to go with her and leave me here or what until he says, "Only if Vanessa agrees to come with us."

His double entendre isn't as amusing as he thinks it is judging by his smirk in my direction.

"No, thanks."

Turning back to the still panting blonde, he gives her the bad news. "Not tonight then, doll. Thank you for the dance."

When he stuffs more crisp hundreds down the front of her minis-cule panties, she gasps realistically as if she's one tap of a fingertip on her clit away from an orgasm.

Straightening up, she says, "My pleasure," with a smile that doesn't reach her eyes. She's obviously disappointed she got herself all worked up, and he turned her down. At least it's over, and she made a few grand in less than half an hour.

After she walks away, Dante stretches his arm across the back of the velvet booth behind my head. He lifts a strand of my hair from my neck and gently plays with it between two fingers. It's all I can do to not tremble at the light touch of his knuckles brushing my skin. Instead, I pretend to not notice or care until he winds the strand around his finger to tug on it hard enough to tilt my head towards him.

"You look bored, butterfly. Not having any fun tonight?"

"I need more alcohol," I tell him as I jiggle the ice cubes left behind in my glass. "And you already know that I prefer to watch men take their clothes off."

"Yes, I'm well aware," he grumbles at the reminder of Gavin.

When there's another tug on my hair, I shove away his hand. Turning to him, I say, "You do know that she only crawled all over you because you stuffed hundreds in her G-string, right?"

His smile is so smug I want to claw it off his face. My fingernails dig into my palm, to remind me that I can't maim a mob boss, especially in public. "Is that what you think?"

"It's what I know, Salvato."

"Okay, then let's do an experiment. The next dancer who comes over here, I won't put a single dollar in her G-string. We'll see what happens."

"Sure. Whatever. You run this show."

Not even five minutes later, a gorgeous woman who could be Halle Berry's younger sister, pixie cut and all, approaches Dante in nothing but a white thong. She straddles one of his thighs then leans down to whisper something in his ear, positioning her swinging breasts in his face. When Dante lifts a hand to clutch her waist, I can't help but blurt out, "I thought you couldn't touch them."

The dancer is the one who peers over at me with an assessing look as if to ask who the hell I am. Instead, she just grabs onto Dante's shoulders and says, "*He* can touch whoever the hell he wants."

And dammit, I hate that. I hate that his hand is on her like he couldn't help himself. Didn't I touch Gavin too when we were on the stage?

When the dancer turns around and rolls her ass over Dante's lap, I realize that she must know the answer to the question I was just asking myself. Is he *enjoying* himself or not?

I shouldn't care. It's a strip club. All the men in here are probably walking around with hard dicks and none of them bother me.

Just the one.

Dante's.

My throat burns and my stupid eyes begin to sting because I'm envious. These tall, beautiful women have perfect twenty-something bodies that I couldn't even begin to compete with.

Mitch cheated on me to be with younger, prettier strippers. They are the epitome of sexy, every straight man's fantasy girl in real life. And while most guys in the strip club would have to beg and pay for them to "finish them off" all Dante has to do is sit here and wait five seconds before they offer themselves up to him.

Sure, they also do it for the money, because of who he is, how powerful he is, but what makes him irresistible are his physical attributes. His intimidating height, the hard-earned, chiseled body of a protector—or an instrument of violence depending on the time of day. And then there's his gorgeous face with those beautiful blue eyes that can flip from cold and terrifying to breathtakingly charming in an instant.

I jump at the unexpected brush of fingers on my bare neck but don't turn to look at him.

"Now that she's finished dancing, and also offered to fuck me without me giving her a penny, I think I've made my point."

"Whatever," I exhale, refusing to look in his direction.

When he stands up, though, my eyes follow him as he swaggers over to the dancer I didn't even notice had left. He slips the rest of his wad of cash down the front of her panties.

Dante turns around to come back, the smug grin on his face quickly fading.

He states the obvious on his approach. "You're ready to leave."

"Have been since before we got here."

"Come on then," he says waiting for me to get to my feet. On the first try, I end up landing back on my ass, nearly dumping my melting glass of ice all over my lap.

"Lightweight. Should've known," Dante comments. He takes the glass from my hand and puts it on the nearby table, then grabs my elbows to help me up.

Shrugging him off, I say, "I'm fine. I just needed both hands to push myself up."

Okay, that's a lie. My legs are a little wobbly at first. But Dante takes me at my word, walking off toward the door. By the time I follow him, I'm walking just fine in a mostly straight line.

There's a wait at the elevator bank, and when one arrives, we're packed in tight. Dante stands behind me in the corner. Slinging his left arm around my waist, he tugs me back so a bunch of other people can squeeze in with us. By the time the elevator doors close, my backside is flattened to the front of his warm body. And there's no way to miss the answer to my earlier question. He's long and thick, poking me in my lower back.

I lift my eyes to the mirrors in front of me to see his reflection. He's watching me as if waiting for my reaction, but he doesn't look ashamed. And he shouldn't be. It's a natural, biological response for men when mostly naked women grind on that particular body part simulating sex.

A few people get off on the second floor, then the third, allowing us a little more breathing room. When I move up half a step, Dante keeps his left arm around my waist to stop me. There's also a touch so light it could've been a breeze of air that starts at my upper back. The lower it goes, making a diagonal progression to follow my tattoos, more pressure is applied until I know it's Dante's knuckles. Or maybe I imagined it because it seems impossible for the busted, bloody knuckles that hurt people to be so gentle.

As he begins the ascent, I can't stop my shiver. Between the tingles on my back and his heavy palm pressing into my lower belly, a jolt of desire surges through me. It's accompanied by a hunger for more of his touch, which pisses me off.

I hate that he has this effect on me, especially now, after I just had to watch perfect women rub all over him like dogs in heat.

Finding his reflection in the mirror again, I lash out at him. "Stop it."

Several people still in the elevator turn their heads in our directions. When they see Dante's towering form in the corner though, they quickly look straight ahead again.

"Why? Is it too...intimate?" he asks without lowering his voice, as if he doesn't give a shit who is listening.

And dammit, there is no right answer to his question. If I say yes, then I'm admitting he's affecting me. If I say no, he'll keep doing it.

I hold his stare in the mirror as I weigh my options. Like he knows he's backed me into a corner, he arches an eyebrow and starts the path with his knuckles all over again.

The air is too thick in the confined space. That has to be why I'm breathing heavily. And the urge to step back against the warmth of his chest, the hardness of his arousal again is so confusing. Does he want me? Or does he want the strippers he made me watch rub all up on him?

Oh my god.

He *made* me watch. If he had wanted to fuck them, he wouldn't have dragged me along tonight. The strippers were just pawns in his little game. He was intentionally trying to make me jealous.

And it worked.

Is this how he felt after he saw me on stage underneath Gavin? Him grinding on top of me? Did Dante do it as payback?

Well, I hated seeing him flirting with those women, so it worked. I don't want anyone else to touch him, to garner even a second of his attention. I want both, his hands on me and all of his attention. Most of all, I want it to be *my* hands on him, over his clothes, under them, roaming over every inch of his muscular body.

Fuck. I don't want to want Dante, but there's no point lying to myself anymore.

Pride? Dignity? Who needs either of those things when I know how good this, being with Dante, would feel?

My only hesitation is whether or not giving in will mean being tossed aside afterward. I need to know once and for all. Either he's the playboy bastard I think he is or he's something more. And there's only one way to find out, right? Actions speak louder than words.

Wetting my lips, I hold his intense gaze in the mirror to say the one word that lets him know I'm giving up fighting him. At least for the time being.

"*When.*"

Dante doesn't bother asking me what I mean. His shoulders slump, as if in relief, and then his right hand grabs the side of my head, turning my face around as his lips come crashing down to meet mine. His tongue forces its way into my mouth, and I taste the sweet, bitter flavor of him, of his whiskey. Warmth spreads through my belly like I drank a gallon of the liquor as I turn all the way around to face him. To get my hands on him. The smooth back of his neck is the first thing I can reach, and I'll take it.

Dante keeps his hand clutching the side of my face as if to make sure I don't pull away. His other hand doesn't waste any time sliding down my back, grabbing a handful of my ass. He doesn't care who is still in the elevator with us, and neither do I.

They probably think we're being rude, going at each other on the elevator instead of waiting until we get to our room. They don't know that this is our first kiss or how long I made an impatient mafia king wait for it. He was so used to getting what he wants all the time before I refused him...

And while the kiss is amazing, the spark slowly begins to dwindle.

I don't know if I could handle his rejection now, after growing closer to him for the past two weeks.

Yes, I want him. I've always wanted him. That was never the problem.

The problem is that I am nothing but a challenge Dante needs to defeat to make everything right in his mafia king world.

21

Dante

Finally.

Fucking finally.

My favorite word just became "when." After agonizing weeks of her insisting it's if, if we fuck, now it's when. As in, when we fuck. It's going to be spectacular.

Hell, I could pick Vanessa up and slam her on my cock right here and now in the elevator and die a happy man. God knows she seemed to like when Gavin dry humped her into the hard floor. And this time at least all her injuries have healed.

Titus, the son of a bitch, was right about ignoring her to make progress. She really is jealous of the other women I spoke to, I looked at, I touched. In the club, I didn't feel a thing for any of those girls who so desperately wanted to ride my cock. I may have even had them before. I can't remember. The only woman in the world who exists for me now is Vanessa.

My palm squeezes a handful of her fine ass about to pick her up when she moans, *"Dante"* against my lips. It sounds like a goddamn prayer.

But instead of asking for more, she groans and slips her hands from the death grip on my neck to slide them down flat against my chest, pushing me away.

Fuck.

The eyes on us look away in a hurry when we stop kissing. I even make my hand release her ass and tug the hem of her dress back down.

"What happened to *when?*" I growl in frustration.

Vanessa lowers her eyes and shakes her head. "I can't," she says to my stomach. "I can't sleep with you."

I grab her chin between my finger and thumb to make her look up at me. "Sure, you can. You've been sleeping with me for weeks now."

No matter how bad the nightmares, the horrible memories, the worry, when I wake up and see her lying beside me, I'm grounded again. The past goes back to the past because I have Vanessa in my present, however temporary that may be.

She sighs and tries to look away, but I don't let her. "That's not what I meant, and you know it."

"Tell me why not?"

"I just can't," she whispers, her green eyes hazy with lust that's quickly fading. "I'm sorry. Flirting with you, teasing you is wrong because *nothing* is going to happen between us."

"Something already has, butterfly," I assure her as I press my lips to hers once, testing the waters. Twice. She doesn't pull away and kisses me back by the third, leaving me even more confused.

Nothing? She thinks our kiss was *nothing?*

The doors on the elevator open, causing a rush of cool air to fill the stuffy space. The elevator is thankfully emptying as we finally get closer to the penthouse. I really need to install a faster, private one.

Since I know I'm not going to get any answers from her on here, I let Vanessa's chin go, and after a second, she turns around again.

The mirror captures the various emotions as they cross her face. She lifts her fingertips to her swollen, kissed lips as if she's not sure if it really happened. Then, her brow furrows like she's as baffled as I am as to why she stopped. But finally, her jaw tightens as if she's determined to continue being stubborn.

As soon as we're locked inside the bedroom alone, I say, "Talk to me, Vanessa."

"I told you," she replies as if I'm supposed to just give up, climb into bed with her tonight, and not lay a hand on her.

"Well, tell me more."

"I don't know. I'm just...I'm not ready yet."

Not ready *yet*. This can't be about her ex, can it? Or Gavin screwing her over, setting up Mitchell. "They're both gigantic pricks."

"I know that! But it doesn't change the fact that it hurt to be cheated on or manipulated."

Ouch. While I assume she's referring to Gavin doing the manipulating, it doesn't mean I'm not guilty of it as well.

"You're not going to forgive Mitchell, are you?"

"No, definitely not. Now that we're over, I realize it never felt right with him."

"That kiss was right, even if you won't admit it," I point out to her. When she doesn't say anything, when she doesn't agree, it blows my fucking mind. The stubborn woman isn't going to budge another inch. At least not tonight, despite the hot as hell kiss on the elevator.

I try not to let my disappointment show. She let me kiss her and grab her ass. That's more than she's allowed in two weeks. That's progress, and I still have sixty-two days left to convince her to give me more. That's why I have no choice but to capitulate, at least for now. "Fine. I can wait."

She scoffs. "You can wait?"

"I've waited this long, haven't I? We can...take things slow if you admit one thing to me."

"What?"

"That you were jealous."

"Did you...did you do that tonight to get back at me?"

"Did you fucking hate watching them grind all over me?"

"Yes," she answers softly.

"Then now you know how I felt finding you under the stripper without him having to do more than crook his finger at you."

"I...Gavin and I spent time talking every day for months in the lounge. It wasn't just one little crook of his finger."

Since I don't want to hear about how much she wanted the stripper, I go back to my original point. "Tell me, Vanessa. Say the words, and I swear I won't let another woman near me as long as you're staying here."

"As long as I'm staying here?"

"Yes. All sixty-something days that are left, right?" I ask like I don't know the exact number.

"And after the sixty-something days? What happens then?"

"Then you go back to your life, and I go back to mine."

"So, if I fucked you tomorrow, you wouldn't throw me out?"

"Hell, no. I'd fuck you as many times as possible in the rest of the sixty-something days."

"But then that's it?"

"That's it. Is that acceptable?"

"I don't know yet," she replies, confusing the shit out of me. Shoving her fingers through her long hair, she adds, "But I will admit that yes, I was jealous of those dancers. I don't want you to be with another woman while I'm here."

Thank fuck.

"And I don't have any experience going slow, but I'm sure I can figure it out," I concede. "You seem to like kissing me, so we can stick with that until you ask me for more."

"That's it? You'll just keep your hands off me and every other woman and only kiss me, nothing else until I ask?"

Closing the distance between us, I sweep her hair over each shoulder. "No. I think I'll make you beg."

"Beg? You think you can make me beg?"

Instead of arguing with her, that she will one day beg me to fuck her, I cup her face in both of my hands to slant my mouth over hers.

She thankfully doesn't push me away. No, she kisses me back, just as enthusiastically as on the elevator. Her hands on my sides even try to pull me closer.

When I press the front of our bodies together, Vanessa moans but rips her mouth from mine.

"It's going to be difficult for me to believe you'll go slow with your hard dick always between us."

Sighing, I stare down at my tented pants and ask her honestly, "What would you like me to do about it? I can't help it if I get hard whenever I see you. It's not like I can tuck all this away."

I really like the way Vanessa's eyes lower to examine my stiff cock. She obviously wants it; she just won't give in. *Yet.*

Wetting her lips, she finally lifts her eyes back to mine. "The other night, you were about to...you know, when you played that video."

"Ah, you want to watch me stroke my dick? In front of you?"

"Yes." Her answer comes even faster than I expected. "Just to different porn, obviously."

I run my index finger over my bottom lip, thinking that over. "I'm not used to having to get myself off."

Vanessa rolls her eyes and sits on the edge of the mattress. "Oh, really?"

"If I want to come, I usually just ask someone, and it happens." There are always women around me, willing and ready.

"But I'm sure you do remember how to do it, right?" She wants me to jerk my dick like a teenager in front of her, when all I can do is imagine how good her mouth or pussy will feel. God help me.

"I guess I can give it a try."

First things first, I remove my jacket and shoulder holster, tossing them both down on the bench at the foot of the bed. Next, my fingers begin undoing all the little buttons on my dress shirt. The entire time, Vanessa watches me like a hawk. I tug my undershirt off over my head at the same time I slip off my dress shoes. Finally, I begin undoing my pants. There's nothing underneath as they drop to the floor, setting my hard cock free. It bobs around as I reach down to remove the pants and my socks.

Unlike the other nights before and after my shower, Vanessa doesn't even pretend to hide that she's examining every inch of me, especially the ones between my legs.

Taking myself in my hand for a long stroke from base to tip, I ask her, "Do you mind finding me something to help get me nice and slick?"

"Ah. Okay." She sort of stumbles off the bed heading for the bathroom, giving me a wide berth, making me bite back a smile.

And when she returns, handing me a little bottle of her cactus blossom lotion, I arch a single eyebrow at her.

Rolling her emerald eyes, she huffs, "It's not like it's prickly like a cactus. It smells good."

Popping the top, I hold it up to my nose to take a whiff. Damn. It does smell nice, sweet, tropical, and warm. It smells like her.

Squeezing some of the white lotion onto my palm, I toss the bottle onto the mattress in front of where Vanessa settles back in to watch, then rub the lotion up and down my aching length.

It feels really fucking good to get some friction, just not as good as a mouth or pussy. Knowing Vanessa is watching does make it hotter than if I were alone. I want to put on a show for her, to make her think about how it will feel when I'm thrusting inside of her.

I place one knee then the other on top of the bench, kneeling facing her to give her a nice view, leaning back a little as I jerk off.

"Do you think about my dick sliding in and out of your mouth?" I ask her as I begin to make long, twisting strokes up and down my shaft. "Because I do. All the damn time. Before we even started our arrangement."

"S-seriously?"

"Oh, yeah. When my dick was in someone else's mouth, I thought of yours."

"Mine?"

"Uh-huh. Your red lipstick? I want it smeared up and down my shaft."

"Why my mouth?" she asks softly.

"Why not your sexy mouth?" Closing my eyes, I conjure up the image of her crawling over and opening her mouth wide for me to use it. My hand moves faster as I get closer to a release. Wanting the show to last a little longer, I reach down with my left hand to tug on my balls, but that just feels so good I moan. On the next slide of my fist, I feel the drops of precum on the tip, so I spread them around with the lotion.

When I open my eyes again, Vanessa's face is flushed, her lips parted, eyes glazed over watching intently.

"If you lifted your dress and shoved your fingers in your panties, I would come so hard."

Surprising me, she actually does what I ask, going up on her knees, and slipping her hand under her dress. Of course, she doesn't lift it for me to see her touch herself, but I know what she's doing under there when she gasps and her hips swivel.

Vanessa drops back down on her heels as her eyes squeeze shut. Her lips part, but no sound comes out as she shudders through the fastest fucking orgasm I've ever seen.

Thinking about her pussy getting drenched with her arousal makes my cock twitch. Imagining that hot, wet heaven throbbing around my dick would be a dream come true.

A few strokes later and I'm grunting from the force of the pleasure bursting free. I catch most of my release in my hand, absently reaching for my discarded tee to clean up the rest before it gets on the bed or my suit.

A sense of sated peace fills me up after the final tremor. The serene look on Vanessa's face says she feels it too.

Now I may actually be able to sleep in the bed next to her tonight without tossing the wall of pillows out of the way to climb on top of her and fuck her into the mattress.

22

Vanessa

Things with Dante for the past few days have been different. A good different.

Now, whenever he runs his fingers up my arm or my thigh when I'm sitting on his lap on the patio or in his office, I get ridiculously horny. Then I have to remind my body to calm down. I endure those moments by turning the tables on Dante, teasing him right back until he ends his call or throws everyone out of his office to make out with me.

So far, Dante and I have just kissed and touched on top of clothes, above the waist. I haven't asked him to jerk off in front of me again, though. Only because I'm afraid I'll put him in my mouth the next time. Feeling him hard underneath me while I'm sitting on his lap is another ordeal where I long to undo his pants to impale myself on his cock.

It feels like only a matter of time before we cross the line into below the waist and under the clothes touching, then full-blown sex.

There's still fifty-six or so days to try and survive Dante. Each day gets a little harder. Literally. I think he gets longer and harder with every day that passes.

Tonight, we got all dressed up to go out again. Only this time, there are no topless women because we're in one of the casino's regular dance clubs. While the patrons here may have more clothing on, it doesn't stop them from humping all over each other on the floor in rhythm with the thumping bass playing through the speakers. The crowd is young, mostly twenty or thirty-year-olds if I had to guess. It's not my kind of place at all. I can't even remember the last time I attempted to dance, and I don't recognize any of the songs. Cole would probably be mortified if he saw me in a place like this with his generation.

Dante and I have just sat down in one of the VIP booths on the second-level when Dante pulls out his phone from inside his jacket pocket.

"Fuck," he mutters while staring down at the illuminated screen in the dark corner of the club.

"What's wrong?" I ask while he types away.

He's still typing when he says, "Eli's coming to stay with you while I go handle some business."

"Business? This late at night?" I know that the mafia king doesn't exactly keep business hours, but he's not usually bothered after he comes into the bedroom around ten or so at night. It's nearly eleven now.

"It shouldn't take long," he says, waving down a waitress to get our drink orders while tucking the phone away again.

When she leaves, I tell him, "I can just go back up to the penthouse."

"No. Stay. Please."

It's the *please* that gets me to concede.

A moment later, Eli strolls into the club, still adjusting the collar of his navy suit jacket like he dressed in a hurry.

"I thought I was off the rest of the night," he says to Dante, giving him more attitude than I've ever heard.

"Something came up," Dante grits out, glaring at the other man. "Stay with Vanessa. I'll be back as soon as I can."

He gives me a quick kiss on the lips, then slides out of the booth.

"Does he need to be here since there are two guards lurking nearby?" I ask as he starts to stride off, adjusting the sleeves of his jacket like it's a nervous habit.

"Eli could take down both guards in less than ten seconds," he says over his shoulder before disappearing.

The man in question sighs heavily, then lowers himself into the booth. "Bastard just had to stroke my ego. But he's not wrong."

"You could take the guards down in ten seconds? Even though they're armed?"

The former MMA fighter grins, then sips Dante's whiskey when the waitress places it on the table along with my whiskey sour. "I could put them to sleep before either oaf could pull their guns out of the holsters."

Shaking my head, I sip my own drink. "Very cocky."

"Very true."

"So why did Dante think I need your protection as well as the guards?"

He shrugs as he glances around the club. "No clue. And no, he didn't tell me what came up."

I can't tell if that's the truth or if he just doesn't want to tell me. "Sorry if he interrupted your plans tonight."

With a puff of laughter, he finishes off the whiskey, then says, "Don't worry. My plans will still be waiting for me right where I left them when I get done babysitting."

"Good. Maybe it won't be long."

"Hopefully," he agrees. "So, what do you think of this place? First time here?"

"Yes. It's definitely better than *Nirvana*."

"I heard Dante took you there the other night."

"He did. I hated it."

"No kidding. I can't believe he took you to his favorite watering hole. Those girls can be cutthroat when it comes to Dante's dick. And I heard you cost at least two of them a ride on it," he adds with a smirk.

"Poor things," I say sarcastically with a roll of my eyes.

Movement in the dark corner of the club draws my eye away from the awkwardness in the booth to a couple pressed against the wall. "Are they...are they fucking over there?"

"Probably just dry humping."

"I'm pretty sure her panties are long gone."

"Holy shit," Eli mutters. While we're watching them, the guy lowers the woman's feet to the ground then spins her around to face the wall before pounding into her from behind. At this angle, you can definitely see her bare, pale ass thanks to the raised back of her dress.

It's impossible to look away as the man plows her. Over the sound of the music, I can almost make out her moans from the deep, energetic thrusts.

Oh, how I miss great sex. I want to get pounded just like that.

God, maybe I should just give in and fuck the mafia king already.

I'm not sure how long the couple goes at it. Long enough that my skin is hotter than the sun, and I'm soaking wet between my legs.

A loud, deep clearing of a throat pulls us both out of our trance.

Dante is back, standing in front of our booth and he looks pissed as he stares down at us.

"Everything okay?"

"Everything is fine. Get up."

Eli quickly slides out of the booth. "Can I go now or..."

"You're dismissed," he tells him as he retakes his seat next to me and slips his arm around my shoulders. Pulling me tightly to his side Dante asks, "What are we looking at so intently?"

"Nothing," I answer way too fast. But Dante easily follows my recent line of sight.

"Ah. I see now." His damp lips brush my ear, making me shiver before he whispers, "I didn't take you for a voyeur, butterfly."

My eyes drift back to the mating couple, even though I can feel Dante's eyes watching my face. "They obviously want to be watched or they wouldn't be fucking in your club."

"This been going on for a while now?" Dante asks as he too becomes mesmerized as well.

"Yes."

"He probably took a Viagra."

"No kidding."

Dante's lips press against my neck, his tongue flicking over the sensitive skin, making me shiver. "I prefer to have multi-rounds in one night to one long one."

"Oh, yeah? Because you can't last long and need time to recover?"

"Only a little. I like to cum in every hole at least once before I'm fully sated."

"Wow. I bet women just love that," I mutter, trying not to imagine him doing those three things, or how I might enjoy them.

Dante's tongue flutters over my neck again. "Since I eat their pussy between each round, they usually let me do whatever I want to them when my cock is hard."

"If you say so," I remark, trying not to sound affected.

"Have you ever watched anyone before now?" he asks while placing his big palm up my left thigh that's crossed over the right one.

"Watched people have sex right in front of me? No."

"And? What's the verdict?"

"The verdict?"

"Are you wet from watching them fuck?" Before I can answer, he says, "Wait. Don't tell me." He slides the hand on my thigh a little higher. "I think I already know the answer, so I'm calling in my debt."

His palm slides even higher, going under the hem of my dress to make his intention clear.

"Right here?"

"Right fucking here." Leaning closer, he whispers in my ear, "Keep your legs crossed. You know how much I love a challenge. I'm going to get my hand between these tight thighs no matter how hard you clench them, and you're going to let me, aren't you?"

Good lord. I don't know if I want to throw my legs wide open or make him work even harder.

"Vanessa? Answer me."

"Y-yes," I agree, not only because it was part of our deal for him to let Gavin go the other night, but because I want him to touch me where I ache. Where I've been aching for weeks.

Glancing around the crowded club, I don't see anyone staring right at us, and there's a table in front of the booth hiding my lap from view, so I clench my thighs as tight as possible.

That of course doesn't stop Dante. His long fingers wiggle their way down, down, down, until...

The first prod of his fingertip wiggling back and forth along the crotch of my panties makes me gasp.

"Fuck, you are drenched," Dante murmurs. My legs open a little more, wide enough for him to cup me in his big hand. "All from watching two strangers fuck?"

"Yes," I gasp as he presses down, finding the spot where I'm the wettest and pushing into it. "And...and from you," I add as I lean my head on his chest and clench his arm. I want him to know it wasn't just them who made me wet.

"You like making me work for it, don't you?"

"Yes."

"*When?*" he says moving those fingers higher to the bundle of nerves where my pulse is throbbing...and pausing.

I gasp and clutch his arm tighter as if I can make him keep going, to keep touching me because I'm so close already. Of course, I can't make him. Even right on the edge I know it'll be when Dante decides to let me finish.

He's waiting for me to say it, to ask him for it.

"When," I whisper.

"It was always *when*, not *if*, wasn't it, butterfly?"

His eyes continue to watch my face, still waiting. I nod until I can wet my lips enough to speak. "Yes. When. Not if. Please, Dante," I beg him. His fingertips thankfully begin moving in circles.

"Have you ever been fucked in public?"

"No."

"Do you want to be?"

"I-I don't know. Never really thought about it," I lie.

"You are right now, I bet. Are you thinking about riding my cock while everyone watches? The women wishing they were you while all the men wish they were the ones inside of you?"

My back arches as my hips begin to rock all on their own, chasing the pleasure that's just out of reach because of his dirty words and talented fingers.

"I've never seen you look so sexy," he says as his lips and tongue tease my ear. "Tell me something, butterfly."

"Mmm?" I whimper, my eyes closed to concentrate hard on the pleasure.

"Should we stop and take this upstairs?"

My eyes fly open at his words that are meant as a threat, meeting his smug stare. "No. Please don't stop," I beg, clutching his wrist to keep his hand where it is, until his fingers finally press into me harder. "Please, Dante," I gasp again just before the first tremor rolls through me.

I hold my breath as I ride them out, hips bucking, desperate to keep the pleasure going, to make that incredible feeling last as long as possible. I don't care where we are or who sees us. It feels too damn good.

When every shiver of gratification has been wrung from me, my body goes limp against Dante's side. I can't even keep my legs crossed at the knee any longer because my muscles are all too exhausted.

"Goddamn," he mutters, lips pressing to my forehead. "The way you say my name when you come is better than any drug I've ever had. I need another hit, and soon. And a fucking cigarette."

Dante finally removes his hand from under my dress. Without lifting my head from his shoulder or opening my eyes I ask him, "Do you think anyone saw us?"

"Which answer would you prefer?"

"I don't know."

"Yes, you do. You're a sexy little exhibitionist, teasing every cock in the room, including mine. Just like on the stage with Gavin," he says with a heavy sigh. "Are you ready to go home?"

Home.

The penthouse isn't my home, but I feel safe and happy inside of it.

"You may have to carry me." My legs are too limp to move right now.

"I've wanted to pick you up and carry you to my bed since the first time I saw you."

"Tonight, you can be my guest," I assure him.

165

23

Dante

Vanessa fell asleep in my arms before I reached the elevator. So, instead of tossing her down on my bed and licking her pussy tonight, I remove her dress and shoes, then tuck her in without getting to taste her. Without getting any relief of my own at all. The pillow wall I voluntarily build between us is even more important tonight since she's only wearing her damp panties.

I've just locked up my gun and removed my suit jacket when Titus texts me.

After the unexpected visit I got from Kozlov tonight in the casino, asking if I've seen his two enforcers, I can't even say I'm surprised to find out another one of my warehouses was raided, this one in California.

Thankfully, it was empty. I wasn't stupid enough to keep product in all the usual places after the hit in Arizona.

Kozlov is obviously coming after me, and someone is helping him. Whoever my rat is, they just don't have the most current information, or they would've warned him about the move. I intentionally kept the details limited to only a handful of people I trust most. Now at least I know it wasn't any of them who betrayed me, making me feel a little better.

"Anything on the cameras this time?" I ask Titus when I step out of the bedroom and meet him on the veranda.

"The IT guys are going through them now."

"I assume you heard Kozlov showed up here tonight asking questions?"

"You think he's behind the raids? There's no way he could've known about his guys when the Arizona warehouse was hit."

"I didn't think so either, but if one of our men got sloppy with the pickup..."

"They weren't. The sun wasn't even up when we grabbed those guys, and all home security cameras were cut before it went down."

"If it's not Kozlov then who the fuck is coming after me?"

"No clue. If I knew, they would be dead by now."

"Put together a list of any guards who may have been involved in this one or with Stevie down in Arizona. Then bring them in for interrogation. Anyone who had a recent deposit out of thin air."

"You think it's one of our own?"

"Somebody on the inside is giving information in exchange for cash. If we can find them, then we find out who they're working for on the outside."

"I'll let you know when we start bringing them in."

"I'll tell Eli to be ready."

"That sick bastard is going to be ecstatic."

"As long as he's around, you won't have to get your hands dirty," I remind him.

"True enough. I'm heading to Cali now. I'll let you know if IT finds out anything else."

I nod and follow him to the door to lock up before looking for Eli in his room. It's still empty so I pull out my phone to text him to get his ass back up here. He's had plenty of time to fuck around tonight.

I'm sitting in the chair in his room waiting when he comes in, his shirt buttoned the wrong way, halfway untucked, his blond hair down around his shoulders for once. He probably thinks he's been sly, but I have eyes and ears every fucking where in this casino.

"Did you have fun playing with Gavin tonight?" I ask.

"Shit, Dante!" he exclaims before flipping on the overhead light and finding me in the dark corner.

"Well?"

"How did you know?"

"A little bird in reservations told me you booked a room for a bachelorette party. I'm guessing you were the lucky lady."

"What I do in my free time is none of your business."

"It's my business when you use my suite to play with one of my employees who is on thin ice." Then I ask the question I'm most curious about. "Is he still alive?"

"Yes."

"While I would love for you to rip his heart out of his chest, if he goes missing, people will notice. And I'll be at the top of the suspect list."

"It's fine. Seriously." Eli scrubs his palms over his face as I search for blood spatter on his clothes or skin, but don't find any.

I get up from the chair to leave, which is when he says, "What happened tonight?"

"Kozlov dropped by unexpectedly asking about his guys, which means he suspects me. Either connected or a big coincidence, a California warehouse was raided tonight."

"Jesus."

"Yeah. Shit is hitting the fan, and I don't have a fucking clue how to stop it."

"You'll probably punch me for saying this, but Vanessa's a distraction you can't afford to have right now."

"I know that," I assure him, clutching the doorknob tighter than necessary. "But she's not leaving, not until her time with me is up."

"I figured as much."

"Just make sure nobody says a word to her about the Russians. She doesn't need to know the two who hurt her are dead, or that it may be coming back to bite me in the ass."

"Right," he agrees. "Can I make another suggestion?"

"What?" I snap, ready to get back to the nearly naked woman sleeping in my bed.

"Maybe it's time to think about calling in reinforcements."

"Reinforcements?"

"Lochlan could be a powerful ally, make the Russians think twice about starting a war if he sides with you."

I hate to admit that Eli makes a good point. I despise asking anyone for help. But the stronger my backing, the less likely Kozlov will attack me directly.

"I'll think about it," I agree before I slip out of the room.

24

Vanessa

I wake up with a shiver. It takes me a moment to realize I'm tucked into bed underneath a mountain of covers, naked other than my panties.

Then I remember the night before, when I let Dante finger me down in his club. It felt so good, too good to care about who may have seen us, like I was drunk on the lust. For a few minutes, I felt wild and free, so different from my constant, uptight, worrisome motherly role.

It was nice to let go, even for a few minutes. It's just a little scary that Dante Salvato is the man who did that to me. For me.

Speaking of the devil, I don't remember what we did afterward. After we left the club.

I'm not sore between my legs, so I'm confident nothing else happened. Dante may be a mobster, but he would wait until I'm fully conscious to have sex with me the first time. If not only so the smug bastard could hear me beg first. Which is surprising. I know the mafia king could've used a release of his own last night. He had to have been hurting, yet he didn't insist I return the favor. Dante's not as selfish as I thought he would be.

"Morning," the man with magic fingers says softly. He's awake and watching me. His messy head of hair still rests on his pillow, on the other side of our makeshift wall.

"Morning. What time is it?" I ask as I pull the covers up to my neck even if there's no point in hiding my nakedness from him since he obviously undressed me the night before.

Dante props his head up on his bent elbow to face me. "A little after seven."

"You didn't go work out this morning?"

"No. I had a late night."

"Oh?"

"I had to handle some more business after I got you back to the room."

"Again? Is everything okay?" I ask, noticing the tension in his jaw, the furrowing of his brow.

"Another warehouse was raided. At least this time it was empty."

"Oh, well, that's good, right?"

"Better than losing millions in product, but it's concerning that the locations of my warehouses are being shared."

Someone betrayed him, which is stupid and dangerous. "Any idea who was behind this one?"

"Not yet, no."

There's no way Dante will stop searching until he finds them, then makes the traitor pay.

"You'll find them. Eventually, they'll make a mistake," I assure him.

"Or I'll twist enough arms to get someone to sing."

"Or that," I agree.

Reaching over, he lifts a strand of my hair from my pillow and twirls it around his finger. The whitish blonde is quite a contrast to his tan skin. "The violence doesn't seem to upset you. Why is that?" he asks.

I shrug. "It's a violent world. And sometimes, I guess it's essential. I just don't believe in hurting innocent people."

He hums, which can be interpreted as an agreement or disagreement. I'm not sure which. "And how are you feeling about last night?"

"Last night was...fine," I reply.

The scowl on his scruffy face tells me he didn't like that answer at all. "Just fine?" He jerks the covers toward him, trying to pull them off me but I cling to them tightly. "You came for me faster than a speeding bullet."

"I did not!" I huff, jerking the covers back.

"I bet one of the security cameras caught it all and could give us a timed playback. Shall we have a look?"

"Ass," I mutter with a grin.

The truth is, I haven't had enough time to think about what we did last night. I enjoyed it, more than I anticipated. It was the best, most erotic experience I've had in years, especially in public. But now, I'm confused. I can't afford to let my body become greedy for, well, any of this particular man's body parts.

What's worst of all is that I want to reciprocate. Not because I think I owe Dante pleasure in return, but because I want to get my hands on him. Every part of him. Especially the long, hard part between his legs.

It would be so easy to toss the pillow wall and touch him everywhere. Maybe that's the reason he skipped his workout, hoping to get lucky.

But no, touching Dante, getting him off, would feel too much like waving the white flag.

"I'm going to get a quick shower, then go see if Sophie wants company on the court."

I turn away before I can see the disappointment in Dante's eyes. It doesn't matter since the displeasure coming off of him in waves is strong enough to nearly knock me over when I stand up with a sheet wrapped around me.

"Wait," he says, causing my feet to freeze while I keep my back to him. This is it; Dante is going to finally snap and demand I get him off by threatening someone's life, possibly my son's, and I'll do whatever he wants despite my convictions. The reminder of why I should hate him will be more than welcomed...

"You play tennis?"

That's it? No death threats or demands, just a question about my athletic skills?

173

"Yes, I played a little with my mom growing up. Even poor neighborhoods have courts, you know," I quickly feel the need to add.

"You lost her and your father as a teenager?" he asks, obviously knowing from his background research on me that my parents were reportedly killed in a car crash that I survived.

"I did," I respond before heading for the bathroom to avoid answering any other questions about my past.

The less Dante Salvato knows about me the better.

Dante

Vanessa acted just as I expected this morning. She refused to admit how good I made her feel last night, turned skittish, and bolted before letting me touch her again.

Everything with that woman feels like one step forward and three steps backward. Just when I start to think I'm making progress, she shows me just how wrong I am.

But Eli is right. Vanessa is a distraction I can't afford to have right now. That's why I decide to focus on the current life or death situation before me, and not my sex life for the rest of the day.

A war with the Russians is brewing, so I need to do everything I can do to stop it. In the meantime, I'll have to make sure my men are ready for anything. That we're prepared for the worst-case scenario.

Being prepared means shoring up defenses and making sure I'm on good terms with all allies. As Eli mentioned last night, there's one potential ally in particular that I've been pursuing for a while now. It wasn't easy at first since his family was thought to be responsible for the shooting that killed Madison's mother Maria. But Lochlan Dunne was a child when that happened. He's not his father, just as I'm not mine. If we could put aside our past, both of us could come out stronger with an alliance.

There's just one little thing holding him back.

It's time to suck up my pride and reach out to the Irishman, despite how much I may hate asking for his support, or caving to his requirement for said support.

Rather than going up to the roof and getting distracted watching Vanessa playing a game of tennis with Sophie, I sit down in my office chair to make the call.

I'm not surprised that he answers by asking, "When do I get to meet my bride, Salvato? I'm not getting any younger."

Pinching the bridge of my nose, I tell him, "I know, Lochlan. But Madison is young. She's still...warming up to the idea of marriage."

"Then don't expect me to side with you when the Russians retaliate for you killing two of their enforcers."

Fuck. If he's already heard that Kozlov is suspicious of me, then I must be his top suspect. "That's pure speculation on Kozlov's part," I lie. "The dead enforcers probably just fucked around with the wrong person."

The bastard chuckles. "I don't doubt that one bit. But until my ring is on your daughter's finger, you're on your own."

"Trust me, I'm doing you a favor right now. If I drag Madison down the aisle before she's ready, she'll claw your eyes out the first chance she gets."

"I do enjoy having my eyes in their sockets."

Changing the subject, I ask him, "Have you by chance heard who is raiding my fentanyl warehouses?"

"No. I heard about the one in Arizona getting hit, but not by whom."

"They came for the California one too, but it was empty."

"At least you're a step ahead of whomever is gunning for you. If I had to bet, I would put money on it being the Russians."

"The Arizona raid happened before I even heard about their two men going missing." Before I killed them.

"Is that right? Wow. It would be unfortunate for you to have war raging on two fronts. I'm not sure if I would want to marry into that kind of messy fucking family. You're also damn lucky the Russians aren't offering me any pretty young brides."

"I'm handling shit," I assure him, meaning all of it. "And our families will come together. Just be patient a little longer."

"If there's no engagement dinner within the next six months, there will be hell to pay, Salvato," he threatens. "And I expect an update when you attend my poker tournament next month."

"I'm not gambling in anyone's casino but my own," I tell him.

"Your ass better be there rubbing elbows with the celebrities. It's for charity, you jackass. And I want you to bring Madison. It's time I got to meet my bride."

"That's a horrible idea." I can't even imagine my daughter at such a public event. "You want her running off with some actor or lead singer in a band?"

"Bring her, or our little truce is over," he says before ending the call.

Fuck.

Rather than adding an ally, I could be gaining another enemy at the worst fucking time if I can't convince Madison to marry the son of a bitch.

Leaving my office, I head up to the third floor and to my oldest daughter's bedroom. All the girls have giant suites. Madison's is at least three times the size of mine. Her door is shut, so I knock on it and wait rather than start this conversation off by busting in unannounced.

"What do you want?" she calls from the other side of the door. When it finally opens her eyes widen. "Daddy?" A second later her surprise fades into indignation. "You actually walked up all the stairs rather than summon me by phone to your office?"

Is that what I do? Lately, yeah, I guess it is. Only because my daughters are teenagers who no longer welcome me into their rooms to play Barbies, have tea parties, or race go-carts in video games. It's been at least seven years since Sophie did any of those things, nearly ten for Madison since she's the oldest. Rather than apologize for my absence they each insist on, I get to the point.

"I need you to make a decision," I tell her.

"A decision on what? Where I'm going to college in the fall? I've narrowed it down to three schools..."

"No. You're not going to college. I meant a decision about marrying Lochlan."

"Oh. Well, in that case you can have my decision right now. My answer is no."

"Let me rephrase that," I grit out. "I need you to *agree* to marry Lochlan right fucking now. The wedding doesn't have to be soon, but you need to accept his engagement ring and agree to see him so he's reassured that it will happen, eventually."

"My answer is still no to all of that. I don't want his ring, or to see him. His family killed my mother!"

"The Irish have always denied the shooting. There was never any evidence pointing to them directly either. And even if there had been, that was Lochlan's father, not Lochlan who ordered it."

"Same thing."

"No, it's not. Lochlan is innocent. Or at least he's innocent when it comes to Maria's murder. I pray that no one ever holds my sins against you."

"So do I," she agrees as if she knows they're too numerous to list.

"Look, sweetheart, I know this marriage isn't what you want. But the Irishman is one of the few men who I trust to actually take good care of you. Lochlan will be able to protect you. He also has the financial means to give you, and your future children, everything you could ever want."

"No! I'm not marrying someone just because you want me to, especially not him!"

"Honestly, I'm dealing with a lot of other shit right now. The last thing I need is to make another enemy by refusing Lochlan's offer."

She crosses her arms over her chest. "Then you should marry him. It's legal now for two men."

"Yes, I know it's legal, but I'm pretty sure he's expecting biological heirs. I'm afraid I can't give those to him."

"I can't either. That's what surrogates are for, right?"

"Madison, if you would just give him a chance, you may even like him. He's not that much older than you, and he's not unattractive."

"Sorry, Dad. It's going to take more than a handsome face to get me down the aisle. I want to love the man I marry and spend the rest of my life with him. I don't want it to be just a business arrangement!"

"The list of men who I trust to keep you safe as well as make you happy is incredibly short. Lochlan is the one closest to your age. The rest are much older men closer to my age. If that's your preference..."

"I don't want or need your help finding a husband."

"Madison…"

"It's not going to happen, okay? Let Cass or Sophie marry the guy instead."

"They're too young to be thinking about marriage yet."

"Then he can wait a few more years."

"I thought you wanted to leave, to get out of this prison of mine, as you refer to it."

"I do. But I want to do it on my own terms. I'm not trading one prison for another."

"Then, I guess we're at a stalemate."

"I guess we are."

"Is there anything I can do to change your mind?"

"Let me go to college for two years, and actually live on campus. I'll agree to date the man while I'm there."

"He'll never agree to that, and neither will I," I tell her. "God, you're so fucking stubborn, just like Vanessa." Madison may look exactly like her beautiful mother Maria, but her mother was so obedient and eager to please me. I never expected her daughter to be so damn difficult.

"How much longer is she gonna be staying here?" Madison asks.

"Several more weeks."

"Weeks? Why? What's so special about her? You've dated plenty of younger, prettier women."

"Don't you dare ever use those words in front of her," I warn her. Knowing she'll do it just to spite me for telling her not to, I add on what the punishment will be for disobeying me on this issue. "You think this is a hellish prison now, but if you offend Vanessa, you'll be living in a stone-age prison with zero technology."

She rolls her eyes. "I don't like her."

"I don't care. You and your sisters *will* tolerate her and be respectful while she's here, or you'll regret it. And you *will* be coming with me to meet Lochlan at his fucking poker tournament next month whether you like it or not. Is that clear?"

"Crystal," she mutters before closing the door in my face.

25

Vanessa

The nighttime routine with Dante may have seemed like it was the normal routine for us, but it was obvious that things had changed.

In bed, pillows still separate us, but the urge to toss them aside to cuddle up with Dante, or do incredibly dirty things to him, is strong.

Still, he doesn't initiate anything after turning the lights out, so I keep to my side of the bed.

Between my raging hormones and his constant flopping around, it's impossible for me to fall asleep.

"Why are you still awake?" I ask him in the darkness.

The mafia king sighs heavily. "Too much shit on my mind. Why are you still awake?"

"Because you are," I lie, unable to admit to him that I can't stop thinking about last night in the club.

After a long, quiet moment, he asks, "Are you hungry?"

"I wouldn't mind a midnight snack. What do you have?"

"Let's go see. There's no point in lying here any longer when sleeping is impossible."

Since Dante doesn't put any other clothes on with his black boxer briefs, I follow him out of the bedroom in just my panties and his oversized tee that comes down nearly to my knees.

The light over the stove is on, giving us enough light to see by, especially when Dante opens the refrigerator door.

"What are you in the mood for?" he says turning to ask me.

Sex is unfortunately my first thought.

"No clue," I answer instead. Dante narrows his eyes at me like he knows I'm lying.

"Is that my shirt?"

Glancing down at the oversized tee, I tell him, "What do you think? The dresses you bought me are smaller."

"I like seeing my shirt on you," he says as he leaves the fridge open to turn to me. His big hands clasp either side of my waist before lifting me up and sitting me on the cool, flat granite surface of the kitchen island. "Sexier than any of that expensive lingerie."

"Is that right?" I ask with a smile.

"Yes." His gaze roams up and down me from my knees to my face several times before he clears his throat and goes back to the refrigerator. This time, he also opens the lower freezer drawer. "Ice cream?"

"Sure."

"That was always the girls' go to midnight snack whenever I caught them up late." He removes a pint of ice cream, then reaches for a spoon from the nearby drawer.

After placing the lid of the container beside me on the island countertop, he digs the spoon into the top.

"Open up," he says, holding the spoonful right in front of my mouth.

Shaking my head as I smile, I tell him, "You just enjoy controlling what I do with my mouth."

"I do, but the only way you're getting my ice cream tonight is if you do what I say."

"What kind is it? Maybe it's not worth the trouble."

Holding the container up to the dim glow of light shining from underneath the cabinets to see the label, he says, "Eh, maybe not. It's cookie dough."

"That's one of my favorites," I admit before I open wide. Of course, Dante doesn't immediately insert the spoon but lets me sit there, my barely covered ass on the countertop, lips parted wide for him. "Ass," I say with a grin. I wrap my legs around the back of his to pull him close enough that I can reach the small pile of ice cream from the spoon.

"That's cheating," he remarks.

I shrug. "All is fair in war and ice cream fulfillment."

We stare at each other for a silent moment before his lips lean forward to brush mine briefly. "What about love?"

"A man must have started that stupid saying because all is *not* fair in love," I assure him. Grabbing the waistband of his boxer briefs, I pull him even closer. "Now give me some more of that fucking ice cream, or I'll cut your dick off in your sleep."

"No, you won't," he says, but he surrenders the spoon and the pint to me. With his hands now free, they start sliding up my thighs while his damp lips make their way up my neck. "You want to ride on my dick at least once before you remove it. Admit it, butterfly. You're half a breath away from begging me to put it inside of you."

Between the ice cream melting on my tongue and his tongue on my skin, I'm not sure which I prefer.

"I'm not in the mood for ice cream tonight," he says against the sensitive skin right below my ear.

"No?"

"No. I want to taste you instead."

He wants to taste me? As in...

His hands slip underneath the hem of the tee, finding the waistband of my thong to pull it down my thighs, demonstrating exactly where he wants to taste me.

When he pushes the bottom of my shirt up to lower his lips to my thighs, he asks, "Any objections?"

"Nope."

But based on how talented his fingers are, I assume his mouth will be even better. Besides, a deal is a deal. I agreed to let him go down on me for Gavin's expedited release at a time of his choosing. That time is now, apparently.

Dante's hands grab my hips to drag me closer, so my pussy is right on the edge of the counter. With one long lick his tongue glides through my slit, making me cry out in pleasure. I put down the ice cream and spoon to grab a handful of Dante's hair as he begins to lick and suck up every drop of my arousal. It's a pointless game since it's constantly being replaced by more and more.

My hips buck, thighs tightening around his head, humping his face without any inhibitions as the pleasure builds. Dante moans against my flesh like he approves of me suffocating him, which only turns me on even more.

"Oh god! Oh, my fucking god!" I scream to the ceiling as my thighs flutter thanks to the tip of his tongue flicking over my clit repeatedly.

It feels like I'm falling or flying. It feels too amazing to even care as I endure the jolts of pleasure exploding through my entire body. So much pleasure it carries me up and away to the heavens.

When I come to again, my back and head are lying on the counter, and my fingers are still in Dante's hair. I lift my head to find his lips pressing kisses to my lower belly while his eyes stare up at me.

"Welcome back to consciousness. Now, come for me again."

Again? I haven't even recovered from the first time.

Dante's long, thick fingers spread my lower lips apart to make room for ... "Oh, god!" My head falls backward again when his tongue dives down, my hips bouncing, trying to get away or get closer.

"Mmm, you're fucking drenched," he says between hard licks.

Two fingers slide inside of me, stealing my breath. "You're so damn tight, like you haven't taken a dick in years. So slick and snug."

"Don't...don't stop," I beg.

His thumb continues rubbing my clit at the same time he fingers me and licks me. "I'm not stopping. I could feast on you all night long."

"I- I can't."

"You will." Dante presses his heavy palm on my pelvis. The weight keeps me still even when the fluttering tip of his tongue returns to my clit at the same time his fingers are thrusting in and out of me.

"Please! Oh god!" I scream even though I'm not sure if I can handle any more. "Please, please, please," I chant, tightening my fingers' grip on his hair.

When he slows down, I stare down at Dante, his eyes once more on mine. His fingertips rub my clit that's soaking wet, and then his wet tongue squirms inside of me. He pauses long enough to say, "Come one more time, butterfly. I'm going to bury my tongue inside of you until you give it a squeeze."

When he sticks his tongue out to demonstrate by fucking me with it, an orgasm slams into me so hard I can't see or hear anything for several moments. My back arches, my legs shake. I clench both sides of Dante's head to urge him to keep going and never stop. This orgasm seems to last longer than any before.

When I come back down the second time, his hum of vibration rumbles through my flesh settling off a few more ripples of pleasure.

"Now you can have your ice cream."

I sit up, tugging the shirt back down, intending to ask him about his turn.

The truth is that while I love oral, giving and obviously receiving, holding back to hurt him is beginning to hurt me. I ache to be full of him, but my head...I just can't cross that line. One fuck and he might walk away, having accomplished his ultimate goal. I honestly don't know why he wants me so badly other than because I refuse him. Once I give in, I'm just like all the others who were used and forgotten by him.

And denying him, knowing how badly I can frustrate this domineering, arrogant, mafia king makes me feel like a goddess.

When I don't make a move to pick up the spoon or pint, Dante retrieves them.

"Now I bet you'll open wide for me," he says again with a smirk, as if he knows I'm thinking about taking him in my mouth.

We stare at each other for a silent moment before I do as I'm told by him for once without complaint.

But I don't get to eat my spoonful before *"Are you kidding me?"* is huffed by a feminine voice. Dante and I both freeze, my head turning toward the source. "Now I can't even leave my room unless I want to see you fucking her?"

I tug the tee down over my knees, but Dante doesn't move away from me, seeming unconcerned we were just caught. His teeth, however, grind together so hard I hear the screech before he glances toward the stairs to the right of the kitchen and the brunette standing at the bottom of them.

"What are you doing down here this late?" he asks Madison like she's a small child wandering the hallways.

"We ran out of ice cream upstairs. I thought I could find some here but now I've lost my appetite." With that, she turns around and climbs back up the steps soundlessly on bare feet. No wonder we didn't hear her.

"Sorry," I whisper to Dante when he sits the ice cream and spoon down beside me. A few seconds later a door slams from two stories up, making me jump. "We probably should've put more clothes on and not done *that* in here."

"She'll get over it," he grumbles as he leans his forehead against my shoulder, burying his face against me. "Or it'll be just one more thing for her to hate me for."

Sliding my fingers up through his soft, messy hair, I tell him the truth. "I doubt she hates you."

Lifting his head, the look in his eyes is the cold blue one that I bet he wears when he kills without remorse. "You hate me too, don't you? Well, except for maybe when I'm getting you off."

"What are you talking about? Why do you assume I hate you?" I ask when my hands drop abruptly from his now messy hair.

"The day that asshole was here he told me flat out that you hated me."

"Who? Mitch?" I ask in confusion.

"There was no reason for him to lie about that."

"I don't...he probably just assumed I did when I bitched about being on my feet all night or complained about the guys who would grab my ass, not you specifically." It sounds like I'm rambling—even to my own ears. I don't know why I'm trying so hard to refute the truth to his face.

"If I knew who had grabbed your ass, I would've sliced their hands off."

"I know that now. Maybe I didn't think you would care if you knew before. Really, I thought you were just as likely to slap my ass without permission."

Backing away from the kitchen island and me, Dante says, "I'm going to bed," and takes off down the hall like he's now pissed at me, and I have no idea what I did wrong.

26

Vanessa

Dante didn't skip his workout this morning. He came back to shower, then was out of the bedroom before I got up.

He's obviously still pissed at me for some reason. Or for several reasons.

I've barely touched him, and certainly haven't given him any relief in the weeks I've been here. That part I can understand. But why he suddenly steered our conversation about Madison last night to me I haven't figured out.

One thing I know I need to do today is obvious. I have to apologize to Madison for making her feel uncomfortable in her own house.

I'm not sure how much she saw of me and Dante last night. Whatever it was had to have been too much.

That's why, after lunch, I sought out Franny, the woman I refer to as the house manager. She buys all the groceries for the family and keeps the fridge and pantry stocked up for their cooking staff. Once that's taken care of, I make the trek up to the third floor, where I was told not to go unless invited. Oh well.

There are several doors open, revealing two empty, expansive bedroom suites. I assume those are Sophie's and Cass's rooms. I knock gently on the closed door and wait.

"Coming!" she calls out.

When Madison cracks the door about two inches, it's enough for me to see her scowl. "What do you want?"

Oh, jeez. I had forgotten how intimidating teenage girls can be. Well, Madison is just out of the teenage years, which makes her even more vicious. I thank the stars above for giving me a son as my fingers fidget, and I try not to let her see how nervous I am talking to her.

"Hey, hi. I just wanted to tell you that I'm so sorry about last night. I also asked Franny to stock up your freezer with ice cream."

She huffs out a laugh. "Don't worry, I won't be wandering down-stairs at night again or any other time unless he commands my presence."

"That's not...we won't do that again, so you can wander wherever you want. It's your house."

"I seriously don't care about where you screw him."

"You don't? And we're not...we haven't...done that together..." Okay, that's probably too much information but I think it's important to be honest with her. Otherwise, she'll never trust me. I'm not sure why it matters if she trusts me or not since I'll be gone soon.

"Whatever. My problem is that he is such a fucking hypocrite!"

Oh. So, she's pissed at Dante for something else, apparently.

"I agree. Your father is very hypocritical. But what in particular is he hypocritical about this time?"

Resting her forehead against the doorframe, her tall frame deflates when she says, "I just want to make my own decisions. I want it to be my choice. I want...I want someone to look at me the way he looks at you."

Okay, she lost me.

"Ah, I'm not sure I know what you mean..." I admit.

"My dad is in love with you, but he's going to force me to marry some asshole I've never even met and don't want to meet!"

"Wait, what?" I ask since I'm confused about every part of what she just said. "For the record, your dad doesn't love me. He's just…a little obsessed at the moment for a ridiculous reason. I can assure you that this is a temporary arrangement for us. There's no love involved."

"Whatever you say, Vanessa." She mutters those words, staring at me with a look of disgust, like she thinks I'm the dumbest woman in the world. While Cole doesn't usually do what I tell him to, he at least acts as if he respects me to my face.

Then again, I know she's just taking her anger toward her father out on me.

"Second of all, I can't believe your father would force you to marry someone you don't want to. That's just…wrong."

"Well, it's either marry the man he chose or live here in this prison forever."

"Those are not great choices," I agree.

"All I want is my own life. I want to go to college, to live on campus without guards, to hang out with friends, and date guys. I'm a twenty-year-old virgin!"

Her admission has me giving her a half smile. "There is absolutely nothing wrong with that, Madison. In fact, it's a good thing to wait until you're absolutely certain you're ready and with the right person."

"It'll never happen if I'm not allowed to be near any men!"

"Did you talk to your father? Ask him about letting you go to college?"

"Yes."

"And he flat out said no?" I guess.

"Yep."

"Because he thinks someone, his enemies, might hurt you?"

"Of course."

"Well, he's right to be concerned," I agree, and she makes a groaning sound before banging her forehead into the doorframe. "You would be much safer if people didn't know who you are or that you're his daughter."

"Yeah, well, that's impossible."

"No, it's not. If you were to use an alias, then you would be as anonymous as anyone else on a college campus."

That has her lifting her head, perking up. "An alias? How would I do that?"

"Well, you probably couldn't. At least not without your dad's help getting all the legal documents to prove to the school administration that you're someone else. That sort of thing, a bulletproof new identity wouldn't be cheap."

"And colleges probably wouldn't be okay with that, would they? Me pretending to be someone else?"

"That's another problem. You would need transcripts and recommendations all in the name of the alias for most universities if you don't want the administration to know who you really are. Even community colleges. My son Cole barely got into Lennox even with a four point oh GPA."

"You have a son? And he's in college?"

"I do," I answer with a proud smile.

"How? You're not *that* old."

"Thanks," I reply, my smile dimming. "I had Cole when I was very young because I made stupid, irrational decisions just to spite my parents. Those decisions ended up biting me in the ass. Not that I have ever regretted having my son," I rush to amend. "I would do anything in the world for Cole. It wasn't easy raising him on my own, having to juggle working with childcare..."

"And his dad?"

Wincing, I admit, "That's another part of where I was stupid and barely got first names. I definitely didn't learn their last names. Even if I did, there are multiple possibilities so..."

"Wow, Vanessa," Madison remarks with a genuine smile. "You're just full of surprises."

Shrugging, I tell her the truth. "I made horrible, irrational decisions, and I had to live with the consequences. But I'm glad they were at least my choices, nobody else's."

Biting her bottom lip, she says, "Do you think you could talk to my dad? Try to convince him to let me change my name and let me go to college? Any college?"

"I can try I guess, although I doubt it will help."

"Thank you!" she exclaims excitedly like it's a done deal.

"He probably won't listen," I tell her honestly.

"He might. And if he doesn't let me leave soon, I'm going to go insane. Cass has her training, and Sophie has tennis to keep busy and out of the penthouse. All I want is to get offline and get out in the world."

"Are you sure you would be ready to be on your own?"

At that question she rolls her eyes. "I couldn't get more ready."

"What would you do without your father's money? And can you take care of yourself? Do you know how to cook? Buy groceries? Wash your laundry? Do you even have a driver's license? How do you plan to get around?"

"I-I don't know. I've never had to do any of those things or thought about it before."

"Exactly. There are basic things teenagers need to know before they head off alone, things sheltered rich girls don't have to do for themselves. It's all just another way to keep you from leaving, right?"

"That's exactly what it is, why Dad never wanted us to learn how to drive or do anything else!" She huffs. "Will you show me how to cook? How to do laundry and some of those other things?"

Dante won't be happy about me showing his daughter how to be independent, but it's the least she deserves. He lives a dangerous life and may not always be around to care for his daughters. I don't like thinking about that, but it's the reality that comes with his mobster world.

"Sure. I would be happy to help. And maybe consider one other thing, Madison."

"Yeah?"

"As long as your father is supporting you financially, his money will always come with strings attached."

She nods but her face looks defeated. Dante won't let her get a job, ergo, she'll never be free of him. While it might have been nice to not have to work my ass off to keep a roof over my and Cole's head and keep us fed, there are zero benefits to allowing someone else to have that kind of control over me.

"When can we start?" Madison asks, swinging her door wide open as if she's ready to hit the ground running right now.

"I've been helping Chef Edward and his crew with dinner most nights if you want to join us?"

"Tonight?" she asks, like the prospect of having to wait to begin is a huge disappointment.

"They get started around four each afternoon. That's how long it takes to have everything ready by seven or eight when Dante wants to eat. They handle the cooking downstairs in one of the restaurants before bringing it all up, even on the nights you don't sit down together."

"Holy shit. It takes that long to cook a meal?"

"Only for mafia kings and princesses," I assure her with a smile. "If you're cooking for a normal group of people, you could probably have it all done in an hour or two, plus cleanup."

"Cleanup?"

"Washing the dishes, pots and pans, and cleaning up messes made in the kitchen."

"Oh. I think I'd rather just have takeout."

"When you're pinching pennies, it can be cheaper, although not as healthy, to go for takeout. Cole and I have had our fair share of value meals."

"Value meals?" the privileged rich girl asks.

"Oh, you have so much to learn," I tell her. "Let's get you caught up on how the world really works for most of us who aren't filthy rich."

27

Dante

"You're late," Vanessa says sweetly when I pull out my chair to join her and my three daughters already seated at the second-floor dinner table.

"Perhaps because I didn't request a sit-down dinner tonight."

"No, but we did," she replies.

"We?"

"I made the salad," Madison announces proudly, smiling and looking happier than she has in probably months.

"A monkey could literally make a salad," Cass informs her sister with a roll of her eyes. "It's just tearing up vegetables and throwing them all in a bowl."

"I cut the vegetables into tiny pieces without chopping off my finger, fuck you very much," Madison replies.

I look pointedly at Vanessa, whom I assume is the one who demanded dinner, and also somehow, talked my oldest into helping prepare the meal.

"Madison wanted to learn how to cook. We had to start somewhere," she replies.

"I want to learn how to cook too," Sophie chimes in.

"Fine. I don't want to be the only one at the table who can't chop shit up without cutting a finger off," Cass says with a huff.

"It can't hurt for them to learn a few tricks, right? In case the chef is sick, and they need to eat."

I have no clue what she's up to, but I don't like it. Still, I keep my mouth shut for the rest of the meal, while Madison tells us all about her kitchen experience down in the casino.

Once we all adjourn from the dining table, I head for my office since I'm not ready for bed. I'm not ready for the torture of wanting Vanessa and being unable to have her either.

The woman doesn't get the hint and follows me inside, shutting the door behind her.

"I have work to do," I tell her.

"Dante, wait." She grabs my elbow to stop me in front of my desk. "I'm not sure what I did to piss you off last night, but you're not really angry about me showing Madison around the kitchen are you?"

"I don't know why you bothered. She'll always have staff to wait on her and cater to her every need."

"Did you not see her face tonight? Being able to do things for herself makes her feel good, like she's capable of anything she puts her mind to."

She's right. Madison did seem happier tonight. I'm just not sure if that's a good thing or not.

"Don't go putting ideas in their heads, making them think they would last a day on their own in the real world."

"Why not?"

"Because I don't ever want them to have to work twelve-hour shifts serving cocktails to assholes who slap their asses or getting beat for dating the wrong men."

My beautiful butterfly scoffs indignantly at me, and I know I just fucked up.

"You think my life is one big failure, and that it somehow proves you're better than me? Just because you have endless amounts of money, doesn't mean shit, Dante! At least I'm free do to what I want, when I want, without worrying about who may have a target on my head. You should want your daughters to escape this world as fast as possible before they become victims of it."

"Watch it," I warn her through clenched teeth.

My message is ignored since Vanessa then has the nerve to say, "You're not actually going to make Madison marry someone she doesn't even know, are you?"

Wow. How did she know about Lochlan? I guess her and Madison had girl talk during their cooking lesson.

"Not that it's any of your business, but arranged marriages are part of this life."

"This life? Being a mob boss?" She scoffs. "Don't force your daughter into a marriage with someone she doesn't want just to elevate territory disputes or bolster your business connections with other mobster families!"

"It's about more than the mobster families. The only way to protect my girls is to make sure they end up with someone who has the money, and the means, to keep them safe."

"Did you even ask them if they would rather be what you consider safe or if they want to find husbands they love?"

"It's more complicated than that. And they don't know what's best for them yet. Trust me, when I was their age, I hated the fucking idea of taking some Russian child bride; it's why I flat out refused."

"You refused, but they can't?"

"My situation was different. She was an actual child."

"Uh-huh. Sure."

"My father wanted me to marry a sixteen-year-old virgin when I was twenty-four. By then I was fucking my way through Vegas, popping any and every pill made, and killing any chance I could get just to make my father proud. Could you imagine me with a teenage virgin?"

"So, you didn't want to be with someone who was young and innocent?"

"Hell, no. I didn't even know the shit was even arranged until it was done, and he told me. My father thought a wedding would be enough to create an alliance between the Italians and Russians and help get me to settle down."

"Again, you refused, but Madison can't?"

"My refusal came with a lot of fucking consequences. It nearly started a war when I backed out. Yuri Petrov took it as an insult to him, his family, and his daughter who I never even fucking met. He threatened to kill me if I didn't agree to go through with the wedding when she turned eighteen."

"You're obviously still alive, so it was an empty threat."

"No, he meant it. But thankfully it eventually blew over. A few weeks after the death threat, Petrov told my father to forget the marriage, that I wasn't good enough for his only daughter anyway. I'm pretty sure he still holds a grudge, though. As long as he and the Russians stay on their side of town, I ignore them. Or at least I try to."

"And then instead of marrying who you were told to marry, you married the girls' mothers?"

"No. I got them all pregnant, so they became my responsibility."

"Did you love any of them?" she asks.

"Does it matter now? They're all dead. I finally grew up, learned from my mistakes, and made sure I couldn't knock up anyone else after the third time."

"I'm sorry," she whispers.

Ignoring her sympathy, I tell her the truth. "None of my girls are cut out for this world, and I don't have any sons. Titus is loyal, but he's not capable of running shit. I had hoped that one of the girls' husbands could take over for me when I'm gone. I won't force them down the aisle until they're ready, but they will remain sheltered here until they marry who they need to marry to stay alive."

"Even if they want to marry boring, strait-laced men who don't want anything to do with the mafia?"

"Those kinds of men won't be able to protect them!"

"I think they would be safer with the boring guy. Boring guys don't have enemies. If you give them to another mob boss, then it's just more of the same, lethal feuds for power for the rest of their lives, and their children's lives."

"Is that why you don't want to be with me?" I ask as understanding finally dawns on me. Does she hate me because of the violence that constantly surrounds me? I thought she agreed that some people deserve to die.

"What?" Vanessa asks softly.

"You don't think I can protect you."

"I didn't...that's not what I said. I just said that boring men don't have the kind of rivals who may try to kill them."

"My daughters are mafia princesses now and forever, whether they like it or not. Just because they leave my household to go live with the boring guy doesn't mean someone won't hurt them to get to me. I can't allow them to be with someone who doesn't have guards constantly watching over them."

"They don't like the guards."

"How do you know that?"

"Because Madison told me she wants to be normal, to go where she wants, to be able to live life without someone looking over her shoulder."

"Someone keeping her alive? I don't care what kind of fucking hardship it is for them to be followed. The guards stay."

"The guards, the house arrest, it's about more than safety and you know it. It's about control. You only let them go where you approve, and you want to know everyone they talk to, right? Do you ask the guards what they do every day?"

"I have to know what they're doing to keep them safe. And this fucking discussion is over, Vanessa. They're my daughters. I'm not going to let anyone hurt them."

"No one except for you is allowed that privilege, right, Dante?"

I don't know why, but those words from Vanessa's mouth flip some kind of switch inside my head. Vanessa turns to leave, and before I realize what I'm doing, my fingers are wrapped around the back of her neck. A second later I have her pinned to the wall, her cheek pressed to it along with the front of her body.

"Don't you ever disrespect me like that again," I growl into her ear. "I have *never* laid a finger on a single one of them. You don't have a fucking clue what this life is really like, how vulnerable they are in this world. *I do.* Madison's mother, Maria, was gunned down in the street in broad daylight while Madison cried in her stroller. Cassandra's mother, Charlotte, I don't even know what happened to her because she went missing, and her body was never found. I would not survive burying one of my daughters."

Vanessa closes her eyes and whispers, "I'm...I'm sorry. I shouldn't have said that."

"No, you shouldn't have. And it's going to take more than a few measly words from your mouth for me to forgive you."

Having her restrained under me like this, her fine ass against my lap, I still get hard even though I'm fucking furious with her.

I want to punish her. No, I *need* to punish her.

"This fucking mouth of yours..." Reaching up with my free hand, I press two long fingers between her parted lips, shoving them down her throat until she gags. "It's going to greedily take whatever I give it in apology, isn't it?" I pull my fingers free to spin Vanessa around by her shoulders.

Her emerald eyes are wide, worried, as I push her down to her knees.

While my trembling fingers work to undo my pants, I warn her, "If you bite my dick, I'll make you watch me remove Mitch and Gavin's with a rusty saw."

Now there's absolute fear in her eyes. She's finally scared of me because she knows I'll fucking do it. Maybe she doesn't give a shit about Mitch, but the stripper is one pretty bastard. I would still cut off his dick to keep it away from Vanessa. All I need is a good reason.

And I hate myself for losing my temper with her, showing her this ruthless side of me.

Does that stop me from pulling my hard cock out, and guiding the head of it to her lips, forcing them apart? Hell no.

It doesn't stop me from cupping the back of her beautiful head in one hand and shoving my cock down her throat either. Her first gag nearly makes me come undone. Vanessa's palms press on my thighs, trying to push me away, urging me to back off. I pull back, bracing my other palm on the wall as I guide her mouth down my shaft a little slower, not as deep. At least not at first. Her mouth is so hot and wet. So perfect.

Vanessa moans or whimpers, the sound vibrating through me. I'm already so close my hips slam forward and back, chasing the release until I feel Vanessa's fingernails digging into my thighs.

How fucking long have I wanted this, needed her to be the one pleasuring me? So damn long. The past few weeks have been agonizing. And for a few moments of overwhelming ecstasy, it's worth the torture.

Having Vanessa kneeling before me, my dick stretching her lips apart as she moans, struggling to take all of me, she's the sexiest thing I've ever seen or heard in my entire life.

"Goddamn perfect," I groan as I press her face to my body and unload the pulsing seed down the back of her throat.

When I hear her choke and splutter, I finally pull my dick all the way free of her mouth, then tug on her hair to make her look up at me. Her mascara is running down her cheeks and my cum mixed with her saliva is dripping from her chin.

I wait for her to call me an asshole, a bastard, a son of a bitch. To tell me she's done with me and leaving...

Her palm swipes over her mouth to wipe up some of the wetness before she finally speaks. "I deserved that."

I don't let the surprise show on my face. "Yes, you did. Are we good now?" I hold my breath, waiting for her response.

She nods, wiping the dampness from her cheeks, smearing the black eye makeup even more.

"Are you sure about that?"

Lowering her face to the floor, she quietly says, "Yes."

I wish I could fucking believe her.

28

Vanessa

Dante lifts me off the floor by my shoulders and thankfully not my hair, but I'm still stuck between him and the wall. I've never seen him so angry, so...terrifying. I thought he was going to hurt me. Other than giving me more of his dick down my throat than I could handle, he went easy on me. What man hasn't done that anyway when a woman goes down on him?

"You have no idea how long I've wanted to fuck this pretty mouth." Dante grabs my chin and rubs his thumb over my bottom lip that's still sticky from his cum. "At least I waited until your lips were all healed up."

"Yes, thank you," I agree. "And, um, I'm sorry about what I said."

Instead of telling me he may have overreacted or that I'm forgiven, he just brushes his mouth over mine, tasting himself with a groan.

When he pulls back, licking his lips, I tell him, "I'm also sorry if I'm not as good at *that* as other women you've been with...."

"What are you...oh." He grins down at me, and it's like most of his anger faded that fast. "You're not jealous of those other women, are you, butterfly?"

At least he's still using the term of endearment after I offended him. I don't think my comments about requiring the girls to marry men went too far. Well, maybe the last thing I said about him hurting them. I didn't mean physically, but it didn't matter either way. Dante took offense to the implication that he would harm his daughters when all he's doing is what he thinks is best for them. After what happened to the girls' mothers, I can better understand his overprotective parenting.

Kissing me, tasting my lips again because of course the arrogant mafia king likes his own personal flavor, Dante says, "I thought you did a brilliant job."

"I gagged."

Dante brushes my hair behind one ear, then the other. "So?"

"I...I don't have much experience. I can't compete with the kinds of women you've been with."

"Vanessa, I haven't fucked any part of a woman since you signed that agreement. I don't want anyone else. And while I hadn't realized it before now, I think I enjoy punishing you by giving you more than you can handle."

"Punishing me?" That's exactly what Dante just did to me, he punished me for disrespecting him. "How...how else do you want to punish me?"

"Make you squirm for my tongue, but not let you come until I'm ready."

"That would be torture."

"But aren't orgasms even better after they're withheld? I'll enjoy making you beg. Your cries when you come for me are a balm to my damaged ego."

"Oh, yeah?"

"Trust me. I don't want to hurt you. Not intentionally. I'm not a psycho like Eli."

"What did he do that was so bad he's now your servant or whatever he is?" I can't help but ask, wanting to change the subject of blowjobs.

Now, the mafia king scowls down at me. "Eli was one of my best MMA fighters. He enjoys hurting people, which made him quickly rise up the ranks in the cage. Then, he started throwing fights to make more money off the bets. He fucked me and fucked my reputation in the process. He cost me hundreds of thousands of dollars and some business acquaintances who lost money and thought I was in on scamming them. I should've killed him. I still haven't forgotten his betrayal or forgiven him. I'm still holding a grudge, making him repent by serving me."

"Why didn't you kill him?"

"I don't know. Maybe because I knew his talent inflicting pain was a necessary evil I needed. He's better at getting people to talk than even my best enforcers. People fear what Eli would do to them, having heard the rumors about him. And that means the smart ones won't ever cross me. Eli sometimes jerks off during torture or watching me, so that's another reason why I didn't want you to watch the other day."

"Ah, okay."

"You think he's fucked up, and I'm sick for wanting to take advantage of his depravity?"

"No, I don't think that," I assure him. "In fact, I think it makes sense for both of you."

"You do?"

"You find pleasure in getting answers, getting revenge using pain as a motivator. He gets turned on seeing you in action as a powerful, vicious mob boss or doing the hurting himself, having that kind of control over someone. You may not enjoy hurting people, but you do it to try and protect the people you care about, right?"

"Yes." Dante pauses for a moment, then says, "I should probably tell you that your stripper friend has found himself tangled up in Eli's web. Whether he's a willing participant or not, I don't know, and honestly, I don't care."

"Wow. Gavin and Eli?" I say in surprise.

"I told you that the stripper is a fuckboy. Yes, he wanted you, but his attention wouldn't have lasted more than a few nights."

"But does Gavin deserve that sort of treatment from Eli?" I ask. "Yes, he was partially responsible for Mitch cheating, and Kozlov's men hurting me. I forgive him, though. He's young and made a stupid mistake. I am glad I didn't do anything with him, thanks to you. Being tossed aside is not what I need right now."

"Is that still what you think I'll do? I told you I didn't go to all this trouble just to toss you aside as easily as a one-night stand."

"It's mostly about the challenge for you too, right? When you win, when you get what you want from me, the thrill of the chase is over."

"Vanessa, I honestly don't think you will ever be easy, even after I fuck you. With you, there are still plenty of challenges left for me to try and win until our time is up, even just trying to make you happy."

Until our time is up.

There's still an expiration date for us, which I hate. Dante and I are only temporary. In a few weeks, everything will go back to the way it was before.

Instead of worrying about that now, I ask Dante, "Why don't you invite Eli to family dinners with the girls?"

"He's not family."

"But he lives here with you all. Whether you want to admit it or not, I think you and Eli are friends at the very least."

Dante opens his mouth to argue that's not true, but then his brow creases in thought.

"Do you care about him? Would you be sad if he left?" I ask.

"I'd survive," he says on a heavy exhale. "But I would miss his unwavering obedience," he says with a grin that quickly fades. "Fuck. He's a friend, even if our relationship is so one-sided?"

"That still counts. It just makes you a shitty friend. Unless, well, will you ever release him?"

"Not until he proves he's loyal to me and is no longer the same greedy son of a bitch."

"How long has he been trying to prove that so far?"

"A little more than a year."

"A year? Wow."

That just goes to show that when Dante gets his talons in someone, he doesn't let them go until he's good and ready.

I can't help but wonder if he'll do the same to me when our time is up.

The worst part is, I don't know which I would prefer—for him to let me walk away without a second thought, or for him to never let me go.

And that scares the shit out of me.

29

Dante

My morning workouts have recently been replaced with sex. It's just oral sex for now, but it's amazing, and so much better than nothing. I enjoy waking Vanessa up with my face between her legs. But I'm not stupid. I know that Vanessa is quick to go down on me after I lick her pussy just to hold back the one thing she refuses to let me have. I need to be inside of her, to fill up that tight, empty part of her body with my own, making her mine. Claiming her. Owning her. Coming inside of her even if I know my seed won't ever impregnate her.

Thank god for that.

As much as I may want to keep my butterfly, I know I have to set her free. I won't let her be taken from me like the other women I tried to love. The women who were unfortunate to cross paths with me, putting a bullseye on their heads.

Eager to push those thoughts away, I slip under the covers. Like usual, Vanessa is sleeping on her back in nothing but my plain tee and a sexy pair of black satin panties I bought her. I hover above her lower body on my hands and knees. Rather than take her panties all the way off, I gently tug the crotch of her thong to the side to flick the tip of my tongue over her clit.

"Dante!" she cries out above the covers in surprise as she tries to squirm away. It never gets old, hearing her wake up shouting my name, like I'm the only man in whatever dream she was having before I interrupted.

I place my palm down firmly on her pelvis to hold her in place as I continue licking her.

Vanessa throws back the covers to see me, and I pause long enough to say, "Good morning, butterfly," then get right back to work, licking her faster.

Her arms flail by her sides, fingers seeking something to grip, settling on the bedding as her hips begin to rock toward my tongue.

When I pump two fingers in and out of her, she chants, "Yes, yes, YES!" Her shouts and shiver tell me I've found the perfect spot. Some mornings I've taken my time, getting her to the height of pleasure, then pulling back, making her wait. This morning though, I'm so hard my dick is leaking, so I'm all about instant gratification.

Vanessa's legs shake on either side of my head, even faster than usual. They clamp down as she moans through her orgasm, tightening around my fingers that are still fucking her.

She's still panting, not yet fully recovered when I move up her body, pushing her shirt up so I can drag my teeth over one of her breasts. At the same time, I shove my boxer briefs down my legs to kick them off. By the time my mouth reaches her neck I'm long and thick, pressing right up against her now soaking wet panties. Her arms come around me, holding me to her, fingernails digging in my shoulders as if she thinks I'm going somewhere.

"Eating you for breakfast gets me so hard," I say as I devour her neck while my hips begin to rock, poking that soft spot of hers that I have to have, or I'll die. This morning I don't want a blowjob, I want this. "I'm gonna come all over your soaking wet panties."

When my cock slides over her still sensitive clit, Vanessa lifts her hips for more pressure, wrapping them around my waist. The move lines our lower bodies up in that perfect way. Nothing but a thin strip of satin lies between me and heaven.

I'm hard enough to plow right through the material too, until Vanessa reaches down, wrapping her fingers around my girth and diverting it away, drawing a growl of frustration from me.

"Come on my breasts," she says as she somehow wiggles her way down my body that's pinned above her, tugging her shirt over her head as she goes.

The sight of her beautiful bare breasts momentarily distracts me, just as she intended.

"I want to come inside of you," I ground out through my clenched teeth as I hang my head to see her face. She slides lower, as if avoiding eye contact.

"Fuck my mouth then," she replies softly before the first swipe of her tongue sweeps over the head of my cock. A groan of pleasure escapes me since my dick doesn't know I'm pissed.

"That's not what I meant, and you know it!"

She sucks on the entire crown, giving it hard pulls, trying to distract me. And it works.

I sit back on my heels to watch Vanessa lift her head to take more of my length, loving the sight of it disappearing into her mouth again and again.

While I want to slam deep into her throat, hear her gag, I hold back. I let her suck me how she wants, making me feel so good and so bad all at the same time because I know it's nothing more than a fucking diversion.

If she insists on keeping my dick in her mouth, then so be it.

My head falls back, my mouth opens on a groan when she takes me deep, and swallows. The third time she does this is the charm. I cup the back of her head, holding her face to my body as my dick begins to throb with my release.

I'm even kind enough to pull back a little so she can gulp it all down. Every drop.

When my cock begins to soften, Vanessa presses on my thighs, urging me to let her up.

"Not yet," I tell her, and her green eyes widen. "You're going to stay right there and keep my dick nice and wet until I get hard again."

Her eyes narrow as if in anger, but she doesn't try to push me off her. After a few minutes, Vanessa's face seems resolved, and my knees begin to hurt.

Keeping my hand on the back of her head, I roll to the right, lying on my side while still clutching Vanessa's mouth to me until she's on her side as well. I adjust the pillow so it's under my head, getting comfortable. I even throw my leg over Vanessa's back and play with her hair. She hums around my shaft, sending jolts of pleasure through me before she reaches around to squeeze my ass playfully. Her other hand slides up my stomach, her fingertips exploring the dips and valleys of my abs reverently.

This may be my favorite punishment yet.

~

Vanessa

Having sex with Dante doesn't have to be a big deal.

We've done plenty of other things, and he doesn't seem to be getting bored with me yet so why should sex be any different for us?

I can give him this last piece of me and not fall for him.

It's just sex—a few more orgasms. We can have amazing sex and then when the seventy-six days are up, I'll be the one who gets to walk away from him.

Or he'll handcuff me to his bed and keep me here day and night.

I didn't think such a thing was even possible for the mafia king until he refused to let me take my mouth off his dick.

The man came, I swallowed, that should've been it. But Dante kept sitting on top of me, staring me down like I had done something horrendous to him.

He's angry that I wouldn't let his cock slip past my wet panties to finally penetrate me. I wanted to, but something keeps holding me back from letting him inside of me. It's probably my heart.

Oral sex is fun and sexy, nothing like making love. Not that I think Dante would make love. No, he would definitely fuck me, at least the first hundred times.

But before my time is up, I believe there would come a day, maybe a morning, when he filled me, then stared down at me while moving slowly, making me think he loved me. That's not what this is between us or ever will be.

If I didn't know that before, I do now as he continues to make me suck on his flaccid cock like it's my new favorite pacifier.

And I know I could stop if I wanted to, I just...don't.

I actually enjoy the way he cradles my head to his lower body, absently stroking my hair. That innocent touch and his leg thrown over me is probably as close to a cuddle as the mafia king can get. Of course, it includes my mouth on his favorite body part as well.

"How long do you think I should make you stay down there?" Dante eventually asks, breaking the silence. "Should I cancel my meetings for the morning? For the entire day?"

An entire day? He can't be serious.

Propping his head up on his elbow, he glances down at me. His scruffy handsome face is so damn smug. He tugs on my hair, and I assume that means he's expecting an answer from me.

I hum and shrug my shoulders, as if to say I don't really care either way. It's not like I had any plans today before he made me his human cock warmer.

The vibration of sound causes Dante's eyes to shutter. His shaft twitches in my mouth, telling me he liked it. I apply suction, which is easier when he isn't long and hard, but getting there.

"Good girl. All day it is, butterfly." He groans. The way he cups the back of my head feels like a loving caress rather than a demand for more.

As if the gangster could ever love someone for anything more than orgasms.

And why does hearing the bastard call me a good girl cause my core to throb incessantly?

"I shouldn't be angry at you," Dante says softly as his fingertips trail down the side of my face. "I told you I could be patient. It's not your fault I underestimated myself. Having you in my bed, feeling your mouth on me, it's more than I deserve."

I don't like seeing this side of Dante. Not because he's being vulnerable, but because it makes me understand him more. I already care for him more than I should.

Sure, he may be rich and powerful, but he doesn't trust anyone around him, and he constantly worries for his daughters' safety, to the point that they hate him for it.

I wonder if anyone has ever loved the mafia king. He never talks about his mother, and his father was a raging asshole, apparently. The girls I'm certain love him, even if they don't agree with his harsh parenting decisions imposed on them. But given the chance, they will gladly leave him to escape this life, the mafia world. Eli stays by his side out of obligation, not love. The same likely goes for the rest of his employees who just enjoy their nice fat paychecks.

The fact is, Dante and I aren't that much different. My parents never gave a shit about me. Mitch was an asshole I should've thrown out of my apartment months ago. Other than my son who is all grown up, living on his own at college, there's never been anyone I loved enough to want them to stick around.

There's never been anyone who asked me to stay either.

Maybe that's why I'm content to keep my mouth on Dante for as long as he demands. It's nice to just be wanted for a little while. Even in such a degrading way.

Except, I don't feel ashamed. Dante has a beautiful cock, and I enjoy the taste of him, the feel of him on my tongue.

Which is why, when he twitches and lengthens again to his hardest, I push my palms to his stomach, urging him to his back. I need a better angle to take him down my throat until he hits the back, making me gag.

"God, I fucking love that sound," Dante moans as he lifts my hair up into a makeshift ponytail. "Do it for me again, butterfly. Take those wet panties off and play with yourself while you choke on my long...hard... cock."

Teardrops race down my cheeks when he thrusts his hips up to shove deeper on each of his last three words.

I've never considered myself to be subservient in any way, shape, or form. But for the mafia king? I eagerly do exactly what he demands, at least for now, shoving my panties down my legs, and easing a hand between my legs.

30

Dante

Vanessa's head rests in the curve of my hip while she sleeps, still holding me in her mouth and making me feel like a god. She passed out lying on her stomach naked between my legs after I came a second time down her throat. She swallowed every drop I gave her, moaning through her orgasm induced by her own fingers.

Sleeping so peacefully with her long, tangled blonde hair spread around my thighs, even tickling my balls, she looks like a fallen angel who went rogue. Or one who was held captive and thoroughly debauched by the devil himself.

Honestly, I'm surprised Vanessa didn't push me away after five seconds of straddling her face the first time I finished.

My butterfly won't let me inside of her, but she seems content to give me this unique sort of intimacy I've never experienced before.

The fact that she's not doing it for money, or because she wants anything else from me, feels oddly exhilarating.

Vanessa is the most stubborn woman I know. She doesn't get

anything out of warming my cock with her mouth for hours now. I know there are plenty of other ways she would rather pass her time, and yet, today she chose to unselfishly submit to me, to my whims.

I would gladly spend days with my tongue between her legs, giving her endless pleasure. The only reason I don't is because of the ache of need for her, and her constant rejection to give me what I'm desperate to have.

Her.

All of her, in every way possible.

Slowly, carefully so as to not disturb the sleeping goddess sucking my cock, I reach to my right, removing my phone from the charging stand on the nightstand.

No surprise, I have half a dozen notifications about calls and shit I have on the calendar. None of it is more important than keeping my ass in this bed with Vanessa as long as possible.

I send Eli a text to go to my office and reschedule everything on the calendar for the day.

His response is instant. **ALL DAY??? Are you sure? Everything okay?**

Vanessa will kill me for it if she finds out, but I can't resist pulling up the camera app to snap a photo of her asleep on me, my cock warm, wet, and cozy thanks to her mouth. I plan to keep the image for an eternity, but I also share it with Eli along with the message, **I'm confined to bed for the foreseeable future.**

Eli's reply is one hell of a buzz killer. **Holy shit that's hot as fuck. I thought she hated you???**

He's right. She does hate me. Although, she doesn't look like a woman who hates me at the moment. No, quite the opposite.

If there is a thin line between love and hate, would it be too much to hope that Vanessa could tightrope walk it? She would probably have to be blindfolded and drunk to fall for me, but anything is possible.

Wanting her to love me is downright evil. Nothing good ever happens to women who attempt to have a future with me.

While it seemed like horrible coincidences to lose all three of the girls' mothers, the more time goes by the more I convince myself that it feels more like a vindictive punishment than karma. At least for

Madison and Cass's mothers. Sophie's mother Stephanie died of natural causes following a difficult childbirth.

Or at least that's what the doctors told me.

If the three deaths were all murders, then I could waste the rest of my life looking for someone else to accuse while knowing deep down that I only have myself to blame.

I was the common denominator in all three women's lives. They just had the bad luck of getting pregnant with my daughters.

And what the hell did I do to deserve being responsible for three innocent girls?

Coincidence or not, I can't condemn Vanessa to an early grave just because I selfishly want to keep her in my bed.

Not that I think she would stay even if I begged her.

No, I just need to accept that our time together is limited, enjoy it while it lasts, and then let her go.

Vanessa

I wake up with a damp chin from drooling in my sleep...and the head of a half-hard cock poking the inside of my cheek.

Again?

He's already come three times! Well, the third was sort of my fault. Dante was napping when I woke up earlier. He would've stayed that way if I hadn't suckled him like I was trying to slurp up a banana split through a straw. Dante popped right up, in the bed and in my mouth, and grabbed both of my swaying breasts to use them as reins. Good times.

Swiping my hand over my wet chin, and then Dante's hip, I glance up to find him lounging against a pile of pillows, all the ones from the pillow wall, his arm thrown behind his head, a Cheshire cat smile on his face showing his straight, white teeth.

Despite how smug he looks, I don't take my mouth off his cock just yet. Instead, I mumble around him, "What time is it?"

"A little after three."

Wow. Three? That means I've been warming his cock for an entire workday.

Tapping a single finger underneath my chin, he says, "We both need to go eat something, then I'm going to have you for dessert. I want to see how many times I can make you come before you pass out."

I hum my enthusiastic agreement with that plan.

Gripping the underside of my chin in one hand, and his dick in the other, he pulls it free, leaving my mouth feeling oddly empty.

"Thank you for giving me a day I'll never forget."

His words, while appreciative also sound like a goodbye. That's why I decide to lighten the mood as I slip off the bed to go use the restroom. "And I will never be able to forget the taste of your cum for as long as I live, so thanks for that."

Grabbing his balls in one hand, and stroking his damp, swelling dick in the other, Dante says, "I've got another cup brewing if you're still thirsty."

"Are you referring to your seed as coffee or tea in that analogy?" I ask over my shoulder. "And how can you be horny again already?"

"Because there's a beautiful, naked woman with an amazing ass strutting around my room with a very dirty mouth," he replies, laying the compliments on thick. "And I'm going to go with a cup of warm milk, since taking my load put you right to sleep."

"Thanks, I may never be able to stomach milk again," I reply with a bark of laughter as I finally go to the restroom.

After that's taken care of, I hop in the shower, needing two rinses with conditioner to get my hair untangled. Before I'm finished, Dante joins me, his fingers digging into my ass cheeks behind me. Spreading them apart, he says, "Let me at least fuck you here, butterfly."

"No way in hell," I quickly reply, turning to face him while rinsing off the body wash.

Seeing him standing so tall and intimidating before me, muscular and tattooed and naked, with his hard, proud cock, I nearly drop to my knees to worship him again.

What is wrong with me? Has Dante been dosing me up with a love potion to turn me into a horny, needy slut for him? I've never been this way with a man before, so obsessed with sex. Not that I've had a lot of it with men. Mostly, I've gotten off with plastic vibrating toys.

And I've definitely never been with a man who enjoys starting most days by waking me up with his tongue licking me until I come.

The relentless oral is nothing more than Dante's attempt to eventually convince me to let him plunge inside of me. He thinks that eventually I'll be so high on orgasms that I'll say yes to anything, even letting him fuck me.

While I'm at war with myself internally, Dante rinses his hair and then starts toward me. I take a step backward, my back hitting the wall with nowhere else to go. The mafia king presses the wet, warm front of his body against mine, including the long hard inches poking my belly. His fingers wrap around my throat, tilting my head up so his lips can brush mine while his other hand reaches around to grab a handful of my ass cheek. "Let me see if you still taste like me," he says before his tongue darts past my parted lips again and again to swipe over my tongue. The whole time he grinds his shaft into me. "Mmm, salty with a hint of chlorine, like swallowing a mouthful of the ocean, followed by a sip of pool water."

"You are sick," I tell him against his lips. He's not wrong, though, about how he tastes.

The fingers on my throat tighten their hold. "I'm sick? You're the one who has a belly full of my cum after sucking my dick for eight hours straight like you couldn't get enough."

"You made me do it," I respond, even though I know it's a weak argument.

"I made you? *I made you?*" he repeats, sounding furious. Dante roughly spins me around by my neck, so my face is pressed to the shower tile. Leaning forward he sticks his tongue in my ear, making me shiver as his cock wedges itself in the crack of my ass. "Is that what you told yourself? That I made you suck me dry? In that case, I should *make you* take my cock like a good little slut."

He pushes his cock between my tightly closed thighs, just like he worked his finger between my crossed legs the other night.

"That's right, make me work for every inch so you can keep pretending you don't want it." When his hard shaft pushes through, grazing my swollen, needy clit, I whimper.

I wait for him to pull back, to shove inside of me, but he doesn't. Dante slaps my pussy lips with his length, teasing me. Desperate for more, I even spread my legs farther apart. He fists himself, dragging his cock through my folds while keeping his fingers around my neck.

"You're so wet I would slide right inside, wouldn't I?"

I shake my head. It's the one part of my body that's not completely on board with letting him fuck me against the shower wall. My traitorous ass is raised, though, as I stand on my tiptoes with my palms braced on the wall, begging him to take me.

That's when I realize what I'm doing. If Dante does this, I'll hate myself, but I'll also hate him too. I would never forgive him for taking what I didn't freely give.

When he notches his rounded head to my entrance, I finally speak up. "Don't."

"Don't?" he asks, resuming stroking himself through my folds faster, harder than before. "Don't what?"

"Don't...fuck me," I whisper breathlessly as he works me up to another orgasm with each pass of his hardness over my clit.

"Why not?" he growls against my ear, slamming his hips into my ass like we're halfway there. "You love when my tongue and fingers are inside of you. My cock will fill you up so damn good."

"Because..."

"Because why?" he asks as he takes me higher and higher.

And just before I explode from pleasure, I tell him the truth. "Because you'll destroy me."

31

Dante

B *ecause you'll destroy me.*

That's Vanessa's explanation for why she won't fuck me.

Hours after our shower when she literally came on my cock without me penetrating her, I'm still fuming.

It doesn't help that I didn't get off that last time. How could I when Vanessa was being so damn confusing? Her body telling me one thing while her mouth said another. She wants me. I'm not imagining that. The woman is just determined to drive me fucking insane.

"Uh-oh," Cass says when we all sit down for dinner. "Trouble in paradise between you two love birds?"

If she thinks what I have with Vanessa is love, then my daughters are even more sheltered than they know.

"No trouble in paradise," I tell them as I slice my knife through my steak. "We're just fuck buddies who don't actually fuck."

"Dante!" Vanessa exclaims, her fork and knife clattering onto the plate.

"That doesn't make any sense," Sophie remarks. "Does it?" she asks her sisters.

"You are all too young to even think about sex," I tell them before shoving a bite of steak into my mouth, giving me something to chew on so I'll shut my mouth.

Madison clears her throat and says, "I baked the potatoes."

"Congratu-fucking-lations," Cass replies. "You learned how to operate a microwave."

"Baked means they were cooked in an oven, dumbass. At least I know the difference."

"Who cares? Do you think you can open your own restaurant now because you throw veggies in a bowl and stick a potato in the oven?"

"I just want to do shit for myself, okay?" Madison grumbles. "I offered to help with cleanup, so can I go?"

"Cleanup?" I ask after swallowing my food.

"In the kitchen downstairs where the chef and his staff cook all our meals?"

"Fine. Just take the guards with you," I grumble.

Once Madison leaves the dining room, Vanessa says, "You three are sisters. You should be supportive of each other's endeavors, not be... hostile."

"Bitches," I finish her sentence for her. "She meant don't be little bitches to each other. You're not kids anymore. Grow up. It wouldn't kill you to try to be nice once in a while either."

"We'll grow up when you start treating us like adults and not children," Cass says. Tossing her silverware down, she slides her chair back then gets up and leaves.

"I know I'm the youngest, but I'm almost legally an adult. It would be nice if you acknowledged that," Sophie says before she takes off too.

"Way to clear a room, Salvato," Vanessa remarks, as if all the women in the house made a pact to be pains in my ass today. And she doesn't even use my first name, as if we're back to where we started weeks ago.

"This is your fault," I tell her, gesturing with my fork to the empty table.

"My fault?"

"You are fucking infuriating!"

"So are you! Should I go too?"

At first, I think she's referring to leaving the dining room before it occurs to me that she means the penthouse. She wants to know if I want her to leave me.

"Stay. Please," I add softly, reaching for her wrist to hold it, as if I can physically restrain her from going anywhere. "I'm not sorry about earlier," I tell her honestly. She knows how badly I want her, yet she continues to send me conflicting signals. I was so close...*we* were so close to finally fucking before she pulled the goddamn emergency brake.

"I'm not either," she replies, which is a fucking relief.

"Good. Now I hope we can try to move past it." I shouldn't have rubbed my dick against her like that, confusing us both. When we finally fuck, it'll be because Vanessa is begging me for it with actual words, not merely trying to appease her needy clit.

"Okay, we can move past it, on one condition."

Great, there are conditions. Just one, but I'm sure it's a motherfucker. "What's that?" I ask, dreading her answer, how she intends for us to not accidentally reach the point of no return while naked.

"No more orgasms. For either of us."

"Wow." I let her wrist go to slide my arm back across the table. "That's even worse than I thought it would be. Why the fuck would you refuse orgasms?"

"Because it's making things messy. I shouldn't be surprised by how you acted in the shower, not after all the mixed messages I've been sending you."

"There's a way to unmix shit."

"I can't," she says, her eyes lowered to her uneaten food.

"If you think I'm an asshole now, wait until you see me after being celibate for weeks yet again. I'll murder anyone who looks at me wrong." Then I can't help but add, "Are you sure you want to give up your morning wake-up calls with my tongue?"

Vanessa sighs like it's a tough decision, even as her cheeks flush. "Fine. One a day. No more."

One orgasm a day after I had four today? It won't be easy, but it's better than nothing.

"Fine."

"So, we have a deal?" She holds out her palm for me to shake it, as if we're finalizing a business deal. I take her hand in mine, then lift it to my mouth to sink my teeth around her knuckles. Frustrated beyond sanity, I bite down hard enough to leave teeth marks but not break the skin.

"Did you forget that I can keep you on the edge for hours, you stubborn fucking woman?" I remind her.

"And I can't do the same to you?" she challenges with a half-smile that makes me feel like we've weathered the worst of the storm. Well, the winds have calmed, but there's still a downpour because shit still feels off between us.

"I would rather have you torture me by keeping me on the edge for hours than you not touch me at all," I admit to her.

"Same," Vanessa agrees. "And you're going to pay for biting me like a rabid dog."

"Oh, am I?"

"For now, let's eat. It's been a long day without any sustenance other than bodily fluids."

"Yes, it has," I agree.

32

Vanessa

After a long, crazy day, I've just changed into one of Dante's tees when there's a rapid knock on the door.

"I'll get it," he says from the bathroom where he's still changing.

"It's fine. Everything is covered," I say, just before I hear the beep of the safe opening, followed by his shout of various swears.

"What's wrong?" I ask going to him because whoever is at the door can wait. He's patting his hand around inside the wall safe frantically.

"Son of a motherfucking bitch!"

"What is it, Dante?" I demand when he continues to ignore me and there's more banging on the bedroom door. One problem at a time.

"All my goddamn cash is gone," he says. "And my other Glock with the clips and bullets!"

I see my gun lying on a shelf, which is a relief. At least for me.

Turning to face me finally, Dante's eyes are the cold blue I hate when he says, "Did you do this? Is this some kind of joke?"

I huff out a laugh. The sound slowly fades away before I realize he's serious. "You're accusing me of robbing you? Seriously? How stupid would I have to be to rob you and keep sleeping beside you, Dante?"

"You and I were in here all day. No cleaners came and went today."

"It wasn't me." When Dante doesn't respond, I remind him, "I don't know your damn code, genius!"

The silence between us stretches as he considers my response until it's interrupted by more pounding on the door.

"God-fucking-dammit," he growls before slipping past me to go answer the door in just his boxer briefs.

"What?" I hear him snap at whoever is on the other side as I return to the bedroom.

"Mr. Salvato, I'm...I don't know how to tell you this. I'm so sorry..." a man's deep voice trails off.

"What the fuck is going on?" Dante demands. "Spit it out!" When they still won't speak, he asks, "Is this about who fucking robbed me today?"

Ah, it must have been a guard. Or Eli. Right? Who else could've snuck into our room while we were having dinner?

"Rob...robbed you?" a second man asks, his voice higher pitched.

"My safe was emptied out today. Are you telling me you two are responsible?"

"No. No, sir. That's not...I didn't...we didn't rob you," I hear one respond. "We were downstairs in the kitchen with Madison."

"Madison? What about her?" Dante asks, keeping a white-knuckled grip on the door.

"She left."

"*Left?*" he roars. "What do you mean she *left?*"

"She slipped out the back door to the kitchen. By the time we noticed she was gone...there was no sign of her."

There's a long, drawn-out moment of silence before Dante erupts. "What the fuck are you doing up here? Go find her!" he shouts at them before slamming the door in their faces.

"We'll find her," I assure him. "I'll-I'll get dressed and go downstairs with you to search," I tell him when he goes to the dresser, jerking open a drawer to pull clothes out.

"No," he says while shoving his legs into jogging pants, then slips a tee over his head. "You go talk to Cass and Sophie, see if they know anything about this, where Madison may be going."

"Okay," I agree.

Spinning in a circle, he mutters, "I need my phone. Where the fuck is my phone?"

I glance around searching for it, but don't see it either. "Is it in the closet where you were changing?"

"Fuck," he says before he jogs through the bathroom to go look. He comes out with it in his hand before I've had a chance to move. "It was Madison," he says when he stops in front of me, his face losing all of its color.

"What..."

"She raided the safe. She took the cash, the gun...I should've known. The code was her birthday."

"Oh, wow. I'm so sorry," I tell him softly. He doesn't seem to hear the words as his mind keeps churning everything over.

"Why would she need a gun, Vanessa?"

"I-I don't know," I say. But I do know. He does too. If she's on her own, she'll need it for protection.

"She wouldn't hurt herself."

"No, she wouldn't," I agree when his mind goes to that dark place. "She wouldn't need the money if...that's not why she took the gun."

"Madison planned this out, leaving, running. Did she...did she say anything to you? Is this why she wanted to work down in the kitchen? I never should've let her...Wait," he says, turning to me with his brow furrowed. "Why the fuck don't you look more surprised?"

"What?" I mutter as I lower myself into the edge of the bed, feeling a huge argument coming on, one that blows the earlier one out of the water.

"Vanessa, did Madison say something to you?" Dante demands as he kneels in front of me to stare me in the face.

"Maybe."

"Maybe?" he repeats. "What the fuck did she say?"

"We were just talking the other day, and she mentioned wanting to go to college, that you wouldn't let her."

"So? I told her she can take whatever classes she wants online."

"I know, but she wanted to leave, to live on campus like a normal kid." Chewing on my thumbnail, I deliver the worst part. "And I, um, I may have mentioned that using a different name to hide who she was, might help keep her safe."

"You did what?" he growls, his blue eyes turning furious.

"I told her it would only work with your help, that legitimate looking documents like that are expensive. Not to mention the SAT scores and transcripts. I didn't think she would try to do it on her own!"

"And how the fuck would you know about those things, Vanessa?"

"Because...because I tried using cheap fake IDs for stupid shit like buying beer and cigarettes when I was young and rebellious. They didn't fool anyone," I explain in a rush. "Look, Dante, I'm sorry Madison left without telling you but leaving was her decision. It's what she wanted..."

Straightening to his full height, Dante towers over me and erupts. "You should've minded your own goddamn business! If anything happens to her..." He spears his fingers through the front of his hair and turns away from me with a growl. "Is this why you've been showing her how to cook and shit, so, she could sneak off and try to make it on her own? Because she can't!"

"Yes, she can," I argue when I get to my feet. "You may not want her to be out in the world alone, but she will be okay, Dante."

"Shut up. Just shut the fuck up!" he bellows as he heads for the door. "Stay away from my daughters, and stay the hell away from me."

33

Dante

Eli is standing in the hall when I storm out of the bedroom.
"What's going on? I heard yelling."

"Madison is gone!"

"Gone?"

"Yes. She raided my safe, took all the cash and a gun, then snuck out the kitchen downstairs."

"Are you sure she's gone? It's a big casino. Maybe she's still nearby."

"She's running," I tell him. "I'll call Titus to get him to review security footage. You call the airlines, bus stations, rental cars, every fucking form of transportation that leaves this city and tell them if they see anyone matching her description to stop her."

"Okay," he agrees, phone already in his hand.

"Where the fuck would she go?" I ask aloud as I pull up Titus's number. Eli doesn't take a guess before Titus answers.

"Yeah, boss?"

"Madison left the casino tonight with cash and a gun. Get to the security room and find everything you can on the cameras."

"On my way now," he says before ending the call.

"You gonna have words with the guards?" Eli asks when he puts his phone to his ear.

"Yes, right after I grill my daughters." I may have asked Vanessa to talk to them, but I don't want her near either of them ever again.

Jogging up the stairs to the third floor, I bang my fist on Cass's door then do the same to Sophie.

They both peek their heads out. "Get out here, now!" I yell at them. When they're both standing in the hall in their pajamas, I ask, "Did Madison say anything to either of you about running away?"

"Running away?" Sophie repeats before slapping her palm over her gasping mouth.

"Madison's gone?" Cass says. "She won't get far."

"Anything could happen to her out there, do you two understand that?" I stare them down and ask again, "Do either of you know where she's going? Did she say *anything*?"

"The only thing I've said to her was at dinner," Cass replies first.

"Same," Sophie says.

"You better hope those weren't the last words you spoke to your sister," I tell them both before heading back downstairs. Maybe they don't know anything. I can't help but wonder if they would lie for Madison. Cass wouldn't. Sophie might.

Back downstairs, I step into the hallway and find two guards plus the two responsible for this shit.

"I told you two to go find her!" I yell at them.

"Every available guard and employee are searching the casino, sir," one of the door guards informs me. "Do you, ah, do you want us to notify the police?"

"I'll handle it," I tell him. "I'll be in my office making calls. Find me if you hear anything, understood? I don't care how late it is, find me."

"Yes, sir," they all agree.

I try reaching out to a friend who looks the other way at Las Vegas Metro. He tells me to send a photo of Madison and he'll spread the word around to keep an eye out for her but keep her name off the record. Nothing official. Notifying the cops she's missing would be like shining a spotlight on her for every enemy.

I tell myself that she's probably wandering the streets of Vegas, dealing with catcalls but nothing more serious than that sort of treatment. One of my men will find her and bring her back. It's just a matter of time.

But hours later, there's not much new information.

The security cameras show she snuck a bag down in an empty covered dish that I'm guessing was full of cash and my gun. Then it looks like she may have grabbed a chef uniform from a closet before she distracted the guards with food to sneak out. The streets were so crowded with tourists that she disappeared into the fray, either getting into a car or going into another casino. I've got every hotel on the strip I can trust searching for her. The only ones I didn't call were the Russian owned businesses. The last thing I need is for them to find her first.

I'm pacing the office floor, sipping whiskey from the bottle when Eli comes in.

"Anything?" I pause to ask him.

"Planes seem unlikely since she won't have ID. Same for rental cars. Buses are being searched before they leave by our men, but no sign of her yet."

"Fuck!" I exclaim, slinging the glass bottle across the room. It hits the wall, shattering into shards. It feels like the same thing is going to happen inside of me. I have to find her...and soon. "She could be in a car with someone, some handsy asshole going who the fuck knows where!"

"Madison wouldn't do anything foolish like hop in a car with a stranger," Eli says confidently. "She might have stolen a car."

"Great. Then the police will find her first."

"As long as someone finds her..."

"I can't fucking believe Vanessa!" I yell. "Who does she think she is? She had no right to talk to Madison, much less fill her head with bullshit!"

"Vanessa?" Eli says in surprise. "You're blaming her for Madison running off?"

"Hell, yes. It's her fault. She gave her ideas; she took her downstairs."

"The guards shouldn't have taken their eyes off of her. If you want to take your anger out on someone, drag them to the basement and take it out on them," Eli suggests.

"Do it. String them up until we find her."

"Yes, sir. Gladly. Stupid sons of bitches," he mutters as he wanders off to do what he does best.

I need to hurt someone. I want to punch the bastards in the face until they're unrecognizable. But deep down, I know that punishing them won't change anything. There are no answers to get out of the guards. They don't have a fucking clue where Madison went, what she was planning.

Checking my phone every ten seconds makes the night go by so damn slowly. That's how I know it's five past three when Vanessa tiptoes quietly into my office in my T-shirt and her panties.

"Any updates?" she asks softly.

"No."

She starts to come toward me but I hold up my palm to stop her. "Don't. There's broken glass."

"Oh." Her eyes search the room, finding the broken bottle. "What can I do?"

"Nothing. There's nothing you or I or anyone else can do. She's gone..."

Despite my warning, Vanessa pads barefoot across the room to me, wrapping her arms around my waist and resting her head against my chest. "I'm sorry. She will be okay. She will, Dante."

"If anything happens to her..." I trail off, unable to even finish that thought. And despite how furious I still am at Vanessa, right now I need her. So, I shove my phone into my jogging pants pocket, then scoop her up in my arms, so her legs are around my waist, feet no longer touching the glass-filled floor.

Carrying her over to the leather sofa, I sit down with her straddling my lap, her head resting on my shoulder, clinging to me tightly.

While I spent the day with Vanessa's mouth wrapped around my cock, I spent the rest of the night with her wrapped around me.

Vanessa

I fell asleep straddling Dante on the sofa in his office, but when I blink my eyes open, I'm lying on top of him like I'm a blanket, and we're in his bed.

At least I'm not drooling this time when I lift my head from his chest to see his face. No surprise, his phone is raised in his hand as he scrolls or answers messages.

"Hey," I say as I sit up, my legs still on either side of his hips.

"Hey," he replies without a glance. At least he's speaking to me. And he doesn't sound like he wants to slit my throat.

"Any news on Madison?"

"No."

I didn't think there would be. She's a smart girl. With the amount of money she took, she'll be fine. Taking a gun for protection was wise too. I just hope she knows how to use it if she has to.

"Did you get any sleep?" I ask softly.

"Not much. I dozed a little. Now I need a shower." Placing his phone back on the charging station, he lifts me up by my waist to sit me on the mattress next to him so he can get up.

"Do you want company?"

"No."

Wow. That was a quick response.

"That's not...I'm not in the mood. Later?" he says as he begins to undress at the foot of the bed.

Later, as in when Madison is back safe and sound. And if he doesn't find her, he'll keep blaming me.

"I'm sorry," I tell him again, knowing the words are empty. He doesn't want an apology; he wants to know his daughter is okay.

Once he's naked, he takes a step toward the bathroom, then stops. "You...You have no idea how much I care for you. How much I trusted you! I trusted you with my daughters when I'm terrified to let anyone get near them! And you know why I'm so goddamn protective of them, the nightmares I have of what could happen to them."

"I know," I say, swallowing around the burning in my throat. "I'm sorry about their mothers."

Turning around, he begins to pace across the bedroom floor with his fingers tugging his hair, not a shred of clothing on. "You have no idea what I've been through. How lost I felt when Maria, Madison's mother, was killed by the Irish in a drive-by while I was locked up in prison on bullshit charges. Then, Cass's mother, Charlotte, was Madison's live-in nanny, the *only* mother she ever knew. I thought she disappeared without a trace when Cass was only two months old. Kidnapped I assumed, but never found out for sure. It's stupid, but I still hope to this day, eighteen years later, that she'll come back. Hope is better than the most likely scenario which is her bones are buried somewhere in the goddamn desert." He pauses in his paces and revelation long enough to scrub his palms down his face. "And Sophie's mom, Stephanie, we were actually going to get married. Yes, I knocked her up too, but I was *finally* ready to settle down, to spend my life with her and our three girls as a family. She never even got to hold Sophie because she...she died in her sleep that night. I couldn't hold Sophie for weeks either because she was a preemie, fighting for her own life every second of the day, while I was left alone to raise three baby girls."

"I'm so sorry, Dante. I hate that those horrible things happened to them, to you."

"This fucked-up world took every woman I cared for from me and left me to raise three sweet, innocent, motherless girls on my own. I can't lose them, Vanessa. I can't let anything happen to Madison, because I'm not sure I could survive failing one of them again."

It's not just his enemies he worries about going after his girls to hurt him. After so much loss, no wonder Dante is overly protective of his daughters.

Climbing out of bed, I go to him like I did last night, doing the only thing I can. I wind my arms around his waist, holding him tight. "I'm sorry," I say yet again. Even though he's angry at me, blames me for his daughter running away, I need his forgiveness. I hate that he blames me, but he's right.

After a moment, he lifts his arms to hold me to him, kissing the top of my head.

Still, I know it doesn't mean that everything is back to how it was between us, and that it may never be right again.

34

Vanessa

It's been a little over two weeks with no sign of Madison. I'm impressed actually. With all the cameras everywhere nowadays, I have no clue how she snuck away without a trace. There's been no sign of her in the city since the night she walked out. I hope she's okay, and that she will at least call to let her father and sisters know she's doing well.

Convincing Dante that she's fine is impossible. He grows moodier each day, spending his free time in the gym sparring with Eli instead of with me. I was able to convince him to let the guards who were on duty live after he let Eli teach them a small, no doubt memorable, lesson. At least they're still alive.

Those orgasms we once had to negotiate down to one are non-existent now. Not that I blame him. If it was Cole who had run away without telling me where he was or what he was doing, I wouldn't know what to do with myself.

Thankfully, that's not the case. And it reminds me of the conversation I've been putting off with Dante.

At dinner that night in the dining room, I interrupt the usual silence to say, "Cole is coming home for a visit this weekend. He's flying in tomorrow."

Dante's fork pauses in pushing around his chicken marsala. "Oh, right. I had forgotten..."

"With everything going on, he can just stay in my apartment."

"No. You want him to stay here. There's plenty of room in the hotel." In the hotel, right, because he wouldn't dare let a twenty-year-old boy near his daughters. Not that I blame him. Boys will be boys and all that.

"Are you sure?"

"You don't have to feel guilty that your son is safe and happy just because one of my daughters is missing."

I wince at his words that feel like an accusation, as if he thinks I should feel guilty for Madison leaving because he blames me for the grown woman's actions. Sure, she may only be the same age as Cole, but she's old enough to be on her own. I survived on my own as a teenager with an infant son.

Since I don't have anything to say in response to Dante's words, I glance toward Sophie and Cass who barely eat more than three bites of dinner lately. "Would either of you mind if my son comes to visit this weekend? He won't be sleeping in the penthouse, obviously."

"Sure," Sophie agrees, giving me a shrug.

"Whatever," is Cass's response without lifting her eyes from her plate.

"Great," I say, forcing a smile on my face. "Could I maybe go pick him up at the airport Friday?"

"Fine," Dante replies with a sigh. "I'll have the guards take you."

"Thanks." Having the guards drive me is better than an absolute no from him.

I never thought I would miss the version of Dante that constantly flirts and teases me, but I do. While I don't think he would let me leave if I asked, he doesn't seem happy about me being here. I'm no longer a challenge for him to conquer. I'm the woman in his bed, in his house, whom he simply tolerates.

After the night Dante held me while we slept, there have been no more pillow walls, yet, he hasn't even tried to touch me which is frustrating.

That's why, that night, when we're both settling into bed, I try to have a conversation with him, hoping to clear the air between us.

"If you're not going to forgive me, then why do you want to keep me here?" I ask him softly in the darkness. "As a punishment?"

"If I were punishing you, you would know it," he grumbles from where his head rests on his pillow, facing away from me. It's as if he can't stand to open his eyes at night and see a glimpse of me.

"What can I do, Dante?"

"Nothing. There's not a fucking thing anyone can do to bring her back, is there?"

Sighing, I slide over to his side of the bed, molding the front of my body to his bare back, being the big spoon as I put my arm around his waist. My entire body is tense as I hold my breath, waiting for his rejection.

How ironic is that?

I came into this arrangement intending to hurt him, to reject him for seventy-six days in a row, and now here I am wanting him when he doesn't want me. My rejection hurt him, more than I could imagine. I know that now.

But Dante doesn't shove me away or tell me to get off of him, so I let my fingertips explore the lines of his abs, the trail of hair leading down into his boxer briefs. My lips are close enough to press kisses to his bare shoulder.

His stomach muscles tighten under my fingers, as if he's at least somewhat affected by my touch.

"Maybe I can't do anything, but you can," I tell him. "Hurt me. Punish me. Fuck me. Just do something because I don't want to be here anymore if you don't want me."

Dante's heavy hand covers mine that's on his stomach. Instead of pulling my palm off him, he slides it under his waistband to where he's long and thick, tenting his cotton shorts. My breath hitches in surprise as I curl my fingers around his hot, smooth flesh.

"Does that feel like I don't want you?" His voice sounds deep and rumbly, making my thighs clench together. His fingers surround mine to squeeze and stoke his shaft. "I have to jerk off every time I think about the sounds you make when I shove down your throat. I explode as soon as I look at the picture of you sleeping so peacefully with your pretty lips wrapped around my cock."

Holy shit. I love hearing him say I still arouse him. After he's been so distant, I thought...wait a second. My hand stills on his erection. "Did you say picture?"

"Of course, I took a photo. It's an image I never want to forget of what was almost a contender for the best day of my life."

Would've been a contender if Madison hadn't run off a few hours later.

"But don't worry, I only sent it to Eli."

"Eli!" I exclaim. Now I try to jerk my hand back from the bastard's underwear, but Dante chuckles and holds it hostage.

"Oh, no. You have to finish what you started, butterfly."

God, how I've missed that name. Even my stupid eyes and throat sting from hearing it again as I resume stroking Dante's cock.

I want to ask him why he didn't come to me if he was so damn horny, but then I realize why. He was angry at me. Thinking about me, my mouth, the photo he took of me before Madison left was the only comfort he would allow himself.

Removing his hand from mine, Dante stretches forward, turning on the bedside lamp before rolling to his back. His fingers come up on the back of my head, grabbing my hair to pull my mouth up to his.

I don't just give him my mouth; I climb on top of him to kiss him. Our tongues meet forcefully, the first time we've kissed in two weeks. When Dante pulls my mouth off his we're both gasping for air. He tugs my tee over my head and off, then tells me, "You know where I need your mouth. I want to fuck your throat all damn night."

I nod eagerly as he grips my hair tighter, shoving me down his body. I crawl down on my hands and knees, rubbing my breasts down his stomach and bulge until my face is above his underwear. I jerk the cotton down greedily to get access to his cock. It bobs free for only a moment before I wrap my fingers around it to hold it still. My mouth covers his wide crown, sucking his head so hard my cheeks cave in. Dante groans as I taste his precum hit my tongue.

"Good girl. You know exactly what I like, what I need, don't you? I'm going to own your mouth all fucking night."

Normally I would lick his shaft up and down, teasing him. But not tonight. No, tonight he doesn't want his dick to leave my mouth. He wants to hear me gag on it, to make me swallow his seed and keep him wet until he's ready to do both of those things all over again.

And I want to do it for him. I want him to use my mouth, to use me however he wants, as long as he wants, because I want to make him happy, help him forget his worry for Madison at least for a little while. I'm not even sure why or how I got here.

The Vanessa who signed that stupid agreement that day in the basement would think I'm pathetic for wanting to suck the mafia king's dick all night long. If Dante had asked me to do that the first night, there's no way I would've agreed.

But now, things have changed. I've changed. Whether that's good or bad, I'm not sure yet. All I know is that the way I feel about Dante isn't something I've ever experienced before. I want him to keep me, to make me his, and never let me go.

The only thing that scares me is that all this may be wishful thinking that ends with a broken heart.

I don't waste any more time worrying about that right now though. I can't when I'm so horny I'll combust as soon as my fingers graze my clit.

My hand moves down between my legs, but Dante says, "Don't even think about touching yourself."

I'm about to bite his dick in protest when his left leg brushes against mine that's next to it.

"The only way you come tonight is on me. Now take your wet panties off."

Understanding what he wants, I shove the thong, down my legs, kicking it off. Once it's gone, I lift my leg to straddle his muscular one. When Dante lifts his knee, pressing the bone between my legs, applying pressure to that bundle of nerves, I close my eyes and groan around his shaft.

His knee lowers, causing my hips to immediately dip in search of it, making Dante chuckle. "Are you that needy, butterfly? So horny you want to hump my leg?"

I grind my pelvis down on his kneecap, not even caring what body part it is as I get closer to an orgasm.

Dante, eager for his own release, grabs the back of my hair to press my mouth down his cock, shoving to the back of my throat with a growl of satisfaction.

My orgasm crashes through me, my body engulfed by waves of pleasure while I'm still gagging. Tears slip from my eyes and drool slides down my chin while my thighs are still trembling. It's all so fucked up. But it's not the last time I ride the mafia king's leg while he shoves down my throat. We barely get any sleep at all between rounds. No, I'm too busy caressing every inch of the man I can reach with my hands. And Dante, he stares down at me the entire time, stroking my face and hair. He looks at me like I'm the sexiest, most beautiful woman in the world when in fact I'm a slobbery, sweaty, mess with one hell of a sore jaw by the time the sun comes up.

It's all worth it, especially when Dante eventually slips from my mouth to worship me between my legs with his tongue, over and over again, until I pass out.

35

Dante

I wake up with my face buried in Vanessa's pussy, the addictive scent and taste of her surrounding me. While half my leg is hanging off the mattress and a pillow under my head would be more comfortable, I'm in no hurry to move.

She came on my tongue at least three times before we both crashed right around sunrise.

The entire night was like an erotic wet dream. One I want to repeat at least once before I die.

My anger at Vanessa faded away as soon as she cuddled up to my back and asked me to fuck her. I knew she didn't mean it, that she was just so desperate for my forgiveness that she would offer me the world. She would've given me herself, everything I've wanted and everything she's refused, as a peace offering.

And I thought about taking her up on the offer for all of about five seconds. Yes, I wanted to finally sink inside of her, but afterward, she would've hated herself, then hated me, ruining everything between us beyond repair. Shit is already fraying as it is.

Besides, I don't want our first time to be a compromise to end a fight. I want Vanessa to come to me on her own, ready, and willing to be mine in every way possible, physically unable to wait another second.

Part of me hopes that day doesn't come. What would be the point of her surrendering to me? I sure as fuck can't keep her after our seventy-six days are up. It would be wrong to let her give herself to me so completely while knowing I'm going to hurt her when I push her out the door.

So, I'll gladly accept her mouth instead. And I love eating her pussy as much as I know she enjoys sucking me off. Other women have claimed to enjoy oral through the years, but only Vanessa sucks my cock for as long as I want her to, forgoing her food, comfort, and everything else to please me. She may make me feel like a god, but that doesn't make her anything less than a goddess.

Of all the women I've met, I never thought Vanessa would be the one to worship me like she thinks I actually deserve her time, her attention, and her adoration.

She actually cares about me. Not my money, or my power. The most stubborn woman I know has fucking feelings for me. No longer feelings of hate but...fondness.

While I wish it were love, I don't think Vanessa would ever allow herself to love me.

If she did...no, not even then would I condemn her to my fucked-up world where there are enemies around every corner, every day, and the violence never ends. Her life would constantly be in danger, which is not something I could endure. I won't let my wants and needs lead her to an early grave.

That's how I know without a doubt in my mind that I'm in love with her.

Giving her up will be the hardest thing I've ever had to do. But keeping her by my side would be so damn selfish.

Glancing up at her naked sleeping form, she's so damn beautiful it hurts. Her pink lips are still swollen and pouty from being used by me for hours during the night. Her brow is furrowed even at rest, as if she never stops worrying about shit even in her dreams. I don't know what parts of her past haunt her, what happened that was so bad she didn't feel safe without a loaded gun within reaching distance at night. And I doubt she'll ever tell me either. Vanessa may have feelings for me, but she doesn't trust me.

I'm surprised she's even willing to let me meet her son.

Which reminds me, his plane is supposed to come in at noon. If I had to guess, it's probably close to eleven or maybe even a little after. That means as much I want to, I can't spend the day eating Vanessa's pussy.

Crawling up over her, I place a soft kiss on her lower stomach, her left breast then right, before I reach her neck. She doesn't so much as twitch in her sleep.

"Rise and shine, butterfly," I whisper close to her ear.

"Uh-uh. Not yet," she mumbles. My butterfly is not a morning person. Now I know why she worked the night shift.

"You wanted to pick up Cole from the airport, remember?"

"Oh, shit!" She sits up so fast we nearly headbutt before she rolls out of bed.

"You have plenty of time," I assure her. "Flights are always delayed."

"I have to shower," Vanessa says as she heads for the bathroom.

So do I.

I lounge and wait for her to warm the shower up before I join her. She barely notices when I slip into the shower that's big enough for at least two other people. No, Vanessa is too busy scrubbing the shampoo into the top of her head.

"We should've got more sleep last night," she remarks, moving on to body wash while letting her hair rinse at the same time.

"We'll sleep when we're dead," I reply before ducking under one of the showerheads to wet my hair.

When I open my eyes to reach for a bottle of shampoo, Vanessa is staring at me, frozen under the steaming water, her lips parted as if she forgot she's in a hurry.

Knowing she's physically attracted to me is one thing, but seeing the raw hunger on her face for me is one of my favorite things in the world.

"I think we could make time for a sixty-nine if you need it."

After a few blinks, she's back to washing herself, pretending she doesn't want me.

"I wasn't...that wasn't...I was just thinking," she stammers.

"Thinking about what?" I ask, turning to face her straight on, certain her eyes would lower to my cock.

"Fine!" she huffs when she turns her back to me, lifting her face to the stream. "It's your fault that I constantly think about sex lately. You got me addicted to multiple orgasms, then took them all away..."

"Oh, I'm sorry. Did this morning not put a dent in your orgasm deficiency I created?"

Keeping her back to me as she rinses off, she says, "I know you have other things on your mind. I get it. But you shut me out for weeks, and now I can't help but wonder if you'll do the same thing again. I don't want to end up a victim in some sort of vicious cycle only you control."

"I never stopped wanting you. And I wasn't punishing you, not on purpose," I admit to her. "It's just...I felt guilty for even thinking about losing myself in you when I should be spending every waking moment searching for Madison."

"Oh," Vanessa says, pausing in her rinse. Turning to face me with her hair slicked back, darker from the water, drops dripping down her beautiful body, she says, "You can miss her and still keep living your life, Dante. I know you'll never stop looking for her. And you shouldn't, even if..." She winces before continuing with her remark. "Even if she doesn't want to be found. But I don't think Madison is in danger or she would've called you by now. So, try not to think the worst or let the search consume every second of your day out of fear. Do it out of love."

"I'll try," I say, which is the best I can offer.

Vanessa nods, swiping the water from her face. "Are you coming with me to get Cole?"

"I was planning on it. Unless you don't want me to come?"

"No, I do. He's excited to meet you."

"Really?" I ask with a grin.

"Yes. He thinks you're a powerful, ruthless businessman." Rolling her eyes, she says, "Don't let it go to your head. What does he know? He's basically still a child."

"He's twenty, right? The same age as...the same age as Madison."

"That's right. And he's been living on his own for the past two years on the other side of the country."

"It's different for boys," I tell her.

"A woman with a gun is just as dangerous as anyone else, right?" she says, reminding me of what I once said to her.

"If she doesn't hurt herself trying to use it," I mutter. "She knows the basics—all my girls do. But it's been a few years. She may not remember."

Coming over to me, Vanessa goes on her tiptoes to give me a quick kiss on the lips. "She remembers," she says before she slips out of the shower to dry off.

I really hope she's right about that.

36

Vanessa

Dante and I have been sitting in the back of one of his SUVs in the short-term pick-up lot for two hours waiting for Cole's flight that was, of course, delayed. There's a second SUV beside ours, just in case. If I had to bet, both vehicles are bulletproof. Only the best for the mafia king.

I'm not sure why I was in such a rush to get to the airport. Planes always arrive late. I just wanted to be in here in case, so Cole wouldn't have to wait. And I was feeling a little out of sorts when Dante woke me up. I didn't get enough sleep following a whole lot of weirdly intimate oral last night and this morning. While I know things didn't magically heal between us overnight, I think we made good progress of getting back to where we were before Madison ran away.

"I'm sorry it's taking so long," I tell Dante who has been taking calls and answering messages and emails on his phone the entire time. "If you want to go back, I can get a cab or an Uber."

"It's fine. I can wait," he says while staring at the screen.

"If you're sure. Hopefully it won't be much longer."

A moment later, my phone dings with a text from Cole saying he's here and grabbing his luggage. I give him the number on the column next to Dante's SUVs, then climb out to keep an eye out for him.

Half an hour later, I finally see the blond hair of my tall, too skinny son.

Cole doesn't come running toward me with arms wide open like when I used to pick him up from elementary school. He just casually strolls over with a smirk on his adorable face, rolling his suitcase behind him, backpack slung over one shoulder.

"You didn't have to come pick me up," is the first thing he says after not seeing him face-to-face for months.

"I wanted to see you as soon as your feet hit the ground," I reply as I throw my arms around his neck to hug him. The distance I have to stretch on my toes to reach him seems even further than before. His father must have been that 6'5" basketball player since he obviously didn't get his height from me. "How are you still growing? And you're so thin. Are you eating enough?"

"Hello to you too, Mom." Cole chuckles as he throws an arm around me. "Now let's get inside. It's hot as balls out here. Where's your car?" He glances around the parking lot, green eyes skipping over the big, fancy SUVs.

"Ah, I got a ride. This is us, actually," I tell him when I start toward the vehicles. The guard in the front passenger seat hops out to open the passenger door for me. Well, for Dante, who slides out adjusting the sleeves of his suit. Staring up at Cole who is maybe an inch or two taller, he says, "Jesus, he's twice your size, butterfly."

"He's still my baby boy," I assure him with a smile as I hug his arm.

"Butterfly?" Cole murmurs, brow furrowed as he stares down at me. I just shrug. I don't think he really wants to criticize the mobster's term of endearment for me in public.

"Dante, meet Cole. Cole, this is Dante Salvato."

Dante holds out his massive hand toward my son who slowly takes it as he stares between the mobster and me as if wondering how the hell we fit together. I can't help him there either.

"It's nice to finally meet you," Cole says. "I heard stories about you when I went to the local high school."

"Oh, yeah?" Dante asks, his eyebrow arched. "Good ones I hope."

Cole laughs and rubs his palm over the back of his neck nervously. "Ah, not really, but they were...entertaining."

"Right. Well, shall we get back to the casino?" Dante asks me.

"Anywhere with air conditioning," Cole agrees.

With a nod of Dante's head, the guard takes Cole's luggage and puts it in the back. Then, he removes his backpack to slide into the backseat first, followed by me, then Dante.

The ride to the casino is odd, sitting between my son and the most dangerous man in the city, possibly state. Maybe this was a bad idea, introducing the two of them. If Dante were to hurt Cole...

No, he wouldn't hurt my son, no matter what happens between us. He *won't* hurt him. Because if he does, well, I'll have to make sure he knows I'll kill him. It would be difficult, nearly impossible after being intimate with him, but I would do it.

Dante reaches for my fist resting on my thigh that I didn't realize I had clenched. Lifting it he places it on his upper thigh, then he pries my fingers from my palm to clasp them. Holding hands with him in front of my son is more intimate than sleeping with his dick in my mouth.

"Relax, butterfly. You're awfully tense all of a sudden. Do you need another spa day?"

"I'm fine," I tell him.

"So, uh, what's going on here?" Cole leans forward to ask us. "I thought you said that you two were 'just friends' when we talked last month."

"Just friends?" Dante repeats. "Is that what you called us?"

Now I'm suddenly caught between a rock and a hard place. "It's complicated."

"Complicated, she says," Dante mutters, giving my hand a squeeze. "Didn't seem so complicated last night. Or this morning."

Since he won't let my hand go, I jab my elbow into his side in warning.

Cole groans and pulls his headphones out of the backpack at his feet to slip them over his ears. "I take back the question. I don't need or want any more details."

Reaching up to pull the headphones down to his neck, I tell him, "That discussion is over, so let's talk about you. When are your friends coming into town?"

"Later tonight," he says. "We're gonna meet up for dinner."

"How many?" Dante chimes in.

"How many what?" I ask.

"How many friends? How many rooms does Cole need?"

"Oh, no. You don't have to do that," I assure him.

"If suites are available, I'll book those for them. Just tell me how many."

"There will be four of us," Cole says, leaning in front of me to talk to Dante while I groan. "What? You may not like free shit, but I won't turn it down. All we need is four beds, if possible?"

"That can be arranged. I'll ask them to be adjoining."

"No parties, Cole," I warn him. "And you and your friends will pay for any damage."

"Jeez, Mom. We're not idiots. Who would be stupid enough to trash a free hotel room owned by a mob boss?"

"Cole!" I exclaim, covering my face with my free hand while Dante chuckles softly beside me.

"He's a smart kid."

Taking a deep breath, I tell my son, "If you're going out tonight then maybe we can do something together tomorrow?"

"Sure. What do you want to do?"

"Since I'm...confined to the casino, we'll have to find something to do there."

"The penthouse pool is always available," Dante suggests.

"Is it like a Scrooge McDuck pool filled with gold coins?" Cole teases with a grin.

Rolling my eyes, I tell him, "No, it's filled with water."

Dante lifts our joined hands to kiss my knuckles. "For your mother, I would build a Scrooge McDuck pool with enough gold coins to swim in them."

"Of all the supermodels and shit you've been seen with, how is it possible you've been whipped by my mother?"

"That's a good question," Dante replies. I can feel his gaze on the side of my face as I stare out the front windshield. "I've never met anyone like her."

"I'm the only woman to ever turn him down," I tell my son truthfully with a sigh. "I'm nothing but a new challenge."

"Not gonna lie, Mom. It sort of looks like he's already won."

"Not yet," Dante says. "Your mother is an incredibly stubborn woman."

"No kidding."

Oh, it's going to be a fun weekend with these two.

37

Dante

Vanessa's son is not at all what I expected. I guess I assumed, based on her size, that he would be a five-foot nothing dorky sort of kid. Instead, he looks like a grown-ass man, taller than me, although on the lean side, with golden facial hair and the kind of cocky swagger that I don't want anywhere near my daughters.

That's why, when I see him by the pool Saturday afternoon, lurking near the edge to gawk at Cass sunbathing, I decide to intervene.

"Aren't you going to join us?" Vanessa asks when I step outside, drawing my attention away from the horny frat boy talking up my daughter. The woman made to torture me is lounging on a long green foam float wearing a black bikini and large black sunglasses over her eyes with her hair all pulled up on top of her head.

My designer suit be dammed, if I didn't have somewhere to be I would drag her ass out of the water right now and let her use me as a towel.

Instead, I talk my dick down. "There's a celebrity poker tournament I have to attend tonight."

"Okay. You're a celebrity now?" she asks with a grin.

"No, but the man hosting it has insisted that I come." Lochlan isn't going to be happy when I show up without Madison, but I'll just have to try and smooth things over the best I can.

"So, it's not down in the casino?" Vanessa asks.

"No. It's at Emerald Paradise."

"Oh." Her brow furrows. "Isn't that the Irish run place?"

"Yes. But don't worry, Lochlan Dunne is a friend." At least I don't think he's turned on me yet.

"A friend?"

"That's right. And I was going to see if Cole wanted to come and bring his friends along."

"Come where?" the kid asks, swimming away from Cass to join our conversation.

"To a celebrity poker tournament," I tell him.

"I didn't think they allowed any spectators, that it was VIP players only."

"They don't allow spectators, but I can buy you and your friends in so you can play." Lochlan won't like that either probably, but he never said I couldn't bring guests of my own.

"Then hell yes."

"I don't know, Cole..." Vanessa starts.

"Don't rain on his parade, butterfly. This is a once in a lifetime opportunity," I assure her. "He could win enough money to pay off his tuition."

The kid is already sold, pulling himself out of the pool to grab a towel.

"The guys won't fucking believe this," he says as he starts drying off. "When should they be ready to go?"

"Now."

"Oh. Okay. I'll go change and round them up. Meet you downstairs in the lobby?"

"Ten minutes from now or I'm going without you," I tell him, because as much as I want him away from Cass, I don't want to show up late. Lochlan will think it was an intentional move to disrespect him.

"See you later, Mom," Cole says as he heads back inside.

Vanessa scoffs. "Did you seriously just steal my son from me?"

"Why not?"

She eyes the door he just went through while chewing on her bottom lip. Turning back to me she says, "Do not let those boys blow any of their own money. And they're only twenty so they're not allowed to have any alcohol!"

"I won't let them piss away any money or drink," I promise her. "They'll be fine. It'll be fun."

"If you say so."

"I do," I tell her. Crouching down next to the pool edge so only she can hear me I add softer, "Try not to burn yourself, butterfly. Red flesh or not, I'm going to lick every single one of your sexy tan lines when I get home tonight."

"And you try to keep your dick in your pants around all those actresses."

"All dicks will stay in pants, especially your son's."

Now she smiles up at me. "Is that what this is about? You don't want my son around your daughter?"

"I still remember how I behaved at twenty, when my dick was every-where *except* inside my pants. Cole may be your son, but he's no different from any other guy in that regard."

She considers that for a moment, then says, "Fine. I'll make sure he knows your girls are off-limits."

"Great. So will I, just to reiterate the point."

"I'm sure you'll scare the shit out of him to dissuade him from doing anything stupid."

With a nod, I straighten back up, then walk around the pool to talk to Cass.

"How are you doing, sweetheart?" I ask.

"Fine."

"Just fine?" I repeat. She doesn't respond, probably doesn't even open her eyes to look at me behind her dark sunglasses. "Did you train this morning with Saul?"

"Yes. Just like every other day. But I don't know why I bother if you're never gonna let me compete."

"The purpose of learning jiu-jitsu is for self-defense, not to prove you're better than everyone else."

"Well, I am better than everyone else, so I want to compete."

My first inclination is a flat-out refusal. But then I remember where refusing Madison got me. It's been weeks, and I still don't know where she is or if she's okay.

"Fine. Send me the information for a nearby tournament, and I'll think about it."

"Really?" Now she removes her sunglasses.

"Yes."

"Because you feel guilty and don't want me to run away like Madison?"

"I don't want to make the same mistake twice."

"You know when Sophie finds out she's going to ask to go play in tennis tournaments, right?"

"I'll cross that bridge when I come to it," I grumble. "And I haven't agreed to anything with jiu-jitsu yet either. I need to know I can trust you to be safe."

"I could probably take out any of the guards if I wanted to," she sasses.

"Your trainer says you're one of the best students he's ever had," I tell her. Not only do I record their lessons to watch for myself, but he sends me a report each day.

"Seriously?"

"Seriously."

"And he's like, really old."

"He's sixty-seven. That's not really old."

"Yeah, it is. You're old and he's really old."

"Thanks for the compliment, Cass."

"You're welcome," she replies with a smile. One of the first I've seen on her face in months, even before Madison left. It gives me hope that I'm not the absolute worst father in the world.

38

Dante

I thought I might be able to avoid Lochlan for at least a half hour figuring that he would be busy trying to fuck actresses. But no, I'm not that lucky tonight. When I see him waiting by the door leading to the event center, I hold up a hand for Eli and our four guards to stay back with the boys.

"Salvato, you finally made it," the Irishman says in greeting, remarking on my lateness, even if it's only five minutes. With his dark auburn hair kept short, he doesn't have the look of a typical soul-less ginger. However, the tattoos on his face and his hands, along with the heavy bulk covered by his plum suit, give him the air of a soulless, dangerous man you don't want to fuck with. He's beyond filthy rich, thanks to the Dunne family's thriving whore houses in Vegas and around the world. Every known legal fantasy or fetish are offered at their establishments. The only reason I agreed to let him marry my oldest daughter is because he's as vicious as he is wealthy when it comes to protecting his people and territory. He's not afraid to fight dirty when necessary, which means he's also not a fool.

"Good to see you again, Lochlan," I reply while shaking his offered hand. Before he releases my palm, he slants his head to the left then the right to glance around me. "I don't see my blushing bride. Where is she, Dante?"

"Madison insisted on doing some last-minute backpacking around Europe," I reply which isn't exactly a lie. She could be on the other side of the world by now as far as I know. When the hotheaded bastard opens his mouth to bitch, I hold up my palm to stop him. "It was all part of our agreement. She gets to travel before accepting your ring and picking a date."

Lochlan's jaw ticks as he clenches his teeth. "Six months. That's my final offer, Salvato. If she hasn't agreed to be my wife by then, I'll have no choice but to start fucking your shit up."

"Understood," I tell him. "For today, let's get to the tables, shall we? Do you have room for my four friends, here?" I nod my head back to the boys who are busy staring at their phones.

"Who the hell are they?" Lochlan huffs.

"They're my...girlfriend's son and his three friends. I'll pay you double for their buy-in and my own. It's for charity, right?"

"Fine. I'll have to have another table brought in, so wait the fuck out here."

"Sure thing," I agree, then call up the most experienced guard. "Frank." I tip my head in the direction of the event room.

Without further instruction, he replies, "On it," then steps forward, following after Lochlan who stops abruptly to glare at me over his shoulder.

"Really, Dante?"

"What good would my security be if they don't make sure every room is secure before I enter them?" It's also the reason why I don't leave my casino often.

"Either you're paranoid or you're in deep shit," Lochlan remarks, his eyes narrowed. "Don't be bringing your drama into my business."

"It's just precautionary," I tell him. "Standard procedure for those of us at the top. I'm sure you understand. I'll expect nothing less when you marry my daughter."

With another mumbled swear, Lochlan storms off into the room with Frank nearly stepping on the heels of his dress shoes.

Going back to the group of boys, I tell them, "You're in once another table is set up. Don't even think about making fools of yourselves. When you're out, you're out, so don't use your own money. And try not to drool all over any models or whatever. They don't like that shit. Ignore them instead. Act like they're the ugliest pieces of shit in the world," I suggest, giving them the advice of how Vanessa treated me for years.

"Speaking from experience?" Cole asks with a smirk, as if he knows I'm thinking of his mother.

"If you fuck up tonight, then I'm in the doghouse," I warn him. "I won't be nice if I'm in the doghouse, understood?"

"Yes, *sir*." His sir is so sarcastic he may as well have said "fuck off" to me instead.

"You seem like a good kid, Cole."

"Ah, thank you?"

"Underneath the manners your mama beat into you, I know you're still just a horny frat boy who makes reckless decisions."

"Uh-oh," Eli mutters softly before he walks away to let us have a heart-to-heart.

"I like your mother, which means I'll tolerate you being around my casino, in my penthouse. But if you ever touch any of my daughters, even accidentally, I'll castrate you slowly with a dull, rusty, knife."

His face pales, letting me know my threat is being taken seriously.

"Damn, man. I seriously don't have a death wish," the kid says, rubbing his palm over the back of his neck.

"I didn't say I would kill you. Your mother wouldn't forgive me for that. I think she would understand if I left you sterile for sticking your dick where it doesn't belong."

"Okay. I've got it. Jeez." Shaking his head, he says, "I still can't believe you're with my mom."

"Why is that?"

"I don't know. She just doesn't seem like your type, and I never thought she would agree to date you. She's never been a fan of yours."

"Is that right?" I ask, my ears perking up. The boy probably knows Vanessa better than anyone else. If I don't break his limbs for staring at my bikini-clad daughter, then he could offer valuable insights into the complicated woman.

"I lost count of how many times Mom called you an arrogant prick or a self-centered asshole." I'm convinced he's just being a mouthy little dick before he visibly winces while glancing around to see if anyone overheard us. He quickly goes on to add, "I swear those are her words, not mine. The only opinion I have of you is that you back up your threats."

"Vanessa told you that she thinks I'm an arrogant prick? A self-centered asshole?"

The kid now shrugs. "Maybe I misheard her, but yeah, that's the gist of her feelings whenever your name was mentioned."

"Well, I hate to admit that you probably heard her correctly," I mutter, wishing I understood. Is it my money and Vanessa's lack of it that makes her hate me? Did I not pay her enough as an employee? I try to offer pay that's competitive to keep the decent staff around for as long as possible. Why did she stick around at the casino for so long if she was unhappy with her wages?

Slipping my hands into my pants pockets, I stroll past the registration desk to the event door to take a peek inside. The room is full of rambunctious drunken elite gathered around tables, well into their own games of poker. I consider texting Vanessa but then I see Lochlan heading toward me.

"About time," I tease him. He flips me off with his finger as he approaches.

"Impatient bastard. As soon as they bring in more chairs—"

He doesn't get to finish his sentence because Frank is suddenly lumbering up behind him, the whites of his eyes showing as he shouts, "*Get down!*"

"What?" Lochlan turns to ask him.

One second the Irishman is standing in front of me, the next, there's a boom louder than thunder that shakes the floor underneath my feet. Lochlan slams into the front of my body so hard I'm knocked backward to the ground. The back of my head hits the floor so hard my vision darkens and blurs. I can't hear shit. It's like all my senses just decided to abandon me.

Then I eventually realize that it's not my vision that darkened the room. The hallway is engulfed in a thick, hot smoke that's quickly filling my nose. I can even taste burning ash on my tongue.

My head is almost entirely under the registration table where two women were working. They're both on the floor, crying and helping each other quickly crawl toward the glowing exit door that leads outside.

What the fuck.

There must have been some type of explosion. Or a goddamn bomb. Something just blew the fuck up in the event room. The room where we were supposed to be...

Cole. I have to find Cole. If anything happens to him, Vanessa will kill me, and I would gladly let her. Thank fuck Madison wasn't with me tonight. I have to get back down the hall to find Cole and his friends. Someone on the outside is bound to have called for help by now. I hope they send every ambulance in the county because I think they're going to need them all.

I have to push half of Lochlan's limp body off of mine to get up. As I fight to squirm out, I realize why he's so heavy. Frank's body is draped over the lower half of Lochlan's, as if the guard tackled the Irishman to the ground. He was trying to warn us but ran out of time.

There are pieces of heavy debris on top of the big man who is bleeding and not moving. Chunks of the ceiling and door to the event room based on the gaping holes in the wall and ceiling surrounding us.

Either Lochlan and Frank are just unconscious or they're dead. There's nothing I can do for them now, so I get to my feet and stumble around the corner of the hallway. It's just as smoky, but there's significantly less wreckage from the building. I don't see Cole or his friends until Eli and the guards climb up off the floor where they must have tried to cover the boys. Once standing, the men offer the kids a hand up. Watching Cole get to his feet, stunned and dirty from head to toe but with no visible wounds is a huge fucking relief.

"Everyone okay?" I ask. Shout maybe. The words echo around in my pounding skull.

They all glance around at each other, then nod. "All good down here. How about you?" Eli asks.

"I'm fine. Frank and Lochlan are still out, though. Come help me get them out." The three guards and Eli rush past me, seemingly unharmed. They return a moment later with Lochlan between two of them, blinking his eyes open, but not Frank.

"He's gone," Eli says. "Shrapnel went right through his back, through his heart."

"Fuck." If not for Frank, Lochlan and I would probably both be dead too. He was a damn good man, always faithful and honest to a fault. He may have known he was putting his life on the line working for me, but that won't make it any easier on his family when they find out he's gone.

"Let's get the boys out of here. I'll...I need to notify Frank's wife before she hears about it on the news."

With every step, my entire body feels bruised and stiff. But I'm up and walking. I'm still alive, somehow.

"What the fuck happened?" Cole asks.

"Some type of explosion. Frank tried to warn us," I reply as I put my arm around his shoulders to urge him to the door I saw the women go out.

Once we're in the fresh night air, I don't let the kids stop walking. "Leave Lochlan and get the boys back to the cars and to the casino. I want security tightened so that nobody goes in or out any door but the main entrance, and everyone, every bag is searched," I order.

"You're staying here?" Eli asks as I pull out my phone. Lochlan is lowered to the curb, able to sit up on his own which is a good sign.

"I'll wait with Lochlan, make sure there's enough help on the way, then see if the responders need help."

"What if it was a bomb and there are more set to go off?"

"Then we're fucked."

"I'll stay too," Eli offers.

"No. You go back and make damn sure Cole goes straight up to see Vanessa. Hopefully before she hears about this and loses her mind."

"At least one guard should stay with you two in case there's a sniper." His neck swivels around, as if looking for the imaginary lone gunman.

"Fine. One guard. The rest go back. Now."

"I'll stay," Mike offers, and I give him a nod.

Legs heavy, I take a seat on the curb next to Lochlan as the sound of sirens fills the air.

"How are you doing?" I ask him.

"Half-dead or I'd be back inside to...fuck," he mutters, lying back on the concrete. Reaching up, he swipes his palms over his dusty face.

"We're both lucky to be alive. I wouldn't let you go back inside if you could walk. Frank gave his life to keep us both breathing. Anyone we try to pull out now could just hurt them worse, so let's leave it to the professionals."

"This is a goddamn nightmare."

"Yes, it really is," I agree just as a firetruck and three ambulances come speeding down the road toward us.

"Who do you think is behind this shit?" he asks.

"Your guess is as good as mine. But if I had to guess...Kozlov."

Dropping his hands, Lochlan slowly returns to a sitting position, eyes furious when he stares me down. "The Russians? Why would they fuck with me?"

"That's what I'm trying to figure out. Did you tell anyone I was coming tonight?"

"What?"

"Who knew I would be here?"

"Oh, so you're just going to assume it was a hit on you that took out two dozen or more A-list movie stars, models, and beloved musicians?"

"Fuck, I don't know, Lochlan. Maybe? If Kozlov found out about you marrying Madison, about our alliance, maybe he wanted to take us both out."

"Fuck you and fuck your enemies! All these deaths are on me, not you, because this is my casino!"

"Hey, don't take this shit out on me. You're the one who was stupid enough to put my name on the public roster, didn't you?"

"How was I supposed to know they would plant a fucking bomb in my hotel to get at you, Dante? Give me a fucking break," he grumbles just as the first group of firemen jog toward the building without the slightest idea of what they're about to walk into.

What a fucking day.

I feel pretty damn lucky to be alive, unlike Frank and who knows how many others.

If there was a bomb meant for me, I will find the fucker responsible and make them pay.

I have to if I want to keep my girls, my employees, and myself alive.

And then there's Vanessa.

I can't wait to hold her in my arms tonight, thanking whatever fates brought her into my life. I had convinced myself that I have to let her go to keep her safe from my world. Now, I can't help but wonder if I should ask her to stay, to let her decide whether or not she can handle my life-style. She's tough as nails, the most badass woman I've ever met. I know she can take care of herself; she has her entire life. Maybe she even thinks I'm worth the risks.

All I can do is promise her that I'll do everything under the sun to protect her, then leave the future up to her.

39

Vanessa

"So...since it's just us girls tonight, do ya'll want to watch a chick flick in the movie room?" I ask Sophie and Cass after the three of us have dinner together. I'm trying not to think about all the women and booze my son and Dante are probably neck deep into at the moment.

Cass frowns at me from across the dining table. "You're joking, right?"

"I'm serious. You two spend way too much time alone. Don't you get lonely?"

"I do," Sophie admits, causing Cass to groan and roll her eyes. "A movie sounds fun."

"Right? Come on, Cass. Don't be such a stick in the mud. We can pop some popcorn. I'm sure you all have some in your gigantic pantry the size of my living room."

"If there's going to be popcorn..." she starts just as the door shuts downstairs.

"Who is that?" I ask them.

"Probably the guards," Sophie says, but I'm already on my feet, heading to the stairs. Cole and Eli are both standing at the bottom of the staircase, covered in...soot?

"What happened?" I ask as I hurry down the stairs to them.

"We're all fine, Mom," Cole says as I grab his face in both hands. When I swipe my thumb over his cheek, it comes away black.

"What the fuck happened?" I demand again.

"There was an explosion at the casino. It was...really bad."

"An explosion?" I whisper as I throw my arms around his neck and squeeze tight, not caring about the soot, just that Cole is okay. He is okay, right?

Letting him go, I pat up and down his chest over his dirty button down. "Are you sure you don't have any injuries? You could have internal ones and not know..."

"I'm fine, Mom. Seriously. We were in the hallway when a bomb or something went off inside the event room. Dante's guards jumped on us to make sure nothing fell and hit us."

"Dante...where..." I ask, looking between Cole and a solemn-looking Eli.

"Is my dad okay?" Cass asks as she now rushes down the stairs with Sophie following.

"Dante is fine, just a little more banged up," Eli assures us.

"Thank goodness. Where is he?"

"He stayed behind with Lochlan who was pretty fucked up," Eli explains. "One of the guards died saving both of them."

"Oh, no," I gasp. When I slap my hand over my mouth, it smells like smoke.

"There are probably going to be more fatalities," Eli says. "Everyone in that room...it was fucking demolished. The ceiling and walls caved in on them."

"Oh my god. What...why would someone do this?" I ask as I wrap Cole in my arms again, unable to believe he was so close to something so horrific tonight. "Was someone trying to get Lochlan?" I ask, before a thought occurs to me. "Please tell me this attack wasn't meant for Dante."

"There's no way to know yet," Eli remarks while rubbing his forehead like it aches. "But I wouldn't be the least bit surprised if it was that fucking Kozlov."

"Kozlov?" I repeat, unable to get enough air in my lungs all of a sudden. "What? Why? Why would Kozlov come after Dante? I thought they were fine. Dante paid off Mitch's debt, and that was that, right? So, it must have been meant for Lochlan..."

Eli's eyes lower before he turns toward the door. "I need to make sure they're tightening security..."

Before he can make it two steps, I release Cole to lunge for him, grabbing his arm to stop him. "Eli, what else do you know?"

"Nothing." He shrugs, still refusing to meet my gaze in the least convincing response ever.

"Ha!" Cass says from behind me. "Welcome to our world, Vanessa, where us females aren't allowed to know anything about what's going on while we're locked up in our tower."

Oh hell no. Dante better not be keeping shit from me. If he has...if he has then I am so done with him.

"Eli, tell me. Please," I beg, still gripping his arm. "I have a right to know if there's trouble, especially when my son could've been hurt because of it tonight."

"Fine. If there was a bomb, it may have been to get back at Dante. Kozlov's been searching for his two missing enforcers, pointing fingers without proof..."

"Missing enforcers..."

Oh god.

Somehow, I inhale so hard I choke on the air while shaking my head. "No. He didn't."

Eli shakes my hand off of his arm. "Of course, Dante took out the two men who hurt you."

"Took out?" Cole asks, as if asking if the phrasing means what he thinks it does.

"Oh shit," Cass mutters in understanding, the understatement of the year.

"Dante's going to be pissed I told you all. Just remember, Vanessa, that you weren't the only woman they beat on. They *deserved* to die."

"Dante shouldn't have been the one to kill them!"

I asked one thing of him during my captivity, that he wouldn't seek revenge for me. And the asshole lied to my face about it.

"When?" I ask Eli. "When did Dante...do that?"

"A few days after you agreed to stay."

"That son of a bitch!"

Dante kept what he did to the two Russians from me intentionally. He's been pretty open with me about nearly every aspect of his business, but this...he did something so drastic knowing the consequences. Knowing that he would be starting a war with the Russians if or when they found out.

And it's all my fault.

"I need go to talk to security," Eli says before he makes a hasty retreat. That's exactly what I want to do too.

"Cole, go...go get cleaned up and grab your things. I'll meet you in the lobby," I tell my son, knowing I need to head down the hall to do the same.

"Vanessa," Eli starts. "Dante went through hell today. Please don't do anything rash right now."

"Rash?" I scoff. "Rash as in killing two mobsters!" When I notice Cole standing stock still, maybe even in shock after the hell he's been through tonight, I ask him again, "Please, please go get your things, honey."

"Why, Mom? I'm fine. My friends are fine..."

"You all were lucky this time. It's too dangerous to stay here any longer. Your friends can come back to the apartment if they want, but I just can't stay..."

"Fine." He huffs before his feet finally shuffle toward the door.

"You're leaving?" Cassandra asks, sounding surprised, and maybe even a little disappointed. I probably imagined it.

"I have to, Cass," I tell her honestly. With a final scowl that reminds me of her father's, she jogs up the stairs.

My hands are shaking when I head down the hallway to get my things, but there's too much. Dante had his guys bring nearly everything in my apartment just to keep me from asking to go pick up shit.

And all the clothes in his closet, the ones he bought for me, they never really felt like mine so I'm leaving them. He can do what he wants with them. So, all I really need are a few toiletries from the bathroom that I dump in a tote bag, along with my purse. I would love to get my gun out of the safe, but I don't know the code. The only thing left for me to grab is my phone. I'll definitely need my phone, but I can't remember where the hell I left it.

I rush to the kitchen, check around the pool, then finally find it sitting on the cleared dining table where I up and left it. My heart is pounding in my chest I'm so anxious to get downstairs and out of here, hoping to be gone before Dante comes back.

And if his guards won't let me leave, then I'll...I don't know what I'll do. All I know is that I don't want to confront him right now. Not when I'm so fucking angry at him.

With my hand on the penthouse doorknob, I feel like I'm in the clear...only to pull it open and find Dante striding out of the elevator with Eli close behind.

Fuck.

His suit has several tears and is covered in more soot than Cole's clothes. The grit on his handsome, stern face makes him look more menacing than usual. But his eyes...well his eyes soften when they see me, filled with an emotion I don't want to label because it will hurt too much. It's quickly replaced by his brow furrowing in confusion when he sees the tote on my shoulder.

"Going somewhere, butterfly?" he asks when he comes to a stop in front of me. He reaches out a hand toward me, and I recoil, taking a step backward out of his reach. There's a flash of hurt in his eyes, but Dante drops his hand. "I'm a fucking mess, I know. I need a shower. Was hoping you would join me. Wouldn't mind staying in bed for the next few days either."

"Don't. Don't even try being all sweet and-and vulnerable with me right now," I tell him. My heart clenches at the sight of him, even if I wish it wouldn't.

"Why not?"

"It won't work on me. I'm so goddamn angry at you I can't even see straight!"

Dante blinks at me in confusion. Great, I thought for sure Eli would have already told him I knew about the Russians and that I was pissed. I guess he preferred for it to be a surprise instead. Asshole. Now this argument will have to be out in the hall with guards bearing witness to it.

"You're angry at me?" Dante points his index finger to his own chest, as if it's so difficult for him to fathom.

"Yes, I'm angry at you!"

His shoulders slump even more. In fact, the mafia king looks more deflated than I've ever seen him. I guess a brush with death will do that to a man. While it's harder to be angry at him in his unusual filthy, disheveled condition, my son's safety overrides that.

"I'm sorry if the shit with the explosion scared you..."

"Scared me?" I interrupt. "Scared doesn't begin to describe how I feel! What were you thinking? Why did you retaliate against the Russians after I begged you not to do that?"

Understanding must finally dawn on him, but instead of responding to me, he turns and charges at Eli. Gone is the calm, sweet, gentle man. Dante's fingers wrap around the former fighter's throat, slamming him back into the wall. Eli doesn't even attempt to fight back. "You fucking told her? I ought to rip your goddamn tongue out!"

I can't hear Eli's muffled response. I'm too busy wishing I could go back in time. If only I had just let Dante kill Mitch, then Dante wouldn't have gone after Kozlov's enforcers, and I wouldn't have gotten myself dragged into his shit. Mitch's blood would've been on my hands, but at least I wouldn't have put Cole's life in danger by playing house with a fucking mafia king.

God, I'm so fucking stupid.

"Don't you dare put this on Eli!" I yell at the bastard. "If it was the Russian's bomb then you only have yourself to blame for every single person who was hurt or killed tonight."

Dante goes still, his head bowing a second before he releases Eli's neck to turn to face me again.

"What happened tonight wasn't my fault. I didn't plant that goddamn bomb, so don't put that shit on me."

"Yes, it was probably your fault if you lit the match that started this whole fucking fire!"

"Those two enforcers...they got what they deserved."

I scoff at that.

"Vanessa, I thought you finally understood that sometimes people have to die. This was one of those times. They fucking deserved it, and you know it."

"Honestly, it's not the killing that bothers me. It's the fact that you killed those two men *knowing* full well it would result in retaliation from the Russians. You didn't warn me. There wasn't a heads up. No, you didn't want me to ever find out. And now your temper may have gotten people killed. How many people are hurt, Dante? How could you put my son at risk by keeping this shit from me?"

"Cole doesn't even have a single scratch on him!" Dante shouts back as he strides toward me. I keep walking backward as he advances until he finally stops in the middle of the entry way of the penthouse. "But can the same be said for my daughter?" he raises his voice. "No, it can't! Because I have no fucking idea where she is thanks to you putting idiotic ideas in her head!"

Oh, no. I will not let him try and gaslight me. What happened to Cole and Madison are two completely different situations.

"Madison is probably better off far away from you," I tell Dante honestly. He flinches at my words that hit him harder than I intended. Still, I'm too pissed to take them back, and they're the truth. Taking a deep breath, I try to explain myself better. "I just meant that if she is using an alias, then nobody will know she's your daughter. My son on the other hand, you decided he and his friends belonged at a fucking celebrity poker tournament. They are the same age as Madison. Would you have taken her to a place like that? No, because she's female and because she's *your* daughter!" A horrible thought suddenly occurs to me, making me so queasy my palm goes to my belly as if to try and stave off the nausea. "Did you know something like this could happen? Are you trying to punish me for Madison?"

"No! God no! I *never* would have taken Cole if I had any inclination that there would be an attack. I should've been more cautious, but my security staff can't guarantee every inch of the earth is safe."

"That's the problem, Dante. There's always a constant threat. That's part of being a gangster. You won't know when or where one of your many enemies will decide to attack you. No one around you is *ever* safe. That's why I can't...I don't want to be a part of your world of endless

271

violence anymore. I am not going to let you drag me or my son into some mafia war that ends with everyone dead."

"I know tonight terrified you, Vanessa. It scared me too. But I'm handling it, okay? This feud with Kozlov is going to blow over eventually, and then..."

"*Eventually* isn't soon enough for me," I explain to him. "I'm going home, to my home, tonight."

He shakes his head in refusal. "No. You can't. We still have twenty-eight days together."

A puff of laughter filled with indignation escapes me as I try to ignore the fact that he knows exactly how many days are left. "I can leave and I am. Kill Mitch or don't, Dante. I really don't give a shit anymore."

For all I know, since I last spoke to my idiot ex, he's probably dug himself into a new hole that ended his own life with his stupidity. Or maybe Dante has since killed him and didn't tell me, like he didn't tell me about the Russians he murdered because they left a few bruises on me.

"Vanessa, if you leave..."

"Oh, no. You finally decide to use *if* in the single instance that is one thousand percent *when*. I *am* leaving. Right now. And there is *nothing* you can do or say to change my mind or stop me!"

His cold blue eyes narrow, his jaw clenches. "You're not leaving. Not until you help me find Madison. You owe me that much."

Ugh, everything is a negotiation with this man. An attempted manipulation. And I have had enough.

"Fuck you," I snarl at him, my built-up fear for Cole, for even the jackass himself, has my anger seething, wanting an escape. "I am done being your hostage. Give me my gun back now so I can go."

"No."

No? I can't believe this man's fucking audacity.

"So, you'll let me leave here unable to protect myself because you're being stubborn? Because you blame me for caging your own daughter in for so long that she couldn't take it a second longer? It's your fault she left, Dante. Yours and yours alone. Not mine. And you know what? I fucking applaud her for refusing to be a pawn in your game for another second. I suddenly feel the exact same way."

"So that's it? You're going to blame me for everything, then just walk out, telling yourself that I'm the villain, and that you never gave a shit about me? That I held you down and made you scream my name over and over again?"

I hate him throwing our intimacy in my face so damn much. And while I can't deny my feelings for him, I refuse to admit them. I never wanted or expected to fall for him of all people.

"You *manipulated* me into staying with you, remember? I didn't want anything to do with you, but you couldn't take no for an answer!"

His blue eyes harden even more. In fact, I've never seen him look so angry, not even when he found out Madison had left. His lips pull back into a murderous snarl when he growls, "Then go. Get the fuck out of my house!"

His booming voice, his callous words ordering me to leave, even if they're what I was planning to do anyway, make me want to cower. But I don't let the distress show on my face.

"I'll go, just as soon as you give me back my gun." My unregistered, untraceable gun has been my safety blanket for years now. I can't imagine being alone in my apartment with Cole without it. I guess I always felt guilty that my son didn't grow up with an intimidating father figure to protect him. With my small build, I have to be armed to try and do a decent job of it.

Dante glares at me for a long moment before he storms off down the hall to the bedroom. Every few seconds there's a loud bang or a smashing sound of something breaking that makes me jump.

I look to Eli who finally dares to enter the penthouse from the hall where the door still stands wide open. He doesn't seem the least bit rattled, just disappointed.

The fighter's voice is still hoarse from being choked when he says, "If you leave him, Van, nobody will be able to talk him down from scorching the earth, and he'll probably get himself killed."

"I *have* to go," I tell him simply. "I won't feel guilty for doing what's necessary."

"Come on, Vanessa. You could at least stay with him while we keep looking for Madison, help us look for her, even if it's not your fault she left."

I shake my head. "No, I won't do that, because she doesn't want to be found."

There are more sounds of glass breaking down the hall, but neither Eli nor I say anything else.

I hear Dante's heavy footsteps before he appears. This version of the mafia king looks so cool and calm, unfazed as if he wasn't just having an argument with me or breaking shit around his house.

He holds out my gun for me to take grip first, his knuckles now scraped and bleeding. When I reach for it, he says, "I loaded it for you. Will six bullets in the clip be enough protection from the entire fucking world?"

Even though he's being a cold, sarcastic ass, I tell him, "I'll make do with six bullets for now. Can you have someone bring me my things tomorrow or should I try to carry it all out with me now?" There are so many boxes I would need to rent a damn U-Haul.

"Eli will have it packed up and dropped off in the morning on his way out of town."

"Fine," I agree.

"Out of town?" Eli asks, as if those words mean more than just running an errand. If I had to bet, it sounds to me like he's being exiled for telling me Dante's secret. I hate that for Eli, but there's nothing I can do to change Dante's mind.

There's a heavy silence suffocating me as I step around Dante to walk toward the open front door. Before I walk out into the hallway, though, I glance over my shoulder at the mafia king one last time. His blue eyes are completely unfamiliar to the ones I'm used to in bed. They're cruel, sadistic, with no fucks to give. It's all a mask to hide the irrational, worried father about to embark on a war with the entire Russian mafia out of revenge. Gone is the man I think may have even loved me if Madison hadn't run away.

That's why I tell him before I leave, "I know you're always going to worry about her, but I really do think Madison will be fine. Cass and Sophie, too. They're Salvatos. Mafia princesses. I bet they can be just as ruthless as you when they need to be."

40

Dante

When Vanessa walks out, I push down every emotion struggling to break free to focus only on the anger.

Anger I can handle.

The rest I'm not equipped for because they're either too debilitating or too new.

Fuck the fear, the panic, the sadness, the loss, and everything else bubbling up inside of me. Missing her before she even leaves the building doesn't make any fucking sense. Whatever we had together, I can feel the bonds of our fucked-up relationship being severed, the knife currently sawing right down the middle. Being physically disconnected from Vanessa hurts like hell.

There's nothing I can do or say to change her mind. No matter how much she cares for me, everything changed today when I put her son's life in danger.

To think she would even accuse me of dragging him there on purpose as payback for Madison blows my mind. I thought she knew me better than that. I thought she understood me, that she accepted that my viciousness was a necessity for surviving and keeping everyone I care about alive.

I bared my fucking soul to Vanessa. For the first time in my life, I let someone see all of me, the good and the bad in the hopes that she would still want me. To have her allege that it was all a manipulation and not mutual, genuine affection on her part is fucking infuriating.

And I really want to take my rage out on someone else since I can't take it out on her.

Finally confronting Eli who is still waiting silently in the foyer, I tell him, "Pack your shit and take it with you when you drop off...her things tomorrow morning." God, I can't even say her fucking name. "If I see you in this city again, I'll put a bullet through your skull."

"You're kicking me out because Vanessa left you?" Hearing those words aloud is somehow even more devastating than thinking them.

Walking up to him, I press both palms to his chest to shove him backward into the wall at his back. "I'm kicking you out because you ran your goddamn mouth!"

"Don't you think she would've figured it out soon enough? You're going to war with Kozlov. Everyone will be able to figure out the bomb was retaliation. You'll need my help, even if you won't admit it, just like Vanessa won't admit she's in love with you. You're both so damn stubborn..."

"Keep her name out of your fucking mouth," I growl in his face in warning. "And the only man she will ever love is her son."

"Come on, Dante. Your girls will always come before anything else, even Vanessa, so don't be pissed at her for caring about the kid more than you. And you can't honestly say that you've completely forgiven her for giving Madison a nudge out the door."

Dammit, I hate when he's right about shit.

"This conversation is over," I tell him. "Find out..." I start before remembering that he's no longer my employee. "Forget it. I'll make the calls myself."

First things, first, I need a shower, then I'll get an update on the casualties from the bombing. I find it hard to believe that Kozlov would be stupid and reckless enough to take out a room full of celebrities to get to me. That's why I want to know what the investigators find at the scene. If there's proof it was Kozlov, then I'll slice off every inch of his fucking flesh for Frank and all the other victims. He will pay for what he did, even if it means risking retaliation from Kozlov's boss, Yuri Petrov. In fact, I may as well start at the top of the ladder and work my way down, while they least expect it.

I was born in Vegas. It's my goddamn city, and I'll be damned if I let them paint the streets with blood.

If I had to bet, Petrov is the one who could be behind it all, using Kozlov's missing enforcers as an excuse to finally come at me like he's wanted to do since my father died.

Petrov's mainly only dealt in heroin and whores which is why we stay out of each other's way. Maybe he's trying to branch out, maybe mix up his H with other shit... like fentanyl to make birria?

Son of a motherfucking bitch.

I'm his biggest competition for fentanyl. For the past nine years, I've overseen the west coast's pipeline of transportation and distribution from China to Mexico. Then there's Lochlan, an only child like me, whose family has always had a lock on running the biggest brothel empire in the world. The two of us are all that's standing in his way of being the west coast's king of drugs and pussy.

Tonight, he tried his best to kill two mob bosses with one stone and missed.

I almost wish I could be in the room to see Petrov's face when he finds out I'm still alive and so is Lochlan, that all he got for his trouble was a world of law enforcement coming after him for killing innocent victims. Not to mention Lochlan's wrath for all the fingers that will point at him as being responsible for not preventing the bomb.

But seeing Petrov and Kozlov behind bars isn't enough. They need to die. Slowly. And I'm more than happy to oblige them.

Planning how to take them down will be a much welcome distraction from missing Vanessa.

Vanessa

. . .

We still have twenty-eight days together.

I add it up and...he's right. There were technically twenty-eight days left as part of our agreement.

With everything going on, I'm not sure why I'm so hung up on those damn twenty-eight days. I sure as hell don't feel guilty for leaving early. It's just...why would Dante know the exact number of days left off the top of his head like that? I should be the one counting them down, marking the calendar, eager to be done with him since I never wanted any part of this arrangement to begin with.

The way he sounded when he threw out the number of days left, it was almost like he was keeping track because he *didn't* want them to end.

"Mom, are you sure you're okay?" Cole asks as I drive us back to my apartment, snapping me out of my mental math. It's the first time I've been inside of my car, or behind the wheel of any vehicle, in weeks. Since the night I went in to work as a waitress and ended up as a prisoner.

"I'm fine," I assure him. Even if my first taste of freedom isn't as wonderful as I imagined it would be that first night of our deal.

"You know what happened wasn't Dante's fault, right?"

My fingers curled around the steering wheel tighten. "He may not have known about the bomb, but he knew there would be consequences."

"There's no way he could've anticipated these consequences, right?"

"I don't know. I don't want to talk about him anymore." I blow out a breath trying to expel him from my mind, my heart, and my soul, and fail hard. "I'm sorry your weekend with your friends was ruined."

"If anything, after such a close call, I think we all have a new appreciation for life, how short it can be, you know? I don't want to waste any time on bullshit."

"Well, I'm glad something good came from something so bad. I'm sorry I put you and your friends in that position."

"Will you please stop apologizing? You don't have anything to be sorry for, Mom. If anything, I should be apologizing to you."

"To me? Why?" I spare a quick glance at him before my eyes return to the road.

"I'm sorry I'm the reason that you ended things with Dante."

"It wasn't your fault. It's for the best. He's...he's not a good man. He's murdered people. That's the reason I left. I would've been out the door as soon as I found out about him killing the Russian enforcers, so the breakup doesn't have anything to do with you."

Cole chuckles. "Why did those particular murders bother you so much? You had to have known that Dante had blood on his hands before. That didn't stop you from holding them."

"I...I was stupid. We shouldn't be having a conversation about the man I was with murdering people. It's insane! God, love can make you so damn blind..." As soon as I realize the words I just spoke, I pinch my lips together, wanting them back. "That...that's not what I meant."

"Isn't it?" Cole asks. "You love him, even if he's a murdering mobster. It's okay to admit it, Mom. Despite who he is or has to be, you still found a way to love him. If I had to guess, not many people have made the same choice when it comes to Dante Salvato. Most people cower at just the mention of his name, and rightfully so. But there's more to him than his worst traits."

"Not when his 'worst trait' is murdering people!"

"So, he's not perfect. It's still possible to love him or want him or whatever you two were. It's not like I have any experience, so maybe I don't know what the fuck I'm talking about. All I'm trying to say is that you seemed different with Dante. I thought you were actually happy for once. Less tense for sure, like you felt safe with him."

Scoffing, I ask, "How could I *ever* feel safe with a murderous bastard?"

"Because you've always been wound tight, on edge, afraid of, well, I don't know what, right? But you looked...peaceful with him, even if he was a dangerous gangster. Maybe because he was a dangerous gangster."

Shaking my head in disbelief, I say, "You think I looked peaceful with a dangerous gangster?"

"You were, weren't you? And I get it. He would probably do anything to keep you safe."

"Dante would've locked me away in his personal prison and thrown away the key so I could never escape. He would've suffocated me until I couldn't take it anymore."

"If so, then his reasons would be sound, obviously, after what happened tonight. He's not being paranoid or overly protective for the hell of it."

"No, I guess not," I concede. "Dante has lost a lot of people in the past, including all three of his daughters' mothers."

"All of them?" Cole asks in disbelief.

"Yes. One died in a shooting, another after childbirth, then one just vanished and is presumed dead."

"Damn. No wonder he's so neurotic. That's a lot of innocent women dying around him. Now with the casino bombing..."

"He brought that on himself," I declare.

"Really, Mom? That's the equivalent of saying that a girl was asking for it when she wore a short skirt and got assaulted. Dante made his own choices, sure, but he's not responsible for how others reacted to those choices."

"He knew what he did would cause problems, and he did it anyway! He's partially responsible for the fallout."

"And he probably feels like shit for that, unlike the people responsible. Not to mention he almost died."

Before a few weeks ago, I never would've believed that Dante was capable of feeling guilt or sorrow for other people's suffering. Now, I know he has a soul that dreads the violence, even if another part of him will always enjoy it. Men like Dante Salvato thrive on being in control of the chaos.

And I hate to admit that I was even attracted to that aspect of him as much as anything else. Dante's ruthlessness is hot. *Was* hot. Which means there is something seriously wrong with me.

When Cole and I finally get home and walk inside the apartment flipping on lights, it feels so empty. I thought I had missed my own place, my sofa, the place I'm most comfortable, but now it's just lonely. Not that Mitch's absence makes it less lonely. That's how I felt even when he lived here. If anything, I'm glad he's not here, that I won't have to deal with him again, thanks to Dante.

After I put on my pajamas, Cole and I both sit on the sofa to watch the news for updates about the explosion.

There's nothing left of an entire side of the Emerald Paradise casino where the event was being held, just a giant, black crater in the earth.

Twenty-two poor souls were killed, at least half of them well-known faces throughout the world. Thirteen more were badly hurt after being buried in the debris or receiving serious injuries.

I had no idea the bomb was that bad. Yes, I knew that there was an explosion and that Dante's guard, Frank, had died to save him and Lochlan. Since Cole, Dante, and Eli were all unharmed I guess I thought it wasn't so bad. It turns out, they were just really fucking lucky.

The next morning, Cole and I are up bright and early to get him on a flight to New York before any other catastrophes happen in Vegas. I was surprised but grateful to find my boxes of things stacked along the railing in front of my apartment. Cole helped me toss it all inside before we left.

On the way to the airport, the roads are empty since it's Sunday and everyone in town was probably up late last night.

"School starts soon, right?" I ask a sleepy-eyed Cole slouched in the passenger seat.

"Yeah, in three weeks. I'm going to try to get in as many hours as I can at work before then."

Work? That's when a thought occurs to me.

"Oh, shit," I mutter. "I have to go back to work at the casino tomorrow. And keep working there until I find another job."

I had been hoping to avoid the Royal Palace at all costs, avoiding Dante. That's impossible when bills will be coming due soon enough, no longer paid by the mafia king.

"Another job?"

"I sure as shit can't keep working for Dante. Ugh, even being in this city is too close to him."

"If you're so adamant about getting away from him, you could always move to New York."

"It may be time to relocate." I've done it enough over the years. At least I won't have to feel guilty about dragging Cole with me, enrolling him in a new school to start all over. "I'm just not sure if I want it to be New York. Besides, you would hate having me intrude on the life you've built there."

"You wouldn't be intruding on my life," he replies. "And the university is always looking to hire. If you insist on staying in the food service industry, there are tons of restaurants and bars around campus."

"Insist on staying in the food service industry?" I repeat. "You say that like I have a choice in my profession."

"You could do so much more, Mom. You're smart and hardworking. I never understood why you stick to the shitty, low-level jobs, that don't pay much."

He wouldn't understand because I've never told him that while my experience is limited, laying low is essential for me. For us. I prefer to blend in with the background, not stand out. And I was excelling at that until Dante Salvato rode a wrecking ball straight into my life.

"I prefer to just be an employee, not supervise anyone. That's as far as I could even go if I wanted to," I explain to him.

"Well, one day soon I'm going to start my own company and be rich enough that you can quit work, and finally just relax for once. You've worked your ass off every day since I was born."

"I like to stay busy," I assure him. "But it's sweet to know you'll think of me when you become a wealthy snob."

Cole chuckles at that. "You fit right in with the wealthy snobs at Dante's. The peacefulness there could've been from not having to work and constantly being pampered."

"I wasn't constantly pampered." I huff. "Just occasionally."

"Admit that you miss it."

"Fine, I miss some parts of the millionaire lifestyle. Just not the mobster one. Never that one."

41

Vanessa

Sunday afternoon is productive. After I get home from the airport, I hop online and start looking for a new job. It's probably too much to hope that I would find someone to call and hire me before my shift at the lounge starts tomorrow night.

At the grocery store that night since I can't sleep, I ask if they need any third shift cashiers. Unfortunately, the manager told me they weren't hiring. Not even for a stock boy position. Yes, I would've accepted anything that earned any amount of money just to avoid Dante's casino.

On the way home, I decide that I'm going to get up bright and early tomorrow to swing by as many businesses as possible on the way to the Royal Palace until I find someone who is hiring.

The idea motivates me, gives me hope that I could find some desperate manager to take pity on me.

I'm so distracted by the hopefulness that when I start to climb out of my car, my purse, and a bag in each hand, I don't pay much attention to the vehicle slowly rolling up behind me in the parking lot. Not until it's too late.

One second, I hear multiple doors opening, the next, thick arms wrap around my neck and band around my own arms and stomach, lifting my feet completely off the ground.

When I get spun around, I see the black SUV with the headlights blinding me. "Goddamn it, Dante!" I scream as I try to swing my bags at the head of my assailant. It doesn't work with the steel band pinning my arms to my sides. Another man takes the bags and my purse, tossing them to the ground, where my flip-flops unfortunately join them. Then he shouts, "Get her in the car, now!"

The man carrying me takes me to the open door of the SUV. I kick my heels at his shins and claw his arms with my fingernails. They're hairy arms, the tattoos unfamiliar. Dante sent his henchmen to drag me back to the casino? Is he fucking insane?

"Put me down! I'm not going anywhere with you, you son of a bitch!" I yell.

He doesn't put me down. He doesn't even let me go when we reach the backseat. No, the goon turns around and climbs into the middle seat backward without releasing me.

"Ow, bitch! You're gonna pay for slicing my arm up and kicking me!" The voice isn't familiar either as he holds me down on his lap. Shit. Dante's guards wouldn't threaten me, would they?

The asshole with shaggy black hair who took my bags climbs in the seat next to us, closing the door which turns off the interior lights. In the sudden darkness, he says, "We're in, go!" directing the driver who accelerates so fast I get whiplash.

What I saw of the faces of everyone in the vehicle is unfamiliar, including the driver and passenger talking on his phone. Glancing over my shoulder, I find two more wide-shouldered thugs in the third-row seat. These are all men who look like their only talent in life is cracking skulls.

Fuck.

Real fear slinks under my skin, making me go still as I try to figure out what the hell is going on. There are six large men in the vehicle. I couldn't take on even one and win, and of course I don't have my gun either. Even my purse is missing, left in the parking lot with my pathetic groceries. That means I'm only left with trying to talk my way out of this shit.

"Who the hell are you?" I ask, just before the passenger says into his phone, "We got Mitch and Salvato's little blonde bitch. Now what?" the moon-faced passenger turns to stare at me with an evil grin that isn't comforting.

Mitch and Dante's bitch? These are definitely not Dante's men...

The man next to me grunts out, "Hold her arms out." I fail trying to escape the monstrosity of a thug when he squeezes my wrists until I cry out in pain. While his buddy wraps silver duct tape around and around my wrists, I feel him harden underneath my ass. My first reaction is to freeze, to stop moving. Gouging out eyeballs won't be easy with my wrists taped together. In fact, I'm not getting away so there's no reason to encourage that...thing.

"Will do," the passenger says to the person on the phone. "The guys and I would love to have a little fun with her first if that's cool with the boss? Alright, I'll let them know," he says then lowers the phone from his ear.

Have a little fun with her...first?

"Go buck wild boys! As long as she stays in this vehicle, boss doesn't care what you do with her tonight. He just doesn't want us playing chase. She's feisty so she probably would try to run."

The boss doesn't care what they do to me?

"Who the fuck is your boss?" I demand but my question is ignored.

"The night is looking up!" the duct taper next to me exclaims. He licks his lips, then reaches a dirty hand toward me, pinching my nipple through my shirt and bra until I scream and writhe.

"Hell, yeah," the one holding me says while groping my other breast.

"When we're done, he wants us to leave her body where it'll be found right away," the passenger announces.

My body. They're going to pass me around, use me, then kill me. Kill me, but leave my body where it can be found. By Dante? They *want* him to know they killed me. This stupid fucking SUV is the last place I'll spend on Earth.

"Make her scream again," someone in the back says before my hair is jerked to the side, giving him what he wanted.

"Who do you assholes work for?" I shout.

"Who do you think? Kozlov," the bastard still pinching and squeezing my boobs informs me.

Kozlov. The Russians. Shit.

"Dammit, Carl! Stop running your mouth," a voice in the back says.

"What does it matter if she knows since she'll be dead soon anyway?" someone replies.

Oh, god. I never should've left Dante. This...I won't blame him for this. No, I blame myself for being scared of my feelings and running from the only man I've ever loved.

Kidnapping me, hurting me, then killing me is in retaliation to try and hurt Dante. How did they know we were together? I don't have a chance to ask. Every thought in my head evaporates when the man holding me starts trying to tug my shorts and underwear down. Thankfully the denim is tight enough the zipper and button have to be undone first. It doesn't take the sasquatch long to figure that out, unfortunately.

"Stop! *Stop it!*" I scream while digging my fingernails into his hand and trying to bend his fingers backward. Nothing works to loosen his arm still banded around my waist or stop him from popping the button.

"Should we gag her?" someone in the back asks as my bottoms are yanked down my hips.

"Nah, nobody can hear her scream in here," the man holding me says. "But somebody needs to hold her wrists down before she claws my dick!"

He's not wrong, I do want to rip his fucking dick off. I'm still infuriated when my arms are twisted and bent backward, going behind the giant's head where they're held by strong hands harder than necessary to make me cry out again.

The pain in my shoulders is quickly forgotten when I hear the zipper of his fly screech down. That's when I know time is running out. These nasty bastards will be the last ones to touch me.

The only alternative is...well, it's almost as bad, but not quite. Hopefully.

Either way, I have to try because I don't want to die tonight.

"Stop!" I shriek so loudly my throat burns when my bottoms are ripped free of my ankles. That's when I feel the man's freed erection being wedged between my ass cheeks. I lift my hips to try and keep him away.

My entire soul aches as I grit my teeth and play the only card I have left. God help me.

"I'm Yuri Petrov's daughter!" I repeat the same words in Russian, even if it's a little rusty.

There's a moment of absolute stillness in the SUV before the deep rumbling laughter starts up in surround sound from every direction. "Yeah, right. Good one. She'll say anything to try and save her life," the passenger remarks. The goon holding me goes still, though. He's unsure. *Thank fuck.*

"My name..." My chest is so tight I can barely take a breath. "My name is Katia Petrov and I swear to you that Yuri Petrov is my father! His *only* daughter, his only...his only heir!"

All these years of hiding from that bastard, and now I'm screaming his name at the top of my lungs hoping it will save me.

"Petrov doesn't have a daughter. Does he?" someone in the back asks.

"Nah, he ain't got no kids," the passenger says.

"I ran away when I was sixteen! I'm-I'm thirty-seven-years-old now," I admit, giving them my real age and not the one on all my fake documents. "I've been using a comatose girl's identity as Vanessa Brooks. Call him! Call Yuri now and ask him!"

There's silence other than the sound of tires on the pavement, the noisy engine that's slowed to a dull roar.

"Do you know what he'll do to you when my dental records, my DNA, and bone marrow prove I am who I say I am? He'll kill you all. Slowly. Painfully. Probably make you watch him kill every member of your family first."

"Fuck," the passenger says as he turns around in his seat to face me. Raising his phone, I hear a click as he takes a picture. "I'll send a photo of her and a message to Kozlov, see if he buys her bullshit."

"It's true. Call Yuri, not Kozlov!"

"Yeah, like we've got the boss's number on speed dial. We're just Kozlov's muscle. He's the only one of us who can make that call."

The grip on my wrists lessens at the same time the driver slows down the SUV even more. They're both second-guessing shit too, just like I wanted. The duct taper doesn't touch me again either, thankfully.

When the passenger's phone rings, I hold my breath waiting for what the other person will say. My fate is in their hands.

"Yeah? Son of a bitch," he grumbles as he turns around to glare at me. "He says it *could* be her."

Oh, thank god.

The hands on my wrists fall away, eliminating the ache on my shoulders as I lower my arms back to my lap.

"Probably not but he's looking into it. Boss says to err on the side of caution until you hear back..."

"Give me my shorts and panties back now!" I yell hopefully loud enough for the man on the other side of the phone call to hear.

Since they're on the floorboard, the passenger is closer to them. He lowers the phone and is about to pick up my clothes when the driver says, "Uh-oh."

"What?" he snaps at him, my bottoms forgotten.

"We've got a tail roaring up our ass!"

Everyone's head swivels to look out the rear windshield, including my own. All I can make out on the dark highway are headlights. Lots of headlights. And they appear to be coming up on us fast.

Dante? No. There's no way.

But the Russians all seem concerned as they all take out their guns and cock them. Even the one holding me grabs his from somewhere with his one free hand.

How could Dante know they grabbed me? That we're on this particular part of the highway? It's impossible.

Unless...unless he had his men watching me, watching the apartment. I bitched at him about not wanting to give me my gun back because it was all I had to protect myself when he didn't have any intention of leaving me unprotected.

While the asshole holding me is busy looking out the back, I squirm my way to the floorboard figuring it's the safest place to be if bullets start flying.

"Fuck! They're already on us! We're blocked in!"

When. When the bullets start flying, because there's a rapid fire *pow-pow-pow* that makes the SUV swerve as if a tire or multiple tires were just hit.

I hear wind noise, all the windows being lowered. Then everyone in the back starts firing their guns.

Idiots. They're telling him where to aim with heads out the windows while Dante's SUVs are no-doubt bulletproof. I just keep my head down as chaos engulfs the SUV.

Not chaos.

Dante fucking Salvato.

"What's the plan here?" the driver asks nervously, voice high while the passenger's fingers fly over his phone. If I had to guess, it's too late for him to call for backup. "They're coming up on all sides of us, Jimbo!" the driver warns.

"Try to run the one on the right off the road!" the passenger instructs. "Take us into the desert if you have to."

There's no way they can outrun the SUVs surrounding them by going off-roading through the desert.

There's a loud scrape of metal on metal then the SUV jerks hard like another one crashed into it before we skid to a stop.

"Shoot then run!" one of the men yells to the others.

All the doors are thrown open while I stay hunched on the floorboard, head down, restrained arms covering it, praying that Dante and his guys are better shots than the Russians.

If not...

No, I can't even think that.

Dante is smart and ruthless. He'll probably take all of these assholes out without getting a drop of blood on his suit.

42

Dante

Not again. *Not this fucking shit again. I can't lose Vanessa. I can't.*
Those words are a chant on repeat in my head. Have been ever since I got the call from the men guarding my butterfly telling me that she was dragged into an SUV. They took off before the guards keeping an eye on her could do a goddamn thing.

It had to have been Kozlov's men, but right now I don't give a shit who it was. They're going to die, that's all that matters.

My guards were at least able to follow the SUV, giving me location updates until our fleet of vehicles could catch up.

Firing guns on a dark highway isn't the way I wanted to stop them, but I didn't want to risk them getting away. Putting bullets in the tires slowed them down enough for my four other SUVs to cut them off in every direction. The lead vehicle hits the brakes, causing the assholes to slam into the back of them. I just hope the impact wasn't hard enough to hurt Vanessa.

Once they come to a complete stop, surrounded on every damn side,

291

all the doors fly open as the roaches flee, firing on us while also trying to run away.

None of them appear to have Vanessa, thankfully. They could've already hurt her...

"Kill them all, but keep an eye out for Vanessa," I order Titus when we finally come to a stop on the side of the road, the headlights illuminating the bolting figures. We jump out, guns in our hands to back up my men in the other four SUVs, but there's no more gunfire.

Diesel, the driver of the totaled front car comes limping over to us. "It looks clear, boss. Six dead men. I think we got them all."

"Good work. We lose anyone?" I ask him.

"Three wounded but nothing vital was hit."

"Get them to Dr. Gates."

"Will do," he agrees.

I start toward the empty SUV with the interior lights illuminating the inside, but Titus puts his palm on the center of my chest.

"You should stay back until we make sure no one's hiding and waiting in the vehicle."

"Fuck you," I reply, as I push past him.

"If you take a bullet to the head trying to save her, she'll be pissed," he calls after me.

Since he's right, I keep my gun up and aimed as I approach the SUV while my guys spread out to surround it.

The closer we get, the more worried I am when there's no movement inside. If I was too late, if she's gone, I'll never fucking forgive myself.

And then I see her.

She's on the floorboard in the middle row, curled up in a tiny ball as tight as possible, her hands over her head.

With her back to me I can see blood splattered in her light hair and down the back of her shirt and fuck...her shirt doesn't completely cover her ass that's bare. Those men better rot in hell for this.

"Vanessa?"

She doesn't move. Not a twitch, nothing. I can't tell if she's breathing, and I can't breathe either.

I crawl inside on my hands and knees to her and lay my trembling hand on her shoulder. She flinches away, and it's a relief and misery all at the same time. She's alive. She's alive, and that's all that matters right now.

"Vanessa. It's me. It's me, butterfly."

Her wrists, there's silver duct tape wrapped around them, keeping them held together tightly. Goddamn motherfuckers deserve to die twice for this shit.

Slipping my gun into my shoulder holster, I grab my knife from my pants pocket, opening it to gently slice through the center of the thick tape. Vanessa's entire body seems to relax when they're apart.

I'm careful not to touch her again, I just put my knife back in my pocket and wait her out. Her now free, but still shaking palms, slowly lower from where they covered her head. Now she glances over her shoulder, looking right at me with wide emerald eyes.

"Dante? You...you came for me?"

"Yeah, butterfly. It's me."

"Is it over?"

"It's over. Are you hurt?"

"No. No, I don't think so."

Thank god.

As she uncurls, she twists around, reaching out her hand for me. *Finally.* I grab her up and pull her to me, crushing her against my chest. Her arms wind so tightly around my neck I can barely swallow, but I don't need to. She's alive, and she's in my arms. That's it. That's everything.

My palms smooth up and down her back, but I don't go lower when I remember.

"Vanessa?" My next question gets caught in my throat and I force the words out. "Where are your...bottoms?"

She shakes her head. "They were on the floorboard before the crash. But I'm okay. They were...Kozlov sent them, but they didn't hurt me," she says with her face still pressed to my neck. "They were going to until...until I told them who I was. Who I really am."

Until she told them who she was. Who she really *is.*

"Who are you?" I ask even though I can only think of one female that the Russians wouldn't harm when they had the chance.

"Katia. Katia Petrov." *Motherfucker*. "Yuri Petrov is my father," she adds just in case that much wasn't obvious.

"Katia." The name is so foreign on my tongue, but so right. She was never a Vanessa; she's Katia. But she chose to be Vanessa, a poor, uneducated waitress who flies under the radar. Unless she tells me to, I won't use the name that son of a bitch gave her.

"I'm so sorry I didn't tell you," she whispers. "I couldn't."

My manipulation, forcing her back into this world, being used by Kozlov to get to me, it's all my fault that Yuri not only knows she's alive but where to find her.

"It's okay, butterfly," I tell her because I get it. It doesn't matter to me who she is. There's nothing she could do or say to stop me from loving her.

"Dante," Titus says from behind me. "I'm glad Vanessa is okay, and that the bastards who took her are all dead, but ah, what do you want us to do with all these bodies?"

Shit. While I don't want to let Vanessa go, I know we've got business to take care of.

"Tell me what you want me to do here, boss."

"You ready to go home?" I ask Vanessa.

"Yes."

I don't think either of us needs to elaborate on which home I'm referring to.

Vanessa doesn't ease up her hold on me as I crawl backward to the door with one arm slung around her back.

When we're free of the vehicle, and I can stand up, her legs wrap around my waist as tightly as her looped arms are around my neck. She's safe. She's okay. She's in my arms.

I inhale a deep breath of fresh night air, so fucking relieved I can barely think straight.

First things first, dead bodies need to be handled. Right.

"Put them back in their SUV and blow it," I tell Titus as I carry Vanessa over to a mound of sand on the shoulder. I don't think she's ready to be thrown into the back of another SUV just yet.

Dropping to my knees on the ground, I rub my palm over her hair, smoothing the strands down, hating that there's blood staining it. That it's my fault she was kidnapped.

"I'm sorry," I tell her. "So fucking sorry for dragging you into this shit."

Vanessa finally lifts her face to look at me, legs and arms still locked around me. There's no anger or blame in her eyes. No tears or even fear in them anymore either, thank fuck. I keep forgetting how damn strong she is, and now I know why.

My butterfly was born a mafia princess.

And she was supposed to be my queen.

Jesus. That's it. That's why she hates me. Hated me?

I refused to marry her all those years ago. I have no doubt that if her father was anything like mine, she paid the price when it all fell apart, even if it wasn't her fault.

"You were so damn young, too young for me," I tell her. "But if I had met you back then..."

She doesn't let me finish my sentence. Her lips cover mine. It's a soft, sweet kiss that tastes like everything is right in the world, like home and sweet surrender. Things I never knew existed before tonight.

Vanessa trusts me, feels safe with me, even though she shouldn't. But I would do anything to keep this woman. To protect her. To just fucking try to make her happy.

After the first swipe of our tongues, it's like neither of us can pull the other close enough. Her fingers weave through my hair to hold my mouth on hers as her lower body grinds down on my lap. When she moans, I remember she's not wearing any bottoms. No panties either. My palms slide down lower as she rubs herself on the growing bulge in my pants. It feels fucking amazing, but I hesitate when I hear the whoosh of the SUV going up in big bright flames behind us.

"Can I put my hands on you, butterfly?" I ask around her frantic tongue thrusting against mine. My fingers fist the back of her shirt until she gives me an answer.

While our lips are momentarily separated, Vanessa lifts her blood-stained shirt up and over her head to toss it aside on the sand. Leaning forward she pulls my head to her breasts covered in lace and says, "*When*. All the *when*s are right now, Dante. I need you inside of me."

"Fuck," I groan.

Using my teeth because I don't want to let her go, I pull one of her bra cups down while my palms lower to grab two handfuls of her bare ass. I swipe my tongue over her nipple and take it into my mouth, earning me more soft moans. I'm about to move over to the other when a loud pop from the blazing SUV startles us both, making us jump. It's not the ideal place for this to finally go down, but I'll be damned if I'll complain or stop. I need her now, not in five minutes or when we're alone with a bed. Vanessa obviously feels the same since she's not wearing anything but her bra as she dry humps me on the side of the highway in front of a dozen or so of my men.

That's when I remember our conversation from weeks ago making me chuckle. "Of course you want to fuck me right here, right now covered in blood with an audience while the world burns around us."

"You were right. I was wrong," she says in a rush, her hands working on my belt buckle while I squeeze her ass. "Make it worth the wait?"

Smiling at her words as she finishes undoing my pants, I rub a finger up her slit from behind. I'm worried she may not be as ready for my cock as she thinks. Between the kidnapping, and shooting, I wouldn't expect her to be wet. But thankfully she is as I pump one finger deep inside of her at the same time she strokes my freed cock.

Her mouth comes back to mine, and gripping my shoulders, she starts lowering herself down on the head of my shaft. I barely remove my finger in time before she sinks down that first inch, hot, wet, and so damn tight.

"Take it slow," I say against her lips, but she doesn't listen. I even try to halt her progress with my hands clenching her ass cheeks.

Vanessa's mouth opens against mine on a moan, fingers digging into the front of my shirt, as she takes me deeper. I'm in fucking heaven, loving the snug fit of her body without any latex to dull the amazing sensation of our flesh joining. It's just so fast it has to be mostly pain and only a little pleasure for her. The woman is in a hurry to get me inside of her, and I'm just grateful to be along for the ride.

She slides up and down a few more times before I'm fully sheathed as far as I can go.

Her forehead presses to mine when she bottoms out and goes still.

"Too much and not nearly enough." I know for a fact she isn't complaining about my size, just that she wants more of me. Her silky walls tighten around my cock, and I bark out her name in warning.

"Too fast. It'll be over too fast if you keep that up," I warn her through my clenched teeth as I force my dick to hold off, to not thrust upward into her yet because she needs more time.

"I don't care." Her tongue swipes over the seam of my lips once. "I'll just sit right here on you...and wait for another ride...then another..."

"Jesus."

Our mouths meet again, tongues now thrusting in the same frenzy as our lower bodies moving together.

When Vanessa begins to fuck me faster, I finally let go. Taking control, I lift her ass up and down my cock, thrusting my hips upward when I'm lowering her.

Her head falls back on a shout. I can't tell if it's good or bad until she says, "Yes! Don't stop!"

Over and over again I slam her down. My mouth finds her neck, her exposed breast, anything I can get it on as our bodies finally collide.

I always knew they would sooner or later.

"This, us, it's destiny," I say against her open, panting mouth between thrusts. "I'm yours, and you're mine. Always have been. I'm never letting you go again, butterfly."

Vanessa's fingers tighten in my hair as she throbs around me. She looks me in my eyes, staring into my soul through her entire orgasm. She rides me, owns me, destroys me, and saves me all in a matter of seconds as I go with her.

I don't even know what words leave my lips or if they're nonsense. It's too good, so good, that I want her again, before I even finish coming inside of her.

And when the last of the tremors have left us, Vanessa lays her head on my shoulder and says, "I'm yours. You're mine. Always."

43

Vanessa

D*estiny.*
　　　That's what Dante called us.

He's right.

Being in his strong arms, feeling him still twitching deep inside of me, there is nothing else. Where we are, who is around, what just happened, none of those things matter. It's just me and him finally surrendering to each other after fighting it for so long.

Over twenty years.

Waiting seems so stupid now. Leaving him does too. The excuses I made to not be with Dante all disappear. The kidnapping, the shooting, the rivalry with the Russians that won't be going away anytime soon, all those things can wait until tomorrow.

I just couldn't go another second without him. I needed his hands on me, his mouth, to feel him moving inside of me.

Dante had already gotten under my skin, invaded every thought in my head, and held my heart hostage. He may as well put his gun to the organ because it's impossible for me to stop loving him. He could shred me apart, and there's nothing I could do about it.

It's a gamble I'm willing to take.

The sound of sirens approaching put a damper on our moment, smothering most of the blissful haze clouding my thoughts, but not completely.

Lifting my head from his shoulder, I actually take in our surroundings again. There are dead men going up in flames within the SUV, ones who just kidnapped me. They all deserve to burn to ashes.

"We need to leave, don't we?" I ask Dante.

"Unfortunately."

When he lifts my bottom up to unimpale me from his still half-hard cock, we both groan at the loss.

I reach down to fix the cups of my bra and then go still when gravity causes a gush of fluids to slip from inside of me. I know Dante can't get me pregnant, and I trust him to get tested for everything regularly with his active sex life. It's just messy. "It would be nice to have underwear now," I tell him. "You left a gallon between my legs."

Chuckling, Dante presses a kiss to my forehead and says, "Cleanup with your bloody shirt then we'll toss it in the fire." He removes his hands from my bottom to fix his pants, then removes his shoulder holster to begin unbuttoning his light blue button down. I didn't even take the time to remove all of his clothing. Later. I will get this man naked later and spend a very long time kissing and touching every incredible inch of him I can reach while he's inside of me. "You can wear my shirt home."

Dante slips the material down his arms and helps me slide his shirt on. He even takes the time to button every little button as if he's not in a hurry even with blue lights on the horizon.

Kneeling in just his snug white tee and dress pants, the dark tattoos on his arms clearly visible, he's not nearly as intimidating. No, he just looks mouthwateringly sexy, not dangerous. No wonder he prefers the suit. If he walked around looking like this all the time, he'd be mobbed by women everywhere he went.

"Where's your jacket?" I can't help but ask when he gets his shoulder holster back on again.

"No clue. It must still be in my office. I can't say it was a priority when I got the call that you had been kidnapped."

"You had your men watching me?"

"Only two. I fucking hate that they weren't fast enough to stop them from leaving with you. At least they were able to follow."

"There was no time to grab my gun either. I was in the parking lot one second and the next..."

"I know. I'm sorry."

"No, I'm sorry I left you. If I hadn't...well, he knows who I am now, Dante. And I'm not sure what he might do." I remind him about the problem with my father.

"We'll figure out a way to take him out together," he says. "I'm not even sure he picked you up in retaliation for me killing his men."

"You aren't?"

"Maybe I'm wrong. It's possible. But losing the three mothers to my daughters, then you are taken...it seems like too big of a coincidence."

"Oh my god," I whisper in understanding as my stomach drops. "You think my father killed them all to retaliate for you refusing to marry me?"

"Yes," he says simply. "We'll talk about this more later. For now..."

"I'll clean up before cum drips all over your pants, then we can leave." I grab onto his shoulders to stand up.

"Too late," he says, holding my waist to stop me from getting up. His handsome face is suddenly crestfallen, solemn, like he lost someone he loved. "You and I...we would've made beautiful babies together."

I didn't cry when I was kidnapped, or when they were about to assault me. I didn't shed a tear when the shooting started or when it was all over. But Dante's words of regret nearly break me.

Cupping the sides of his face, trailing my fingertips down his scruffy beard, I tell him, "I know we won't ever have any children together, but we can share the four beautiful, pain in the ass ones we do have. And then our grandkids someday soon..."

"Don't even joke about that shit, butterfly."

Smiling, I give him a quick kiss on the lips, and he releases my waist so I can go clean up with my destroyed shirt.

~

Dante carries me through the casino, both of us such a mess that all eyes follow us. There's blood in my hair, and all I'm wearing is his blue button-down that's swallowing me whole. Dante's in his snug white T-shirt and has dirt all over his pants, his gun visible in his shoulder holster.

The elevator is packed and slower than usual, or at least it seems that way.

And when we finally walk through the penthouse doors, I wasn't expecting to be confronted by anyone. Sophie and Cass both stand up from where they were sitting and waiting on the stairs at the entryway.

"What happened?" Sophie demands.

"Is Vanessa okay?" Cass asks.

"I'm fine," I assure them.

"Vanessa was kidnapped by six Russians before the two guards I had watching her could do anything to stop them." I can tell by his tone that Dante wants them to remember how horrible I look and how badly it could've ended so they don't try and run away like Madison. "She was lucky. They took her clothes off and were about to...hurt her when we caught up to them. I'll let you both fill in the blanks about what they would've done to her, what they would do to *you* if they can get their hands on you."

"Dante," I whisper because he shouldn't scare them like that.

"We're going to wash the blood off of us. You two should go to bed."

Sophie turns and heads upstairs without another word, but Cassandra says, "I'm glad you're okay, Vanessa."

"Thank you, Cass."

"Do you think Madison..." she trails off and looks to her dad.

"Madison wasn't kidnapped by anyone. She ran away on her own," he reminds her. "If my people can't find her, then I'm certain nobody else knows who she really is either."

Sophie who was waiting on her father's response exhales a breath of relief. "I miss her."

"Me too," Dante says as he starts down the hallway. "Maybe she'll call when she's settled..."

I don't think he actually believes that, but I bet in a few days or weeks he'll lie to the girls and tell them she reached out and is fine just so they won't worry.

"Let's get you cleaned up," he says, dropping the topic for now.

Taking me into his bathroom, he sets me down on the sink counter to turn on the shower spray.

Dante gets undressed in the closet while the water warms up.

Even though I've seen him naked plenty of times, he still takes my breath away when he returns to the bathroom. Stopping in front of me he lifts both of my hands gently and turns my wrists over, frowning down at the sliced duct tape still covering them.

"Quick like a Band-Aid?" he asks.

"Sure."

I barely wince when he rips the tape from my left hand, then my right, tossing the silver pieces into the trash bin. Lifting my hands, he rubs his thumb over the red skin. "I'm sorry they didn't die slower for what they did to you, butterfly."

"I'm just glad they're dead," I admit honestly.

Dante then picks me up to carry me into the shower. I think he would've kept holding me except he needs both hands to wash, so he sits me down on the shower seat. I don't complain since my legs still feel weak from the earlier orgasm. I never thought I would be the type of woman to have sex with a man in public, in front of other men, but I don't regret it.

"Can you hand me the shampoo?" I ask.

Instead of passing the bottle to me, he pulls one of the showerheads free from the mount and brings it over to wet my hair.

I tilt my head back to keep it out of my eyes. And wow, the warm water feels amazing.

When my hair is completely saturated, Dante lets the showerhead hang against the wall to grab a shampoo bottle from the built-in shelf. He squirts some liquid into the palm of his hand, then begins massaging it into my scalp.

"I can't promise this will be the last time there will be blood in your hair," he says as he works up a lather. "But I'll try."

"I know." I stand up, clutching his damp biceps and going up on my toes to place a quick kiss on his frown. At the same time Dante's large hands nearly envelop my entire waist. "I'm willing to take the good with the bad. You're worth the risks."

"You didn't think so a few days ago."

"I panicked before. The bombing was an excuse to walk away before you broke my heart."

Guiding me over to one of the still mounted shower heads to rinse the shampoo from my hair, he says, "I promise to never break your heart."

My lips part, getting ready to tell him not to make promises he can't keep when Dante's hand slips between my legs, cupping me possessively, making me forget how to speak for a moment.

"I can't make the same promise for your pussy," he says with a hint of a smile that I return.

"So romantic."

His long middle finger penetrates me, stealing my breath. He pumps the digit in and out, slowly, teasingly. "Now that I know how good you feel, how I fit so perfectly in your body, I want to bury myself inside of you and never leave again."

"How about we start with you being buried inside of me all night?" I ask, gripping his biceps tighter as his talented fingers move inside of me while his thumb strums my clit.

"That's not nearly long enough, but I'll take it." Dante lowers his mouth to mine, the kiss soft and sweet, the opposite of his fingers moving faster, pressing harder, working me into a frenzy.

My fingernails dig into his hard biceps as our tongues collide. Soon my hips begin to buck, chasing a release. I close my eyes and lean into Dante's warm body when the waves of pleasure nearly obliterate me.

A moment later, my back is pressed to the cool tile as Dante hoists me up by the backs of my thighs. Spreading them apart, he lines up his cock to my entrance and slides the first few inches inside of me, setting off more fireworks as my body stretches to accommodate his immense size.

"*Dante!*" I exclaim in praise and gratitude. Wrapping my arms around his neck, I squirm as much as I can with him pinning me to the wall, even clenching the muscles around him. I try to pull him impossibly closer, needing him deeper, greedy for more of him, right now, even if it hurts. I want all of him.

"So impatient," Dante mutters against my lips as he leisurely fills me. "You'll get every inch soon enough, butterfly. I think you'll enjoy keeping my cock warm inside your pussy even more than you liked it in your mouth all night."

"Yes!" I agree, totally on board with that plan.

As soon as he bottoms out, grinding his pelvis against my clit while he stretches me, I pulse around him with another orgasm.

44

Dante

Vanessa screams my name again when she throws her head back against the shower wall. Her pussy throbs around my cock, trying to pull me in deeper as I fuck her slowly.

The urge to slam inside of her hard and fast creates a battle of wills. But since I meant what I said about staying buried inside of her all night, I know I have to go easy. In the morning, when the sun comes up, I'll take her hard. Until then, I'm going slow and easy, moving just enough to make us both crave more, to make Vanessa keep coming for me.

Her green, heavy eyes blink open again once the last of her tremors pass. "You feel...so good. Don't stop, even if I fall asleep."

"I wasn't planning on it," I tell her honestly. "You're mine. Your body belongs to me. In the morning, neither you nor your pussy will be able to forget who fucking owns it now."

Rather than be indignant that I'm laying claim to her body, Vanessa just gives me a satisfied smile before she says, "Good."

We hold each other's gazes with our bodies joined. I continue moving gently in and out of her, lifting her up and down the wall. It feels good to not be in a rush for the finish line, to just enjoy her slick warmth embracing me, every second of the buildup because she made me work for this. It feels like I earned it. Earned her.

For once, I'm not just going through the motions that are part of the act of fucking someone. No, this is our night of reckoning.

After twenty years of fighting fate, Vanessa is finally mine.

And when I come inside of her for the second time with her staring into my soul, I feel stripped bare, more naked than I have ever been in my entire life.

Vanessa knows how much I love her, that I would do anything for her, and that there's no going back now.

By the time I turn the water off and wrap a towel around us to dry us off, Vanessa's head is slumped on my shoulder. She's still sound asleep when I take her to bed, the glow of the nightstand lamp the only light in the dark room. With both of us lying on our sides facing each other, I pull her close to my chest. My palm runs up and down her leg that I eventually hike up over mine. Taking my half-stiff cock in my hand, I swipe the head over her damp entrance, then sink home again.

Her tight, wet pussy surrounding my flesh makes me lengthen and harden again in a hurry. I rock in and out of her body three times before Vanessa wakes up and moans.

"Yes. More." Eyes still closed, she swivels and thrusts her hips searching for more friction that I withhold on purpose.

Brushing the damp hair back from her face, I say, "First, tell me what happened back, what, twenty-one years ago?"

That question has her waking up fast. Her eyes are wide open and clear again in an instant. "You...you want to talk about that? Now?"

"Yes. Tell me. The faster you talk the faster we can..."

"Ah, okay," she quickly begins. Her gaze lowers to where her fingertips are travelling over my arm that's resting on her raised leg thrown over my own. "Well, I crushed on you hard from afar, or at least I crushed on the *idea* of you. And you, you flat out rejected me."

Reaching up to lift her chin so she'll look at me again, I tell her, "I was never rejecting you personally. I'm sorry if you thought that was the case."

"It felt personal to me. I was a silly, sheltered, barely sixteen-year-old girl. My father wanted me to meet you, to try and seduce you before you refused, but I wouldn't. I was too nervous, had never even dated anyone before. So, then of course he blamed me for the arrangement falling apart."

"He hurt you?"

"It wasn't like it was the first time he took his temper out on me. He did the same to my mother, beat her so much that eventually she just kept her head down and her mouth shut unless she was pouring bottles of wine down her throat."

Cupping her face in my palm, I tell her, "I'm sorry he did that to you. Is that when you ran away?"

"Yes. I had to...I hurt three guards to get away, maybe even killed them. I never found out..."

"You did what you had to do," I assure her. "Those men, if they worked for Petrov then they weren't saints."

"Still. I had to live with the guilt, the selfish thing I did, hurting others to escape."

"Put all that blame on Petrov for what he did to you, no one else. My father beat the shit out of me too."

"He did?"

"When your father was so pissed that he wanted me dead, my father beat me then sent me to stay with distant relatives of his in Italy. My old man hated me, but he knew that if I died, Petrov and the Russians would take over his territory when he was gone. He considered me a better option than losing his empire entirely. Then, weeks later, Petrov suddenly called a truce."

"That was because he couldn't find me to drag me back even after months of being on the run," Vanessa explains. "If you had changed your mind, there wouldn't have been a bride at the altar when I turned eighteen."

"Where did you go?"

"I got as far away as possible at first. But then, after I had Cole, I came back to Nevada. I knew he was probably still searching for me and wouldn't think I would still be in the state."

"And coming to work for me four years ago?" I ask, wondering what the hell she was thinking.

She shrugs. "I did need a job, and I saw the job posting online for a cocktail waitress, so I applied. I thought that if I got it, then I might get a chance to finally meet you face-to-face."

"Meet me or tell me off?"

Smiling, Vanessa says, "I was planning to throw a drink in your face, call you an asshole, or something along those lines. But then you came into the lounge one night, and I couldn't move. I just froze. You were this intimidating man with a commanding presence bigger than the entire casino. And then you spoke to me..."

"I remember that night." I slide my hand around to squeeze Vanessa's bare ass, then thrust into her hard enough to make her gasp and moan. "You looked like a doe in headlights. I asked if you were new because I was certain I had never seen your beautiful face around the casino before."

She nods with her lips parted as I slowly thrust in and out of her. "And when I said yes, you offered to show me a good time."

"I remember that too. Your black dress was so short and tight. You were so petite. I wanted to bend you over and take you hard right then and there on the table." My cock twitches as it gets even harder inside of Vanessa. She must like the sensation because her walls clench.

Sinking her teeth into her bottom lip she nods, and says, "Yes. You made it *very* clear that you wanted me. And I was so thrown off by that because I had assumed for years that I wasn't your type, that you weren't attracted to me. Then I realized you probably slept with every woman you meet. But at that moment you wanted me, and I finally had the chance to reject you back."

"So, you did." I remember how shitty all her rejections felt, how I thought I would never get to have the one woman I wanted more than any other. The memories have my hips pumping into Vanessa a little faster.

"I-I did." Her words are breathless as if she's getting worked up again when she glances up at my face. "Mmmm. And it felt so good.

Better than throwing a stupid drink in your face and you killing me for the insult."

That makes me freeze, my dick included. "You thought I would kill you for throwing a drink in my face?"

"Yes. Possibly. There were rumors about your lovers and guards..."

"That I killed them?"

"Yes."

"I've never killed a woman."

Vanessa presses her palm to my chest. At first, I think she's trying to push me away, until I roll to my back, and she follows with me still inside of her. Now she's naked and riding me with her damp hair trailing over her bouncing tits. She's the sexiest thing I've ever seen.

"I know that now," she says as she begins to move on me. It takes me a minute to remember what we were talking about. Then I wish I didn't remember. "Back then, you were just so scary. But I kept working here because I knew my father still hated you and wouldn't ever think to look for me in his town, so close to his turf, on your property."

Gripping her hips, I thrust up into her, unable to wait any longer, ready for this conversation to be over.

"And then I manipulated you into an agreement for Mitch's life that put you front and center on the mafia stage again," I grit out between my clenched teeth.

"I-I didn't think anyone would figure out who I was after so many years had passed," Vanessa says, bracing her palms on my chest while rolling her hips. "And nobody did. Not even the Russians, until I told them. They...they didn't even believe me at first. None of them knew my father had a daughter."

If we keep talking about this shit, I'll lose my hard-on. Still, I tell her, "The crew who knew you have probably all died out."

"Probably so. The ringleader in the SUV called Kozlov... sent him a picture he took of me. He told them to give him time to look into it."

"So Kozlov knows who you are, and we have to assume Petrov and the rest of the Russians know too."

I slam her down on my dick while thrusting up hard.

"Yes! I'm so sorry! If I had known...if I had known you would find me, that you would stop them..." she trails off.

Sliding my hands up to cup both of her breasts, I tell her, "You did what you had to do to keep their fucking hands off you. I don't blame you. I'm glad you spoke up, because I would've lost my mind if they had touched what's mine."

Leaning forward, she says, "Now I'm done talking, and so are you," before her lips slam down on mine. Our tongues clash as Vanessa rides me, until she slows down, about to get herself off.

Needing another release of my own, I sit up so we're chest to chest, grabbing her ass to move her how I want, harder, faster.

Vanessa's fingers thread through my damp hair and pull it. "Yes! Yes! Oh god! I'm so close."

"Come on my cock, butterfly." I reach underneath her to press my fingers to her clit, setting her off instantly.

With her head thrown back, heavy breasts bouncing in my face, she's the most beautiful woman in the fucking world.

And she's mine.

45

Vanessa

A fter my...however many orgasms I've had tonight, Dante lays back down on the pillow with me still draped over his body.

When his arms come around me, holding me tightly to him, he says, "Stay right there, just for a little longer, butterfly."

"Mmm. Not going anywhere," I mumble resting my cheek on his rising and falling chest. "You feel so good. So safe."

Dante doesn't reply for a long moment, then says, "Safe?"

I nod without lifting my head. "I always felt safe here with you. Even the first night. I'm sorry that I didn't appreciate it at the time."

His big, warm palms gently coax up and down my spine.

"You've spent your entire life constantly looking over your shoulder. I know how that feels. You make me feel safe too."

"I do? Little ole me?" I tease with a smile on my face he can't see.

"Other women I fucked, I wouldn't dare fall asleep with them, knowing they could rob me or slit my throat. I never worried about that with you. Well, it took a day or two to be confident you wouldn't slit my throat."

"I don't blame you."

"But I also knew that if someone were to sneak past the guards and attack me in the night, you would shoot them to save me."

"Oh yeah? You thought I would save you, even the first few days?" I ask in disbelief, surprised to hear such a tough man admit that he thinks I could save him.

"Even the first few days. As soon as my men found the gun hiding under your mattress, I knew not to underestimate you. I still didn't fully trust you not to fuck me over until I started giving you screaming orgasms."

"Right, because only a crazy woman would kill the man who gets her off," I joke. I do believe him, though, that he trusts me and even thinks I could be dangerous in my own right. He thought so before he found out who I was, the life I was born into.

"How did you become Vanessa Brooks?" Dante asks.

"Her parents really did die in a car crash. They were traveling in an RV, on their way from Texas to Washington state on a family vacation. They wrecked in California, the parents dying instantly. Their fifteen-year-old daughter was in a coma until the doctors pulled the plug. No family or friends came for any of their bodies. I had been waiting so..."

"When you heard about them, you decided to take over her identity?"

"I was homeless, crashing in an empty dorm room nearby, hiding there, when the accident happened. Then I just had to find a tech genius on campus who could get in the system to delete her death certificate."

"I don't want to know how you convinced this tech genius to help you," Dante grumbles making me smile.

"I hated using her death for my gain, but I didn't have any other options."

Which unfortunately reminds me of other deaths....

Trailing my fingertips over the black wings tattooed on his chest, I voice the unpleasantness he mentioned earlier. "You think my father could be responsible for killing the girls' mothers?"

Sadly, his palms soothing up and down my back stop suddenly.

"Yes. It's just too big of a coincidence to lose them all. Petrov could've set up the Irish to take the fall for Madison's mother getting gunned down. I wouldn't be surprised if Cass's mother was killed by him when she disappeared, or he kidnapped her. And Sophie's mother, the doctors said she died from a complication of the C-section, but she was fine the last time I saw her."

"I wouldn't put something so horrible past my father. But why wait until these women had your children before killing them?"

"I don't know. To torture me even more?" he mutters. "Maybe because he couldn't keep up with who I was seeing until my name showed up on the birth certificates."

My throat burns at the thought of my father doing something so cruel, hurting innocent women just to torment Dante. "He killed three innocent women, three new mothers, because he wanted to punish you for not marrying me."

"If I had realized it before, well, he would've been dead a long time ago. Once you were kidnapped by his men, I became even more certain. After the bombing too."

"What do you mean?"

"I believe Yuri has been hitting my warehouses. He wants to take over the fentanyl trafficking from me, and the whore trade from Lochlan. That's why I think he planted the bomb where he did, to try and take us both out, cause rifts between our people. Best of all, he could use the excuse that he was just retaliating for me killing his two enforcers to get his men to agree."

"So, the bombing, it wasn't about the loss of his two men at all," I remark. "God, Dante. I'm so sorry that I blamed you."

Wrapping his arms around me tightly, he says, "And I'm sorry that I put all the blame for Madison leaving on you. You were right. It was my fault she left. The tighter I hold on to the girls, the more they'll try to push me away to be free."

"One day you will find Madison safe and sound," I promise him, placing a kiss on his throat. "Until then, maybe you could think about giving Cass and Sophie a little more freedom?"

"I'll think about it. I already told Cass I might let her compete in a tournament. Only after we handle Yuri."

"Agreed," I say with a sigh. "He has to die."

"Of course, he does."

Lifting my head to stare down at Dante, I tell him, "But you can't go after him in a blind rage. We need to have a foolproof plan to make it happen."

"I couldn't agree more, butterfly." He brushes his lips over mine softly. When he pulls back, his brow furrows as if he had a sudden thought he doesn't like.

"What?" I ask. "Well, other than the obvious?"

His long fingers strum against my back as if figuring out what to say before finally speaking. "Once Yuri is gone, he'll probably be replaced by Kozlov who does all his dirty work and could be even worse than him. Have you thought about stepping up, taking over?"

I shake my head. "No. I never wanted this life for myself. He knew that, and he picked you out of all the men to marry me, to have your son or daughter who would rule the Italian and Russian underworld."

"Yuri probably doesn't know about Cole yet. You should warn him."

"I will," I agree.

Kissing the top of my head, Dante says, "I'll send someone to the school to look out for him."

"Thank you. I sure as hell never wanted this life for Cole either. It's why I ran and never looked back."

"Well, it's too late now. You're back in it, at least with me, which means it's Cole's world too now."

"I plan to keep him as far away as possible. This is the first time I've been glad that he's on the other side of the country. My father is going to know that you're coming after him," I warn Dante before resting my cheek on his chest again.

Dante's palms also return to their soothing caress. "Yes, he'll be anticipating a direct attack."

"So how about an indirect one?" I ask.

"What do you mean?"

"Yuri doesn't know you and I are together."

Dante sighs heavily. "Of course, he does. That's the reason he had you kidnapped."

"True, but plenty of people also know that you manipulated me with the deal to let Mitch live."

A growl of frustration is Dante's response, as if he still doesn't care for the m-word. Lifting my head I tell him, "Like it or not, this, our relationship, began from your manipulation. Not that I'm complaining now," I add when I clench my inner walls around his shaft that's still buried within me, making him groan and his dick twitches to life again.

In the blink of my eyes, I'm on my back with Dante's weight pressing on top of me. His lips and tongue are feasting on my neck while he lengthens and thrusts deeper inside of me. "You already know the perfect way to distract me from my anger, butterfly."

"Yes, I do, but before you start making me forget my own name, let me finish my thought."

Dante goes still. "Fine. Make it fast."

"All I'm saying is that we use that information, the truth, to hurt him. Kozlov knows that you paid off the debt for Mitch, right?"

"Yes."

When he applies suction to my neck, I grab the sides of his head to stop him. "No visible hickeys. That'll ruin my idea."

"Then I already hate your idea." Dante still lifts his mouth from my neck to look at my face. "But do continue, so we can continue. What are you getting at here, Vanessa?"

"What if you bargain a truce with him?"

"A truce?" Dante repeats with a scowl that says there's no way in hell.

"A truce to stop the violence, the attacks on your business empire, in exchange for you giving me to him."

Sitting back on his heels, his palms slide down my legs on either side of him as he says, "You *want* me to hand you over to your father willingly? I thought that was the last thing you wanted. All these years you've tried to avoid him..."

"Yes. Well, I'm still his daughter. His possession. He'll want me back, then want to use me for his own purposes."

"No, Vanessa. He'll hurt you..."

"He'll underestimate me. And he won't hurt me. Not after I tell him I had the son he always wanted—smart, charismatic, a little ruthless, and with the potential to be business savvy. I'll dangle the carrot of the perfect heir."

"Why would Petrov buy you coming home to him with open arms now after all these years?"

"Well, I won't be. Not at first. You'll be handing me over against my will. And then, well, I'll let him convince me that I'm tired of the daily grind of poverty. I'll reluctantly tell him I've decided that I want more for Cole—a better future for him now that he's grown. I'm sure even my father can understand that I didn't want my son exposed to his dangerous lifestyle as a child. But now..."

"Now you'll let him think you're ready to let Cole take over the family business," Dante finishes.

"Exactly."

"One problem. If he does welcome you back, he's not going to let you leave."

"Oh, I'll leave."

"How, butterfly?"

"I plan to step right over his dead body," I reply with a smile.

"You're going to kill him?" With those words, Dante's dick doubles in size, taking up all the available space within me. For the mafia king, murdering assholes who deserve it really is an aphrodisiac. His blue eyes darken as the arousal overcomes him. When he lifts each of my legs straight up to rest on his chest, I know we won't be talking much longer.

"I'm...I'm the only one who can get close enough to do it," I say in a rush just before Dante pulls nearly all the way out to slam deep inside me again.

"We'll need to plan all of this...carefully," he says as he starts to move slowly, methodically in and out. His thumb circles and presses on my clit, scattering my thoughts.

"*Yesss,*" I agree, with his statement and fingers.

Dante is still thinking things through as he moves. "And why would he believe I would be willing to turn you over based solely on his word that there won't be any more attacks on me?"

"Because you don't want to look over your shoulder more than usual, and you want him to stay out of your fentanyl business."

"I guess those are good enough reasons..."

"What do you mean? You think we need something better?"

"I was thinking I could agree to the offer he made me twenty years ago," Dante explains while hitting the deepest spot inside of me.

"What?" I ask since he's lost me. I'm too close to coming now.

"I could tell him he can have you back, if he makes you marry me."

That grabs my attention away from the pleasure. "Makes me marry you?"

Dante stops moving too, which I hate. "Even if he has to drag you down the aisle in a white dress and twist your arm until you say those two words."

"He wouldn't have to twist very hard," I admit, arching my back to roll my hips faster and faster, fucking him from the bottom.

Dante groans to the ceiling, jaw clenched tight, but he doesn't move, letting me have my way with his cock.

Then I ruin the moment by voicing a concern. "One problem with that plan is...he wanted you to give him an heir to the empire. Now... now he probably knows you can't have any more children."

Dante's massive hand strokes down my leg, over my stomach, between my breasts before squeezing the right one. "I don't think that would be a problem."

"Why not?"

"Not if I agree Cole will be my heir too."

"That's not even a little funny," I scoff. "And you're ruining the mood."

"My dick can wait. We've got all day," Dante replies with a grin.

"Well, no need to make your dick wait. This discussion is over."

"You won't even consider asking Cole what he wants, letting him make his own decision? What if he wants to be a part of this world?"

"No."

"So, you'll fuck and love a gangster, but it's not good enough for your son?"

"That's not..." I try to lower my legs but Dante grabs both of my ankles, holding them tight to his shoulders so I can't move them.

319

"Not what? The truth?"

"Those two things aren't even close to being the same. Now let my ankles go and get your dick out of me."

"No."

"No?" I repeat with an indignant huff.

"I'm never letting you walk away angry from me again," he says, placing a kiss on the inside of my ankle. "I just got you back. I don't want to lose you again."

"Then don't ever bring up my son again, especially while we're fucking!"

Dante presses my legs together so he can wrap one arm around them both, making me impossibly tighter with him still buried deep. Then, the bastard shoves his thumb into his mouth, sucking on it before lowering it, pressing it to my clit.

"Asshole," I grumble while trying to grab his thumb and squirm away. His tattooed hand is unmovable. And the more I squirm, the better it feels until I relent, my head falling back on a moan.

"I know how to distract you from your anger too, butterfly," Dante informs me, his handsome face smug as hell. "Now, I'm gonna flip you over to your stomach and fuck your brains out until you scream my name and come on my cock. Then, we'll make a plan to kill your father, and table the discussion about your son's future for the time being. Agreed?"

I nod since forming words seems impossible at the moment.

"Good girl," he replies. Those two words make me want to give the mafia king anything he wants, which is confusing and ridiculously arousing. "Now squeeze my dick tight while I turn you over without pulling out. Not being inside of your hot, wet pussy for even a second is too long."

"How—oh god!" I groan as he makes good on his promise. At first Dante rolls me to my side. Then, with a little adjustment of his knees, I'm flat on my stomach with him straddling both of my legs that are pushed together tightly. His weight presses down on me, pinning me into the mattress, as he slams into me over and over again in that perfect way.

46

Dante

Sex with Vanessa is even better than I imagined. I can't get enough. Thankfully, she seems to feel the same way.

Unfortunately, after about twenty-four hours of rolling in the sheets, we both have to leave the bedroom to handle business. And while I don't particularly care for Vanessa's idea for me to hand her over to her father, I don't have any better ones.

That's how we ended up in the basement tonight, with her being tied to a chair.

"Don't even think about restraining her wrists," I warn Titus when he picks up the stack of zip ties from the workbench.

Titus oversees all the guards. He had a come to Jesus meeting with them about not saying a word to anyone about what they see or hear while in my service. Then he picked the three he trusts the most to join us for part one of our plan.

"It's okay, Dante," Vanessa says softly, even though I know that's a lie. Her palms slide forward ironing out invisible wrinkles in the lap of her simple lavender dress. After having her wrists bound with duct tape by those assholes who kidnapped her, I can't imagine she would want to relive that, even to pull off a convincing performance for her father.

"No. Just keep your hands behind the chair," I instruct her. "He won't need to see the back of it."

"It's fine. Just gag me and restrain my wrists and ankles. We can't risk any mistakes selling this big of a lie to my father. Being cautious and overly paranoid about every little thing is how he's managed to stay alive this long."

"Are you sure you can handle those things, though?"

"We haven't had a chance to explore this topic yet, but I don't mind being tied up if it's you who is restraining me."

"Is that right?"

"Besides, it'll be nice to replace the memories from the other night with something...better."

If I couldn't grasp the sultry meaning behind her words, her hard nipples poking through her cotton dress would've done the trick.

"I'm more than happy to oblige in replacing those memories after we finish this call, butterfly." Going over to Titus, I snatch the handful of plastic from his hands. "I'll take care of the ties."

"Go for it," he agrees. "I'm still not sure who you two think you're gonna fool here."

"You and the three guards just need to stand around looking stern and keeping an eye on Vanessa, as if you expect her to try to bolt. She'll be acting the part of a hostile captive who hates me and would rather be anywhere but here in my torture dungeon."

"Good luck with that, boss." He chuckles. "Right now, she looks like she's begging for your dick with her pointy nipples and thighs wide open."

Hearing his remark, Vanessa quickly snaps her knees together. "Sorry. Give me some tissue to stuff in my bra?"

"I've got you," I assure her as I head for the back of her chair. Vanessa offers me both wrists that I wrap the plastic zip tie around and fasten loosely. So loose she could easily shake them off if she wanted. "That feel okay?"

She nods her head and rolls her shoulders. "Yes."

Walking around to the front of her chair, I kneel down to clasp her right ankle to one chair leg with the plastic ties, then the left while Vanessa watches me work silently.

"Good?"

"Yes." She sounds a little breathless now, like she is enjoying being at my mercy.

Pulling my blue silk handkerchief from the front pocket of my suit, I rip it in half to make two pieces. I fold the first half into a small rectangle then slide it down the front of Vanessa's dress, into her bra cup. She gasps when my fingers brush over her nipples before covering them with the material on her right breast, then the left.

Vanessa squirms as I stand up, taking a few steps back to look at my handiwork, making sure the lines of the newly added fabric aren't showing through her dress.

"No more nipples showing, and with the ankles attached to the chair legs, it looks like you're shyly, desperately trying to clamp your thighs together but can't. All that's missing from making you the perfect victim is a gag. Unless you think it's too much?"

"No. Gag me. The less I talk, the less chance I say something to fuck this up."

"Something like, *Dante, I hate you, but I love your tongue. Will you pretty please lick my pussy while I'm your powerless captive?*"

Vanessa rolls her eyes but smiles. "Right. Exactly that."

Pinching my bottom lip between my finger and thumb as I imagine it, I tell her, "Just so you know, if we manage to convince the bastard on this call, I plan to do just that to you before cutting the ties."

"Oh, Jesus," Titus mutters from behind me. "This is never going to work. She's about to make a puddle of pussy juice in that chair."

"He's not wrong," Vanessa replies. She then whispers loudly, "And I'm not wearing any panties."

Every male in the room groans at those five fucktastic words, myself included. I know exactly what game she's playing at now. She wouldn't have said that for them to hear if she didn't want them to know her secret too. Vanessa doesn't just want me to lick her pussy while she's tied up; she wants to let them watch me eat her out.

"My butterfly is an exhibitionist. And since I don't mind showing the world exactly who she belongs to, I'll gladly indulge her fetish after the call."

Vanessa pretends to look surprised and dismayed, already breaking out the acting skills.

"Gag her with something so we can get this over with," I instruct Titus.

"Fuck yes," he agrees as he turns back to the workbench.

"Preferably something clean," I add.

"How about this?" He turns around holding up the two-foot long, nylon bungee strap.

"If you wrap it around two or three times then hook the ends together it could work," I agree. "Vanessa?"

"Better than the splintery, bloody rope over there," she replies, nodding her head toward the pile on the end of the workbench.

"Fasten it, then I want the three guards to get into position, one standing on either side of her and one behind. Titus with me."

"Sure thing, boss," Titus agrees. He jerks his chin to call the three guards over, then positions them before stepping behind Vanessa to secure the rope. When she stares at me while opening her mouth wide for him, I nearly postpone this whole thing until after I fuck her throat to remind her who it belongs to.

After.

After I lick her pussy and get so hard when she comes on my tongue that I'm ready to explode, I'll fuck her throat. Yeah, I wouldn't mind letting my men see that encounter either.

I have a feeling that after all this shit with Petrov is over, Vanessa and I are going to be giving my employees more free shows than they'll know what to do with.

Clearing my throat, I wrench my eyes from Titus fitting the rope to Vanessa's mouth to scroll through the contacts in my phone, searching for the number I've only used a handful of times since I took over for my father.

When I glance up again, the rope is wrapped around Vanessa's head twice, cinched tight so it forces her lips and teeth apart. Oh, hell yeah, I'm going to leave that in place while I eat her out.

324

"Everyone ready?" I ask. The guards nod and so does Vanessa. We hold each other's gaze as we both take a deep breath, ready to get into our roles. Vanessa's warm eyes now glare at me with a bone-deep hatred. I know it's actually for her father, but it stings a little.

And I know I have to put on my own mask of indifference for her now. For a few minutes, I need to act like she's nothing but a prized possession to be owned or sold at my sole discretion. An object like my cell phone that I can toss aside, easily replace, or trash without a second of guilt. During this call, Vanessa can't be the woman I love, but an insignificant pawn being used in a bigger game.

Eager to get this over with, I make a video call to Yuri Petrov, certain he'll be too curious not to answer my call.

It rings several times before his face fills the screen, my own tiny image in the bottom corner. His thick head of hair and full beard are both snow white when they used to be light blonde, just like Vanessa's.

"Dante. You're still alive after that awful bombing. What a relief," he says sarcastically, his face expressionless, not giving anything away. Not even blinking at the mention of his own attack that killed so many innocent men and women. I don't sleep well every night even though I've never killed anyone who didn't deserve it. I'm not sure how Yuri Petrov even closes his eyes without seeing the faces of all those he hurt for the hell of it. I hope they haunt him, if not now then in his afterlife that's just around the corner. The girls' mothers shouldn't give him a moment's peace. They didn't deserve what he did to them. My daughters didn't deserve to lose their mothers before they even knew them because this motherfucker had some vendetta against me. And if Vanessa hadn't spoken up, she would've joined them in their graves.

Forcing those thoughts down, I try to keep my face devoid of emotion, refusing to show him my anger, my sadness, my guilt for even a second.

"I know it was your fucking bomb, and that Lochlan and I were the targets. But as you can see, I'm alive and well. And I'm also in possession of something I believe you lost." I quickly steer the conversation where I want it to go, to Vanessa, before I promise to rip his head off his shoulder or some other violent threat he'll see coming from a mile away.

"Is that right? What possession would that be?" he asks, playing dumb.

"I always wondered what happened to that daughter of yours. Katia was her name years ago. She goes by Vanessa now..."

The old man's left eye twitches, an uncontrollable tick that lets me know I hit a nerve. "Her name *is* Katia. How the fuck did you end up with her anyway?"

Yes, I do believe he's angry at Vanessa for not only running away but being smart enough to never allow him to find her. God, and now Madison is doing the same damn thing to me. I will find her, though.

"You're really going to pretend like you didn't send her to spy on me, to tell you where I would be and when so you could try to take me out?"

That exaggeration was Vanessa's idea, reminding me to think like a gangster—that she came to my hotel with ulterior motives and played the long game. I know that's bullshit, but if I had found out who she was on my own, I may have considered her a spy.

"I haven't seen her in over twenty years!" Petrov raises his voice, letting out some of his frustration with her before reeling it back in, straightening his red tie as he gets his emotions back under control. "I didn't send her to spy on you. Hell, I didn't even know she was still alive until recently."

Until recently when his men were about to rape and kill her to hurt me.

"Oh, she's still alive," I assure him with a smirk. "For now."

"How did she end up with you, Salvato? How did you find her?"

He's so damn curious. The man hates not having all the answers.

"I didn't find her. And it's a long story." Now, I feed him the lie, using the name she goes by, not the one he gave her to piss him off. "Sweet little Vanessa thought she could walk out on me while I was distracted by the bombing, weeks before our contract was fulfilled. My men were on their way to snatch her back up when yours swooped in first. They followed them and you know how that turned out."

"What contract?" he snaps, jumping right over the reminder of his six dead employees, as if they don't matter.

"Kozlov didn't tell you?" I ask, even though I'm certain he has by now. "I paid off her slacker boyfriend's debts with Kozlov in exchange for seventy-six days and nights with his woman. Vanessa hated the idea, but he jumped right on board. I had no idea I was in possession of such a prize until the other night."

"That's not the story I've heard," Yuri mutters, face sour like he ate a bowl of lemons. "Yes, I knew about you paying off some loser's debts, but Mitch claimed that you and my daughter are not only...intimate but sickeningly so. He says you're obsessed with her."

Obsessed, sure. But how the fuck would Mitch know we've been sickeningly intimate? He's a double-crossing son of a bitch, that's why. I knew I couldn't trust that motherfucker. He's a problem for another time.

"Intimate? He thinks I've been intimate with her?" I turn the video angle on the phone around so he can see Vanessa tied up in the chair, gagged, and scowling with rage before quickly turning the camera view back to my face. "The only time she lets me touch her is when I threaten to put bullets in the people she cares about. Of course she claims she doesn't enjoy our trysts, but we both know how women can be. They don't know what they want until we give it to them."

I know Vanessa would cut my dick off if I tried to force myself on her. In Yuri's world, though, that's how him and his men treat their women.

"Since she ran out before I was done with her, I've had to keep her tied up to make sure she doesn't stray again," I add to sell our lie.

"Is that right?" the bastard asks. "Who does she care about so much? That Mitch fucker?"

I'm not surprised that he skipped right over me admitting to forcing myself on his daughter or restraining her. Instead, he wants to get right down to her weaknesses and how he can exploit them for his own bullshit.

"Mitch? Not anymore. But there are a few co-workers she wants to protect. And she gets real nasty whenever I threaten her precious little boy."

"Her boy?" Petrov's widening eyes confirm that he didn't know about Cole yet.

"Yeah, her son, Cole. You knew about him, right?" Before he responds with a lie, I call him out. "Oh, fuck! You didn't until just now. How the hell did she not only hide from you but keep the kid away for twenty goddamn years?"

"Her son, he's twenty years old? How..." Now his face pales a little when he realizes she got pregnant right after running away. I really hope Madison won't be that reckless.

"That's right. Her son is twenty, going to college on the east coast. Vanessa still thinks he's her baby boy even though he's bigger than I am. You see, I've done a thorough investigation into him to get all the details I need to twist Vanessa's arm." His green eyes, the color of Vanessa's go distant, as if trying to imagine the boy. Just as we hoped, the mention of a grandson distracts him from everything else. An heir is the one thing he's always wanted, but never had. I wouldn't be surprised if not having a blood relative to take over the family business is the only reason the ornery bastard is still alive and kicking.

"What I didn't know about Vanessa, until one of your men begged me not to hurt her before I killed him, was that she's your daughter."

"Bullshit," the old man spits, blinking his eyes clear as his head returns to the conversation to call me a liar.

"You think I'm lying? I thought you sent her as a fucking spy! She lived with me in my penthouse for weeks. If I had known she belonged to you, I would've offered a trade sooner. That's why I'm calling now..."

His eyes narrow, trying to figure out my angle. "What are you playing at, Salvato?"

He uses my hate-filled last name just like Vanessa used to do at first. I loathed the sound of it then because I wanted her to know me for more than the mafia lifestyle, and to still want me for all that I am. I wasn't sure if it was possible to change her mind. Thank fuck, she did.

"I'll tell you exactly what I want, Petrov. I want a truce."

"What are the terms?"

"I'll either keep her and do what I want with her while you try your best to kill me, or you can have her back. If you want her back, though, you'll have to back the fuck off me and my fentanyl trade. You have until this time tomorrow to decide."

I press the red button to end the call on him, ensuring I got the last word in, then let out a sigh of relief.

"What do you think?" I ask.

Vanessa shrugs, as if to say, we gave it a shot, and that the ball's in his court now.

And my balls are about to be in her mouth.

47

Vanessa

Being gagged and tied to a chair, suppressing the memories of being restrained and manhandled by my father's men is easy compared to having to deal with the emotions of hearing *his* grating voice again.

A voice from my childhood telling me I was a whiny spoiled brat, a stupid little bitch, a silly, weak girl who could never fill his shoes. He never failed to remind me that he wanted a son instead of a daughter or stopped blaming my mother for not being able to give him any children other than me. He's probably the one infertile if he couldn't impregnate any of his whores either. The asshole thinks he's a king, when in reality he's nothing but a ruthless gangster who grabs and holds on to whatever power he has by sheer terror.

The only thing I hate more than hearing him speak, seeing the brief image of him on the phone, is the fact that he now knows Cole exists. I've spent my son's entire life trying to keep him away from that monster. The only reason I agreed to let Dante use Cole as a distraction was because I know that my father will be dead soon. I'll find a way to kill him before he ever gets a chance to see Cole.

Dante walks up to me and grasps my chin between his finger and thumb to lift my face to his, pulling me out of my dark thoughts. "Do you want to go back upstairs?"

I shake my head no. I want a distraction, and I think he could use one himself after having to remain calm while talking to the man who killed the mothers of his daughters.

No, neither of us want to think about any of that right now. Instead, I would rather think about all the dirty things Dante might do to me while I'm tied up and his men are watching. That will make me forget everything else. Everything except for Dante's name. He'll be the master of my body and mind, the one who gives me pleasure or takes it away. I'll be completely at his mercy, and I can't wait.

Sure, I could squeeze my wrists free from the tie behind the chair if I wanted, but I don't. I trust Dante to give us both what we need right now.

"Very well," he says when he leans down to press a kiss to my cheek since my mouth is full. "There's nothing to do now but wait, right? May as well enjoy ourselves."

I can't help but wince when Dante kneels before me on the dirty, bloodstained floor in his flawless suit.

As if reading my thoughts, he grins as his palms squeeze my knees then slide up my thighs, pushing the hem of my dress as he goes. "A few grand is worth the price of admission to eat this gourmet spread, don't you think?"

The time for thinking is over when both of his thumbs graze either side of my slit because I'm not wearing any panties. My dress is bunched up around my waist when Dante leans forward to swipe his tongue just once over my flesh then lifting his head, teasing me, teasing the men in the room who may not be able to see my pussy, but know damn well what he did to it.

Since I can't speak, I part my knees wider in invitation, as far as they can go with my ankles tied to the front chair legs.

"I know what you want, butterfly, but we have to give the men a chance to prepare themselves. Should they be allowed to jerk off while I eat your pussy, or should we make them wait until later for relief?"

I shrug, leaving that decision up to him.

His lips trail over my inner thigh, so close but too far away from where I want them. "How about letting them tug on their dicks if they want, but they can't come until I do?" he suggests.

I nod, already fairly certain how Dante plans to come. His eyes darkened when Titus was gagging me. And I know how much he loves to gag me with his cock, how long he can last. He wants to torture these poor men, but I don't think they'll mind. I sneak a peek at the guards, at Titus. All four of them are standing around frozen in place with hungry eyes on me and Dante, as if they're afraid to blink and miss something.

"Do you like seeing how much other men want you?" Dante asks as his thumbs spread me open for another stroke of his wide tongue.

"Mmm," I moan in answer to his question and in appreciation when he slowly licks me from bottom to top again like he's lapping up an ice cream cone.

"Let me taste how much you like it," he says before aiming the stiff, pointed tip of his tongue to my clit to attack it.

I moan again around the cord, my neck going limp like the rest of my body as I melt into the chair. My hips try to lift and tilt toward his tongue to get more contact, but Dante already knows exactly what I need.

One of his thick fingers penetrates me, making me cry out in surprise.

"She's drenched," he informs the other men. "Vanessa loves being watched, don't you, butterfly?" I would maybe even be embarrassed if his tongue hadn't resumed its ministrations.

My head falls backward and my eyes close on a whimper of need. Dante groans against my flesh like he's enjoying himself. When he adds a second finger, my thighs flutter because I'm so, so close. With my hands behind my back and ankles tied to the chair, there's nothing I can do to chase the orgasm but squirm. I can't even beg Dante to make me come. All I can do is wait, not so patiently, while he brings me to the edge over and over again until finally my inner walls bear down on his fingers, and I explode.

My orgasm slams into me so hard I can't see or hear anything for several moments. My back arches, legs shake, clenching on either side of Dante's head. This orgasm seems to last longer than any before. It feels like I'm falling, I think the chair even tips backward, but Dante doesn't let me fall over.

When the last of the wonderful tremors fade, I blink my eyes open and find his dark head still between my legs, nose pressed to my damp flesh as he continues to lap up my arousal. I shiver, my senses over-whelmed, which causes him to stop and look up at me.

"My turn? Or should I make you come again?" he asks while swiping the sleeve of his expensive suit over his mouth to dry it.

I shake my head, because I can't believe he wiped my juices on his suit, and also because I don't think I could survive another orgasm. My limbs are still weak, unable to move even if they weren't tied up.

"Fine. I'll fuck your mouth and finish eating you later," he says as he stands up. Straddling me in the chair with one leg on either side, Dante undoes his pants to pull out his long, hard cock right in front of my face.

Holding himself in one hand, he grabs the back of my head in the other to remove the cords from my mouth. As soon as they fall away, he presses my head forward.

I tease him, licking his crown instead of opening wide. Impatient, Dante says, "Open your pretty mouth and gag for me at least once, butterfly."

I part my lips to let him slide over my tongue, to the back of my throat, where I do just what he wants.

Dante groans above me, and so does someone else in the room with us.

God, that's hot. I know Dante would never let anyone else touch me, but I love that he doesn't mind letting other men see him pleasure me or watch him fuck my mouth like he owns it.

He pulls my hair as he begins moving in and out, usually slow shallow strokes until he can't help himself and shoves deeper to make me choke. My eyes water until tears slide down my cheeks. While my throat may protest his length, I don't mind. In fact, I moan around his shaft in approval.

"Fuck," Dante grits out, feeling the vibration. I taste his salty flavor before he pulls his dick all the way out. "Not yet. They don't get to come yet."

I glance around and find the men all breathing heavy as their hands pump their cocks either inside their pants or out. Even Titus's pants are unbuttoned and unzipped, his dark pubic hair leading the way to where he's fisting himself.

"Show her your cocks, gentlemen. Let her see how hard she made them while her mouth is full of my balls."

There's another groan as Dante presses my head lower. I do what he asked, giving his sac a few teasing flicks of my tongue. When my tongue rolls over one of his balls, I close my lips around it and apply suction.

"Both. Now," Dante demands while stroking his shaft. I open wide again taking as much of his sac as I can, sucking on them until he swears and pulls back.

He slaps his dick on the underside of my chin. "Where should I come, butterfly? Down your throat?" He jerks the top of my dress down to reveal my bra. "On your beautiful tits?"

"On my tongue," I suggest, which is rewarded with several swears around the room. I want to taste Dante, but at the same time, I also want the other men to see him finish, filling my mouth with his seed, branding me.

"God, yes," Dante agrees as his hand pumps his shaft faster. It doesn't take long until he growls, "Fuck, here it comes."

I open my mouth wide and even stick out my tongue. "So fucking perfect," Dante says followed by a long, drawn-out groan of my name as the first rope of cum lands on my tongue, followed by three other pulses. I swallow his release down as he growls and swears, then open again for him to wipe his head on my tongue, licking up the last drops. Now that they finally have permission to finish, the grunts and swears of the other men echo around the basement while Dante puts himself back in his pants. I watch the guards stroke themselves faster while they watch me with hungry eyes full of desperation for the release they're chasing.

"They all wish they were coming in your hot little mouth or cunt instead of coming in their own dry fists," Dante remarks, making me feel like a goddess being worshipped.

While observing the guards take turns coming, I ask the mafia king, "Can we do this again sometime? Exactly this?"

Grabbing the side of my face to make me look up at him and him alone, Dante says, "I'm the only one who *ever* gets to touch you."

"Agreed," I reply with a very satisfied smile. "Take me upstairs?"

Dante doesn't respond right away. Instead, he pinches his bottom lip, obviously thinking dirty thoughts. Bending down, he picks up the bungee cord. "With or without the chair and rope?"

"With the chair and rope," I easily announce. "But only if you can figure out a way to fuck me in it? I'm so very, very wet. You'll slide right in..."

Groaning, he says, "You're going to be the death of me, butterfly."

"The feeling is mutual."

"Then challenge accepted." While still staring at me, about to pull his lip off, he tells the guards, "Put your dicks away and carry Vanessa upstairs to my bedroom in the chair. I've got more work to do."

48

Dante

After a small adjustment, Vanessa had to free her wrists long enough for me to slide underneath her in the chair seat and take her dress off, I was able to accomplish her challenge.

God knows I've wanted her to ride my cock while sitting on my lap since the first morning I put her on it to eat breakfast. I even got to braid her hair again between rounds while we caught our breath. Tugging on it while buried deep inside of her was just as amazing as I imagined it would be.

I only used the rope to gag her the first time because while I enjoy hearing her muffled moans, I love making her scream my name even more.

When I finally release her hours later, we get a shower together then have dinner with the girls. That's when I get the bastard's response. Still, I hold off telling Vanessa until later, when we're alone, watching the sun set over the city from the single chaise lounge on the bedroom balcony. It should be peaceful to have her stretched out between my legs, taking in the view of the city, but it's anything but relaxing thanks to my growing anxiety.

Tightening my arms that are wrapped around her waist, I breathe in her clean tropical scent and press my lips to her hair before finally telling her, "Yuri's texted back."

"Yeah?" She twists her neck around to look at me. "When? Why didn't you tell me? What did he say?"

"The message came in during dinner, but I wanted us to be alone when I told you. He said he wants to meet tonight and provided an address."

Now Vanessa sits all the way up. "Shouldn't we be getting ready?"

"We do have somewhere to be in about an hour, but it's not to meet Yuri. I don't trust that fucker as far as I can throw him, so I'll be damned if I let him set the meeting up that could easily turn into an ambush in the middle of the night." And I'm not ready to let Vanessa go just yet. I know it's only going to be a temporary separation, but I fucking hate it. "I responded to his message with my own, telling him that I'll give him a time and location tomorrow."

"Tomorrow?" she repeats.

"Yes. During daylight hours, at a place of my choosing. I wanted one more night with you, and I wanted to remind him that he's not in control of this situation."

"Okay. Tomorrow then." Vanessa's shoulders relax, then she leans her back against my chest again. She may pretend to be all calm and brave about seeing her father, but I know she's dreading it as much as I am.

Resting my chin on top of her head, I tell her, "You don't have to go. We could come up with another plan."

Covering one of my hands encircling her waist with her own, she gives it a squeeze. "This plan will work. I probably won't even be gone but for a few days."

That's the thing. Days could turn into weeks. I hate the unknown, especially when it comes to her.

"You don't know how long it will take to get your hands on a weapon, to get him to trust you enough to be alone with him, away from his guards. Then you have to figure a way out once he's dead. And you don't know how awful the son of a bitch will treat you until you get a chance to kill him either."

Vanessa shrugs. "True, I don't know any of those things. But I really do think I can take him out in less than a week. I can pretend to be an obedient daughter for seven days to get him to trust me."

I wish it was that easy to take out the bastard, but I think she's being a little too optimistic. He hasn't seen her in over twenty years, so he's not going to trust her easily. I'll give Vanessa seven days to do this her way, but that's it. If she's not back in a week, then I'll go into his compound for her if I have to. Not that I'll tell her that now. She'll just get pissed, tell me I don't believe she can kill her old man or that it's too dangerous for me.

"While I'm gone, you should try to focus on finding Madison," Vanessa says, changing the subject on purpose no doubt.

I sigh so hard loose pieces of her braid blow around in front of my face. "I didn't think you wanted me to find her, sort of like how you hid from your father for two decades."

Vanessa's fingernails drag up and down my arm gently. "You're nothing like Yuri, Dante. And Madison doesn't have to struggle through life alone. Now you've both had a chance to figure out that changes need to be made, but nothing worth keeping you apart."

"I'll try my best to find her," I assure her. "But if she doesn't want to be found yet..."

"Then she will eventually."

I don't respond to her assumption. There's no way to know if Vanessa is right or not about Madison. I just have to believe that she's somewhere safe. That she's happy. It's the only way I can get through the days and stay sane.

"So where do we have to be later?" Vanessa asks. She then squirms her ass against the crotch of my pants, taunting me. "I'm surprised we still have our clothes on and that you would want to leave the bedroom tonight."

Kissing the side of her neck, I follow it up with a swipe of my tongue along her skin, making her shiver. "Trust me, butterfly, we will get plenty of quality bedroom time again before you leave tomorrow. But first, I have a surprise for you."

Now she goes still in my arms. "A surprise? What kind of surprise?"

"If I told you, it wouldn't be a surprise, would it?"

"And we have to leave the penthouse for it?"

"Yes."

"How long will we be gone?"

"Not sure."

"Okay.... What should I wear?"

"Anything you want."

Slapping lightly at my arm, she huffs, "That's not very helpful. I don't want to be underdressed or overdressed. I should go start getting ready."

When she starts to sit up, I pull her back down to my chest. "Not yet. I have something for you."

"Another surprise?" she cranes her head around to ask.

"A little gift." Reaching into my inner suit pocket, I pull out the simple rose gold band and hold it in front of her between my finger and thumb for her.

"You bought me a ring?" she says softly, frowning as she studies it. "Is that..."

"It's a smart ring. A way for me to know that your heart is still beating, that you're still breathing. I'll even know when you're asleep or awake like a demented Santa Claus."

"Oh." Maybe I'm mistaken, but she sounds a little disappointed when she plucks the ring from my fingers to look at it closer. I don't bother to hide my grin.

"I got one for myself too."

"Yeah?"

"The best part? With a full charge it should last you a week."

"A week. Okay. So, it's a way for you to spy on me without being obvious about it."

"It'll keep me from doing something rash," I reply. Resting my chin on her shoulder, I take her right hand and slide it onto her ring finger.

"It fits," Vanessa remarks as she spreads her fingers to examine it. "And it looks innocent enough that my father won't notice it."

"Probably not."

I don't bother telling her that if it goes dark, I'm coming for her right then and there.

Vanessa twists around placing her legs on either side of mine to straddle my lap. Her arms wind around my neck to lean in and kiss my lips. "Thank you for caring enough to stalk me," she says against them.

"I love you, butterfly," I tell her as my palms slide up and down her perfect, hourglass curves before pausing abruptly.

Damn, that's the first time either of us have ever said those words to each other. How is that possible? I don't have any more time to worry if she feels the same because Vanessa kisses me again and says, "I love you too. I should've told you that before now."

"I'm so fucking glad to hear that because once this is all over, I want to spend the rest of my life with you, however long or short that may be."

"You do?" she asks, flashing me a smile.

"Yes. Do you think you could endure forever in this fucked-up world with me?"

Tilting her head to the side, she holds my gaze as she considers my question for a brief moment. "Yes, I do."

Her words seem like a good omen for what I planned later.

"As long as you stay honest and faithful to me."

"I will," I assure her as I tuck a loose strand of her light blond hair behind her ear. "Now, do you remember the phone number I gave you earlier?"

She rolls her eyes. "Yes. I'm not that old."

"It's nothing to do with your age. I know you have a lot on your mind, so I want to make sure you can reach me if you need to. Repeat it back to me." She does, three times in a row, so I can make sure she's memorized it. "Good. That's an untraceable burner phone. I'll have it on me at all times."

"At all times, huh?" she asks, pressing her breasts to my chest when she leans in to kiss my lips. "Even in the shower?"

Grabbing a handful of her ass cheeks in each hand I give them a squeeze. "Yes. The phone will be waiting on top of my towel."

"I'm going to be fine."

"I know you're going to be fine," I agree. To think otherwise would have me locking her in the penthouse and swallowing the key. "And I'll have confirmation of that now, thanks to your ring."

"Right." She looks down at her hand that's resting on my shoulder. "Is it waterproof?"

"Yes?"

"Really? Should we shower together again and test it out?"

Groaning, I remove my hands from her ass to rest them on her waist. "If we get naked and wet, we won't make it downstairs tonight."

"Downstairs for..."

"The lounge. We're just going to the lounge," I confess.

"Oh." Again, she sounds disappointed. "Then, I can just wear whatever."

"That's exactly what I told you."

"Why the lounge?"

"You ask a lot of questions," I mutter. "Don't you want to see your friends? Co-workers before you leave?"

"Sure, I guess."

"If not, I could close it to the public and we could have it to ourselves. I could fuck you in the booth where you constantly cock-teased me."

"If that's what we're going down to do then we should just stay up here."

"What if I didn't close it to the public, and I fucked you in the booth? Would that be more appealing?"

Vanessa sinks her teeth into her bottom lip. "I don't know. Maybe."

"You would have to pretend like you don't want it, you know, in case your father found out about it from someone."

"I could do that," she easily agrees. "Yes, I want to do that. This morning was...well, you know I'm an exhibitionist now. I only want you, but I like when we're being watched."

It's risky, but if the guards confiscated phones from onlookers, it might be worth it. Vanessa sounds excited by the idea, which excites me. I decide to agree but give her my one and only caveat.

"Okay, naughty girl, I'll give you what you want, but only if you give me what I want."

"And what do you want, naughty boy?" Vanessa asks, grinding her pussy down on my bulge. Yes, I want sex, but that's not all.

With a grin, I grab the back of her neck to pull her forward, whispering the words in her ear.

"Dante!" Vanessa exclaims when she pulls back to examine my face as if to see if I'm serious.

"Oh, and I also want to hear you scream my name when I'm fucking you in front of a room full of people."

"You're serious?" she asks, and I know she doesn't mean about the screaming. That is definitely going to happen.

"It's not *if* but *when*, butterfly. All you have to do is say the word."

With an enormous smile on her face, she answers like there was not a single doubt in her mind.

"*When.*"

49

Vanessa

L ast night with Dante was...well, it was a night I'll *never* forget. But no matter how great it was, it's been pushed to the back burner today.

"You look gorgeous in pink," Dante tells me, referring to one of the dresses he bought me weeks ago.

"Thanks," I reply absently, flashing him a smile before my finger-nails go back to drumming on the passenger door panel. The frantic rhythm keeps pace with how fast my heart is beating as I think of all the shit that could go wrong. What if I screw this up? What if Dante is walking into a trap?

"Vanessa, you know you don't have to do this if you don't want to." Sensing my hesitation, he reaches for my twitching left hand, raising it to his lips to kiss my knuckles above my new ring. He twists the band up and off to slide it onto my right hand instead. "In fact, I would prefer if you didn't do it. We could turn around right now..."

"I can do this. I need to do it," I tell him with a heavy sigh. "As long as you're certain that Cole is safe?"

"He and my girls are now all safe and sound on a private island with his friends. Nobody gets on or off the island without the guards knowing."

"Good. That's good. He's probably having fun, doesn't have a clue what's going on here..."

"I'm sure he is having fun," Dante agrees with a smirk.

Narrowing my eyes at him, I have to ask, "What does that mean?"

"I sent them some company, you know, to keep the boys occupied and distracted from my daughters."

Now my jaw drops to the floorboard. "Oh my god. You sent my son whores?"

"No, not whores. Island staff, a few housekeepers, waitresses, some masseuses, even a couple of lifeguards who just so happen to all be young, beautiful, and up for a good time."

"Right," I mutter with a roll of my eyes.

"Your son isn't an angel, and you can bet your ass he's not a virgin."

"I know that!" I huff. "I would just rather not know about any of... that. You could've kept those details to yourself."

"I refuse to keep any secrets from you from now on, no matter how uncomfortable they might be."

"Well, at least I'm not as sad about leaving you now. I can't believe you paid women to...to..."

When I turn my head toward the window, Dante lifts my hair from my neck to leave a scruffy kiss on it. "Are you sore from last night?"

Shaking my head at his sudden change of topic, I tell him, "Oh, I think you know I'm sore, just as you intended, right? So, I can't help but think about you and remember all the dirty details." Grabbing the top of his hair, I pull his mouth away from my skin. "And you better stop that before you leave a beard rash."

"Like the one between your thighs?"

"Yes, like that one, but one on my neck would be visible for everyone to see."

"You didn't mind all the people who saw the beard rash I gave you last night? How many was it? Two dozen or so?"

"That's a good guess. I still can't believe you did that," I tell him with a chuckle, unable to help my lingering smile.

"Do you regret it?" he asks softly, seriously.

"No. Do you?" I ask, watching his face.

"Never." Grabbing my chin, he rubs his thumb over my bottom lip. "Don't forget that when I have to act like an asshole in a few minutes."

"I won't," I assure him.

He gives me a soft kiss on the lips, then releases my chin. "We're almost there."

"Okay. I'm ready." At least that's what I tell him and myself. "Are you sure the location is safe? What if he tries to shoot at you?"

"We're in the middle of the flat desert in broad daylight. There's nowhere a sniper could hide. My men have had their eyes on the location since before I even gave the coordinates to Yuri. He sent a crew to check it out, but they drove by and left without getting out of the vehicle."

"Good, but..."

"He knows I could put a bullet in his head too. That's how this works. He'll accept the truce. Even if it's just for today so he can get you back." Pulling out his phone from his suit jacket, Dante adds, "He arrived two minutes ago, and we're running late on purpose."

"Right. Power play and all that. He'll also be pissed you kept him waiting."

"That's exactly why I did it."

Staring out the window, I ask the question I've wondered for years. "Do you think he killed my mother?"

Squeezing my hand, he asks, "Do you?"

"I don't know. The memorial page I saw online twelve years ago said she died peacefully in her sleep. She would've only been fifty, ten years younger than my father. I guess it could've been natural. She did pop pills and drink a lot. But he was always getting caught with other women, giving my mom the same old excuse that he has to fuck younger women who can give him a son. I wouldn't be surprised if he just got tired of having her around."

"Do you miss her?" Dante asks.

"She wasn't evil like my father, but I think that just makes her something worse," I explain to him. "She stood by and watched him be so cruel, to me, to his men, to the house staff. She knew he would punish me for so-called slights to him by starving me for days or backhanding me across the room. Yet she never tried to stop him or sneak me something to eat. She didn't do anything but sit there and watch it happen. I know she was scared of him too. Everyone was. *Is.* But she never even tried to stand up to him for me."

"I'm sorry," Dante says quietly. "I'm sorry I didn't get you out of that hellhole when you were a teenager."

"I wasn't your responsibility, but I was hers."

"I know, but looking back, I was a selfish asshole. If I had known, I would've taken you in, even if you were too young to marry."

I don't bother telling him that I'm glad he didn't because I don't want to hurt his feelings. The truth is, though, if he had taken me in, I never would've learned how to fend for myself, to work for an honest day's pay. Most of all, I wouldn't have become a mother. Having Cole gave me someone to love with all my heart for the first time in my life. A love that was good and pure that nobody, not even my father, could take away from me. And for that, I wouldn't change a single thing. The struggle, living in poverty, it was worth it all for a chance to grow up and raise my son on my terms. The worst punishment I ever gave him was taking his phone away when he skipped school in the eighth grade with his friends. He didn't speak a word to me for two weeks after that, but he never skipped school again. Maybe I got lucky, but I couldn't have asked for a better son. He was nothing like my angry, manipulative father, despite shared genetics, which is what I worried about most throughout his teenage years.

"My father beat my mother to death," Dante says, ripping me from my thoughts. "I found her body, her face so bruised...I could barely recognize her."

Oh wow. No wonder Dante got so upset when he saw the bruises on my face, why he overreacted by killing those two men.

"I'm so sorry that he did that to her," I tell him as I rub my thumb over the top of his hand, unsure what else to say. "How old were you?"

"Fourteen. She was a good mom."

"That must have been so hard."

"I wanted to kill him for it then," Dante mutters as his fisted hand scrubs across his chest. "Eventually I did."

"The, um, angel wings on your chest, are they for her?"

"Yes."

I'm not sure why, but I'm glad they weren't for one of the girls' mothers.

Before I can ask anything else about her, about him killing his own father, Dante says, "We're here," just as the SUV slows down and pulls off the road.

I'm so ready to get this over with. All of it. But mostly ridding the world of my father.

Dante offers me a new cell phone, one that's clean as we discussed. No contacts or search history. Nothing that my father can glean from it about my life or Cole's.

The SUV slowly creeps up a little way further on the shoulder before coming to a complete stop. Through the windshield I can see what I assume are my father's vehicles. The tires on all of them are angled toward the road, as if he's planning to make a quick getaway.

"Keep me in front of your body," I tell Dante, clutching the new phone in my hand. "He probably wouldn't kill me to get to you."

"I'm not using you as a shield," he says, releasing my hand to grip my arm. "You're supposed to be a reluctant hostage, remember?"

I nod my agreement. Yes, I do need to remind myself that I'm not supposed to like Dante.

"Be careful, butterfly. Call me if you need me or smash your ring."

"I will," I promise him. With one last shared look at each other, Dante opens his door to climb out, pulling me along with him, none too gently.

Once I stumble out of the SUV, not entirely acting, Dante releases my arm to grip the back of my neck harshly. His grip even pulls my hair harshly as he shoves me forward. Well, alongside him, but not in front of him. I try to swerve in that direction, but he hauls me back over to his left side.

I give up the fight when I see my father and several men in suits climb out of one of the waiting cars. He stands behind the open door, as if using it as a shield. Or like I'm not worth stepping foot into an open space to retrieve.

As soon as I see the perpetual scowl on his long face, I'm right back to being an awkward, shy sixteen-year-old girl again.

"Good-fucking-luck with her," Dante mutters, yanking me out of my thoughts.

I'm not a teenager anymore. I'm a grown ass woman. And I'm going to kill that bastard for hurting me, for killing every innocent woman in Dante's life, all the people at the poker tournament. He will never touch my son or try to kill Dante again.

"She's been nothing but a pain in my ass." Dante sounds legitimately annoyed with me when he shoves me forward so hard, I stagger. He still doesn't let me get in front of him, stepping up beside me instead.

Steeling myself, I square my shoulders to glare at Dante, memorizing his face, his massive, muscular, powerful body before I have to leave him. I already miss him, and he's still standing next to me. But I can't let it show.

"You're just pissed you confessed all your secrets to me before you figured out who I was, you greasy bastard. That's what you get for being so distracted trying to get into my panties."

For a second, Dante even looks shocked by my statement. Good. It'll seem more authentic to my father.

"I don't know what the fuck you're talking about. You don't know shit about me, other than how big my cock is. Isn't that right, princess?" Now he gives me that cocky smirk he used to try and get me to sleep with him for years. How I resisted for so long, I honestly don't know.

My father, though, I hate to admit, looks pleased with me. His white brows are raised in interest as he watches me and Dante. Convincing him to trust me so I can get close enough to kill him won't be easy. I need to make him think I can be useful to him, that I know Dante's secrets.

"Katia," the fucker says with a fake smile. He eyes me up and down, taking in my pale pink dress and high heels. I didn't dress up for him. The heels are the only weapons I figured I could get away with having. They're not much, but better than nothing. Other than the phone in my hand, and the ring on my finger, I don't have any other belongings. "You're all grown up. I barely recognize your face."

Asshole. He just insulted me, called me old.

"I've had a long, hard life," I admit to him with my own insincere smile.

"Well, let's go catch up," he says. Then to his men, "Search her."

"Search me?" I huff as two large meatheads come ambling toward me. They remind me of the ones who kidnapped me, although I know it can't be the same ones since those men are dead. My father is just like Kozlov. He would let his goons assault a woman before killing her.

Without anything more to do, I hold my arms up and let the bastards feel me up and down.

I don't dare glance at Dante but see him standing stock still in the corner of my eye. I have no doubt that he's struggling not to blow this whole lie when he sees another man's hands patting my breasts and ass, sliding up between my thighs. I blow out a breath when the hands are off me, relieved Dante didn't even flinch.

The other guy runs some little device over every inch of me from head to toe, most likely checking for wires or tracking devices. Neither pay any attention to my ring. The one with the scanner plucks my phone from my hand.

"Hey!"

"You'll get it back once I've gone through it," my father replies, already treating me like I'm a child again. He says something in Russian that I think translates to "filthy little whore" but I'm not entirely sure. Followed by, "Come, Katia."

God, I hate that name. The way he says it especially, because it always makes me feel like I'm his dog he's calling to heel.

But it's now or never.

As I walk around to the other side of the car where a man holds open the back passenger door waiting, I glance back at Dante. His face is blank, giving nothing away as he turns to his SUV. I want him inside the bulletproof vehicle sooner rather than later. First, though, I raise my hand, flipping him off, certain he'll take the "fuck you" middle-finger gesture exactly how I meant it—that I can't wait until he's literally inside of me again.

Inside the car, the door has barely closed behind me when my father asks without facing me, "Where's my grandson?"

351

50

Dante

It's been the longest fucking week of my life. Six slow ass days have gone by since I sent Vanessa back to her fucking father, and I haven't heard a word from her.

If not for her ring, I wouldn't know if she were dead or alive.

She is definitely alive. She's stressed out, and not sleeping much according to the device, but she's alive.

Not that I've gotten any sleep either lately.

To keep myself busy, rather than fucking up Vanessa's plan before giving her a chance, I've been contacting more PIs all across the country, hiring them to search for Madison.

And I've also spent my time getting updates from my men about the coming and goings of two pieces of shit. Tonight, I finally told them to drag their sorry asses down to the basement. They may not deserve all my wrath, but they're the ones who are going to get it for now. Vanessa's ring probably only has another day's worth of charge on it at most. And if I have to see her pulse and blood pressure spike one more time, I'm going to lose my fucking mind. I don't know if it's her father or his men hurting her, but they're all going to be dead soon.

"Mitchell," I drawl as I pace in front of the bastard, swinging a metal bat in my hands. Sitting under a fluorescent light, the rest of the basement bathed in darkness, he looks scared shitless, as he should be. "I wish I could say it's nice to see you again, but we both know that would be a fucking lie."

"What am I doing here this time?" the slacker whines. "I moved out of Van's apartment; I stayed away from her; I don't have any new gambling debt. Why did you drag me out of a gorgeous woman's bed to do this same old song and dance?"

That's right. For the past few days, he's been shacking up in a hotel with some young girl, barely legal drinking age, who is enjoying blowing her trust fund in Vegas with late night partying.

"You see, Mitchell, I have techs who noticed some very large deposits in your bank account recently. Which is odd, isn't it, since you still don't have a job?"

"You're hacking my accounts now? What the fuck?"

"Vanessa gave your sorry ass a second chance you didn't deserve, and you went and fucked it up."

"I don't know what you're talking about. I've got a new girlfriend who is loaded."

"Oh, shut the fuck up. The deposits didn't come from the girl you're mooching off. In fact, I already know who gave you the money. I just want to hear the words come out of your mouth."

He doesn't respond, so I lift the bat to my shoulder, then swing it down with all my might, nailing both of his shins at the same time.

"Ow! Fuck! Motherfucker, that hurts!" He winces and squirms in his restraints, unable to do anything to stop me from hurting him with his hands restrained behind his back, ankles tied to the legs. It's similar to the way I tied up Vanessa the other day, but not nearly as sexy. Mitchell has stains all over his tee, there's still bits of food in his long, untidy beard, and I've been around dumpsters that smelled better.

"Now do you want to tell me who you talked to and why? Or should I give you a little more motivation?"

He presses his lips together, pissing me off because he's wasting my time.

"Eli..." I start before remembering the deranged fighter isn't here anymore. Maybe I was too harsh with him after my fight with Vanessa.

In fact, he may actually be able to help me with my plans for later. If I had to guess, the kid's still in town, despite me ordering him to leave.

"Titus," I say instead. "Flip the lights on and then reach out to Eli. Tell him if he can find me four or five cage fighters who want to earn a million each tonight, then all will mostly be forgiven."

"Yeah?" the big guy asks.

"Yeah. I'm in a forgiving mood," I reply. To Mitch, I place the end of the bat to his chest. "Just not for you. And you see, I already know you ran your mouth about me and Vanessa to Kozlov. I just need to know who your source here in the casino was before I kill you. So, you have two choices. You can either die fast, or you can die slowly."

With the phone already to his ear, Titus flips the switch to light up the other side of the basement. When Mitchell sees the man hanging upside down, he swears under his breath.

"Kozlov decided he wants to die slowly, the blood gradually dripping from his minor wounds that I'll open up again and again, using various, painful methods, every day until he's dead."

"Jesus," the grungy fucker mutters as he stares on in horror.

"Not even Jesus can save you now. So, fast, or slow? What's it going to be, Mitchell?"

Turning his face to me, I can see the white of his eyes when he says, "Look, Dante, I'm sorry, okay? I was pissed at you and her. We had a good thing going, and you came along..."

"You were pissed at me and her? I paid off your goddamn debts!" I lean down to yell in his face. "And you think you had a good thing going with Vanessa? She never gave a shit about you. The only reason she saved your sorry life was because she's a good person, unlike me, and unlike her father, Yuri."

Gaping at that, he whispers, "Holy shit! Her father is Yuri? Yuri Petrov? Then why didn't she just pay off my debts?"

"God, you're a fucking idiot," I tell him. "Too bad for you, Vanessa isn't here to stop me from putting a bullet in your head this time."

"What? Wait! She'll be pissed if you hurt me!"

"Good thing I learned a few tricks for making her forget why she's angry. Now. Who. Told *you*. About. *Us?*" I grit out each word slowly.

When he doesn't answer my question, I drop my bat. The loud aluminum on the hard cement floor echos around the empty basement, startling the bastard. I reach into my suit jacket to pull out my gun from the shoulder holster instead.

"I can put a bullet in plenty of body parts that won't instantly kill you," I warn him. "You've got three seconds to decide. Three. Two—"

"Wait! It was Gavin! Gavin told me that he's the one who set me up with Kozlov's girls, and that you were obsessed with Vanessa and shit. He said he heard that she loved sucking your dick. That's it. That's all I told Kozlov."

Wow. It looks like Gavin is a dead man too. Was he with Eli when I sent that photo of Vanessa's mouth on me? That was stupid of me.

Since the jackass told me exactly word for word what Kozlov eventually confessed Mitchell told him, I decide to give him a quick death. Vanessa would want that for him, even if he's the reason her father may not *ever* believe we weren't fucking consensually. I should've brought Mitchell and Kozlov in sooner, even if it meant Yuri finding out. No telling what Vanessa has been through this week because of this son of a bitch running his mouth.

"Enjoy hell," I say to Mitch before I lift my gun. Aiming it at his head from less than five feet away, I pull the trigger. My ears are still ringing when his head falls forward, gone in the blink of an eye.

"Damn, Dante," Titus mutters when he comes over. "That's the second suit you've ruined today."

"Worth it," I tell him as I sheath my gun. "Were you able to reach Eli?"

"Yeah. He's on his way, sounded certain he could get the four or five fighters you asked for within an hour."

"Great. Get this mess cleaned up." I lift my arm to wipe the moisture from my cheek on my suit sleeve, leaving a crimson stain on the material.

"Then what, boss? You got plans tonight for Eli and those fighters?"

"Oh, I've got plans, all right," I tell him as I head for the elevator. "Tonight, I'm going to get my wife back."

51

Vanessa

"Where is he?" my father asks me yet again.

"I told you..." My words are whispers because my mouth and throat are so dry. It's been hours of questions like this each and every day. I can't remember exactly how many days it's been since I've had anything to eat. I've been telling myself it's a good thing to lose those last, stubborn ten pounds.

I'm not even hungry anymore. I'm just weak, living off of water from the faucet. I'm so weak I have to be held up by two men when my father comes to "visit" me in the groundskeeper's storage building he's keeping me locked in on the edge of the property. Even if I had the energy to try to run, there are always guards watching me. I have to wash off and drink from a utility sink and use the bathroom in a goddamn bucket.

"He's not at the school! He's nowhere to be found in the whole goddamn state!" Yuri exclaims. "Not a soul has seen him in days!"

He sent people to search for Cole on campus the first day he brought me here. By then, he had already used my fake name to hack my bank account and track down Cole's school from my tuition payments.

"Where the fuck is my grandson!" Yuri roars.

"I haven't...talked to him in...weeks. I don't know."

"Yes, you do. I have the phone records!" Either his fist or the back of his hand slams into the left side of my face. All I know is that my jaw and lip hurt worse than before. I taste copper on my tongue a moment later. I'm just glad that Dante made Cole and the others leave their phones behind before leaving New York so my father couldn't track them.

"You're keeping my grandson from me on purpose. But I'm going to get it out of you one way or another."

It turns out that getting my father alone, gaining his trust, was impossible from the start. I never even got to step foot in the mansion I grew up in. He's always with at least four guards, and they're all heavily armed. I haven't been able to even get my hands on a fork since I got here. If I die before I get out, Dante will be so pissed. Thinking of him, I decide to spin a new lie. One that has a ring of truth to it.

"Dan...Salvato has Cole."

"Bullshit!"

"He does. He really does," I assure him. And that much is true. Dante knows where Cole is even if I don't. "You think...Salvato doesn't have his own...torture techniques? He's even more vicious...than you."

That's not a lie either. Dante is more vicious when it comes to getting vengeance for someone he loves. And he loves me. He loves me so much he asked me to marry him. No planning. No prenup. He fucked me while we said our vows before the officiant in the lounge. It was crazy hot and sort of romantic having him inside me when he promised to love and cherish me for the rest of our lives. I, on the other hand, refused to say I would obey him, which resulted in my ass getting a slap. Dante may wish I was more subservient, but he would get bored with a wife who always agreed with him and did everything he asked of her.

"You love that bastard, don't you? *Admit it!*" my father bellows, followed by another hit to my sore cheek. This one hurts even my neck from the whiplash. Probably his fist that time. I don't know why he hates the idea of me loving Dante so much, but he does.

"He didn't want you before; he doesn't want you now."

"I know," I agree.

It's true. Dante doesn't want me. It's more than a simple *want* for the two of us. He *needs* me, just like I need him. He's a necessity, a basic requirement like oxygen. I need him to survive.

And I need him now more than ever before I starve to death.

But I would rather die than have him barge into the compound guns blazing and get killed on a suicidal rescue mission. His girls need him. Cole...he's all grown up. Dante will take care of him for me.

"What's Salvato planning for me, huh? Tell me the truth this time!"

Each day I give him another lie to keep him good and paranoid of his own people.

"Poison."

"Poison?" he repeats. "Did she say poison?"

"Yes, boss, that's what I heard," one of the men holding my arm replies.

"How the fuck does he think that will work?"

"Kitchen. Supplies. Retailers. I dunno. Give me food...and I might remember." There, that's enough suspects to keep my father busy. I just hope he doesn't kill anyone he finds suspicious. He probably will. But he would do that even without my nudge because he's a goddamn monster.

"You don't deserve to eat, you filthy whore!" That's right, now that I'm all grown up, I've graduated from being a spoiled little bitch to a filthy whore.

He's so certain that Dante and I were fucking like bunnies, and I have no clue *how* he knows. Someone must have heard about us or seen us at the resort. But he still doesn't know I'm married to his enemy.

Dante paid people to keep it out of the public record for now, for exactly this reason.

I use what little strength I have to try and lie better. "Fine! He used me, okay? I didn't want him to touch me at first. Then...then he got what he wanted...and moved on to other women right in front of me. I hate that asshole!"

Thankfully, my father's lips curl up, believing me. His shoulders even relax as if he's not quite as concerned about Dante coming after him for me. He still believes he's a playboy.

"Why did he agree to give you back to me, huh? He could've asked me for money, property, anything."

My father would've given anything, not to get to me, but to have a strong, male heir to groom into a manipulative bastard like himself.

"Business," I say simply. "He cares about his business...more than anything. Money. Greed. He was...furious about the warehouses."

"Good," Yuri replies with a broader grin. "Let her go. I'm done with her for now."

"Food?" I ask, hating myself for begging him for anything.

"Not until you tell me where Cole is."

"If I die..."

"You won't die. You have enough meat on your bones to make it at least another week or two without food."

"Asshole," I mumble as the guards lower me gently back down to the ground. An old towel is the only cushion between me and the cold concrete floor. My body aches all over from sleeping on the hard surface and my face constantly throbs from the beatings.

Despite what my father thinks, I don't know if I can survive another week or two here. But I'll try my fucking best.

"We'll get you out of here tonight," it sounds like one of the guards whispers while lowering me.

"What?" I ask, blinking up at him. He looks familiar. I think he's the one who patted me down the first day. But then again, all the guards are tall and bulky with face tats and military crew cuts.

The guy looks to the door. As soon as my father walks out he says, "He'll be occupied all night. We'll get you into the house. Find you some food. Let you get a bath and sleep a few hours in a bed."

"What? Why? Why would you do that? If he finds out..."

"He won't find out. And I'm doing it because he's a dick who got my brother killed when he tried to kidnap you," is what the man says before he slips out with the other guard, the two nodding at each other.

I don't want to get my hopes up, but with a little food in me, maybe I can come up with an actual plan to get out of here.

Dante

"Do you really think Eli and five other grapplers can take out all the guards around the entire parameter?" Titus asks as we wait in an SUV a mile away from the Petrov estate.

"Guess we'll find out soon enough."

For a million dollars each, Eli and his buddies are knowingly risking their lives sneaking up and silently choking out the guards. They're working in pairs, coming from three sides of the property, before they all meet up at the front which has the heaviest security presence.

Our IT guys are running a replay of last night on all the security cameras rather than taking it out completely. That way, anyone watching the feed will think everything is fine.

"Well, I guess this is better than going in hot, losing as many men as we take out," Titus says as he stares down at his phone, waiting for updates.

Since he's in charge of the guards, he's closer to the guys than I am or ever will be. He'll send them into danger if I order him to, but he doesn't like watching men die for bullshit. I don't either. But sometimes, violence is the only thing that works in this lifestyle.

Before I met Vanessa, I probably would've always gone with the quicker, bloodier route. But she makes me want to be a better person. She also showed me what it is to love someone with your entire heart and soul. Knowing what that feels like, hell, I don't want to risk the lives of my men, taking them away from their wives, sons, or daughters. And part of me doesn't even want the men who follow my enemy to endure that kind of fate either. Yuri's crew deserves to keep living their lives even after he's dead. That man isn't worth dying for, and I plan to give them a chance to change sides once he's been dealt with.

The screen of Titus's phone lights up as he reads a text. "The gate is clear. Security has been dropped and zip tied. Eli's corralling them all into the guard house."

"Good. Let's go. Get everyone in position," I tell him as we all jump out of the row of SUVs to go join the party. I knew the first step, getting into the estate without raising the alarm, was going to be the biggest challenge. They'll never see us coming now.

"Make sure everyone waits for me before going inside the main house, and not to fire a single shot without my permission," I tell Titus when he catches up to me.

The last thing I need is for Vanessa to get hit by friendly fire. She barely escaped the bullets during the car chase and shootout with Kozlov's crew. I'm not taking that chance again. This time of night, I'm betting on Vanessa and Yuri being asleep in bed, without the slightest idea that we're taking over the house.

We pass the guard house which is exactly as described. A man in all black, including his face mask nods to us as we walk through the opening in the gate of the ten-foot-tall fence.

There's not a single guard on the property as we cross the fake grass and decorative hedges. Flood lights are already on, helping us find our way to the front of the mansion.

Two men in black wearing the same attire as the one at the guard house are leaning their backs against the columns as if they're hanging out on a smoke break. Under the portico, four brawny men are on the ground, faces absolutely furious. I would be too if I were hogtied. I doubt these guys could bend in such a way if they even wanted to. Not to mention they're also gagged with...belts. Possibly their own since I only provided Eli's crew with zip ties.

One of the lounging men steps forward, peeling their mask up. *Eli.*

"The grounds are secure. No unnecessary bloodshed as ordered," he says. "And if there are any guards inside, they haven't come out to check on these fuckers."

"Nice job," I tell him. "It's good to have you back."

"Good to be back," he replies with a wicked grin. I bet the bastard did miss inflicting pain. Unless he was doing that in his free time. "Now what?" he asks.

"Now we go find Vanessa and deal with Yuri."

Walking up to the double front doors, I try one of the knobs...and it opens with a faint creak.

"Huh," I mutter.

"Why would the door be locked if the guards are constantly coming in and out?" Titus remarks.

"True. Let's go. Quietly."

Our footsteps on the marble floors are soft and slower than I would've liked, but necessary. Since I would assume the man is too paranoid to sleep on the first level, I take the lead up the marble stairs.

The second floor seems to go a mile in each direction. So many doors to try until I find Vanessa.

When I hear sounds coming from the far end on the left, I head in that direction, gesturing for Titus to halt the men behind us. On the off chance they get trigger happy, I don't want it to be when they open a door and find Vanessa.

I twist each doorknob I come to, finding them all unlocked. Some were even open, and of course empty. The closer I get to the one on the end, the louder the noises get. Grunts and groans. A woman's high-pitched moans and shouts for god. No wonder Yuri didn't hear us coming. He was too busy getting some ass.

The doorknob of the last door, as expected, is locked. I could either try to bust it down with my shoulder, which may or may not work, alerting him to my presence. Or I can shoot the lock for quicker entry. Here's hoping I can get the drop on the old man before he pulls out his own gun. I have no doubt he sleeps with one close to him. I just pray he doesn't keep one in his hand while he's fucking.

Thanks to the silencer I put on my gun, it doesn't make much of a sound, but it's definitely noticeable when it blows a hole through the locking mechanism. I kick the door open with my foot and steady my gun with two hands, ready to pull the trigger again.

"Hands up!" I yell in warning to the occupants of the bedroom. All... three of them. "Wow." That's the only word I can say when I take in the scene.

Yuri doesn't lift his hands, but I'm not too concerned. He doesn't have a gun in them. The only thing he's currently holding is his dick. And when he lets it go, it's small, shriveled, and limper than a wet sock.

To make this even more embarrassing for him, he's not even in the bed with the naked brunette who was yelling for god. No, he's sitting in a brown leather chair beside the bed, watching. A young, also naked, twenty or thirty-something guy with a flabby dad bod is frozen in place in the middle of the king-sized bed. The woman in front of him is on her hands and knees, getting fucked from behind. Both of them crane their necks to look at me standing in the door, holding them at gunpoint.

"Trouble getting it up, Yuri?" I can't help but ask, unable to hide my smirk. Serves the bastard right. To the man and woman, I say, "Get out."

They don't have to be told twice. The couple scrambles off the bed, not even bothering to try and pick up any clothes before rushing out the door past me.

"Where's Vanessa?" I ask first and foremost.

Even in the compromising position he's in, he still manages to scowl indignantly at me. "That's not her name."

"Where is she? Which room is she in?"

"She's not here."

"What?"

"I knew I couldn't trust that little whore."

"Watch your fucking mouth. My wife isn't a whore."

He snorts. "Your wife, huh? So, you finally think she's good enough for you?"

"It was never about that. She was a child before. Now, well, you finally got what you wanted. The two of us are going to rule this city from now on, you just won't be there to see it."

"Dante," Eli says stepping up behind me. "I just saw Vanessa."

"She's not here!" Yuri exclaims again.

"Yes, she is," Eli replies.

"Where?" I ask.

"She's standing at the other end of the hallway."

"Restrain him," I say to the fighter, as I turn to go find her.

52

Vanessa

The roast beef sandwiches on rolls were the best meal I've ever had. It was all the guards could scavenge to bring up before the kitchen staff noticed. I didn't mind. I was just happy to have something in my belly.

Soaking in the tub in the bedroom on the farthest end of the house from my father's felt amazing. I feel like a new person. Like I could lie down on the thick mattress and sleep for days. One of the guards even gave me a shirt to sleep in so I wouldn't have to put on that damn pink dress I've worn all week. I handwashed it and hung it over the tub, hoping it'll dry some before I have to leave in the early morning to go back to the shithole storage building.

Until then, maybe I can finally get a good night's sleep.

But as soon as I lay my head on the pillow, I hear voices. Distant but shouting voices.

Sliding off the bed, I tiptoe to the door, wondering if I should chance a peek. The sounds are far enough away that I unlock the door to crack it open. There are no guards on my end of the long hallway, but there's a crowd gathered at the other end. Right outside my father's bedroom.

My eyesight isn't great, but I swear that from afar one of the men looks like Titus and another, with long blond hair, looks like Eli. But that's crazy...

The Eli lookalike turns his head as if he heard my thoughts and waves me over. Is he insane? I'm not going anywhere near my father's room. I don't ever want to know what happens in there.

The same time I have that thought, a woman comes streaking out of the gathered group of men, followed by an equally naked man hot on her heels. They both run down the stairs as if the hounds of hell are after them.

What in the world is going on?

Then I hear it. Someone says his name.

I take a tentative step forward, then another, hoping, wondering if maybe I'm dreaming.

But then the crowd parts and there's no mistaking his tall, intimidating frame for anyone else as he strides toward me with purpose.

"Dante." He came for me. He's here. How? I didn't hear a single gunshot.

The closer he comes, the blurrier he gets.

Instead of wrapping me in his arms, he stops three feet away.

"Oh, butterfly. I should've come sooner."

"What? No. You shouldn't have come at all!" I say as my throat begins to burn thanks to the moisture filling my eyes. God, I'm so damn glad he came for me. "How?" I whisper, still not sure this is real, that he's real.

"With a little help from Eli's ninja friends."

Okay, this is definitely a dream if Dante Salvato is talking about ninjas. Besides, he exiled Eli.

The blurry dream Dante's jaw clenches tight. "Where else?" he asks.

"Where what?"

"Where else did he hurt you?"

"Oh." I touch my face, remembering the swollen mess, busted lip, and black eye I finally saw in the mirror a few minutes ago. I look nearly

366

identical to when Kozlov's men beat the shit out of me, but at least my ribs don't hurt this time. My face will heal. I may need plastic surgery on my nose to get it straight again...

"I'm...I'm fine."

"You're not fucking fine!" Dante shouts so fiercely that I recoil instinctively.

Dropping like a ton of bricks to his knees before me, Dante says, "I'm sorry, butterfly. I just...I don't know if I can touch you without hurting you."

I reach my shaky hand out toward him, to see if he's real, afraid that he won't be. But my fingers slide into his soft black hair, and he closes his eyes. They're still shut, when he says, "Why are you wearing another man's shirt?"

Glancing down, I realize that's definitely not something dream Dante would ask.

"Vanessa?" He uses my real name when I don't immediately respond.

"My dress was dirty."

Now his ice-blue eyes open to stare at me, a tick in his cheek from his tightly clenched teeth. "Take it off. I need to see..." he trails off, but I know what he wants. He wants to see if there are more bruises.

My muscles are slow and stiff from sleeping and sitting on a hard floor for days, but I manage to lift the hem of the shirt up and over my head, tossing it aside.

Dante's gaze sweeps up and down the front of my completely naked body.

"See? I'm fine."

His eyes continue to take in every inch of me, even my bare toes.

"Turn around."

I do as I'm told, turning my back to him so he can see that for himself.

A second later he asks, "How?"

I had forgotten that there may be a bruise or two on my butt and hips. Turning back around to face him, I tell him the truth. "From sleeping and sitting on the floor of the outdoor storage building."

"Oh, butterfly," he says softly. Hearing the heavy sorrow in his voice, seeing the distress so clearly in his face, finally breaks me.

I can't stand another second apart. I throw my arms out wrapping them around his neck, praying he doesn't disappear into thin air, like a mirage.

He doesn't disappear. And when his strong arms come around to hold me to him, the last of my fears that this isn't real subside.

"What are you doing here?" I ask him. "I told you...I told you I could do this."

"I know that you could endure anything he did to you; I know you could kill him," he says into my hair. "But you shouldn't have to. I can carry that burden for you. I'll carry all your burdens for you from now on, okay?"

"Okay," I easily agree, breathing in his familiar scent.

"I missed you. One night with my wife wasn't enough."

"I missed you too," I tell him.

"We should be on our honeymoon."

"We should," I agree. "Get me out of here, and we'll go anywhere you want."

"Deal. Just as soon as we finish shit once and for all with this son of a bitch."

I pull back from Dante's embrace to see his face. "He's still alive?"

"Yes."

"And the guards? Some of them helped me..."

"They're all alive. Restrained for now. I'll give them a chance to leave town with their families or stay and work for me."

"That's...nice of you."

"It's the butterfly effect," he says with a smile. "I'm trying not to kill as a first resort. I want to be a better man for you, for my girls. I won't ever be a good man, but I can always be better."

"I love the bad parts too," I assure him.

"I know you do. And I'm going to give you all the filthiest parts as soon as every bruise on your face heals."

"That could take a while. There are plenty of other parts that can handle your filthiness for now."

"Fine. I'll kiss your pussy until your lips heal."

"Deal," I agree.

Dante's arms leave me, just long enough for him to remove his suit jacket. He helps me slip my arms inside the sleeves. It's so big that the bottom of it comes down past my knees.

Getting to his feet, Dante takes my hand to lead me down the hall where his guys are still waiting. "First things first, how do you want to handle your old man?"

"I'll let you decide. You're way better at torture than I am."

"We could give him to Eli as a welcome back present."

"That actually sounds like the perfect punishment for him. Just as long as he ends him, eventually."

"Absolutely," Dante agrees. "And you won't believe how I found him."

Shaking my head, I tell him, "Nope. I don't want to know."

EPILOGUE

Dante

Six months later...

Married life is nothing like I thought it would be.
I've never been happier than I am with Vanessa. And while some may think being in love has made me go soft, I think it's only made me harder, yet smarter.

The city has been calm and quiet since the news of Yuri's death was announced. About half of his men joined my ranks where they continue to be closely watched, and Vanessa inherited everything since the bastard never wrote her out of his will.

Yuri "disappeared" for weeks then was suddenly found dead in his bed. The coroner I paid off declared that he died of natural causes.

That's not exactly a lie.

Fire occurs naturally. Rodents, snakes, and other revolting animals are also part of nature. All of the above played a part in Yuri Petrov's slow demise. Eli is a sick fuck.

The rumors from his torture and death alone have been enough to keep the peace in Vegas.

Gavin still hasn't paid for his betrayal yet because he's laying low. He will one day soon.

Now, if I could just find Madison and convince Vanessa to let Cole learn the family business, I think my life would be perfect.

The bombing and Madison's absence has continued to cause strain between my potential alliance with Lochlan.

I haven't opened his most recent correspondence. He sends shit every few weeks.

Who the fuck sends actual mail nowadays?

I haven't read any of the letters, but when I've got my beautiful wife naked bent over my desk, she knocks a pile onto the floor when her fingers reach for the edge of the desk to hold on.

Draped over her back, I reach a hand underneath her petite body to rub her clit to get her off before I come.

"More. Harder!" she begs.

"God, you take my cock so damn good," I tell her as I give her exactly what she needs, slamming into her tight, slick cunt. Grabbing up a handful of her hair, I lift her head off the desk, forcing her to turn her face to mine so I can shove my tongue in her mouth, filling her every way I can. When I pull back, I tell her, "I always knew you would be able to take it all. Every. Last. Inch." The last three words are punctuated with my thrusts.

"Yes, so good," she moans, her eyelids heavy.

I rub her clit faster, telling her, "Come for me, butterfly. Come for me so I can fill you up. Afterward, I'm going to sit back and watch my cum drip down your thighs."

"Oh, god! I'm...I'm...*Dante!*" she exclaims when her pussy clenches around me, throbbing in that perfect fucking way. Her small body shudders underneath my weight, her hips bucking wildly, setting me off.

My release is so intense I have to bite down on her shoulder and growl while my wife milks every last drip from me.

I only lay draped on her for a second, placing a kiss over the teeth marks that didn't break the skin, then a butterfly tattoo on her shoulder before I pull out. Pressing my hand on her upper back, I tell her, "Stay right fucking here until I tell you that you can stand up."

"Yes, sir, Mr. Salvato," she pants.

Satisfied beyond belief, I slump down into the desk chair behind her to do exactly what I said I would. I stare at her amazing ass and slick cunt, waiting for my seed to gush out. Thanks to how big my load was, it doesn't take long. When the thick liquid drips down her inner thigh I swipe my fingertips through it, rubbing it around her pussy lips, then over her asshole, just because I like the way she squirms and whimpers, begging for more.

Since I still want more too, I open a desk drawer to pull out a new toy I've been wanting us to play with. I rub the pointy end through her wetness, over her slit, teasing her, making her writhe. Since I haven't told her she can stand up yet, she has to endure it. When the beginner-sized anal plug is soaking wet, I press it to her puckered hole and push it inside.

"Oh!" she exclaims in surprise.

"Keep this inside of you for the rest of the day. Tomorrow you'll take a bigger plug and so on until I can fit my cock in your ass," I tell her. I give her right ass cheek a smack, making her gasp. "Oh, and I can make it vibrate from anywhere in the penthouse, whenever I want."

"Mmm," she moans.

"You can stand up now, butterfly. Come sit on my lap, while I try out the vibration settings."

Vanessa pushes herself up and staggers back a step, sending more mail to the floor.

"Pick that up," I order her just so I can watch her bend over.

She looks over her shoulder to roll her eyes at me, but does as she's told, even turning her ass to me. Twice in one day might be a record for her to comply without complaint.

"Ooh, fancy," Vanessa says as she gathers up the paperwork and mail. I groan at the sight of her bare ass in the air wondering if I should fasten my pants or keep them open for another round. Like always, even after I just had her, I want her again. When she straightens, she shuffles through the stack of envelopes. "Some of these are from Lochlan."

"I know."

"You haven't opened any of them?"

"He wouldn't take my call for weeks. The only reason he's contacting me now is to ask about Madison, and since I don't have anything to fucking tell him..."

"This looks like..." Vanessa trails off before she tosses the stack onto the desk to rip open one of the square envelopes.

"Looks like what?"

She pulls a piece of cardstock from inside. "Oh my god. Oh. My. God," she repeats while slapping a palm over her gaping mouth, her green eyes wide. And since my wife isn't usually so dramatic, her reaction is concerning.

"What is it, Vanessa?"

"It's Lochlan's wedding invitation." She holds up the card.

"That's great. He's finally giving up on marrying Madison."

"No, Dante. It's *not* good." She turns the invitation around for me to read it. It takes a second to decipher the words since it's in the raised, fancy blue, cursive font.

"Join us as we celebrate the union of Lochlan Dunne and Sophie Salvato on June first," I read aloud.

"You're forcing little Sophie to marry him?" Vanessa asks.

"No. I would never agree to that! She's still a child."

"Then...what the hell is he thinking?"

"Lochlan's trying to force my hand. He must have found out Madison is missing," I grumble. "Which means we have to find her fast, because there is no fucking way I'm going to let that son of a bitch near Sophie."

The End for Now...

COMING SOON!

Thank you so much for reading *Savage Little Games*!
Would you like to read Dante and Vanessa's steamy wedding scene? You can find it here:
https://dl.bookfunnel.com/4gr50kyksa

Ruthless Little Games, Lachlan and Sophie's book, is coming soon!
Order your copy now: https://mybook.to/RLG

ALSO BY LANE HART

While you wait, start reading the <u>complete</u> Savage Kings MC series!

"The rugged men of the Savage Kings Motorcycle Club are hardened and ruthless — especially when it comes to protecting the women they love! A sizzling series featuring a brother's best friend, a sexy second chance, a determined single dad, and more."

https://mybook.to/SKChase

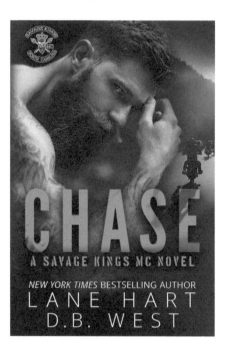

Chase Fury, the VP of the Savage Kings MC has dealt with his fair share of tragedy over the years. He never wanted the responsibility that comes with being at the head of the table, preferring to leave that to his brother, Torin. But after an unexpected attack on the Kings sends his brothers on a path of vengeance, Chase will have no choice but to take on the burden of being the man in charge.

Reporter Sasha Sheridan has steered clear of any and all bad boy bikers wearing the bearded skull for the last ten years. While investigating a story, she suddenly finds herself back in the crosshairs of the Savage Kings. Uncovering the secrets that the club's president is trying to keep hidden may very well put her life in danger. She may be able to handle the threat, but she can't escape the man who broke her heart.

Chase hasn't forgiven himself for hurting Sasha and causing her an unbelievable amount of pain. He still wears her name on his chest, a reminder of the night that he wrecked his bike and everything the two of them had together. Now, with secrets, lies, bloodshed, and violence causing chaos in the club, Chase is determined to use his second chance with Sasha to keep her safe. He never imagined that the best way to do that would be to get her as far away from him and the MC as possible.

Read now: https://mybook.to/SKChase

ABOUT THE AUTHOR

New York Times bestselling author Lane Hart lives in North Carolina with her husband, author D.B. West, and their two children. She enjoys spending the summers on the beach and watching football in the fall.

Connect with Lane:

Author Store: https://www.authorlanehart.com/

Tiktok: https://www.tiktok.com/@hartandwestbooks

Facebook: http://www.facebook.com/lanehartbooks

Instagram: https://www.instagram.com/authorlanehart/

Website: http://www.lanehartbooks.com

Email: lane.hart@hotmail.com

Find all of Lane's books on her Amazon author page!

Sign up for Lane and DB's newsletter to get updates on new releases and freebies!

Join Lane's Facebook group to read books before they're released, help choose covers, character names, and titles of books! https://www.facebook.com/groups/bookboyfriendswanted/

Made in United States
Troutdale, OR
03/18/2024

18566692R00216